MW01687147

JUST FOR THE SUMMER

Sue Moorcroft writes award-winning contemporary fiction of life and love. *The Little Village Christmas* and *A Christmas Gift* were *Sunday Times* bestsellers and *The Christmas Promise* went to #1 in the Kindle chart. She also writes short stories, serials, articles, columns, courses and writing 'how to'.

An army child, Sue was born in Germany then lived in Cyprus, Malta and the UK and still loves to travel. Her other loves include writing (the best job in the world), reading, watching Formula 1 on TV and hanging out with friends, dancing, yoga, wine and chocolate.

If you're interested in being part of #TeamSueMoorcroft you can find more information at www.suemoorcroft.com/street-team. If you prefer to sign up to receive news of Sue and her books, go to www.suemoorcroft.com and click on 'Newsletter'. You can follow @SueMoorcroft on Twitter, @SueMoorcroftAuthor on Instagram, or Facebook.com/sue.moorcroft.3 and Facebook.com/SueMoorcroftAuthor.

JUST
for the
SUMMER

SUE MOORCROFT

avon.

Published by AVON
A division of HarperCollins*Publishers* Ltd
1 London Bridge Street
London SE1 9GF

www.harpercollins.co.uk

This paperback edition 2020

20 21 22 LSC 10 9 8 7 6 5 4 3 2 1

First published in Great Britain by HarperCollins*Publishers* 2017

A catalogue copy of this book is
available from the British Library.

ISBN: 978-0-00-838517-0 (TPB)

Typeset in Sabon LT Std by Palimpsest Book Production Limited,
Falkirk, Stirlingshire
Printed and bound in the United States of America by LSC Communications

Acknowledgements

I'm glad to have this opportunity to thank everybody who played a role in bringing *Just for the Summer* to life. I'm so grateful for their time.

Andrea Crellin, during one of our evenings at the Kino, reduced me to tears of laughter about her holiday from hell and didn't bat an eye when I asked to borrow a little from her story. Andrea was also very helpful with information about the teaching profession and its obligations.

Julie Shardlow not only welcomed me into her home in Alsace for several days but also entered into the research process with gusto, introducing me to Strasbourg, coypu and (too much) local alcohol and cuisine. This story would have been set in the Dordogne if I hadn't suddenly remembered Julie saying 'Come and stay any time'. For added local knowledge, Julie also introduced me to Corinne Huchet who was so kind as to read my manuscript for stray facts and French language errors.

David Roberts shared his knowledge on medical matters; Rosemary J Kind and Eilidh McGuinness did the same on matrimonial.

A special mention for Martin Lovell of SkyTech Helicopters who advised on all things related to Ronan's career and the hard landing he suffered. He introduced me to Matthew Bolshaw, who kindly shared his extensive knowledge of aviation insurance, and aviation medical examiner Dr Kevin Herbert, who helped me make Ronan's injury what it should be and advised on the pilot/AME relationship.

Martin Lovell also generously treated me to the flight of my life. See the bonus material at the back of this book for more!

Pat Walsh allowed me to give Alister her leg injury and advised on the recovery process.

A variety of Facebook friends obliged with information on annoying teenspeak, Goths, hair dye and school attitudes to certain student behaviours.

Scott Matthewson bid generously at an auction in support of Narcolepsy UK for the opportunity to have a character named after him. As the real Scott Matthewson is a barrister I wasn't entirely comfortable with his invitation to make 'my' Scott Matthewson a villain but I had fun and I hope that the real Scott enjoys the result.

Beta readers Mark West and Dominic White did their usual great job with an early draft of the book, asking awkward questions and making pithy observations that enabled me to make the next draft better. I never tire of this process.

Fabulous Juliet Pickering of the Blake Friedmann Literary, TV & Film Agency is everything an author could possibly ask for in an agent. Her support is there for the asking and her advice on point. She also understands the importance of champagne.

Helen Huthwaite, my lovely editor, gathered the fantastic

team at Avon Books behind me with fabulous results such as #1 spot in the UK Kindle chart for my last book, *The Christmas Promise*. (No pressure everybody, but please could we do that again?)

Thanks as always to Team Sue Moorcroft members who are tireless in their support of me and their advocacy of my books, and Manda Jane Ward for naming Curtis. I'm constantly amazed and humbled by this. (If you think you might like to be involved in the street team you can discover more at www.suemoorcroft.com.)

I'm grateful to, and in awe of, the incredible book bloggers who do a tireless job of supporting authors and their books. Their community is amazing. I could talk to book bloggers all day – and, at blogger/author meet ups, frequently do. Thank you for reviewing my books and inviting me onto your blogs.

I'm lucky to be part of an awesome family, evidenced by the number of my books dedicated to its various members. We frequently communicate with insults and mickey-taking but I'm not joking when I say how much I appreciate their love and support. Especially when they sell my books to their friends.

Most importantly, thank you, the readers, for whom I spend hours every day, shut away, making stuff up. Thank you for buying my books, for the lovely reviews and for the wonderful comments and messages on social media.

There are few things that give me more pleasure than people enjoying my books.

As *Just for the Summer* features Leah the Cool Auntie it seems fitting that I dedicate this book to my nieces and nephews

Véronique, Lucy, Ashley, Dan and Ryan

who bring fun and laughter with them whenever we meet.

Prologue

Michele: *Re holiday . . . Alister wants to come! Says he's never visited that region of France, it was planned before the break-up, he paid, there's room, and what's he supposed to do for most of August with the kids away? The gîte has good wifi so he can do his pre-term admin, blah blah. The children will hate me if I say no. Would you mind? Pleeeeeease don't mind! x*
Leah: *Happy to step aside. Only said I'd come because you'd be alone with the kids. Maybe you and Alister will make up? *hopeful face* ☺ x*
Michele:☹ *We absolutely WON'T make up and I NEED you there to defuse the TENSION. Pleeeeeease? xxxxxx*

Leah Beaumont read the final message with a sinking heart. A few weeks ago, in a shock move – shocking even to husband Alister, apparently – Leah's sister Michele had ended her marriage. Since then, Leah's role had been to provide emotional support for Michele and the kids, Jordan and Natasha. Even Alister had turned up at Leah's place for a long open-heart discourse on the hideousness of having to leave – 'being kicked out of' – the family home.

In the end-of-relationship wasteland, the family's trip to Alsace had slipped down the 'needs attention' list until Michele received a cheerful e-mail beginning *Soon we'll be welcoming your family to our fantastic gîte, Mrs Milton. Here are a few things you'll want to know!* and instantly phoned Leah. 'Will you come in Alister's place? You know I can't drive on the wrong side! And you don't mind doing outdoorsy stuff with the children.' Michele's voice had been squeaky with tears and it would have taken a harder heart than Leah's to refuse, though it would mean a dreary drive to France in Michele's lumbering seven-seater known as 'The Pig' because Michele had had it sprayed pink. On *purpose.*

Leah's phone beeped again.

Michele: *Really absolutely definitely PLEASE don't back out! Can you come round? xxxxxxxxxxxxxxxx*

Leah sighed.

Ten minutes later she was sitting in her sister's kitchen. Michele's curly bob corkscrewed randomly above one eye and the top button of her jeans was undone. 'You're not going to back out. *Are* you?'

Though Leah understood that 'Yes' would not be the correct answer, she wriggled feebly on the hook. 'But now Alister's going –'

'If you don't come, I'll shoot myself,' Michele promised, eyes swimming with tears. 'But if you're there to make the holiday bearable, maybe Alister's presence might actually help the children. If we're friendly and civilised they'll know that whether we're together or apart our love for them is the same.'

Though Leah didn't see children as quite that easy to

reboot, she knew better than to theorise when Michele scored fifteen years' parenting and twenty years' teaching to Leah's nil. She propped her elbows on the oak table. 'There may be enough rooms but it would mean taking two vehicles.'

'Alister can drive The Pig, as it's bigger than his hatchback, and I'll be your passenger.'

A road trip in Leah's middle-aged Porsche Cayman was definitely more of an incentive than being obliged to drive The Pig. 'But putting me in the middle of your marital distress –'

'It's just for the holidays and you're on gardening leave! You've landed a great new job and you're being *paid* to stay away from the old one. It's a free holiday!'

Leah's neck prickled at the familiar sensation of a sisterly squabble brewing. 'I did already have plans for my gardening leave – redecorating my lounge, a trip to see Mum and Dad and a track day with Scott.' They hadn't been firm plans, but they'd been plans.

'Scott's not even a boyfriend!'

'What difference does that make? He's my friend.'

Michele sucked in a long, wavering breath, eyes huge and tragic. 'But – I'm pregnant again.' And she burst into noisy tears.

Leah's jaw dropped. '*Pregnant? Michele* –!'

'I know, I know!' Michele's shoulders heaved. 'It's come at exactly the wro-wrong time. But tha-at's why I nee-ee-eed you. Everythi-ing's such a mess.'

'If your life gets much messier, soap operas will be stealing your storylines,' Leah agreed, though not without compassion. 'Does Alister know about the baby?'

'Of course! The poor man thinks I've undergone a personality transplant. I've still got to find a way to tell

Jordan and Natasha! And what about Baby Three? What kind of family life is she or he going to be born into?'

Leah slid a comforting arm along Michele's shoulders. 'Is the baby Alister's?'

Michele flung herself upright, tears on hold as her best indignant teacher's voice cracked out. 'Leah! If even *you* think the worst of me, I might really shoot myself!'

'Sorry.' Leah backtracked hastily as her sister's face crumpled into a still more tragic mask. She did love Michele, no matter how much they jokingly referred to themselves as 'Chalk' and 'Cheese', Michele being eight years older, the very married and motherly Mrs Milton; Leah the resolutely single and child-free Ms Beaumont. Michele having a sensible job in teaching; Leah having what Michele termed 'a silly job' in chocolate products – though it paid better than Michele's sensible one. Despite having the bossy and manipulative tendencies that she seemed to feel the right of an elder sister, Michele had also stuck up for Leah a million times and provided whatever was needed in the way of bolthole, wise counsel or shoulder to cry on.

'All right, I'll come,' Leah capitulated, 'if I get the garden annexe, as agreed. I'm not used to family life and I need my space.'

'It would be better if Alister was out there.' Michele grabbed a fistful of kitchen roll to trumpet noisily into. Then, catching Leah's eye, 'Oh, OK, if that's what it takes. Thank you.'

Leah ignored the whiff of reproach. Her claiming La Petite Annexe would force Alister and Michele into proximity in the main house. Maybe Michele's uncharacteristic decision to hurl her family into upset and confusion might yet prove to be a feature of early-pregnancy hormones?

Away from the daily stresses of home, of Michele being a teacher and Alister a head teacher, things might improve.

Then Leah could quietly pack up her car and give them privacy to realign their relationship. Behind her back, she crossed her fingers.

Chapter One

Three weeks later

Leah loved her sunglasses, and not just because they made her look cool or made driving her Porsche in the mellow sunshine of France more pleasurable. No. Those sunglasses were currently allowing her to pretend to leaf through a magazine in the sunshine outside La Petite Annexe while actually watching the first-floor balcony of the house next door where a workman had bared his tanned back to the morning sun.

His sure and easy brushstrokes were transforming the walls of the house from dirty grey to the gold of unclarified honey but Leah's anxious gaze was trained on the youth behind him. Everything the youth wore was black and decorated with studs or chains. Having perched himself on the wooden balcony rail and hooked his feet around the uprights, he was now arching backwards into scarily thin air. Flexing his spine, he swung gently, chains dangling and winking in the sun.

Leah bit her lip against an urge to shout a warning, scared of startling the youngster into falling.

Then, as if possessing a sixth sense, the man turned. Demonstrating commendable reflexes, he dumped his paint pot and made a grab for the gangly figure. Bellowing with laughter, the youth allowed himself to be hauled to safety. Leah let out the breath she'd been holding and grinned at the man's obvious exasperation as he gave the youth a tiny shake before dragging him into his arms for a hard hug. Finally, the man managed a laugh as he loosened his embrace, his dark hair lifting in the breeze.

Then his gaze snagged on Leah and, after a moment's contemplation, he raised his voice. '*Bonjour!*'

Unnerved at being spotted through the leafy trees, Leah lifted her head as if she hadn't been spying on them. 'Oh! *Bonjour.*'

'*Vous êtes en vacances? Restez-vous ici en Kirchhoffen?*' The man settled his forearms on the balcony rail as his voice rolled over the sunny air. His front view was as pleasing as the back had been.

Leah smiled. Her French was just about equal to the conversation so far. '*Oui.*'

But then, '*Enchantés*' launched him into a speech of fascinating undulating rhythm punctuated with *urrrr* and *airrr,* of which Leah caught about ten per cent. She did at least understand that when he paused it was to invite her to respond to a question.

Both *oui* and *non* carrying equal risk, she prepared to offer a shrug and her stock phrases, '*Désolée, mon français est très mauvais. Parlez-vous anglais?*'

But then Natasha bounded out through the door of the main gîte. 'Dad says, aren't you coming in for breakfast? We want to go kayaking.' Both man and boy swung their heads to gaze Natasha's way as, message delivered, she dashed back inside again.

Thus saved from confessing to her rubbish command of the native language of her host country, Leah put her shrug to good use and called '*Excusez-moi!*' to the occupants of the balcony and went to join the family.

Curtis craned over the rail to watch the woman and girl out of sight. 'Hot.'

Ronan quashed the reflex to call out a sharp 'Don't lean too far!' His heart might not have recovered from Curtis's last stunt but Curtis was one big growing pain these days and making it abundantly clear that he no longer expected to be treated like a child. He was *a teenager* and had embraced the language, rituals and social conventions with the fervour of a religious convert to a sect.

Instead, Ronan hazarded a suitably laddish reply. 'Obviously, I won't comment on a teenage girl, but the woman was hot.'

Curtis rolled his eyes. 'How d'you know I didn't mean the woman?'

Ronan tried to decide whether his teenage self would have had this conversation with his own father. It had been just him and Dad for a long time and Ronan had only good memories. But no, he couldn't imagine openly staring at a thirty-something woman with long bare legs and a rope of streaky hair. Even when Ronan had been old enough to spend university holidays on big, bluff Gordon Shea's building sites, he wouldn't have sprouted four facial piercings, as Curtis had done this summer holiday. And what Dad would have thought of Curtis's long hair at the front and shaved patches at the side . . .

Ronan took up his brush. 'The hot woman seems to be the mum and the girl mentioned a dad so she's taken anyway.'

Curtis jingled the four chains he wore in place of a belt. 'Try not to be intimidated by convention, Dad.'

Suppressing simultaneous compulsions to laugh, scold, and suggest Curtis get himself a paintbrush and direct his energies to something more productive than being a smartarse, Ronan replied gravely, 'Try not to gawp at other people's wives, Curtis.'

With one of the lightning changes of mood that came with his teenaged landscape, Curtis began to whoop like an ape, 'Oo oo oo!', crossing his eyes and swinging his arms.

Glad they were joking around rather than arguing, Ronan tucked his left arm into his pocket to relieve his sore shoulder of its weight as he turned back to his task with a wry 'How could she resist?'

The roomy kitchen was bright with colourful tiles and fabrics. Alister was attacking the shiny crust of a baguette and Leah realised guiltily that he must have been down to the *boulangerie* while she'd been lazing in the sun.

Natasha was already at the table, buttering chunks of bread, tutting as her knife made a hole, while Jordan stabbed at his phone with the intensity reserved by fifteen-year-olds for anything with a screen. 'You're coming kayaking with us, aren't you?' demanded Natasha.

'Sounds fun.' Leah washed her hands before opening the fridge in search of cheese and cold meats. She glanced at her brother-in-law. 'Does Michele know kayaking's on today's schedule?' It didn't seem the obvious activity for a forty-three-year-old in the early stages of pregnancy.

Alister sawed energetically, his eyes fixed rigidly on the baguette through the lenses of his glasses. 'Haven't seen her this morning.'

'I have,' Natasha piped up. 'She's a bit under the weather so she's going to stay here and rest. If the boats are two-person, can I be with you, Leah? Then it'll be girls against boys.'

Jordan glanced up from his phone. 'We'd spend all day waiting for you. It'll be better if I go with Leah and you go with Dad.'

Natasha pointed an indignant butter knife. 'I said Leah first. Just because Mum's not here –'

'Jordan, would you make the coffee, please?' interrupted Alister, in his head-teacher voice that managed somehow to be both mild and authoritative. 'Natasha, how many more slices?'

Leah followed Alister's lead in distracting the kids from bickering. 'We'll take the advice of the hire staff regarding distribution of paddlers between kayaks, shall we?' As they sat down at the refectory-style table and she sliced Munster cheese onto her bread Leah added, 'I could eat so much of this that I wouldn't fit in a kayak.'

Jordan grinned. 'You do have the appetite of the average gorilla.' The conversation loosened with laughter, though Leah's thoughts were less than cheery.

Three days they'd been in Kirchhoffen. For two of them, Michele had managed to contrive that the family went out without her. So far nobody had openly questioned it but Leah knew the oddness of this behaviour wouldn't bypass the kids for long.

When breakfast was over, she slipped out into the hall and up the wooden staircase, its open treads sweeping up between thick spindles to the first floor, then up again to the rooms tucked beneath the gabled roof. Michele and the children had rooms on the first floor; Alister had been allocated space at the top, where there was only his room and the games room.

By treading at the edges of each step Leah found she could glide almost silently to Michele's quarters. Without ceremony, she thrust the door open.

Dressed only in pretty underclothes and a towel swathing her hair, Michele jumped guiltily, pressing a button on her phone. 'Come in, won't you?' A yellow summer dress was laid out on top of her neatly made bed.

Leah closed the door behind her. 'Do you need anything before we go out? Natasha says you're under the weather.'

Michele lowered her voice. 'You know I feel lumpy in the mornings.' Her skin did look pale and waxy.

'We can hang on until you feel well enough to come with us.'

Michelle belted on a blue robe and dropped her phone into its pocket. 'I can't go kayaking in my condition and I don't want to tell the kids why yet.' She unwound the towel and began to rub her hair.

'We can do something less energetic.'

'I'd hate to ruin things for them. I'll put my feet up today, have a lovely dinner ready for when you come home, then spend the evening with the children.' Michele began to brush her wet hair sleek against her head. She looked different without her curls. Harder.

Or was that just how she was, these days? Harder?

Although Michele picked up the hairdryer and paused, poised, as if to hint she had other things to do than chat, Leah meandered to the bedroom chair and plumped down into its depths. 'It's turned out to be a good thing that Alister's here, with you having morning sickness. I know you wouldn't have put on me to take the kids out all the time.'

Michele's eyes glinted oddly. 'Alister told me last night that I'm acting like a stranger so I suppose I might do anything. What do you think? Do you still know me?'

Leah's sympathy warred with exasperation. 'Of course I do. I just don't really understand what's going on with you.'

Blinking, Michele fidgeted with the hairdryer, dropping her gaze. 'Maybe you should.'

Leah leaned forward and covered her sister's hands to still her fretful movements. 'But all our lives you've known what you wanted. To be a wife and mother with a home in a nice area and a sensible car to ferry your kids around in. Now you're suddenly less cautious than I am.'

Michelle shrugged. 'Your choices are just as carefully thought out as mine. It's just that they're all about how to avoid having kids or a husband who would stop you from indulging yourself with car races or stunt driving. Why shouldn't I want my life to be all about me, sometimes?'

'Because you gave that up to have children. Shell, even if you stop being Alister's wife you can't stop being a mother. You're in a strange place but none of this is easy on Jordan and Natasha.'

Michele's shoulders began to quake. 'I know. I'm the worst mum in the world.'

Though aware she was being manipulated, Leah was unwilling to damn Michele's hitherto conscientious parenting. 'You're absolutely not, or the kids wouldn't be so keen to spend time with you.' She jumped to her feet and assumed a bright tone and matching smile. 'Look, take today for yourself. Put on your pretty dress and flake out in the garden. Read, paint your nails, snooze. There's even a hot workman next door to watch. Then maybe you'll be ready to go out with the family tomorrow.'

'Maybe.' Michele managed a watery smile, picked up her hairbrush and switched on her hairdryer.

* * *

Unfortunately, the day's kayaking on the River Ill in the forest of Illwald achieved a poor rating on the fun scale. Natasha, though she achieved her aim of sharing a boat with Leah, became tearful every time she was splashed, Jordan called her Gnasher, or one of the ugly grey bugs that plagued the river took a bite of her. As a result, she spent most of the day sporting damp eyes. Every ten minutes she'd sigh, 'I wish Mum was with us,' which made Jordan snap, 'Shut up, Gnasher.'

Alister emerged from his thoughts long enough to say, 'Bit kinder, maybe, Jordan?' and Jordan fell to silent scowling, stabbing the khaki surface of the river with an angry paddle.

Leah drove home longing to hide away in La Petite Annexe and treat herself to a huge glass of pinot gris. Instead, as she shifted down a gear to encourage The Pig up the slope towards the gîte, she cast around for something to improve the mood. 'Do you kids want to make mug cakes when we get back? Your mum's preparing dinner but we could make dessert.'

'Are mug cakes like cupcakes, only bigger?' Jordan's expression lightened.

'No, a mug cake's made in a mug, in the microwave.'

Natasha who'd managed to bag the front passenger seat coming home, looked more cheerful, her nose red from the sun. 'Chocolate mug cake?'

'Of course. Nice and gooey. We can put some cola in the mixture to make it moist.'

'Any chance of coffee in mine? Good and dark?' Alister smiled at Leah via the rear-view mirror. Smiling wasn't something he'd done a lot of today and Leah grinned in return. Alister was a nice man. He'd been her brother-in-law since she was seventeen and it was painful to see him so sad, yet trying to cover it up. 'Coffee, cola, nuts, orange, strawberries – everyone can choose.'

The atmosphere lightened as Jordan suggested 'Marshmallow and Haribo' and Natasha countered with 'Banana and lime. And chocolate, obvs.' Amazing what cake could do to lift the spirits.

When they pulled up in front of the gîte, Leah spotted that the workman from earlier had moved his area of endeavour to the front balcony of the house next door, while his studs-and-chains young companion leaned on the rail, playing with his phone. Both turned at the sound of the car. The workman flashed his grin, giving an airy wave of his paintbrush before turning back to his work. The teenager just looked.

'Who's that boy?' hissed Natasha.

Jordan tugged her hair. 'Someone too cool for you.'

'He's not!' Natasha responded in indignation. 'He's just Goth. We've got loads of Goths at school. They're not allowed to wear their piercings in school but they put up with it because Goths are big on tolerance.'

'Being excluded if they don't comply has a lot to do with that kind of tolerance,' Alister observed.

He and Leah began to clear The Pig of the cans and bottles accumulated during the day. Jordan and Natasha dawdled off down the path at the side of the house as if the mess was nothing to do with them.

Overtaking the kids, Leah followed Alister through the back door and into the kitchen. The room was cool and quiet. She paused, listening, becoming aware of Alister listening in the same way.

She glanced at her watch. Six thirty. The kitchen looked exactly as it had when they'd left it this morning. No salad washed, nothing cooking. She glanced out of the window. No barbecue alight.

'What's for dinner?' Natasha bumped through the door

behind them. 'Or can we start the cakes straight away? I'm staaaaaaaaaaarving.'

'Can I have crisps?' demanded Jordan.

One glance at the apprehensive expression that had settled over Alister's face and Leah smoothly picked up the slack. 'Dinner before the cakes,' she suggested brightly. 'I'll whip up a risotto and we'll have it with salad. There's some of that fab bread left, too, I think.'

'I'll find Mum.' Natasha trotted off through the hall.

Alister cleared his throat. 'I thought Michele said she'd cook?'

'She's probably having a nap.' Leah hoped. But, somehow, she didn't think so – the house had had an empty air. She slopped a little olive oil into a heavy pan, popped it onto the hob to heat, took out two onions and topped, tailed and peeled them. With swift, machine-gun movements, she passed them under her flashing blade, *ch-ch-ch-ch-CHAH*, using the back of the knife to scrape the pieces from the chopping board into the pan, stirring briskly, then turning to the fridge for bacon, mushrooms, parmesan and cream.

Natasha bounded back into the room, eyes wide. 'I can't find Mum!'

Somehow Leah wasn't shocked to hear it. She just tried to smile reassuringly as the delicious smell of sizzling bacon filtered into the air. 'She's probably gone for a walk.' *But she'd had all day. Why would Michele leave it until now, when she'd promised to have dinner waiting?*

She glanced at the others to try and read their expressions but Jordan was frowning ferociously at his phone while Alister moved wordlessly to the fridge, took out a tall green bottle of Crémant d'Alsace and lifted down two glasses from the rack. He filled both and passed one to Leah. Unnerved by his silence, and in no way treating the sparkling liquid with the respect it deserved, Leah took a couple of big gulps. 'How about one of you kids text your mum and see where's she's got to? Tell her dinner will be ready in forty minutes.'

Jordan and Natasha began to squabble about who should do the texting. Under cover of their noise, Alister hovered close to Leah. 'Do you know where she is?' His wineglass trembled slightly.

Her heart squeezed at his evident misery. All Alister had ever done was be Alister, steady and kind. Even if it wasn't massively exciting, that had once been what Michele wanted. Leah took another slurp of wine, beginning to wonder if she might need a lot of it before this holiday was over. 'No idea,' she whispered.

'Shit.' Alister gave a short, bitter laugh. 'I don't even know why I'm surprised. What's a forgotten meal when you can shuck off a marriage like an unfashionable coat?'

'Mum's on her way!' cried Natasha, saving Leah from having to think of a response. 'She says she'll be ten minutes. I'll go outside and wait.'

As she banged through the door Jordan observed loftily, 'Natasha's such a baby.'

Leah weighed out the rice and made up a jug of stock, remembering thirteen being a pretty confusing age even without the shock of a parental separation. 'Good job she's got a brother who's a whole two years older to be kind to her, then. Eh, Jordan?'

'Big brothers are meant to be kind?' But he grinned sheepishly, as if taking Leah's message on board.

It was nearly twenty minutes later that Michele finally strolled in, Natasha clinging to her arm. Leah looked up from grating parmesan. 'Are you better? I thought you promised to make dinner.'

Michele looked better – except, perhaps, for a little guilt around the eyes. 'Sorry! I forgot the time.' She ruffled Jordan's hair, as much as his hair would ruffle now he'd taken to lacing it with gel or gum or whatever was that week's favoured product.

Under cover of topping up his glass Alister muttered to Leah, 'Promises, eh? Like "Till death us do part"? Turned out to be crap.'

Leah stifled an inappropriate urge to giggle, though nothing about the situation was actually funny.

'And I see it's wine o'clock.' Michele reached for an empty glass.

Alister halted his drink halfway to his mouth. '*Really*?' He shifted his gaze meaningfully to her mid-section.

For a second Michele looked thrown, as if the existence of Baby Three had slipped her memory. Silently, she turned to the fridge and filled her wineglass with orange juice.

Chapter Two

'I hope Mum comes out with us today.' Head on hand, Natasha was playing with her croissant instead of eating it, a sheen on her skin from where the morning sunshine streamed in through the kitchen window.

Jordan had already wolfed a cheese doorstep sandwich and two croissants. 'Yeah.' His expression was hidden, absorbed as he appeared to be in fraying the bottom of what he termed 'shorts', despite their ending halfway down his calves. Calves that seemed too hairy to belong to someone Leah still thought of as a boy.

Anxious that the kids might be beginning to pick up on Michele's uncharacteristically evasive behaviour, Leah debated whether to suggest a visit to the water park in nearby Muntsheim. Even if Michele was supposedly feeling delicate it surely couldn't be too taxing to read or snooze while the kids hurled themselves down the chutes?

Alister got in first with a simpler plan. 'How about we hang out in the garden? Then Mum won't have far to go when she feels well enough to join us, will she?'

A smile lit Natasha's face. 'I'll tell her.'

'Cool,' agreed Jordan.

'But you'll do something more active than playing Minecraft, won't you, Jordan?' Alister said, employing his mild-but-inflexible voice.

Jordan sighed and climbed to his feet. 'OK. I'll get my supersoaker to shoot Nat with while she plays boules.' He sent Alister a challenging look but Alister, who picked his battles wisely, merely smiled.

The kids gone, Leah began to clear the table, admiring the delicate pale blue and green of the crockery. 'I'm perfectly happy to play boules or get into water fights but are you and Michele going to be able to do it without . . . an atmosphere?' She managed to bite back the urge to call it 'public displays of animosity'.

Alister watched her load the dishwasher. 'I'm sorry. This is crappy for you. My suggestion we stay here today is an experiment.'

Leah abandoned her tower of crockery to give him a friendly hug. 'I'm not going to ask about the nature of the experiment or what data you hope to collect. I'm just sorry it's all gone wrong between you.'

His body seemed to sink in on itself as he sighed but whatever he opened his mouth to reply was lost in Michele's entrance as she banged crossly in, throwing back over her shoulder, 'No, stay up there, please, Natasha. I want to talk to Dad.'

'I'll leave.' Leah turned for the door to the garden.

'Appreciated,' murmured Alister.

'Why should you?' Michele snapped simultaneously. 'You're involved in this Happy Families plan for today.'

Alister met her ire with coolly raised eyebrows. 'Basing ourselves here will enable you to see something of your children without worrying about feeling queasy in the car or doing anything too active for your delicate condition. Does that cover whatever excuse you were about to trot out?'

Acutely uncomfortable as Michele and Alister glared icicles at each other, Leah resumed her escape. 'I'll get more loungers from the summerhouse.'

She closed the door on Alister's low-voiced 'Think what's best for the *children*, Michele.'

Intent on keeping clear of the battleground, Leah dawdled as she set out the wooden sun loungers. Casting around the capacious summerhouse she located a paddling pool and a hose and dragged them out, too. The gîte and its neighbour were the only residences this far up the lane and there seemed to be nobody next door but the workman and his young assistant so she doubted it mattered if they had a water fight and it got a bit screamy.

She watched the clear water burble into the pool. *Think what's best for the children* . . . If not for the kids, she'd reverse her car out of the garage and make a break for it instead of sticking around to share the death throes of Michele and Alister's marriage.

But, as she was here, Leah could – probably – prevent spilled blood, and that definitely came under the heading of 'best for the children'. Mentally polishing her halo she let herself into La Petite Annexe to change into her bikini. It didn't cover as much as she would have liked, but she hadn't had much time for holiday shopping and she was amongst family.

After slathering on factor 50 and grabbing her magazine, she reserved herself a lounger and settled down to try and Facetime Scott during his morning break. Scott had been her best friend since school and she usually saw him several times a week, sharing their love of all-things-car. She missed him. If anyone knew her deepest, darkest secrets, it was Scott.

'Hey, you,' he answered snippily as his image leaped to the screen, brown hair shining and spiked at the front. 'Finally found time in your holiday schedule to remember the existence of your bestie?'

'Don't be grumpy. I'm feeling homesick and I wanted to hear your voice. As lovely as Alsace is, I'd rather be back in Bettsbrough enjoying the gardening leave I'd planned. Got to support Michele and family, though.'

'Oh. OK.' He looked mollified. 'So what's the place you're staying like?'

Leah directed the phone screen towards La Petite Annexe so the camera would capture it for him. 'This is my bolthole.' Then she lined up on the gîte, panning around so he got the full impact of all three floors and the impressive timberwork on the outside. 'And this is where the others are.'

'FFS, it's massive! Have you got a rugby team visiting or something?'

Leah laughed as she turned her phone so they could see each other again. 'There aren't quite enough spare rooms for that but it's certainly not cramped.' And she told him about the long drive over and the frost occasionally twinkling between Michele and Alister.

Leah's spirits rose as, in return, he gave her a jokey rendition of his latest run-in with his boss, including his outrageous excuse that his work was suffering simply because 'his bestie' was in another country. Scott always made her feel better with his uniquely snarky affection and she sighed along with him when it was time for him to wind up the conversation with 'Got to get back to work, I'm afraid. Get yourself home as soon as you can.' He blew a kiss and disappeared.

Regretfully, Leah put away her phone as Natasha and Jordan burst into the garden, Jordan armed with a Rambo-sized water gun and Natasha with plastic bowls from the kitchen.

'Girls against boys!' Natasha yelled, frisbeeing a bowl in Leah's direction.

With little choice but to join the fray, Leah snatched the bowl from the air and, taking outrageous advantage of Jordan's exposed position at the pool as he filled his supersoaker, scooped up a healthy bowlful of glistening water and sloshed it down his bare back. 'Girls against boys!'

'Waaaaah, freezing!' Jordan heaved harder on the plunger that loaded his weapon. 'This means water war!'

'Water war!' Natasha, screaming like a chimpanzee, leaped into the middle of the paddling pool just as Alister emerged from the house. With no respect for his sombre expression she scooped a wave of water in his direction.

The arc of water hung in a shimmering rainbow in the air before sloshing over Alister's head and chest. He flinched. Blinked. Then, resignedly, he dragged off his T-shirt, laid his bespattered spectacles away and calmly took up the garden hose. 'OK, water war.'

'You can't have the *hose*, Alister, it's not fair to outgun us by that much!' Leah tried not to trip over her flip-flops as she raced to remove herself from the firing line.

'Who said life was fair?' Alister spun the tap to the 'on' position and pulled the hose trigger at the same instant as Michele stepped out from the house. The powerful jet of water met her head with an audible *splat*.

'Oops.' Alister took just a second too long to shift the jet away. 'Sorry.'

'Oh –!' Michele gasped, one side of her hair plastered to her head and the corresponding eye streaming mascara.

Natasha screamed with excited laughter. 'You got splooshed!'

With a Tarzan yell, Jordan aimed his supersoaker at his mother. 'Girls against boys! Choose your weapon.'

For a second, Leah thought Michele would give everybody a good scolding or whirl around and retreat to her room. Time seemed to stutter while water glistened on bare skin and lush lawn.

Then Michele wiped her face and slicked back her hair. 'Girls against boys,' she growled dangerously, yanking the bright green hose off the tap, leaving Alister with an altogether empty weapon. Jamming her fingers into the stream of tap water she sent it spurting in his direction with deadly aim.

'Unfair!' he bellowed, slipping on the grass as he floundered to escape at the same time as attempting to rearm himself by stealing Jordan's water gun.

'Get your own weapon, soldier,' snapped Jordan, wrestling it back and aiming at his sister.

'Eeep! Noooooo!' Natasha flew across the garden with the water playing square between her shoulder blades. 'All onto Jordan, girls!'

For the next hour the air was filled with screams, protests, laughter . . . and a lot of water. It was sufficient to swill away the tension – temporarily at least.

Finally, puffing hard, Michele held up her hands. 'Enough! Ceasefire or I surrender or whatever I have to do.' She fell onto one of the now damp loungers.

Glad that the atmosphere had warmed a degree or two,

Leah flopped down on another, wringing out her hair. 'I'll get drinks when I've caught my breath.'

Michele closed her eyes and tipped her pale face to the sun. 'Thanks. I think perhaps I overdid it.' Her clothes clinging damply didn't deter her from plummeting almost instantly into sleep.

Alister regarded his estranged wife sheepishly. 'Maybe she did overdo it. She's zonked.'

'It's to be expected, I suppose. She's very pale.' Leah's eyes darted towards the youngsters, their heads bent over their phones as they recovered from the water war via their world of constant communication. When were they to be told about their brother/sister-to-be? Would they leap on the news, hoping against hope that the baby would reunite their parents? Her heart twisted to think of yet another bitter disappointment to poison their young lives. Since the first shock of their parents splitting up, when Natasha had cried for days and Jordan had shut himself in his room, they'd coped almost unrealistically well. It was as if they'd been able to grow thin protective shells.

But if those shells were put under pressure they'd surely shatter.

Keeping these uncomfortable thoughts strictly to herself Leah managed to bask in the sun for an hour before Natasha announced herself once again to be 'staaaaarving.' Michele stirred but sank back into her slumbers so, stifling a sigh, Leah laid down her magazine. 'We'll eat out here. Lots of lovely salad.'

'And cakes?' Jordan suggested, hopefully.

'With ice-cream?' supplemented Natasha.

'For afters,' Leah agreed.

She wasn't sorry to go indoors and get a break from

the powerful sun. The smooth tiles of the kitchen floor felt cool beneath her feet as she put eggs on to boil, then washed watercress and lamb's lettuce for the *salade verte*. Humming quietly as she moved on to slicing big firm tomatoes that were so red they glowed, she became conscious of a man's voice speaking French outside. Then Michele, evidently restored by her nap, replying. Alister joined in. Leah didn't bother trying to follow a conversation that was way above her command of simple French phrases. Her sister and brother were Francophiles; French Language was Alister's teaching commitment in his junior school and Michele loved to compete in airing her command of the language.

As Leah whisked together the ingredients for a quick pecan toffee pudding, covered it with brown sugar and poured boiling water over it before sliding it into the oven, she did catch Michele insisting, '*Oui, oui, il est notre plaisir!*' It was good that something was giving Michele pleasure because not much seemed to, these days.

There was a little rice left from the risotto and Leah made a quick rice salad, chopping in tomatoes and spring onions with almonds while the eggs cooled, pausing only to call through the back door, 'Could someone carry the table and chairs onto the lawn, please?' and check that they did.

Finally, she grabbed napkins and cutlery and stepped out once again into the shimmering heat of the garden. 'I'm ready to bring lunch out, if someone wants to help me.'

At the same moment, Michele called, expansively, 'Welcome! Come and join us.'

'Pardon?' Leah halted in confusion.

Then two figures rounded the corner of the house and a deep voice replied. 'Thanks. This is nice of you.'

Leah jumped as she recognised the workman and the teenager from next door. 'Oh!'

'This is my sister, Leah.' Michele beamed.

The workman's dark hair looked as if the wind had just blown through it, his even darker eyes smiling from his tanned face. 'I'm Ronan Shea and this is my son Curtis. Great to meet you.'

'You're not French!' Leah exclaimed.

'No, indeed.' If anything, she could detect a touch of Irish in his voice.

'But you spoke to me in French!'

He grinned disarmingly. 'I'm a big fat showoff.'

'Leah, I've invited them to join us,' interrupted Michele, 'so they've brought their lunch and we're all pitching in.'

As if to prove her words Ronan opened a cool-bag to display three different hunks of cheese, a whole cooked chicken, a portly loaf of bread and bottles of wine and cola. 'I hope it's not too inconvenient?' His gaze remained steadily on Leah's face, whereas his son seemed unable to lift his eyes above Leah's neck. Although they weren't far below it.

She felt colour sting her cheeks at the sudden realisation that she was standing chatting in her *bikini* for goodness' sake. She forced a smile. 'No, of course not. Just excuse me for a minute.' Acutely aware of what felt like acres of flesh on display Leah tossed the cutlery on the table and set off for La Petite Annexe, forcing herself not to break into an undignified gallop.

Michele, perhaps realising belatedly that Leah wouldn't have chosen to be wearing only a purple high-leg bikini when introduced to a strange man and his wide-eyed adolescent son, called after her, 'You take your time and we'll bring the food out.'

'Good of you,' Leah muttered, bolting through the annexe door.

Having let her embarrassment cool under a tepid shower before covering herself in cropped jeans and a T-shirt, Leah rejoined the party to find the table was busy with conversation and everybody had already heaped their plates. Leah quietly took the only vacant chair.

Which was between Ronan and Curtis. It would have to be.

'Thanks,' she murmured, when Ronan passed her a plate and napkin. She poured herself a glass of lemonade. Only Alister seemed to be doing damage to the wine bottle in the centre of the table.

Ronan fell into easy conversation with Alister, and as Curtis, Natasha and Jordan had found common ground in the belief that all software should be free, Leah's residual bikini embarrassment began to fade.

Curtis, she discovered by listening in, was, incredibly, only thirteen, despite being six feet tall and wearing head-to-toe black Goth gear. Leah wondered at a boy quite that young being allowed piercings in eyebrow, nose and both ears, and his alternative hairstyle dangling perpetually in his eyes. Whenever he was offered anything from the table he replied with an endearing 'Yeah, yeah, yeah, fanks.' Aside from their height there wasn't much similarity between father and son: Curtis sandy and hazel, Ronan uncompromisingly dark.

Curtis politely helped Natasha and Jordan clear the first course as Leah brought out dessert. The sight of the steaming pudding with its accompanying chocolate sauce and fresh fruit silenced the gathering momentarily.

Alister passed around clean plates. 'Leah makes fantastic desserts.'

Ronan turned his dark gaze on her. 'You're surely not baking on holiday?'

'It's something incredibly easy –'

Michele broke in. 'Leah only has to look at food and it jumps around and becomes something delicious.'

'But still.' Ronan smiled. 'Surely nobody works on holiday?'

'You're painting a house.' Leah reached for one of the local yellow plums called mirabelles and bit into its sweet juiciness.

Ronan watched her lick juice from her lips. 'We're only kind of on holiday. My dad built the house when my mam was still alive and, hilariously, they named it "Chez Shea". After she died, he and I spent a lot of time here and eventually I inherited it from him. As I'm off work for a few weeks I thought I'd come out and give it some TLC. But anyway, why does food jump around and make itself delicious for you?'

'I trained as a chef but I work in chocolate products.' Leah reached for another plum, her hair swinging over one shoulder.

'She's a chocolate taster!' giggled Natasha. 'It must be the coolest job in the world.'

Curtis's eyes grew round in astonishment. He stared at Leah. 'Seriously? You taste chocolate? For a job?'

Leah's eyes twinkled. 'Before you apply, there's more to it than just scoffing chocolate down all day. I source ingredients, come up with new recipes or test other people's. I'm lucky to possess the correct palate.'

'So much so that when her last employer discovered she was moving to Chocs-a-million she was instantly put on gardening leave to remove her access to planned products,' put in Michele, drily. 'All right for some.'

'Like teachers don't get paid for taking the summer off?' Leah sent her sister a sidelong look.

'But "desk" isn't a four-letter word for me as it is for you –'

Jordan interrupted, evidently focused on the important stuff. 'She can make *amazing* cakes, Curtis. Talk to her nicely and she might make you something.'

Curtis gazed at Leah hopefully.

'She's on holiday,' Ronan reminded him.

But Leah obviously recognised suffering when she saw it. 'Maybe if we have a bad-weather day we can have a bit of a bake off. The kitchen in the gîte has a big oven and hob.'

'Yeah! Bake off!' gloated Jordan.

'Bake off, bake off!' sang Natasha.

Curtis switched his hopeful gaze to Ronan and Ronan softened. 'Sounds as if you're in luck.'

'Yeah, yeah, yeah, fanks!' breathed Curtis. 'I like making stuff. 'Specially stuff I can eat.'

'And we could have a chocolate tasting –'

'I'll get the chocolate.' Jordan raced off towards the gîte, leaving Leah halfway through her sentence.

Ronan felt his mouth stretch in a grin, in no doubt that she'd had no intention of the chocolate tasting taking place on the instant. Catching his eye, she managed to pull her face out of its expression of dismay, giving only a small eye roll before Jordan came loping back to the table, cradling three coloured packs in his hands.

'I'll have to move my stash to La Petite Annexe,' she observed, drily. She set one of the packs aside. 'This is open and, anyway, we need only two. OK, those who are taking part in the tasting, you need to drink water and eat a little dry bread to cleanse your palate.' Alister declared himself a spectator, Michele occupied herself with her phone, but Ronan joined Curtis, Jordan, Natasha and Leah in nibbling on crusts of bread while Leah went on. 'I'd normally taste in quite different surroundings. A product development kitchen's a cross between a kitchen and a science lab. It's clean and quiet and free of other tastes and smells. But this is only a demonstration so we'll pretend we can't see the remains of lunch or each other.'

She picked up the first large slab, enveloped in a deep brown paper with a dull sheen. Her hands were shapely, the nails short and plain. 'I'd normally make sure it was room temperature but France in August is hotter than I'd keep my kitchen so this has been in the fridge.'

Ronan found himself unexpectedly engaged. He enjoyed chocolate as much as the next man but his attention was more on the subtle shifts in Leah as her professional persona took over, showing itself in the confidence in her voice and body language. 'What difference does the temperature make?' he asked.

'Partly consistency but mainly that over-cool temperatures hinder my ability to detect flavours.' She gave him a quick smile. He found himself watching her mouth again. 'So here's the speed-dating version of how I'd assess a chocolate that's new to me, starting with the packaging because quality chocolate usually gets quality wrapping. This looks good to me.' She slipped a finger under the brown paper and pulled back the foil beneath to expose a dark slab of chocolate divided neatly into rectangles. 'Of the chocolate itself, I note that the surface is smooth and free from bloom – the whitish marks we sometimes see on cheap products, those that have been around too long or stored badly. The colour's good. The surface has a sheen which, in dark chocolate like this, lets me see other colours. It's a sort of brown rainbow visible to the practised eye.'

Ronan inspected the slab. He saw dark brown. No rainbow. Curtis flicked him a *what's she on about?* look.

'The precision in the moulding is another sign of quality. Then I listen.' She picked up the slab and broke off a rectangle, then broke it again. 'It should resonate when it snaps. Hear it?'

'Seriously?' Curtis demanded. 'Talking chocolate?'

Leah laughed. 'Buy a cheap bar and you'll be able to hear and see the difference. You won't get that snap and the product will be grainy and without lustre.' She turned the pieces of chocolate in her hands. 'See how this snapped? It has a sharp edge. That's how it should be.' She broke off four generous portions and handed them out. 'Don't eat it yet. Smell it. Enjoy the aroma and prepare your taste buds.' She inhaled, her eyes half shut. 'Smells good to me.'

'Yum,' agreed Natasha.

'So now – being glad that at a chocolate tasting we don't have to spit, as we would at a wine tasting – place a piece on your tongue. Don't chew unless it needs breaking slightly to release the flavours. Letting it melt on your tongue releases the cocoa butter and counteracts any bitterness. We're not eating, we're tasting. Close your eyes. Let yourself experience the flavour.'

Instead of closing his eyes, Ronan watched her close hers, observing her focused expression, and Jordan snaffling a second piece while Leah wasn't looking, then blushing when he realised Ronan was.

Slowly her eyes opened again. 'A beautiful, rich flavour.

This is good chocolate, high in cocoa solids, well presented, great aroma, just the sweet side of bitter. I'd expect it to temper well and I could make high-quality chocolate products from it.'

'What's tempering?' Ronan put in.

'It's a faffy procedure involving heating and cooling the chocolate slowly to avoid the cocoa butters separating out or crystallising. A product development kitchen for chocolate products will have a machine to do it with precision because it ensures smooth glossy chocolate for dipping and coating.'

'Your sensory perceptions must be well developed.' Ronan just stopped himself from using the word 'sensual' instead of 'sensory'. The sensual experience had been his, watching her.

'Can we try the other bar?' demanded Jordan.

'It is interesting to compare,' she agreed. 'It often helps me fully explore my impressions of one product to compare it to another. We need to cleanse our palates again, though.'

Nobody objected; in fact Jordan almost knocked his glass over in his haste to co-operate. Soon they were running through the process again, everyone closing their eyes and solemnly sucking chocolate. Unanimously, they scored the first bar higher than the second and Leah pointed out economies in the packaging of the second that hinted at a slightly lesser quality.

Generously, she let the kids 'taste' chocolate until it had all disappeared, then Curtis, Jordan and Natasha wandered over to the shadier part of the garden – 'which means they don't want us to listen in,' observed Alister – and Michele stowed her phone and did the polite-company thing in asking Ronan all about himself. 'So are you being paid not to work, this summer, like Leah?'

Ronan caught the faintly exasperated look that Leah sent Michele. He'd worked out that the two were sisters but thought some of Michele's digs were a bit uncalled for.

Before Leah could respond, however, her phone buzzed to claim her attention, and Ronan responded courteously. 'I broke my clavicle and had to have it pinned. Luckily it was my left side and painting uses my right.' He rubbed the dull ache that made his shoulder heavy and stiff. From the corner of his eye he could see Leah tapping rapidly at her phone screen. The phone buzzed again almost straightaway and she snorted with amusement before resuming her tapping.

'Poor you,' said Michele. 'How did that happen?'

'I'm a helicopter pilot and I had a bit of an incident, but in a few weeks I should be passed fit to fly again.' He deliberately glossed over what had happened. Those who didn't fly treated it like a big deal to get an ailing helicopter to the ground rather than the simple good airmanship that it was. Now the op was over and the healing well under way he didn't want to indulge avid requests for information. He just wanted to enjoy the extra time with Curtis.

Happily, Michele seized on his job as the interesting element of his explanation. 'Helicopter pilot? Glamorous! Makes teaching look boring.'

Alister smacked his lips over his wine. 'Ha! Maybe, though that depends on the teacher.'

Michele sent him a death glare and Leah hastily put away her phone and butted in. 'A helicopter pilot? That's cool.'

She had her work cut out as peacekeeper between her sister and her husband, Ronan decided as he smiled at her. 'Flying's my life. I work for an air tours company called Buzz Sightseer, flying tourists over London. I'm the chief pilot and helped build the company up from day one.'

Leah found herself fascinated as Ronan talked, relaxed and easy in his chair, long legs crossed at the ankle.

He lived on the southeastern fringe of London's urban sprawl, was divorced, and shared Curtis's care with ex-wife Selina. He'd been brought up in Ireland, 'the rocky bit, right at the top', but his dad had moved the family to England, where he helped Ronan through university and on his way to his commercial pilot's licence before he passed away. 'Dad would've been pleased that I got the career I love,' he concluded. He gave the impression of calm control, of not wasting words, except to occasionally inject flashes of dry humour into the conversation.

When Leah finally glanced at her watch the time had whizzed around to almost four. Regretfully, she searched around in the grass for her sandals. 'I'd better get off to the supermarket, unless we're eating out tonight.'

Ronan sat up. 'The supermarket in Muntsheim? I don't suppose I could beg a lift? My car's having work done and the garage said it should be ready round about now. I was going to call a cab.'

Alister sloshed more wine into his glass. 'You can leave Curtis here if he wants. He seems to be stopping our two from bickering.'

Ronan grinned. 'And miss a ride in your pink car?'

Alister snorted. 'Not my car.'

'I did think it was a bit pretty.' Ronan went to check with Curtis, who looked up only long enough to say that the others had given him the password to the wifi and he was quite happy where he was. Ronan going off without him was, apparently, 'Cool beans'.

'I'll come with you.' Michele began to get to her feet.

Although she understood the eye-roll Michele directed towards Alister, Leah suddenly found she'd used up her quota of sisterly compassion for the afternoon. 'Sorry, no room, I want to give my car a run,' she whispered. Once she'd dropped Ronan at the garage she could blast out into the countryside, letting her satnav bring her back to Muntsheim to do the shopping when she was happily chilled. Surely she was entitled to snatch a few moments from this tense, unholidayish holiday, to open her car windows and let the wind blow it all away?

Refusing to hear Michele's 'But –!', Leah ducked into La Petite Annexe for her keys and purse then emerged with a brief ''Bye!' and a hasty 'C'mon' in Ronan's direction.

Ronan, with a last word to Curtis, allowed himself to be collected up and chivvied out of the garden.

From his position, prone on the cool grass, Curtis watched his dad follow Leah up the path beside the house.

He turned back to his new friends. 'Your mum's a MILF,' he muttered, too quietly for the adults to hear. He'd been waiting to use the line ever since he'd seen *American Pie* on DVD when his mum and Darren had been out one evening but, frankly, mums usually weren't.

'What's a MILF?' Natasha screwed her neck to try and see what Curtis was doing on his phone.

Jordan groaned. 'You must need your eyes testing. And don't even think it. She's our *mum*.'

'Still a MILF.'

A throaty roar emanated from around the house. Jordan

cocked an ear. 'Leah's taking the Porsche. Hope your dad doesn't scare easy.'

Curtis stared. Jordan had short back 'n' sides dark hair. Curtis wished he, too, had dark hair, like his dad, instead of being sandy with freckles, like his mum. 'Why do you call her Leah?'

Propping his chin on his hand, Jordan treated him to a condescending stare. 'Because . . . it's, like, her *name*?'

'Duh! But why don't you call her Mum?'

Jordan frowned. Then he began to laugh. He laughed so hard he had to slap the ground making that 'Huuuurgh!' sound between peals that people did when they couldn't even inhale for mirth.

Curtis gave Jordan a shove. 'What?'

Although she giggled, Natasha was more helpful. 'Leah's not our mum. She's our cool auntie.' She nodded to where Michele was talking in a low voice to Alister, who was brandishing the nearly empty wine bottle. 'That's our mum.'

Jordan laughed harder. 'Do you still think our mother's a MILF?'

Face burning, Curtis realised he hadn't even thought who Michele was in relation to the rest of the group. Yet Michele was much more his idea of a mother – old and a bit plump, wearing a frown most of the time. 'Erm, sorry.' The 'No' was implicit in his tone.

'Leah can't be a MILF because she's not a mother,' Jordan pursued, with unanswerable logic. 'She'd have to be an "AILF", which you can't even say.' His voice was rich with the superiority a fifteen-year-old reserved for thirteen-year-olds.

Scowling, Curtis hunted for a way to redress the stupidity scale. 'Does she ever look after you?' He ripped up a handful of lawn to throw into Jordan's face.

Jordan coughed up a blade of grass before mashing Curtis's head playfully into the ground. 'I'm a bit old to need looking after. She used to though.'

'If she's a babysitter she's a BILF then,' Curtis said smugly, and got the Urban Dictionary up on his phone to prove that 'BILF' wasn't something he'd made up.

Natasha clamoured, 'But what *is* a MILF? And what *is* a BILF?'

In the vicious tone siblings seemed to reserve for moments of inexplicable irritation Jordan suddenly snapped, 'Look it up, Gnasher.'

Glaring at her brother, Natasha snatched up her phone. 'I will, then, in the Urban Dictionary!'

But as Curtis could see she was spelling it 'erban' she had no success. Soon she shoved her phone in her pocket and went off to the woman that Curtis now understood to be her mother, complaining that the lemonade was warm.

As she drove out of the village, Leah relaxed into the driving seat of the Porsche and glanced over at where Ronan lounged in the passenger seat. 'I didn't want to subject you to The Pig.' As if she would, when she hadn't driven the scarlet Porsche Cayman since washing the dust from her after the long trek to Kirchhoffen.

Ronan ran his fingertips over the stitching in the leather. 'I can understand why.'

'I love this car. I never get tired of driving it.' Feeling a surge of proprietary delight to be behind the wheel, Leah began to accelerate up the lane out of the village, slotting into third gear as the engine note climbed.

'And Alister doesn't mind?'

'What?' Flicking into fourth, Leah felt the day's irritations slithering from her shoulders, glorying in the power of the engine that thrust her back in her seat.

'He doesn't mind you driving it?'

The irritations thudded smartly back. 'Mind? Not at all.' Leah kept her eyes on the road, turning over in her mind the realisation that Ronan, who handled a truly cool machine as his job, appeared to have leaped to the conclusion that the Porsche could only belong to a man. Her foot steadied on the accelerator and she reined herself in to a stately forty-five miles per hour.

Leah butted heads with dismissive men every time she went on a track day, especially when she was the only female participant. It had created in her a burning need to prove herself in the eyes of the condescending male. In fact, most males. The need was burning particularly fiercely right at this moment, urging her to make a stand on behalf of snubbed women drivers everywhere. And though they were currently sailing past neatly laid-out fields that rose up to meet more distant tree-clothed hills she knew they'd soon come to a half-finished business park on the outskirts of Muntsheim with a very different kind of wide-open space. One that would provide the perfect arena to challenge Ronan's assumptions.

As she formulated her plans Ronan made up for her silence with a helpful rundown of the tram system into Strasbourg and where to find the 'office de tourisme', near the cathedral. 'But perhaps you've visited Strasbourg already?' he prompted.

Leah, attention not really on city tourist traps, replied absently, 'I expect we'll get there but Alister's more into cycling and active stuff,' and Ronan retreated into silence, too. Maybe he was worried Leah wasn't capable of talking and driving at the same time, she thought, grinning to herself.

Ten minutes later the fields petered out and the road became broader and busier, street lighting and advertising hoardings signalling the town's approaches. The business park came up on their left. Leah slowed to give it the once over. Work at the site looked to have halted some time ago. Red skips and depleted brick stacks were corralled behind temporary fencing but she saw no sign of a workforce.

Would the owners mind her borrowing their big empty car park for a few minutes?

No, she decided, as she indicated and turned across the traffic to nose the car through a drunken line of plastic cones.

Ronan glanced across at her, expression perplexed. 'You'll need to go on a bit for either the supermarket or the garage.'

'Oh, dear!' Leah tried to look as if she were gazing about helplessly while actually assessing the area for hazards. 'I'll turn around.' She straightened the car up, confirmed it was in first gear and made a last check of her mirrors. Then she stamped on the accelerator.

'Whoa!' gasped Ronan as the engine, howling in joy that it was playtime, catapulted them across the tarmac.

'Oops,' crooned Leah, relishing the feeling of acceleration. Settling her left hand on the handbrake she gathered power for another few seconds. Then she simultaneously yanked up the handbrake, stamped on the clutch and spun the steering wheel hard left. The Porsche changed direction like a dog chasing a rat.

Flung against the door, Ronan gasped. 'What the fu—'

Standing on the accelerator again Leah sent the car flying back the way it had come, powered up, yanked the car into a doughnut that made her tyres screech, slammed into reverse, J-turned, and screamed to a halt neatly facing the exit.

'It's not Alister's car,' she pointed out, breathlessly. 'It's mine.'

Chapter Three

Ronan checked all his limbs were still attached and that his head could move from side to side. All OK.

But his shoulder was on fire, stopping his breath. Heat was building in his temples, too, but that wasn't medical.

It was simple good old-fashioned fury.

Slowly, he turned to contemplate the woman beside him. She was removing her sunglasses; grin blazing, eyes dancing, as she awaited his reaction.

He didn't keep her waiting for long. 'What part of "I broke my clavicle" didn't you understand? I'm still healing! My career is hinging on my recovery and you throw me around like an insane fucking idiot!'

The grin flicked off and Leah's eyes widened with horror. 'What?' she gasped. 'I didn't know you'd been hurt!' She actually clapped her hand to her forehead like a sitcom actor.

'How could you not know? You were sitting right there when I explained! And, anyway, you don't put someone through your stupid antics without knowing their medical history. You could *kill someone*!' The final two words emerged in a kind of strangled roar.

White to her hairline, she swallowed hard. 'I am so sorry. Should I get you to a doctor? Should you lie down? Do you have medication?'

'As far as I know, I'm in one piece,' he allowed grumpily, sliding over the peak of his anger as he eased his shoulder up, down and round, laying tender fingers on his collarbone. 'It's still working, which is better than I'd expect from being hurled into a series of car stunts without warning, helmet, harness or other rudimentary provision for my safety.'

She hung her head but not before he saw tears well in her eyes. 'I can only apologise. I was showing off.'

Silence, apart from the smug purr of the engine, while Ronan fought with himself. Probably she had been expecting him to be impressed by her prowess but it had been an idiotic piece of exhibitionism and part of him wished the driver had been a man so he could drag him from behind the wheel and vent. Leah being female – the bikini had left him in no doubt about that – physically relieving his feelings was not an option.

He drew in a slow breath. And then another. 'In my job I take safety extremely seriously and to have someone do that for a joke in my current circumstances—'

'—is *unacceptable*,' she agreed, wretchedly. 'Unacceptable in any circumstances. Showing off is exactly what my instructor told me never to do. I completely understand.' Her voice had thickened. 'Should I take you to the garage? Will you be able to drive home? Are you certain you shouldn't see a doctor? There might be a hospital in Muntsheim or I could take you into Strasbourg.'

At her obviously miserable guilt he felt the remains of his fury drain away. He flexed his arm experimentally. It worked fine. 'Let's just go. I think I'll be OK to drive.'

'Right.' Gently, she put the car into gear and pulled away like a granny with a full load of eggs on board.

Ronan glanced at her as she rejoined the traffic. She'd replaced her sunglasses, so he couldn't see her eyes but he could see her hand tremble on the gear stick and he began to wish he hadn't been such a diva. She'd only meant to have fun at his expense and when he was fit he liked fun. Every pilot had adrenalin-junkie tendencies beneath the control and precision that governed the job. If the episode had occurred six months ago he would probably have howled with laughter as she'd flung the powerful car around like a pro.

But since he'd had a stark reminder of his own fragility and the way that his career, like a helicopter, depended on everything being in top working order, he was more cautious. 'Left at the square, then the garage is at the top of the hill.'

She nodded.

He tried to think back to the moment when he'd explained his injury in the after-lunch social chatter. Alister had been soaking up the sun and the wine in equal measures. Michele had been asking Ronan twenty questions . . . and, damn, Leah had been texting, frowning in concentration as her thumbs flew.

She hadn't been listening.

Before he could acknowledge this they pulled up at Garage Zimmermann to be greeted by a deserted forecourt and a padlock shining dully on a big blue sliding door. Ronan sighed. 'Great. My car's probably the other side of that. But it looks as if there's a note.' He left her sitting silently while he hopped out to squint at the few scrawled words on an envelope taped to the door.

In moments he was letting himself back down into the

passenger seat. 'I think it says that they'll be back at five but the note appears to have been written with a blunt pencil held between the toes.'

'Shall we hang around?' she queried, ultra-politely. 'Or would you prefer to wait alone? Unless you think you shouldn't be left alone,' she added.

Her woefulness made his conscience twinge anew that he'd been so heavy on the self-righteous indignation. 'I probably shouldn't be left alone, actually.' He smiled, though it was wasted as she was looking anywhere but at him. 'There's a nice café on the square where you can keep an eye on me.'

At least his words made the corners of her mouth relax. 'I could use a shot of caffeine,' she confessed.

He directed her to the Rue des Roses where he felt sure of Muntsheim's sometimes complex parking system and they strolled through to La Place de la Liberté, a pretty, popular square surrounded by shops. They took a table outside Café des Trois Cigognes where they could watch the sun making diamonds of the splashing water in the fountains.

Leah ordered espresso and he was glad to see some colour return to her cheeks as she sipped the black brew.

He added milk to his Americano. 'Now I've got over myself, I'm in awe of your driving. Are you a stunt woman in your spare time?'

Her smile was so faint that it was hardly there. 'I like going on experience days – stunt, drifting, performance, that kind of thing. I don't usually do it in my own car and I've left some expensive rubber on that car park. That, as well as putting your health in danger, will teach me not to show off.' Under the shade of the parasol she'd lodged her sunglasses on top of her head, allowing him to see the contrition in her eyes. 'I don't know where my brain went. Whenever I do an experience day I have to fill in a huge medical questionnaire so I know that before you start throwing a car around you have to be sure there are no issues for anyone who might be in it.' She clattered her cup on its saucer.

'If being up yourself is a medical condition, I certainly suffered a severe episode,' he observed, gravely. 'Honestly, I'm usually more adventurous.' He was rewarded by a glimpse of a proper smile, a big improvement on the wretched mask she'd been wearing for the last half-hour. 'I apologise–'

She cut across him. 'No, don't. I was the one in the wrong.'

He leaned a little closer. 'But I could have put my objections across without being a gobshite.'

The smile flickered again so he was encouraged to continue. 'Here are the highlights of the conversation you evidently missed. At the beginning of July I had what's known as "a hard landing" in a helicopter. I did my collarbone and now I can't go flying until the doctors say so.'

'When's that likely to be?' Her gold-brown gaze shifted to him.

'Maybe September if, by then, the pain has gone, my orthopaedic surgeon says I'm OK and my Aviation Medical Examiner agrees. I'm on full pay so I expect my boss, Henry, will want me back in the air as soon as possible – as I want to be. Flying's one of those things that isn't so much what someone does but what they are. If I can't fly . . .' He lifted his hands in a gesture of despondency.

At this stage, most people demanded details of the

landing, whether he'd hurt anyone else and whether he'd made the news. The answers were 'No' and 'Yes'. Inevitably, a fascination with the sensational would then lead them to demand to know whether it was his fault. When the answer to that was also 'No' it was beyond irritating to see their faces fall at discovering no juicy incompetence to chew on.

But Leah's mind obviously trod a different route. 'But your shoulder was well enough for you to drive all the way over here?'

He flexed his shoulder. 'We flew with an airline. Dad's old BMW's kept here and it's an auto, so I can manage local journeys.' As she'd brought up the subject of cars he decided to broach the elephant in the café. 'I presume our exciting tour of the car park was prompted by my assumption that because the Porsche is a powerful machine it must therefore belong to your husband? I apologise for falling for sexist stereotypes but, in my defence, Alister had been quite emphatic about the big pink car not being his. As I'd seen you driving it, I therefore assumed it was yours.'

Her eyebrows flew up. Then clanged down. 'My what?'

'Your car.'

'No. Before that. Husband?'

He tried to work out what had prompted her aghast expression. 'Have I committed another solecism? Your *partner*. Significant other. Boyfriend. Baby-dadda. *Alister*.'

Suddenly her smile was back, full strength and dazzling along with dancing eyes. 'Alister's my brother-in-law. He's married to Michele.'

He couldn't hide his astonishment. 'Alister and Michele are married?'

A short laugh. 'Well, separated. It's very recent, hence

their interesting decision that both should be included in the family holiday. My presence here is to defuse tension – though I'm not sure it's working. What on earth made you think I'm married to Alister? He's a lovely man, of course,' she added, quickly, 'but a lot older than me.'

'The first time I saw you – when I was the one showing off, jumping in like a callow youth to air my French – Natasha fetched you to join your family and mentioned "Dad" so I mentally pigeonholed you as the mum.'

'A mum to two teenagers? I obviously need to upgrade my moisturiser. Michele's eight years older than I am and Alister's four years older than her.'

'You look miles and miles too young,' he agreed, grinning as she rolled her eyes at his flattery. 'But you could have started early or Natasha and Jordan could be your stepkids. Families come in many permutations. I saw you going out with Alister and the children, and with Michele having a boyfriend – though that's explained now that I know of the separation – I drew the conclusion that you and Alister were a couple.'

'Boyfriend?' she repeated blankly. 'Michele has a boyfriend? As in . . . *boyfriend*?'

Uh-oh. Uh-bloody-oh. Leah was looking as shocked as if he'd just keyed her precious car. He could only think that he'd just let a particularly scabby cat out of an inadequately fastened bag. He'd escaped his own distressing domestic strife too recently to involve himself with anybody else's and his first instinct was to backtrack. 'Hasn't she? Perhaps the stunt driving affected my brain. Shall we try the garage again? I'd hate the mechanics to have finished for the day by the time I get back. And you have shopping to do.'

'Tell me why you think she has a boyfriend, first.'

He shifted uncomfortably. 'I'd much rather not.'

She gazed at him for several seconds, then slumped back into her chair. 'I understand.' She took up her coffee cup as if she had nothing more on her mind than savouring its richness. Until she tacked on: 'I'll simply confront Michele when I get back to the gîte. I put aside my own plans to come on this holiday and supposedly save her from shooting herself.' Her sentences began to rise both in speed and volume. 'I've driven her ugly fat car and played mum while she, she said, was under the weather. I've endured her bitching with Alister, I've taken on most of the domestic drudgery, I'm doing everything I can to support her family. But a boyfriend is a detail she hasn't shared with me and, frankly, it does put things in a different light.'

Her colour stormed from chalky white to angry red. 'And if I lose my temper it may involve shaking my sister by the throat. So if you want to avoid me being thrown into a French prison I'd really appreciate it if you'd tell me what you think you know so that I have a chance to calm down before I get back!'

Though taking a second to note that Leah looked amazing with her eyes snapping angrily, he could understand her feeling that she had a right to the truth. Also, if he refused to explain, it would surely mean a chill between them. And as he was already bound for Michele's shit-list when Leah tackled her because the only ones around to report her activities were Ronan or Curtis, there seemed no point in hacking Leah off, too.

He gave in. 'I was painting the front of the house. A car pulled up and Michele rushed out and got into it. A man was in the driving seat. They kissed.'

'Not a peck on the cheek?' The sun picked out the gold flecks in Leah's eyes.

'By no means.' Not unless Michele kept her cheek halfway down her throat. Then, because Leah obviously wasn't going to give up before she'd drawn out the relevant details, he added, 'An intimate, passionate kiss. Or ten.'

'Right.' She turned to gaze over the square.

Ronan gave her time to absorb this obviously unexpected and unwelcome news, trying not to glance at his watch. He truly was beginning to get fidgety about his car.

'Was your divorce amicable?' she asked, suddenly. 'I'm beginning to wonder whether they ever can be.'

Though surprised by this tangent, he answered neutrally. 'In my case, it was exasperating more than anything, much in keeping with Selina's usual way of doing things. Time had already proved that we hadn't made a heavenly match. I would have stuck with her for Curtis's sake, but she met Darren and I was left with no real choice but to accept it and help Curtis with the realities of the break-up. I settled for "reasonably civilised" rather than "amicable" – considering how aggrieved I felt that my desire to hang on to Chez Shea meant Selina coming in for most of the equity from the marital home. It had been funded from what Dad left me plus the sweat of my brow before Selina ever moved in.

'Anyway, that's the way the law works. For nearly three years we've lived apart but in the same part of Orpington, close enough that we can share custody and Curtis can stay with me as my work rota allows.'

Her gaze softened. 'How's it working out? I'm anxious for Natasha and Jordan.'

He felt the familiar tug of unhappiness. 'It's not the same as living together full time. It's hard, part-time fatherhood.

Not able to see your child every day, being excluded from swathes of his life. It's no wonder that Curtis is growing away from me.'

'Is he?' She propped her elbows on the table as she watched his face, seeming to have completely set aside her beef with her sister while she concentrated all her attention on him.

He had to force a laugh so as not to choke at the sympathy in her eyes. 'Maybe it would have been the same even if we'd still been a family. Teenagers are teenagers. I hate his Goth look and his obviously cultivated mispronunciations. He's been able to pronounce "thanks" perfectly well till now.'

She groaned. 'But that's just teenspeak, isn't it? Like Natasha with "obvs" instead of obviously and "forevs" for forever. I expect it's just the new "fing".'

'I don't know about Jordan and Natasha but Curtis is full of new "fings", like turning up at the beginning of the holiday with all that ironmongery on his face, for which Selina gave permission without consulting me. I was furious but I had to swallow it for the sake of good relations with them both. I told myself that piercings can grow over once the hardware's removed, so not to make a big thing out of it, and hope it's just a phase. What if Selina had let him have tattoos?' He felt his jaw tighten. Then he saw that Leah had two rings in each ear. 'Not that I've got anything against piercings per se. He's just too young.'

'If he's like Jordan he loves to do things he's too young for.' She jumped to her feet, switching with dizzying speed from deep conversation to decisive action. 'Let's reunite you with your car. We both have things to do.' She dropped some euros on the table without giving him a chance to contribute and strode off towards Rue des Roses.

When they returned to the dusty collection of buildings that made up Garage Zimmermann the doors had been pushed back and Ronan could see the aging BMW inside. 'Looks like I'm good to go. Thanks for the lift.'

Her hand on his arm stayed him as he went to open her car door. 'Thanks, Ronan. I put you in a difficult position about the boyfriend and I hope you understand why I was angry. I won't really attack my sister.' Her smile wobbled. 'The kids have had enough to put up with.'

He nodded. 'It's always the kids.' Then he kissed her cheek, because why the hell not? He might as well get something good out of an afternoon that had left him with his shoulder thumping like a bitch. He didn't want to make Leah feel bad by going over to the pharmacy to buy painkillers, though. He had some in the car and he'd ask for water at the garage to take them after she'd gone.

In fact, by the time Ronan made it back to Kirchhoffen his shoulder pain had subsided to a dull ache, thanks to managing the steering wheel mainly one-handed. He found Curtis still sprawled on their neighbour's lawn between Natasha and Jordan, heads close together as they played something incomprehensible on their phones. Alister was nowhere in sight but Michele looked up from a magazine to greet him.

Ronan, returning a polite response, wondered if her smile would be quite so wide if she knew what beans he'd just spilled to Leah. He nudged Curtis with his toe. 'We'd better get something sorted for dinner.'

Curtis didn't even look up from the game he was playing so furiously. 'We're eating here. Natasha, get the wither skeleton skull.'

‘What do I do with it?’ Natasha frowned as her thumbs darted over her phone screen.

‘Put it on the wither skeleton!’ Curtis and Jordan chorused scornfully.

‘Oh, yeah.’ Natasha looked abashed and the three laughed together as if Ronan had become invisible.

‘Curtis,’ Ronan said quietly, in the voice that meant he wasn’t enjoying invisibility.

Curtis paused his game with a put-upon sigh, the heading-for-a-storm expression Ronan was getting to know lurking in his eyes. ‘Natasha and Jordan’s mum has invited us to have a barbie with them.’ Then, perhaps realising from Ronan’s frown that the use of manners might help achieve the result he was looking for, ‘Can we stay, please?’

Michele called. ‘Do! Leah will be home any time with the food. She does a mean barbecue.’

Ronan debated. Leah wouldn’t tackle her sister about the boyfriend in front of the children and Curtis having company was exactly what Ronan wanted as, so far this summer, the only other teens around the village had been French, and Curtis’s language skills weren’t quite good enough to keep up. And Ronan was prepared to put up with Michele now if it meant gaining a little more of Leah’s company later.

‘Thanks.’ He pulled up a garden chair and assumed a politely attentive expression as Michele launched into her impressions of Alsace, thinking, as he listened, how little resemblance he could discern between the sisters. Michele’s hair was shorter, curlier, and highlighted an improbable silvery blonde. Taller and more thickset, she was pallid compared to Leah’s sun-kissed glow. If Ronan had to pick a descriptor for Michele it would be ‘self-orientated’, whereas there seemed no single term to express Leah. She was complex, fun, unexpected, valiant, interesting – not to mention so hot and curvy that she'd look just as at home sprawled over a bonnet at a car show as she obviously was behind the wheel. And she'd probably be extremely hacked off at him if she knew that he'd let the thought of her as a hood ornament stray across his mind.

Still, he tried to turn the conversation to his topic of interest. 'Your sister loves her car.'

'Leah's pose-mobile.' Michele wrinkled her nose. 'Proper petrol-head is Leah. Spends half her life at circuits with Scott Matthewson.'

'Is that her boyfriend?' Damn.

'No, just her ever-present best buddy. I'm quite glad, really,' she added, frankly. 'He wouldn't be the best boyfriend for Leah. Heteroflexible,' she added, meaningfully.

Reassured by 'buddy' and not needing 'heteroflexible' explained to him, Ronan decided not to make his interest obvious by enquiring whether there was a boyfriend as well. Hearing a deep engine note approaching, he jumped up. 'Sounds like Leah. I'll help unload.' He strode around the house, intercepting a frowning Leah as she yanked shopping from the Porsche's boot.

He made his voice low as he threaded his fingers through the handles of several bulging bags. 'Heads up. Michele's invited us for a barbecue and Curtis was keen so I agreed. Sorry if that creates an obstacle to you shaking her by the throat.'

She managed a one-cornered smile. 'I haven't finished brooding so she's safe.'

'Good to know.' Following her around to the kitchen door, he let his voice return to social volume. 'That boot takes more than I'd have guessed.'

‘Enough for me,’ she agreed. Passing through the garden, she shouted hellos.

‘I thought we could barbecue,’ Michele called, without moving a muscle.

‘Already got the news. On it.’

Not intending to get stuck with Michele again, Ronan elected to hang out with Leah in the kitchen. Soon the kids piled in and there were four pairs of helping hands. Or one pair of hands, plus three eager potential diners making menu requests and getting in the way.

Leah made no complaint that Michele didn’t budge from her comfortable spot, or that when Alister reappeared he was grouchy because he’d drunk too much wine in the sun and, despite a nap, his head was clanging. She just laughed and joked with the children and calmly managed to barbecue in the garden as well as preparing a salad *and* steam a chocolate and marshmallow melt-in-the middle pudding in the kitchen.

Ronan buttered bread and carried whatever needed carrying, earning an approving nod from Leah. ‘A kitchen porter who doesn’t forget, avoid or bitch about the task at hand; you’re a priceless commodity.’

‘Glad you’re impressed.’ He was enjoying his arm brushing hers as they manoeuvred around each other so he forbore to point out that fetching and carrying wasn’t hard compared to his normal job of delicately controlling the height and speed of a complex piece of machinery in the air, reading instruments, navigating, communicating with the ground and simultaneously giving his spiel to exclaiming tourists about the Gherkin Building and the London Eye.

He helped clear up after the meal when Michele excused herself in pursuit of an early night and the children went off indoors somewhere to play pool. Alister dozed over more wine and Ronan was glad all over again that Alister and Leah weren't married. It made Ronan feel better about hanging on for coffee with her and remembering how good she'd looked in that purple bikini.

Chapter Four

Natasha, Jordan and Curtis were already strapped into The Pig and Alister was loading the day's supply of drinks and snacks when Leah, reasoning that the end justified the means, dropped the bad news on him.

'Alister, do you mind taking the kids to the aerial activity park on your own? I'm feeling too bleugh to whiz down ziplines. First day of the month, you know.' Smiling apologetically, she counted on the reference to her cycle to discourage protests or questions.

Alister flushed slightly as he took the car keys but was unable to resist enlarging her French vocabulary. 'Of course I don't mind taking the kids to *le parc accrobranche*. You stay here and, um, recover.'

Though she suffered a pang of guilt at jumping ship – or jumping Pig – Leah waved farewell as the vehicle reversed out of the drive. Jordan and Natasha, mouths forming Os of surprise, were obviously questioning their dad as to why Leah was left behind. Then, evidently satisfied with whatever reply he made, Natasha waved back and Jordan turned to talk to Curtis.

Once they were out of sight, Leah let herself back into the house silently and padded through the kitchen to the salon, a formal room the family hadn't much bothered with. Its window gave a good view through the shrubs and down the empty drive to the lane though, and Leah sank onto the sofa to worry gently while she waited.

Her patience was rewarded twenty minutes later when a blue hatchback pulled up in the lane outside. Heart ticking anxiously, Leah watched the driver take out a phone and tap at it. *A text to announce his arrival*, she thought. Sure enough, she heard an upstairs door open – *Michelle's room* – and footsteps dance down the wooden stairs. Another opening door – *back door* – and, moments later, Michele came into view, skipping down the drive – *wearing one of her most flattering dresses. Hair freshly blow-dried.* A hop into the car, the driver leaned towards Michele – *kissing* – for a long minute – *ages* – and, finally, the engine note rose and the car roared off.

Despite seeing exactly what she'd been warned she would, Leah felt sick with disappointment and dismay.

Michele had been constantly lying about her state of health to get rid of her family so that she could meet up with her lover.

It was several minutes before Leah could coax movement from her heavy limbs. What could she – or should she – do? The existence of a boyfriend made Michele's mess worse, destroying as it did any lingering hopes of reconciliation.

Poor Jordan and Natasha. Poor Alister.

Poor, *poor* Alister – because Leah had recognised the car before she'd recognised the boyfriend. The metallic cobalt-blue boyracer hatchback with alloy wheels, spoilers and skirts belonged to Bailey Johns, a buff personal trainer and coach at Peak Fitness, the gym-cum-community centre used by the Milton family. Bailey coached Jordan's soccer team and was high on his hero-worship scale; Jordan could often be found in the crowd of adolescents hanging around the car. As a fellow petrol-head, though she preferred her cars without giant air boxes or pointless light arrays, Leah chatted to Bailey on the odd occasion she picked Jordan up.

Michele, too, knew Bailey as Jordan's footie coach. Leah remembered how Michele had seemed a reluctant joiner of Peak Fitness a year ago but soon developed unexpected gym-bunny tendencies. Leah had put it down to her realising that, at forty-three, she had to make more effort. Now, when viewed along with a growing predilection for having her hair and nails done professionally, Michele's gym visits made a different, disappointing kind of sense.

In a fog of misery, Leah sought comfort in the familiarity of the kitchen but couldn't even settle to baking. Her eyes burned every time she thought of Natasha's uncertain little smile when confronted with uncomfortable situations and Jordan's scowl when his feelings were hurt. They were young to be asked to cope with one heartache after another. They'd been so brave. But Leah would have had to be blind not to notice Natasha sometimes on the edge of tears or Jordan being especially grouchy and Alister quietly gathering them into comforting hugs.

Michele was an adult and there was nothing Leah could do about the way she chose to live her life. Yet . . . nothing was exactly what she couldn't do. She took out her phone.

Leah: Can you come back to the gîte now, please? Important.

The reply pinged back after a few minutes.

Michele: ??? Aren't you at this zipline thing? :-/
Leah: *No. But Alister and the kids are.*

A much longer pause, long enough for Leah to make and drink a cup of coffee, then:

Michele: *On my way.*

Leah passed the time wiping kitchen surfaces that didn't need wiping, feeling uncomfortably like an angry parent waiting up for a misbehaving adolescent. The sensation was unreal and unfamiliar.

Finally, Michele stepped tentatively through the back door like a cat sensing trouble, gaze wary. 'What's up?'

Leah had to swallow unexpected tears. *This isn't about you. It's about them.* 'You didn't mention that you had a boyfriend.'

A pause. Michele fiddled with the buckle on her bag strap. 'No.'

Leah refused to allow the single clipped word to wall her out. 'I'm going to ask you again: is Baby Three Alister's?'

Michele heaved a great sigh. 'No.'

A fresh heart-sink. 'Certain?'

Michele nodded.

'Poor Alister. Does he know?'

'He knows he's not the father. Obviously.' Michele gave a mirthless laugh, drifting drearily into the room as if realising there was no longer any hiding place. 'Not difficult to deduce when we haven't had sex in a year.' She threw down her bag and dragged out a chair. 'He says I have to tell the kids; he won't do it. He's given me a deadline of the end of the holiday, before I begin to show and they guess. It's part of why he's muscled his way into the holiday, to support them when I do.'

Stricken, Leah plumped down to face her. 'Michele! No wonder he's so broken. It must be agony for him, not just knowing you're carrying another man's child but worrying about how the kids are going to take it too. Why did you lie to *me* about it?'

Gaze shifting, Michele shrugged. 'I didn't. I just acted outraged and you took it as a denial.'

'Deliberately making someone think something when it's actually untrue is a lie. Did you think it might change whether I'd support you?' Leah moved on to the next issue. 'And it's Bailey Johns. He's all but a generation younger than Alister. And how do you think Jordan's going to react when he finds out? He considers Bailey supercool.'

'I keep telling you it's a mess.' Michele wiped a tear from beneath her eye. She didn't look surprised that Leah knew Bailey's identity. She'd probably worked out that letting him pick her up from the gîte had been a complacent step too far.

'I don't know whether to be indignant, envious or reluctantly impressed,' Leah went on. 'Bailey's in his *twenties*!'

'He'll soon be thirty.'

Leah's mind was buzzing as she tried to put together the pieces of the puzzle. 'How on earth does Bailey come to be in France, anyway?'

'He wanted to be near me. It's not as if I invited him or planned it. But once he was here . . .'

'Is he staying nearby?'

Michele nodded. 'A hotel in Muntsheim.'

The sisters stared at one another. Anger began to prickle beneath Leah's skin. Her voice dropped. 'What the hell are you thinking? This midlife crisis is equal parts selfishness and insanity! You're the Unstepford Wife, leaving your marriage, bringing your twinkie on holiday when you're supposed to be with your family–'

'My what?' Michele looked confused.

'Twinkie,' Leah snapped. 'Younger lover. Toy boy. You're depriving your kids of their father for a *fling* with a *twinkie*.'

Michele dropped her chin on her palm and met Leah's gaze. Now the horrible moment of discovery was over she was beginning to look relieved, almost relaxed. There was even a hint of defiance. 'You're trying to diminish what we have with scornful words but I'm in love. I'm in love in a way I've never been in love with Alister – unless it was so long ago I've forgotten. I got to know Bailey properly and suddenly all that was important was the next time I'd see him and the expression in his eyes when he looked at me. He knew I was married with children. He tried to keep away from me but I never tried to keep away from him because nothing else seemed to matter.' Her eyes shimmered with tears. 'I fell in love and the world changed.'

'Love? Or infatuation?'

'Call it what you want. I know what I feel.' Michele looked defensive and rose to clatter around restlessly with the icemaker, dropping cubes into glasses, pouring iced tea from the fridge. 'My contraception failed and I found myself pregnant like some clueless teenager. It plunged me into a nightmare of telling Alister we were over, and Natasha and Jordan we wouldn't be living with their father any more. I hated myself for what I was doing to my children but there was no way back.' Her laugh was like a sob. 'Then I had to tell Bailey he was going to be a parent. But he wasn't scared off, because he loves me.'

She brought over a glass of tea, mint and lemon floating

on the top, and placed it before Leah like a peace offering. 'Forgive me for not telling you the truth, Leah. I did need you on my side, here, supporting the family. Selfish and insane I may be but I know when I've got too much on my plate – and you have so little on yours. Your life's just about you.'

'That's not fair!' Leah jerked upright, stung by this offhand dismissal of her life choices.

But Michele was already onto the next point on her agenda, grabbing Leah's hands across the table for emphasis. 'I understand that Natasha and Jordan need their father . . . but Baby Three's entitled to a father, too.'

Leah's stomach felt lined with lead. She hadn't been thinking through the Baby Three situation. But he or she was on the way, not just a little pudding mound under Michele's dresses, not just a life-changing shock, but a tiny person-to-be. Inconvenient, unexpected, but as much Michele's child as Jordan and Natasha. 'Shit,' she groaned. 'What the hell are you going to do?'

Michele's gaze grew beseeching. 'I know you're going to be even angrier with me – but I'm going away with Bailey. I need time to talk about the future and make the right decision for my kids. All three of them. And for me.'

'No, Michele–!'

Michele steamrollered on. 'It would be wrong to pretend my marriage can be saved. I'm done with pretending, with lying. I'm even going to admit to Bailey that I'm not thirty-nine.'

Leah felt pressure weighing heavily on her shoulders. 'And while you go off and explore your options with your twinkie, I suppose you're going to ask me to stay and help Alister look after your kids?'

'Short term,' Michele protested, a fresh tear forming

beneath her eye. 'Please. The children like and trust you. And it's such a brief period out of your carefree life.'

Leah snatched back her hands. 'Don't make me sound like the irresponsible one!'

Michele hunched a defensive shoulder. 'I just mean the way you've avoided having a partner or kids so you never have to put anybody else first. Even your job's easy.'

Holding a deep breath for an instant before letting it hiss out slowly, Leah took stock. No matter how exasperated she was – for 'exasperated' read 'wanting to shriek with rage' – Michele's family was in chaos and Leah couldn't indulge in a hissy fit. 'I'll take issue with you about whether my job's "easy" some other time,' she managed, fairly calmly. 'But it's true that I've chosen the single life. You made different choices. *You* married Alister and *you* conceived Jordan and Natasha. *You* had an affair with Bailey and *you* conceived Baby Three. You don't get to say now that it's somebody else's turn to live that life while you flirt with a new one.'

Michele's gaze faltered. 'But don't say you won't do it.' The lonely tear suddenly had company, rolling down her face. 'Please, Leah! I know I've messed up, and it impacts my family. I know I fell in love with the wrong man, gave way to my feelings and got pregnant but I'm buckling under the strain here. Please!'

Watching her sister begin to cry in earnest Leah tried and failed to resist being manipulated. Jordan. Natasha. Baby Three. All were her flesh and blood. The only aspect of this turmoil Leah could control was the support she could offer them. 'Do you have any further bombshells to drop? Lies to confess? Omissions to correct?'

Michele's head shook wildly. She wiped and blew, blew and wiped in an apparently inexhaustible flow of grief.

Her skin waxed to the pallor that seemed a feature of this pregnancy and she clapped a piece of kitchen roll to her lips, shoving the remains of the iced tea aside.

'OK,' snapped Leah. 'Just as long as *you* explain to your kids and husband before you go and you realise that *this is only temporary*.' She tapped Michele's hand to make certain of her attention. 'On September the fourth I begin my new job. On September the ninth I've booked a track day with Scott. On the tenth I expect to be on my sofa watching the Italian Grand Prix in peace and silence. I chose those things and they're my life. You need to be clear that I'll be returning to it.'

Michele nodded wildly. 'I understand. It won't be for ever.'

'It can't be.' Leah scraped back her chair. 'Your life is *yours*.'

Chapter Five

When Curtis knocked on the gîte's kitchen door it was Leah who answered, wearing denim shorts and a thin strappy top. Her eyes were red.

He thought of the MILF remark he'd made to try to impress Jordan and felt a bit cringy. Leah was, like, nearly as old as his dad. 'Hello,' he began politely. 'Got hay fever?'

She gave him a wobbly smile. 'Just sore eyes.'

'Oh. Only I've got some stuff for hay fever.'

Her smile warmed. 'That's sweet of you but I have everything I need, thanks. Have you come to see Jordan and Natasha?'

At the thought of Natasha he felt his blood hit his face in an embarrassed rush, which was an improvement on where it might otherwise have rushed to. Feeling stupid and about four years old – although he suspected that four-year-olds didn't worry about what was happening in the boxers department when they thought about girls – he managed to mumble, 'Only they said they were coming to ours to hang out. Dad said they could, if they didn't mind the decorating mess. Then they didn't turn up.'

Leah glanced behind her. 'Um . . . come in and I'll see what their dad says.'

She slipped from the kitchen to the hall, closing the door behind her, leaving Curtis hovering and uncertain whether to sit or stand or stay or go. This afternoon, when they'd been balancing on bridges and rope ladders, Alister had seemed fine with the idea of Jordan and Natasha hanging with Curtis but now he began to wonder what was up. The skin around Leah's eyes had been all blotchy, which never happened with him with hay fever.

Before he could decide whether to wait, Leah reappeared. 'Alister says would you mind if it was here, rather than at your place? The kids are in the games room.' She was smiling but her eyes still looked funny.

'Where the pool table is? Cool beans.'

'Had you better text your dad and check it's OK?'

'Yeah, yeah.' He passed her in the doorway and set his long legs to the sweeping staircase. He liked these big stairs; it was cool the way you could look over the banisters and through the middle of the house.

At the very top, the second landing opened out into the games room. Jordan was there, chalking a pool cue and not looking at Curtis. 'Stripes or spots?'

Curtis said, 'Spots, fanks,' confidently, although he'd only been introduced to the game of pool the day before and knew nothing would prevent the more practised Jordan from beating the crap out of him. Yesterday, even Natasha had whupped him.

Keeping his gaze averted, Jordan racked the balls noisily while Curtis chose a cue to chalk and stole a surreptitious glance at the older boy. Maybe hay fever ran in the family because Jordan had red eyes, too. 'All right?' he enquired gruffly.

'Yep. Break.' Jordan gazed fixedly at the balls he'd racked.

Curtis couldn't think of a better plan than to lean over the table and hope the triangle of balls was as easy to hit as it looked.

He'd just slammed his cue into the white ball to send it hard into the pack, balls spinning angrily in all directions except the pockets, when Natasha blundered up the stairs, cheeks tear-streaked. 'Did Jordan tell you?' Her voice wavered thinly.

Jordan heaved an exaggerated sigh, lining up the white on the blue-stripe ball, one eyebrow curling angrily.

Curtis looked from sister to brother. 'What?'

Natasha's face puckered. 'Our mum's got some horrible boyfriend and she's gone off with him to talk about the future. They're going to have a baby!' She began to cry in chest-heaving sobs, lips creasing back from her teeth.

The hay-fever eyes and Jordan's scowl slammed into focus. Curtis felt a turning over in his stomach, an echo of the shock of when it had been his family that had been blowing itself apart. 'That's crappy.'

'Curtis doesn't need to hear this, Natasha.' Jordan stabbed his cue at the white ball and it spat the blue-stripe into the pocket before ricocheting away.

Curtis leaned his cue against the table and moved a few uncertain steps closer to Natasha. She tugged at his heart, a drooping little figure standing alone and weeping. 'My parents split up three years ago. It's bad to start with.'

Jordan hurled his cue down onto the baize, balls crashing and clattering into each other. 'Like it doesn't stay being bad?' he demanded aggressively, as if Curtis was somehow head of the parental split-ups department.

Curtis shrugged, though he went all hot at the anger

ringing in Jordan's voice. At least it had been the table Jordan had slammed the cue onto, not Curtis's head. 'Well, they stay split up but otherwise it's OK. I hated it at first but it happens to everyone, doesn't it?' He went over to the kitchen alcove and pulled sheets off a roll of blue kitchen paper to hand to Natasha.

'Thanks,' she said, sniffing and scrubbing at her face. 'But I don't *want* them to split up.'

'Too late,' Jordan bit scornfully. 'They did that weeks ago.'

Natasha's tears began to fall faster. 'Po-or Dad!'

Jordan turned his furiously flashing gaze on her. 'Shut up, Gnasher! You give me shit ache.'

And all at once Curtis found himself fighting for control of his facial muscles. It totally wasn't funny. Natasha was bawling and Jordan was obviously the kind of unhappy that made you want to smash things. The back of Curtis's nose began to hurt as he tried to swallow the words that burned in his throat. But out they came on a gurgle of laughter. 'How can your shit ache?'

Jordan switched his glare to Curtis. Then an unwilling smile tugged at its corner. 'Things have to be really really crap.'

Natasha gave a huge revolting sniff and a giggle-sob. 'You give me shit ache, too, Jordan. And so does Mum.'

'She's shit-ache central,' allowed Jordan. His twitchy smile developed into a grin.

'But, mostly, the horrible boyfriend.'

'And the baby.' Jordan picked up his cue just to slam it down again with a roar. '*A freaking baby*!'

Natasha wiped her face. 'But it's going to be our brother or sister.'

Natasha's voice being hoarse with tears, Curtis decided

no one would mind if he investigated the contents of the drinks fridge. Discovering a fat lemonade bottle, he reached for glasses from the draining board. 'Surely all babies give you shit ache? They just scream all the time and go red and smell. Are you going to have to live with it?'

Jordan glazed over with horror. 'Live with the baby? That's proper shit ache. I bet we will. Did your mum have any more kids?'

Curtis watched the lemonade hiss up the sides of the glasses. 'Nope. She lives with another bloke though, Darren.'

'Yeurgh!' Natasha's face began to crumple anew. 'What if Mum goes to live with whoever she's having the baby with? What if we don't like him? What if Dad gets someone new, too? We could have horrible step-parents and horrible stepbrothers and sisters and–'

Taking too huge a glug of lemonade Curtis belched loudly, surprising Natasha into a pause. He grinned as if he'd summoned the giant burp just to cheer her. He crossed to the big brown L-shaped sofa by the window and flopped down, looking out over the garden. From where he sat he could see the woods behind the annexe, laced with footpaths to the park. 'But there are upsides. If either Mum or Dad has shit ache with me–' he paused for them to snigger '– I can make an excuse to go stay with the other one. I get to go on two holidays. Last year it was the Dominican Republic with Mum and Darren, and coming here with Dad.'

'That's cool,' Jordan admitted. He plumped down on the sofa, side-on to face Curtis. 'We just come to France every year.'

'Maybe that'll change.' Natasha pulled the sofa's big end cushion onto the floor and plopped down onto it.

'Maybe whoever Mum's going with will take us somewhere else.'

'Hasn't your mum told you her boyfriend's name?' Curtis tried to think back to when his parents had split. Mum, brightly positive, had introduced him to Darren right from the first. Darren, who'd seemed a horrible intruder in those days, had been brightly positive, too, no matter how rude Curtis had been. Only Dad had been grave and quiet.

Natasha gave another big gross snorty sniff. 'Dad just says it's all out of his hands.'

'Which is code for "It was her who wanted to split up, not me, so she can tell you."' added Jordan, gloomily. He cocked a considering eye at Curtis. 'Richie at school says he gets loads more birthday and Christmas presents since his parents split.'

Curtis grinned. ''Sright. From Darren's family I've got like a spare nan, grandad, aunts and uncles. They all give me stuff. And I get two Christmas Days, one with Mum and one with Dad.'

Natasha wiped her swollen eyes and dumped the tissue on the floor. 'My friends Alicia and Rowan say the same. And at least we've got Auntie Leah here for the holiday.'

Jordan rolled his head back on the sofa. 'Yeah, better than just being with Dad. He's got enough shit ache for all of us.'

Unwilling to be in the house but not quite comfortable with closing herself off in La Petite Annexe, unconcerned about everyone else's unhappiness, Leah lay on a garden lounger, a bottle of rosé pamplemousse nestling amongst ice in a blue plastic jug beside her, a good slug of its contents gleaming in her glass. Alister had taken himself off to brood in the silence of the salon, the kids were elsewhere in the gîte with Curtis, while Leah vibrated with the swimmy-trembly feeling of unreality that came with disaster as she attempted to assimilate the day's events.

'You kidnapped my boy?'

The voice mock-growling through the twilight made Leah jump, slopping her wine in a chilly splat onto her legs. She twitched around to find Ronan leaning over the fence. The last solitary ray of evening sun fired red lights in his dark hair.

'I did ask Curtis to text you. He's with Natasha and Jordan. He came to invite them to your house but Alister said would he mind being here, instead.'

'He has an instant memory wipe available for such requests. Is he in your way?'

She shook her head. 'Alister thought it might be good for the kids to have someone their own age to talk to.' The tears tightening her throat made her words come out on a sort of gargle.

Ronan's expression changed. 'What's up?' He slung a leg over the wooden fence and landed on his feet on her side of it, though he winced and flexed his arm.

Knowing she must look a sight she smoothed her hair and wiped at her cheeks as he crouched down to gaze into her face but her chest convulsed on a sob as she explained the day's events.

'I feel sick that she's gone. I got angry and challenged her. By the time the others got home she was all packed. She justified herself to the kids, giving them loads of kisses and promises to be back soon, then carted her bag out of the house and around the corner, where, I presume, her boyfriend picked her up. Everyone's gutted but Michele says she has to be fair to Baby Three. It's a mess.' Though relief had been mixed with the guilt on Michele's face as she left.

'These things always are.' He sighed, sombrely, letting himself down on the grass and propping his back against the next sun lounger. 'But, for the record, I agree that the new baby's paternity should be considered. Did Jordan and Natasha know about the pregnancy?'

'Not till today. If I'd just left well enough alone–'

He moved nearer, closing his hand comfortingly on her shoulder. 'It's not your fault! Michele must've been formulating her plans. Being pushed into admitting the existence of the boyfriend just gave her the opportunity to put those plans into action. And she must trust you implicitly.'

His reassuring logic eased some of the tightness in Leah's chest. 'It sounds as if you're trying to put a positive spin on me being Deputy Mum while she goes off with her twinkie.'

His eyes softened. 'No spin. I just know how hard it can be to entrust your child to others, so relying on you is a kind of a compliment.'

Leah snorted. '*Putting* on me.' Taking another gulp of wine, she welcomed the slight weight alcohol added to her limbs. Nothing about the hideous situation had changed, yet somehow Ronan was steadying her. She tried a smile. 'You've no idea how much I admire parents. I'm awed by the sacrifices you make, staying calm when the shouty little people you've created disrupt your every plan, or when they're upset or ill and your heart's in tatters for them. But I chose not to be responsible for the next generation.'

'So,' he answered mock-solemnly, injecting a lot of Irish into his voice, 'will I go to Muntsheim and find a shop that will make you a medal and a plinth to stand on while we all admire you for your sacrifice?'

She let out a strangled laugh.

He returned to his normal voice. 'Are you sure you don't want me to take Curtis home?'

Leah tipped back her head to drain her glass. 'I think I'd prefer you both to stay and eat with us. It'll distract the kids. Alister's done his best but he's . . . upset.'

A shadow passed over Ronan's face. 'Humiliated, is my guess. Whatever the state of the marriage, it's bruising to know that your wife prefers someone else. When the kids learn you've been rejected you feel like shit.'

She stole a glance at the hardness that had taken over his face. 'Sorry if anything I said touched a nerve.'

His grin flashed, dispelling the lines of pain. 'Don't worry. Those nerves have been covered by nice tough skin for quite a while now. It's all in the past.'

Chapter Six

The next day, Leah was woken by an incoming text. She groped sleepily for her phone.

Michele: *Is everyone OK? How are the children? xxxx*

A tide of hurt swept over Leah. She got up and showered, rather than trusting herself to reply. Under the fall of water she practised breathing deeply and counting to ten. She reminded herself that Michele was in a tough place and that she genuinely did have a responsibility to Baby Three as well as to Natasha and Jordan.

When she was dried and dressed she typed a return message.

Leah: *It's v early morning and I haven't seen them since last night when they were sad and tearful but talking to Curtis as he's an old hand at parents splitting up. Alister's gutted and I'm feeling petrified and put upon.*

Then she deleted it unsent and, instead, returned a more sensible and conciliatory:

I'm doing my best, and so is Alister, but they're bound to be upset. Perhaps you could talk to them each day so they're reassured you haven't disappeared completely?

To keep the channels of communication as friendly as possible she added an *x*, whilst muttering, 'This is not about you, Leah, it's about them. By early September you'll have your life back.'

She'd just begun to text Scott to bewail her bloody sister and the bloody holiday when, after a perfunctory knock, Natasha burst through the door into the kitchenette of the annexe.

Fair hair screwed into an untidy ponytail, she looked pale and panicky. 'I'm so glad you came on holiday with us. You are coming out with us today, aren't you? If we go somewhere. Are we going? Can Curtis come? Jordan isn't so horrible when Curtis is there. Will Dad come? Are you staying right to the very very end of the holiday? The very end? You will, won't you?'

After a big comforting hug, Leah gently turned Natasha around so that she could brush out the tangles from her hair and Natasha couldn't see the guilt on her face. 'I don't know anything about today, sweetie, till I've talked to your dad. But I expect to be here as long as you guys are.'

'Yes! Can we have *pain au chocolat* for breakfast? And *pains aux raisins*?' Natasha clutched Leah's hand to tow her up to the gîte. She got underfoot, whined when Jordan snapped at her and asked peevish questions about her mum, which Leah, understanding how thoroughly her niece was rattled, did her best to answer without allowing the least impatience to creep into her voice.

Apart from Natasha, breakfast was a near-silent affair. If Natasha was Leah's shadow, Jordan was more of a black cloud.

Alister was quiet but composed. 'I think we should go out today. Let exercise take our minds off things.'

'So long as Leah comes,' stipulated the shadow.

The black cloud just shrugged.

Leah pinned on a bright smile. 'Yes, let's go out and do something fun!'

Both shadow and black cloud looked at her as if she must be kidding.

Nevertheless, an hour later she was driving them all, plus Curtis, to a local lake described in the guidebook as 'a perfect place for families' where Alister hired bikes to ride along the cycle track alongside the water's edge.

Natasha was all sorts of sulky from the first turn of her wheels. 'It's far too crowded and I've got a stupid bike that's stuck in one gear.'

At the same time, Alister made an effort to keep the pack together as Jordan and Curtis surged heedlessly ahead. 'Not so fast, boys!' The boys, tyres hissing, showed no sign of hearing.

The floundering Natasha was acting like a chicane, obliging other cyclists to ring their bells and swerve around her. Leah cast around for a way to improve the situation. 'I don't mind if you swap bikes with me. I can't get excited about anything without an engine, anyway.'

'But yours has those stupid brakes.' Natasha slapped furiously at her gear lever.

'They're easy once you get used to them. You just pedal backwards instead of the brakes being on the handlebars.'

Leah back-pedalled to demonstrate how the wheels were slowed.

Natasha was in no mood to be mollified. 'How come Jordan and Curtis have scored 21-gear trail bikes? It's not fair.' She glared after the boys.

Alister shouted again, '*Jordan! Curtis!*' as their back views disappeared around the next curve.

'You go after them. I'll stay with Natasha.' Leah pulled aside to let a family past while she resettled her helmet, which persisted in swivelling until its strap sat over one eye. She pointed to a Nestlé's flag fluttering above the trees. 'Looks like there's an ice-cream place not far off. We'll meet you there.'

'I'll never make it on this thing,' whined Natasha as Alister hared off around the curve after Jordan and Curtis. Blinking back tears, she wrestled anew with the lever. Then, with a triumphant 'Done it!', she found a co-operative gear and began to pick up speed. 'C'mon, Leah, keep up!'

Mindful of it being a family area, Leah smothered the curse that leaped to her tongue, standing on the pedals as she obeyed Natasha's summons and tried to be thankful for the lightning change of mood.

Finding her pedalling rhythm, she began to feel the wind in her face. The next bend saw her whizzing up behind Natasha who, in turn, was gaining on Alister. The two boys were again out of sight. Leah's feet whirled faster and faster, her wake marked by reeds swaying at the edge of the lake.

Natasha glanced around, wobbling precariously. 'Dad, Leah's catching us!' she shrieked. 'Go, Dad, go!'

Alister tucked his head down and pedalled harder, putting on a big booming Gandalf voice. 'You shall not pass!'

Leah laughed, her legs going like pistons, her hair blowing over her face, helmet strap once again over her eye. 'I'll be first in the queue for ice-cream!'

Giggling and gasping, Natasha crouched over her pumping legs. 'No, no, I will!'

Alister panted, 'You shall not pass!' less convincingly, as Natasha and Leah drew level.

Three abreast, howling and laughing, wobbling and swerving, jockeying for the lead, they flew around the next bend.

Which was when they met Jordan and Curtis flying back.

'Whoa!' the boys bellowed, sliding sideways in a screech of brakes, flinging up clouds of dirt but ending up more or less on their feet and astride their machines.

'Waaaah!' screamed Natasha, swerving wildly towards the reeds.

'NO!' After a heart-stop moment of grabbing at the handlebars for brakes that weren't there, Leah remembered the unfamiliar braking system and back-pedalled. Hard.

The bike bucked her off like a pony.

She had a split second to be thankful for her helmet, skew-whiff or not, before the ground flew up to thump all the air from her body. 'Oof!' As she lay and crowed for oxygen, she heard a splash. And then a piercing scream.

'Natasha!' On a surge of adrenalin Leah hauled herself to her feet and staggered dizzily to where the reeds fidgeted in agitation at being disturbed.

But no Natasha stood in the water among them.

'*Natasha*! Tashie?' Leah's heart hammered, and she had to hold her ragged breath to listen. After a terrifying moment, she heard whimpering.

'I'm stuck.' A choking cough. 'I can't!' Splutter. 'Lea–' More coughing.

'I'm coming!' Leah splashed into the water, shoving blindly at the reeds that, nightmare-like, grabbed at her arms and legs. Endless seconds of battling took her up to her waist in icy lake water and suddenly she could see Natasha's neon green helmet bobbing frighteningly close to the surface.

'Legs stuck– Bike–' Natasha gasped, flailing bravely to keep her mouth above water.

Heart pounding, Leah fought her way close enough to scoop an arm beneath Natasha's shoulders. 'OK, I've got you. Breathe, sweetie. Just breathe.' She took a couple of moments to follow her own advice as Natasha's panic began to calm with a few last heaves and coughs.

'Can you kick free if I hold you up?'

'Think so.' After a lot of splashing and 'Ow! Ow!' Natasha was able to slide her legs out of the bike frame and tremble her way to her feet. 'I couldn't br-breathe. I thought I'd drown.' Reaction setting in, she clung wetly to Leah and burst into tears.

'I know. You're safe now.' Leah closed her eyes and cuddled her niece close as she waited for the fear to subside. It was several moments before either of them felt strong enough to yank their feet free of the lakebed and turn back towards the dry land. Jordan was just striking out towards them through the reeds, looking uncharacteristically anxious.

'Leah–'

'I've got her. She's had a fright but she's OK.' Gaining dry land, after a cursory check of Natasha's person and finding nothing worse than barked shins and bruises, Leah pressed her niece's hand firmly into Jordan's. 'Look after your sister for two minutes while I drag the bike out. Don't move an inch.'

'Leah, Dad's hurt his leg.'

'One thing at a time.' Ignoring the fact that her elbow was beginning to throb fierily Leah waded back into the chilly water, slipping over painfully between the reeds. It took all her strength to haul the bike up from its watery bed and back to shore. When she allowed herself a moment to catch her breath she noticed that not only were Jordan and Natasha still holding hands and standing exactly where she'd left them, but Jordan was dead white. Her heart gave an extra thud. 'Did you say Alister's hurt?'

'Really hurt. Curtis stayed with him and I came after you and Tash.'

The sun was beating down but Leah's blood ran cold. She'd been so focused on her mission that Alister's absence hadn't hit her. For him to abandon his daughter in a lake he must have been physically unable to–

'Right, let's check him out,' she said briskly to disguise the slimy feeling of apprehension slithering through her belly. Leah jogged back towards the track as fast as suddenly wobbly legs would allow, surprised to see how far she and Natasha had plunged after the mass collision.

She found Alister sprawled in the dirt, face an unpleasant grey-white, Curtis crouched beside him.

'Oh, shit.' Leah almost gagged as she saw the unnatural angle of Alister's leg.

'Hurts.' Alister's breath hissed through gritted teeth either side of the single word.

'I'll get an ambulance. The French for 999 is 18, isn't it?'

Alister sucked in a breath. 'But we left all the phones in the car to save them from getting damaged – my bright idea, I think.'

'Right. We'll have to . . .' Leah faltered. The track, so

busy just a little while earlier, was empty. Her mind hurtled through the possibilities. Which was closer, the ice cream place or The Pig? Should she leave Alister and take all the kids? Leave all the kids with him? She'd just made up her mind to leave the boys but take Natasha, who was wailing again at the sight of her dad's leg, when, to her swamping relief, two men in Lycra shot around the corner on serious cyclists' cycles. They swished to efficient halts with exclamations of '*Merde!*'

'*S'il vous plait*,' Leah stuttered, jumping up, '*mon bon-frère est blessé* —'

'*Beau-frère*.' Alister couldn't resist correcting her, be it through white lips. He even took over the explanations, his French flowing impressively despite his agony. In moments one man was hunkering down beside Alister while the other flew back along the track, wheels whirring. Alister, grimacing all the while, translated these developments into English. 'There's a ranger's station as well as a café. The gentleman's gone there for help.'

Leah huddled with a shivering Natasha as the lake water in their T-shirts and shorts became too cold to be outweighed by the warmth of the sun. Jordan sat on the track with his father, and the Frenchman who'd remained with them introduced himself as Théo and chatted reassuringly with Alister in French and with the others in fair English. A few minutes saw the rangers bowling up in a pick-up truck with *Garde Forestier* on the side, the second Frenchman and his bike in the back.

Théo nodded approvingly. '*Les pompiers* come also, soon.'

It felt like ages before the red ambulance edged along the track. *Les pompiers* seemed to be firemen, to Leah's surprise, in navy uniforms with red and yellow flashes.

They took control with easy efficiency and when Alister was splinted and in the ambulance the rangers piled the rented bikes in their truck and Théo escorted Leah and the kids back to The Pig to guide her to l'Hôpital Civil in Strasbourg.

'But you are cold, I think.' He frowned at Leah and Natasha's wet clothes.

'I can put up with it.' But Leah cast a worried glance at her niece.

'Here, Natasha.' Curtis gallantly pulled off his black T-shirt decorated with snarling wolves then turned to gaze out of the window while Natasha, thanking him shyly, pulled off her wet top and changed into his dry one, long enough on her to pass for a dress.

Leah, not wanting to pause to accept similar offers from Jordan or Théo, pulled swiftly away. Or what passed for swift, in The Pig.

Earning her undying gratitude, Théo located a parking place and the entrance to the correct hospital department – Leah wouldn't even have known that A&E was called *Urgences* – bought them drinks from the vending machine, found them an English-speaking nurse and indicated the wet clothing and what Leah suddenly realised was a giant, sticky, gritty graze on her arm. Waving away thanks, he left to wait outside to be picked up in his cycling buddy's car.

The nurse provided white scrubs for Leah and Natasha and Curtis took back his T-shirt. While the nurse bustled off on some other errand, Leah tried to ring Michele but could only leave a message.

Natasha, hoiking at her waistband to stop her hems trailing, declared, 'I look like I'm in *Casualty* on TV!'

'Wrong colour, gonk,' began Jordan. Then he caught Leah's baleful glare and subsided.

Grateful just for dry clothes, whatever they looked like, Leah dropped into a chair in the glass-walled waiting area and tried to assess their situation. 'OK. We're all together and in the same place as Alister. The lovely nurse speaks English, for which I'm pathetically grateful. We have our phones back. We'll survive. Curtis, text your dad and tell him where you are and not to worry. Now, please.'

'Yeah, yeah, yeah,' Curtis grumbled, fishing out his phone.

Leah's arm throbbed like a bastard but she could cope if she didn't think about it too much. Not thinking about it wasn't easy and it seemed a long time before the English-speaking nurse reappeared. 'Come,' she said, gently taking Leah's arm and inspecting it. 'I will check it for you.'

Alarmed at the idea of leaving the teenagers Leah snatched back her limb – ouch! – and flexed it. 'It's not broken, just bruised.'

But the nurse, demonstrating her profession's magical people-management qualities, somehow agreed, disagreed and got her own way. 'I think so, too. But we will clean and dress it.'

After at least seven assurances from each child that they'd be fine sitting on their bums and drinking fizzy drinks, that they wouldn't leave, particularly with strangers, or be a nuisance to others, particularly with pointless bickering, Leah allowed herself to be ushered towards a cubicle, where she put up with the nurse persuading chips of gravel from her flesh and covering the fiery graze with an antiseptic dressing.

When Leah finally returned to the waiting area it was to find a charming French doctor in a white coat laughing and chatting with the kids who, bizarrely, had stacked their empty drink bottles tidily on a seat, totally ignoring the nearby bin.

The doctor rose. 'Miss Beaumont? May I trouble you to follow me, please?'

They were borne off to an office, Leah managing to snatch up the rubbish and transfer it to the correct receptacle in passing, to be informed that Alister had smashed his ankle in some complex manner that also included significant damage to tendons and ligaments. He would shortly be transferred to the city's other hospital, Hautepierre, for an operation, and could expect to be there for about seven days.

An entire week.

As sentence was passed Leah knew how Natasha must have felt as her bike tried to drag her under the water. But her burden came in the form of the kids gazing at her in the evident expectation that she'd know what to do next.

So, chips down, Leah gave it her best shot. 'OK, I'll get the kids home shortly but can I see my brother-in-law first? He'll need to tell me what he wants from his room so I can take it to the other hospital tomorrow.'

'Of course, of course,' the doctor beamed. 'Families. We must look after each other, *hein*?'

Stifling an urge to reply, 'Must we?', Leah just smiled.

When Curtis had texted that he was at a hospital owing to Jordan's dad having made an unscheduled switch from bike to ambulance, Ronan had asked whether Leah needed help. Though Curtis had relayed a message that she could manage, thanks, ever since Curtis had arrived home with details of the day Ronan had been battling an urge to rush next door.

The sight of Leah sprinting down the garden and into

the little annexe, wearing white hospital scrubs and a hunted expression, had brought him up short. Nothing in her stricken appearance had given him the idea that she needed company, but to give himself an excuse to hover in the vicinity he set about taming the monster rambling rose that threatened the fence with its weight. Lopping its thorny arms, he chopped up the amputations to cram into the bin. As if in revenge, the fragile white blooms sent out their fragrance onto the early-evening air, enticing bugs to dive-bomb him.

He was jolted from batting away his tormentors by a drawn-out, muffled but definitely distressed '*Aaaaaaaa-rrrrrrggh*!' emitting from the annexe.

He tossed down his secateurs, grabbed the top of the fence and scissored over, swearing as his shoulder wrenched with a burst of fire, but hitting the ground running. Next instant he was hammering at the annexe door.

'Leah?' He glared at the green-painted wood that was keeping him out. 'Are you OK?'

Just as he was about to ignore the niceties and rattle the handle the door jerked open and Leah, still in hospital scrubs like a crumpled paper bag, gazed back at him, eyes wild and golden brown hair unravelling.

'What's up?' His eyes flew to a business-like dressing that graced the angle of her arm. 'You're hurt – is that why you screamed?'

Stepping back to let him into the kitchenette, Leah clenched shut her eyes for a long, slow breath. When her eyelids flipped open again her usual sane self was staring back at him. She answered politely. 'I'm OK, thank you.'

He rubbed his shoulder resentfully, feeling foolish at his headlong dash. 'Why scream, then? You frightened me to death.'

'Sorry.'

Seeing only unhappiness in her face he let his voice soften. 'It's bad news about Alister.'

Her shoulders sagged. 'He needs an operation but they're not sure when. They have to transfer him to another hospital. I'm about to move into the main house while he's gone because I can't leave Natasha and Jordan there alone.'

Comprehension began to dawn. And with it, sympathy. 'So you're left being Deputy Dad as well as Deputy Mum? Now I understand the scream.'

Her laugh strangled. 'OK, I admit to a tiny letting-off-steam scream. I didn't mean to be overheard. It's just that I like my space and I can't have it because I have to do a load of parenting that, despite loving the kids to bits, I don't want to do. I'm not parent material. I let Natasha half-drown today.' Then she squared her shoulders, though so much tension radiated from her he could almost hear her buzzing. 'But there's no one else. I'll move into Michele's room and look after the kids until Alister comes out of hospital. Then I might have to look after him, too, until I can get us all back to England, which, as we have two vehicles here, will be a challenge because Michele's freaked out about driving on the right and refuses to do it.'

Despite the wobble in her voice, he found himself admiring her, not just for stepping up to the plate but for so disarmingly admitting her discomfort in doing so. One of his hands found its way to her arm above the dressing. *Soft, smooth,* his fingertips told him. Almost shocked at his hand for transmitting that message at such an inappropriate moment, he let it drop. 'I'll help you move what you need into the main house. Then let's all eat at the little restaurant in the village tonight and worry about tomorrow when it comes. You look as if you've taken quite a bump yourself.' He winced as he got a proper look at her grazed and contused arm.

She touched her swollen elbow gingerly. 'It's sore.'

'I'll bet. Why don't you just point me in the direction of whatever you want carrying?' His left shoulder gave a throb as if to remind him it had been injured, too. 'As long as it's not madly heavy,' he amended.

She gazed around sadly. 'I just need a few clothes and toiletries. It's not as if I'll be far away.' But her sigh was all about leaving behind the most precious item – space.

After several more attempts, Leah gave up trying to get more than her sister's voicemail and turned to text instead.

> ***Leah:*** *Michele, ring me ASAP. Alister's had an accident and is in hospital. His ankle's badly broken.*
> ***Leah:*** *It's just me with the kids and they're upset. A's got to have an op and will be away about a week.*
> ***Leah:*** *Ring me now!*

In half an hour she was checking her phone for the hundredth time. Nothing. To reassure herself her phone was working she clicked on Scott's avatar, showing his one-sided smile and tousled hair, and sent a long, groaning text to spill out the day's events.

The reply arrived in seconds:

> ***Scott:*** *You need to give your sister a kick up the arse. Btw, do you know you're only 2 hours from the Merc museum in Stuttgart? *tongue hanging out* x*

Briefly, she dreamed of the luxury of jumping into the

Porsche and crossing into Germany to spend tomorrow admiring amazing cars. Then shoved the dream away.

Leah: *Very helpful. Not. x*
Scott: *Does Alister's accident mean you're coming home? x*
Leah: *I wish. x*

Hearing Ronan and Curtis knocking at the door and shouting to announce themselves, she shoved the phone into her pocket and ran downstairs. She found Jordan and Natasha in the kitchen ahead of her.

Over their heads Ronan sent her a smile and mouthed, 'OK?' She rolled her eyes but nodded as Jordan shoved his feet into unlaced trainers and Natasha crawled beneath the table looking for a missing pink flip-flop.

When everyone was finally ready to leave, Ronan said to the teens, 'We're walking into the village. Don't get too far ahead, you guys.' This pretty much guaranteed that they got as far ahead as they could along the lane without being out of sight, leaving Leah and Ronan to enjoy the peace and tranquillity of bringing up the rear, Ronan entertaining Leah with tales of childhood holidays in Kirchhoffen until they reached the village restaurant.

À la Table de l'Ill was in the centre of the village where Rue Paul Deschanel widened into a crossroads. Painted blue and bedecked with white petunias and red geraniums, it was evidently popular with the locals. Wine bottles gleamed on tables beside jugs of water that clinked with ice. Inter-table banter filled the soft evening air and Leah supposed that in a place the size of Kirchhoffen you fell over your friends and neighbours – which was companionable or claustrophobic, depending on your point of view.

Ronan chatted to the pretty waitress as she showed them to a table in the courtyard, his deep voice rolling over the rhythms of the French language and making the waitress smile.

Once the kids were engrossed in their own whispering and sniggering, Ronan dropped his voice to ask Leah, 'Have you managed to get in touch with their mum?'

Leah pitched her voice equally low. 'I've tried several times, but no reply.'

'Worried?'

She considered the emotions prompting the butterflies waltzing tensely in her tummy. 'I've been focusing on terror with a touch of anger but, yes, I'm uneasy. In the furore of her leaving, I never thought to ask where she was headed. Bailey could have minced her up and stuffed her in his boot for all I know.'

Ronan's eyes smiled. 'If that was his plan I think he'd have done it at home, saving the expense of travelling to France.' He went on more seriously. 'She couldn't have foreseen what was about to happen and she'll probably come back when you get the chance to explain.'

'I hope she does, but the Michele who's infatuated with Bailey is not the one I've known all my life.' She put her glass down on the wooden table, too on edge even to enjoy the wine. 'It's scary enough for me, with the kids, the language and the French medical system, but goodness knows how Alister feels, in pain and abandoned in hospital. We don't even know when his surgery will be. I'm to ring in the morning for an update, which will be fun if I don't get an English speaker. I'm more worried about the prospect of trying to make myself understood in French than driving in a strange city on my own, which I'll have to do to find this new hospital.' She wiped suddenly sweaty palms on her dress.

Beneath the table, Ronan's hand found hers. 'I can telephone the hospital for you. And why drive into Strasbourg when the trams and buses are so fantastic? Hautepierre's website will have directions for public transport and Curtis and me would be happy to come along to familiarise you with the system.'

Some of Leah's tension seeped away. 'Would you mind?' She had to swallow a wimpy urge to cry in gratitude. 'I wish I hadn't dropped French as soon as my school let me. Even Curtis knows more than I do.'

He picked up the menus and passed them around the table. 'We can't all be good at everything. I can't do handbrake turns.' He winked.

Blushing at this reminder of her inglorious hour Leah turned her attention to selecting her meal.

However, when her food arrived she found herself doing more brooding than eating, reminding herself to pack Alister's bags then checking her phone in case she'd somehow missed a call or message from Michele.

Ronan's voice jolted her from her thoughts. 'Is that sauce as good as it looks?'

Not even sure she'd tasted it properly, sufficient professional interest stirred for her to swirl a forkful of duck in dark-red sauce and pop it in her mouth. 'It's unusual. Mushroom base, owes something to pine nuts and a lot to red wine.'

His eyebrows lifted. 'Impressive analysis. What about mine? It's a local speciality, *baeckeoffe*, a kind of hotpot of more than one meat.'

As the kids laughed because '*baeckeoffe*' sounded like 'bake off', she tried a few bites. 'Mutton, beef, pork, onions, carrots, leak, celery, bay leaf and clove. White wine, probably Riesling.'

They continued tasting, discussing ingredients, and it was only when most of both dishes had vanished that she realised it had probably been a ruse to get her eating. She narrowed her eyes at him but definitely felt better for the food.

Natasha dragged her chair closer so that she could rest her cheek against Leah's arm. 'Are we having dessert here or are you going to make something?'

'Here,' Ronan replied, firmly.

Leah, smothering a yawn, didn't protest at his answering for her. Her elbow was throbbing and she was beginning to feel a lot of other bruises.

Finally, full of plum *clafoutis* and wilting fast, they trailed homeward along the cobbles, past the *tabac*, a mini-market, a pizza vending machine – to the fascination of the children, who had to be dissuaded from trying it there and then – and the *boulangerie-pâtisserie*, which was also a *salon de thé*. Beginning the climb up the hill, Jordan and Curtis, with legs young and long, strode ahead into the darkness.

Natasha hung tiredly on Leah's arm. 'What are we doing tomorrow?'

Leah recognised the onset of anxiety. In uncomfortable situations Natasha sought reassurance by testing the knowledge and control of those around her. 'Hopefully, we'll be able to visit your dad.'

Natasha yawned. 'Will Mum go?'

'I haven't heard from her yet. I'll probably get her tomorrow.' Apprehension squiggled like a snake in Leah's belly but she refused to let it betray its presence to Natasha.

'Have we got food for breakfast?'

'Yes, don't worry.'

'What is it?'

'Eggs, cheese, meat, bread. All the usual.'

'Have we got enough money, with Dad in hospital?' It was as if Natasha woke every morning with a quota of questions to ask and she'd just seen bedtime approaching.

'Yes, don't worry, we have money.' It just wasn't in Leah's purse.

'Will you drive to the hospital?'

'Ronan says the tram will be easier. We haven't been on one so that will be cool, won't it?'

'Do you know the way?'

'Ronan's going to show us.'

'Will you like the tram more than The Pig?'

'Hugely,' said Leah, frankly. Beside her, she heard Ronan give a quiet snort of laughter.

Natasha dragged even more heavily on Leah's arm – luckily not her sore one. 'What's a MILF?'

Leah halted to stare at Natasha, whose eyes were full of her usual guileless curiosity. She cleared her throat. 'What?'

Natasha started forward again, dragging Leah with her. 'Curtis said that you're one,' she said, chattily. She frowned. 'Oh, no, he *thought* you were a MILF. Then Jordan told him he was stupid because you're our cool auntie, so Curtis said you were a BILF, but I didn't get it. Are MILF and BILF words in French? I could ask Dad because you don't talk much French, do you?'

Leah floundered. In her cool auntie role she'd occasionally encountered awkward questions from Natasha or Jordan – mostly Natasha – and had had no hesitation in referring them to a parent. As Deputy Mum she realised she ought to take an active part in the conversation but, gripped by a paralysing combination of horror, mortification and the urge to giggle, had no idea where to start.

Ronan stepped in smoothly. 'Curtis shouldn't be using either of those words, Natasha, and I'm sure your parents would prefer it if you forgot them. I shall explain to him why.'

'Oh.' Natasha digested this. 'But shouldn't I make up my own mind? Dad's always telling me I should.'

Stifling more mirth at Ronan's perplexed expression Leah scrabbled around for a distraction technique. 'I'd much rather you looked up yummy chocolate recipes.'

'Le-ah,' Natasha chided, proving diversion worked even when in pursuit of the truth about MILFs and BILFs, 'you probably wrote half those recipes!'

'I never give up the search for more, though,' Leah replied solemnly. 'I'm thinking about trying chocolate ice-cream with peanuts and caramel. What do you think?'

Natasha gave her a hard stare. 'That sounds just like a Snickers ice cream.'

'Oh, yeah.' Leah pretended to look crestfallen but was glad she seemed to have diverted Natasha from the previous topic.

Their conversation had carried them to their own driveway, where Jordan and Curtis were waiting to invite Natasha to play Minecraft.

'Yesssss!' Natasha rushed to join them, fatigue forgotten in the joy of being included with the cool kids.

Leah snorted. 'Bet the boys think they're fooling us into saying, "Ahhh, isn't it nice that the children are getting on together? We'll let them stay up." Let's pretend to fall for it. I desperately need five minutes' me-time.' She rounded the corner of the house and made for the open back door, the kitchen light streaming out like a rock festival for moths.

Ronan halted her, pitching his voice in the *I do not wish*

to be overheard register. 'I cannot apologise enough for Curtis with his "MILF" remarks. I'll talk to him.'

'Oh, boys will be boys,' she began airily. But, somehow an unladylike snort of laughter escaped.

'For crying out loud, don't,' he groaned. 'What the hell will he say next? I'm entirely mortified. As if I can't get in enough bother on my own, without having to go around apologising for the little person. Can you imagine the conversation I have to have with him, now? "And what do those words mean, Curtis? And why is it wholly inappropriate for you to be using them about anybody, never mind a woman so much older than yourself?"'

'You make me sound about ninety.' Leah felt better for having something to grin about. 'I'd be tempted to pretend I didn't know he'd said it.'

Ronan ambled over to where the garden loungers stood shrouded in darkness and let himself down into one, rubbing his shoulder absently. 'Don't think I'm not. But it's not responsible parenting. I don't mind about the language so much as the lack of respect, saying such a thing to Jordan and Natasha when he thought you were their mother! Worse, saying it to someone who would bring it up to nearly kill me with embarrassment.' He closed anguished eyes.

Leah let herself stiffly down onto the lounger beside his. The wooden slats seemed to hold an echo of the heat of the day and she eased her sore body against them.

Ronan turned his head to watch her. 'As he's put the subject of your appeal on the table, though . . . I'd like to say something.' The light from the kitchen left most of his face in shadow but for the gleam of his eyes. 'I've not been as attracted to anyone for a long time.'

Leah's heart put in a double beat of surprise. The few

inches separating them came into sharp focus, the smell of his shower gel combining with the grassy freshness of the dewy evening. 'That's very . . . direct of you. Do you usually work this fast?'

His laugh was low. 'We only have the holidays, right? Direct and fast seems the best way. We're mature enough to admit feeling sparks, surely? You've no idea how relieved I was to discover you're not married.'

Her stomach gave a pleasant little swoop. 'Despite me nearly rattling your brains out with my handbrake turns?'

'Could have happened to anyone.'

'Despite most of my attention being on surviving the morass of family problems I've been sucked into?'

The laughter left his voice. 'Probably because of it. Your resilience is enticing. That, and your looks – I am a man, after all.' His fingers found hers as he added encouragingly, 'I think this is where you tell me if you have a boyfriend/girlfriend/urge to extricate yourself from this conversation.'

The skin of his hand was slightly rough and she could feel a tiny pulse on his thumb. It felt comforting to be held, even in such a minor way. 'None of those,' she admitted huskily, heart bouncing gently at the direction the evening had taken. 'What about you? You should know that I once got involved with someone who turned out to be not as divorced as I thought he was and I'm not up for that again.'

'I'm completely divorced. Selina's happily partnered up. I haven't been in a relationship since she moved out.'

She felt her eyebrows shoot up. 'What? No women at all?'

His smile gleamed. 'I didn't say that. "Want to see my helicopter?" is a pretty reliable chat-up line, but I'm not in the market for anything other than brief encounters.'

He hesitated. 'The common thinking amongst single parents is you don't go introducing your kid to every person you have a thing with. Even if, eventually, you decide the "thing" is more than a brief thing, you don't get hot and heavy in front of your kid and you keep the private side of things private.' He waited, and when she didn't speak, he added, 'Are you looking for something more committed?'

'No!' she replied frankly. 'I'm dodgy enough at relationships without having to worry about kids being involved, even if they're not actually my kids.'

He looked relieved. 'Tell me about the married man.'

Leah felt her smile slide away and the familiar chill, like icy breath on the back of her neck. 'A depressing story of naïveté. I was twenty-five. His name was Tommy. I met him at a track day; we quickly got involved and began to book the same events. He worked in sales and wangled a patch near where I live, which often meant overnighting at my place, so we saw a lot of each other. Until my friend Scott grabbed me at a track day to warn me Tommy's wife had turned up. Not *ex*-wife.'

A light came on in an upstairs window and illuminated the hard line of Ronan's mouth. 'What happened?'

'Tommy's wife was . . . hideous to me.' She paused to swallow, shying away from confessing the whole truth about the day she'd been irrevocably scarred by betrayal so brutal it had never stopped stinging. 'So now I make damned certain I don't mess with people's marriages.'

'Tommy's loss, but I'm glad you're single.' He leaned in closer, hovering, giving her time to pull back. When she didn't, he brushed a single kiss beside her mouth.

Leah closed her mind to the wretched memories and let desire ripple through her at the warmth of his lips. 'I'm glad, too. Very few people love being single as much as I do, which is fortunate because my relationships never work out. Sooner or later the man begins to want me to compromise, to give up my life in favour of 'our life', to stop me going to track days or to record that weekend's Formula 1 race and watch it later.'

He drew back. 'Outrageous!' But he was laughing. 'Tell me about your friend Scott.'

'He may be another reason my relationships don't work out,' she admitted, adding, hastily, as Ronan's eyebrows shot up, 'I don't mean he gets intimidating. I don't think he knows how to intimidate. And it's not necessarily because boyfriends don't like me having a male best friend, although it does happen. It's because Scott's such undemanding company that boyfriends seem high maintenance in comparison.'

'I don't see why that should apply to me,' murmured Ronan, kissing her again. 'After all, it would be just for the holidays.'

Ronan called up the stairs. 'CURTIS!'

He heard a groan and something that sounded suspiciously like 'Gotta go. The old man's yellin'.'

Ronan watched Curtis come clumping down the broad wooden staircase and, knowing the conversation that lay ahead and because Curtis remembered to say 'Thanks for letting me stay round' to Leah, let being called 'the old man' slide.

Outside in the warm summer evening, Curtis began to yawn and, once home, he headed straight for the stairs, calling, 'Night.'

'Just a moment.'

Curtis turned, looking apprehensive at Ronan's tone. ''Sup?'

Ronan pushed open the sitting-room door and beckoned

Curtis through it. 'What's up is that I'd like a word with you.'

The sitting room walls had already been repainted and the furniture was in roughly its rightful place. Curtis flopped into a chair, looking defensive.

Ronan fixed Curtis with an unsmiling gaze. 'I'd like to know why you'd call Leah a MILF or a BILF.'

Jaw dropping comically, Curtis floundered around for an answer, eventually hitting on nothing more constructive than a sheepish 'Sorry'.

Inwardly, Ronan sighed. Did any parent actually enjoy this side of parenting? It would be easy to say, 'That's all right, then' and add it to his 'let it slide' list, but he hoped he was a better parent than that. Selina was sometimes too easy-going when it came to making Curtis a good citizen and Ronan was never happy with the result. 'Suppose you explain what you think those words mean.'

Curtis cleared his throat and mumbled reluctantly, 'Um . . . MILF means "mother I'd like to f-word". BILF means the same but "babysitter".' Though he'd avoided saying the whole f-word, blood roared to his face.

Ronan was reassured that Curtis's mortification indicated that he at least understood his crime. 'You know how I feel about you using bad language so let's focus on the disrespect in you saying these things about Leah. Can you imagine her embarrassment when Natasha asked Leah what MILF meant and told her why she was asking?'

Even Curtis's ear tips were glowing. 'She never said it in front of *Leah*?'

'Afraid so.' Ronan let his stern expression relax. 'Are you embarrassed by knowing Leah knows?'

'Proper! And I've got to face her for weeks.' He shut his eyes and groaned.

'These things do come back to bite you.' Ronan could remember being a cocky, klutzy teenage boy. He almost grinned at his son's chagrin.

Still sheltering behind his closed lids, Curtis nodded.

After a moment's study of his son, Ronan judged the message had got home. 'OK. I suggest you just let it drop. An apology will only embarrass her more.'

Gloomily, Curtis nodded again, probably all too aware that no matter how much they both pretended, he and Leah would both *know,* next time they met. He climbed to his feet.

Ronan decided on a touch of sympathy. 'Curtis, I do understand that you have feelings. You have to express them in a socially acceptable manner, but the feelings are perfectly normal.'

Dragging his feet as he made for the door Curtis tossed back, 'Yeah? I think it's you who has "perfectly normal" feelings for Leah, Dad. I've seen the way you look at her.'

Wrong-footed into silence, Ronan listened to his son's moody progress on the uncarpeted stair and sighed. Navigating burgeoning attraction to a woman was a delicate enough undertaking and now Curtis's snippy comeback reminded him, had he needed reminding, that everything he did had the potential to affect his son.

Aping Curtis's actions of a moment ago, he closed his eyes and groaned.

Chapter Seven

For the second morning running, Leah was awoken by her phone. This time it was a call. ***Michele.***

Leah raked her hair out of her face and pressed the handset against her ear to hear over a noise that she suddenly realised was rain pounding on the window. At least it would make a change from the unbroken sunshine they'd enjoyed since their arrival. 'So you've finally turned your phone on? Well done.'

'Sorry. We've been driving in the mountains. The signal's rubbish and we had to stop every five minutes for me to be sick. My morning sickness is lasting all day long, Leah. I did mean to call the kids last night but they would have been asleep by the time I made it out of the bathroom so I just flopped into bed. I didn't know anything had happened until I switched on my phone this morning.'

Slightly mollified by the explanation and realising that a journey interrupted by constant hurling couldn't be fun, Leah smoothed the irritation from her voice as she launched into a description of yesterday's accident and Alister's current circumstances. Michele kept gasping 'Oh, no!' and 'Oh, dear!', but otherwise listened in silence.

'I'll know more when I ring the hospital this morning. Ronan's going to make the actual call – unless you feel you should do it, of course,' Leah concluded.

She eased her position on her pillows and waited hopefully for Michele to declare that *of course* she'd make the call instead, and *of course* she'd drive straight back to be with her kids at this tricky time. Then her mind clicked back to Michele's opening words. 'Hold on, what mountains?'

'The Karwendel Alps.'

'And where the hell are they?'

'Austria and Germany.' Michele sounded amused at Leah's ignorance of mountain ranges. 'We're in Innsbruck but as the journey seems to have kicked off a constant need to throw up, I've done nothing but sit in the bathroom feeling wretched.'

Leah bolted upright, catching her sore elbow painfully on the nightstand and swearing. '*Innsbruck?* Austria? When you said you were going "away to talk" I didn't know you meant two countries away!'

Michele sniffed dolefully. 'I didn't either, to be honest. Bailey booked it.'

The sisters listened to each other's silence.

Irritation began to bubble back into Leah's voice. 'So how long will it take you to get back?'

'It took us about seven hours to get here–'

'I can expect you tomorrow, then?'

Another silence. Then Michele made a sound that was suspiciously like a sob. 'I can't face that journey back on those twisty turny roads until I'm feeling less nauseous. And I do need to talk things through with Bailey, Leah. The situation I'm in isn't to be taken lightly.' She gulped, piteously. 'We haven't talked yet because I'm hanging over the loo most of the time. I'm really, really sorry'

Leah took a slow breath. 'It does sounds miserable,' she allowed, 'but when I agreed to help look after your children I didn't bargain for being left with them on my own, hauling them into Strasbourg to visit their dad in hospital, and hoping they're coping emotionally with everything that's going on. I don't even know whether Alister will be able to come back to the gîte when he gets out, or whether his medical insurance company will want him flown home. In either event, it's going to be a bastard to get both vehicles back to the UK, isn't it?'

A low groan echoed down the telephone line. 'I can't think about that. I can't even think of getting back in Bailey's car until this disgusting sickness passes.'

The rain became heavier, drumming against the glass behind Leah, and thunder rumbled in the distance. Her hand tightened on her handset. 'Just as long as you're aware that your children have only their fairly clueless auntie to turn to.'

'They adore you! They'd much rather be with Auntie Leah who bakes and jokes and does cool stuff with cars than with their parents, who make them do as they're told and act sensibly. I'll bet they're having a fantastic time.'

However sympathetic she was trying to be, Leah couldn't let that go by. 'Actually, they're having a horrible time. Their mum's left them and their dad's in hospital. The holiday's hardly living up to expectations, is it? In fact, it's less a holiday and more like being stranded.' Leah had to raise her voice over the escalating hiss of the rain. 'Judging by your last pregnancy it could be weeks before the sickness passes. How about coming back by plane? I'll fund the ticket if necessary.'

A mulish note crept into Michele's voice. 'I can't. I'm sorry. I have to wait for this extreme nausea to pass, both for my sake and the baby's.'

Leah gave up. She couldn't push back against any possibility of damaging an unborn child. Resignation stole around her like dreary fog. 'At least leave your phone on so your kids can be in touch with you. *All* the time. *All* the time, Michele. No exceptions. All. The. Time.'

Michele agreed faintly, then added, 'I have to go back to the bathroom.'

When the call ended, feeling in need of a jolt of caffeine, Leah padded down to the kitchen in her pyjamas. She barely had time to get the coffee machine going before first Natasha then Jordan turned up, barefoot and bed-headed. She gave them bright smiles. 'We're all early birds, aren't we? Juice?'

Natasha got the glasses while Jordan sat at the table, scratching his head and watching Natasha slop orange juice on the work surface, then stoop to lick it up instead of getting a cloth.

'Good one, Gnasher.'

Leah shot him a look of reproof but decided not to point out to Natasha that 'licking up' wasn't approved in any hygiene training. Instead, she passed her the cleaning things then opened the fridge in search of eggs. 'Good news! I talked to your mum on the phone this morning. She's been in a low signal area. Less good news is she's still quite under the weather. She's very sorry to hear about your dad, of course, and sent loads of hugs and kisses to you both.'

Natasha gazed into her glass, watching the orange pith settle. 'When's she coming back?'

'Not sure yet.'

Jordan scratched his chin. 'Where is she?'

'Austria.' Leah elected to be truthful but try to sound airy about it.

'Why?' Natasha looked puzzled.

Leah gave her a big hug. 'Because that's where she went to talk but she didn't realise that she was going to feel so ill. She needs to feel better before she can start the journey back to be with you.'

Natasha's brow crinkled anxiously. 'So she's very very ill?'

Leah had no idea how many 'verys' were applicable to extreme pregnancy sickness so hunted for a calming comparison. 'She's vomiting a lot. Like a bad tummy bug.'

'Bleurgh.' But Natasha looked reassured.

'Do you know who her boyfriend is?' Jordan's sombre eyes followed Leah's movements as she returned the eggs to the fridge.

Silently cursing Michele for creating an appalling muddle and leaving Leah the unwilling keeper of secrets, Leah grabbed a slab of dark chocolate instead of answering. 'Let's make our own pastries. I have a mad craving for *pain au chocolat* and double espresso.'

'Cool!' Natasha jumped up.

Jordan, though, wasn't so easily distracted. 'Hasn't she told you, Leah? She tells you everything.'

Feeling a dismally disloyal piggy-in-the-middle she tried to avoid an outright lie. 'What she told me is that she'll explain everything when she comes back. I would have preferred her to clear things up before she went but I had to accept her choice.'

Jordan didn't look reassured and Leah felt worse than ever. To add to her guilt that confronting Michele had sent her literally running for the hills, Leah couldn't stop thinking about the words she'd spoken to Michele: *Deliberately making someone think something when it's actually untrue is a lie.*

Ronan appeared promptly after breakfast to make the promised call to the hospital, leaning on the kitchen counter. Although he had to frown his way through a great deal more repetition than when conversing face-to-face, he was soon able to pass on to Leah that Alister was comfortable, eating adequately, and the visiting hours of *service orthopédique et de traumatologie* were in the afternoon and evening.

'And his operation?'

'No news on that yet.' He frowned as he studied Leah's arm. 'Your elbow's so green and swollen this morning it looks like a conference pear. Shall I drive us all to the tram stop in Muntsheim?'

Leah winced as she flexed her damaged arm, all too aware of it because it felt as bad as it looked. 'That would be fantastic,' she accepted gratefully.

When they all met on Ronan's drive after lunch Leah realised from Curtis's dark red blush and his close inspection of his metal-bound boots that Ronan must have had the MILF talk with him. Her heart going out to him at his unhappy embarrassment she looked for a way to resolve the issue. 'As the weather's so miserable I thought we'd do some baking after the hospital. You up for it?'

Curtis peered through his hair cautiously. 'Yeah, yeah, yeah. Fanks.' He looked a bit less tortured as he climbed into his dad's car. Cake was a great healer.

Ronan's BMW was old and well-loved. He drove decisively but without risk as the windscreen wipers laboured to clear the rain. For once Leah found that even leaving aside her pulsing elbow she didn't mind someone else driving. It gave her the opportunity to relax for the first time that day and let her mind wander. His hands were firm on the wheel, and she watched the muscles moving in his forearms as she revisited the memory of last night's kisses in the garden. They'd been gently intense kisses rather than deeply passionate but she had a feeling passion was just waiting for the right opportunity to ignite. Or even explode.

The frisson between her and Ronan was about the only bright spot in the holiday, and the fact that he wasn't looking for anything heavy was perfect.

Ronan shot her a smile and brought her back to the moment. 'Their chatter's kind of soothing in its inconsequentiality.' He indicated the back seat occupants with his head.

'It's great that Natasha and Jordan have hooked up with Curtis,' she agreed. 'It gives them things to think about other than the disintegration of their parents' marriage, their dad's injury, and bickering with each other.' Leah listened contentedly to the kids for the rest of the short journey, watching the rain-swept fields flash by.

After parking the car in Muntsheim they splashed their way to the tram stop.

When the tram arrived it was sleek and silver, quiet and smooth. They whooshed along the tracks gazing out through the large windows with Ronan pointing out the bridge over the River Ill, a school, and allotments with cute sheds and children's play things. Once among the busy streets of Strasbourg they jumped out at the stop for Hôpital de Hautepierre. With aid from Leah's phone app they plodded through the puddles to the sprawl of buildings where acres of rain-spattered glass reflected the lowering sky. Inside the hospital, Ronan and Curtis took themselves off to the cafeteria while Leah and the kids located Alister's ward or *service*.

There was only one other bed in the bright and airy room but Leah only noticed poor Alister. Her heart shifted at how sorry for himself he looked, how drawn and defenceless, his leg immobilised by a big black boot and elevated on pillows. A walking frame stood beside the bed.

'It's for when I want to get out to the loo.' Alister pulled a face. 'Which is the only time I'm allowed out of bed because of the danger of clotting in the damaged tissue if it's not stuck up in the air all the time. It's awful!'

Swallowing down rising panic because it was so uncharacteristic of Alister to be anything but stoical, Leah handed over his sponge bag, pyjamas, the Dean Koontz novel from his bedside and his phone and wallet, which she'd been required to take home while he was transferred between hospitals. 'Try not to worry. All you have to do is lie there and get better.'

The kids were overawed by their rumpled, unshaven and bleary-eyed dad. Natasha whispered, 'You look like you're in *Holby City*.' But then she looped her arms around him in comfortable familiarity. 'Mum's in Austria and she's not coming back, and we're having a bake off later. Are you OK? Is there a tea trolley that comes round? Does it have sweets on it? Why do you think Mum went to Austria?'

'Probably to get away from your yapping,' Jordan scowled. '*Are* there any sweets, Dad?'

With a smile that looked as manufactured as Leah's felt, Alister fumbled in his wallet. 'Here's ten euros, five for each of you. Pop down to the cafeteria and buy something, but be back in twenty minutes, please. Stay together.'

The pair turned and left, for once in perfect accord

that signs to *la cafétéria* should be easy enough to track.

Alister gave the kids time to get out of earshot before bursting out, '*Austria*?'

Miserably, Leah nodded. 'Innsbruck. Sorry.'

Alister looked away, mouthing something that looked a lot like *fucking woman*. Leah regarded him uneasily as he took a deep breath. Then several more. 'And she's not coming back?'

'Yet,' Leah offered, cautiously. 'She's constantly nauseated after the journey there and says she can't turn straight around. She had this constant sickness when she was expecting Natasha, didn't she? I'm sure she'll be back when she's sorted herself out . . .' She tailed off as she read bleak disappointment in her brother-in-law's face. Unless she had a way of turning back the clock to a point before Michele fell for Bailey, nothing Leah could do or say was going to make Alister feel better.

Alister heaved a huge sigh and fell to gazing miserably out at rain that hosed the windows like a car wash. Leah fidgeted, feeling again that Michele's absence was at least partly her fault.

Then he swung back and took Leah's hand, something she could never remember happening before. 'Thank goodness you're here to look after the children! I'm more grateful than I can articulate.'

'I'm doing my best,' Leah managed. 'But—'

'Why is she doing this?' He cut across Leah's attempt to share her worries. 'I must have made her very unhappy for her to abandon her kids while she chases off to another country on some wild odyssey. I thought the worst had happened when she told me she was carrying another man's child but *this* . . .' He squeezed his eyes shut but not before Leah saw the sheen of tears.

'It's horrible for you,' Leah croaked, biting back a whirl of inappropriately honest responses. *She just fell in love with someone else . . . You're going to feel even worse when you know who he is . . . I may have helped trigger that wild odyssey.*

Alister drew in a long shaking breath and opened his eyes. 'I've no idea when I'll be out of here because I'm not even *seeing* a surgeon until Monday, let alone having my op.'

'But today's only Friday.' Leah was unable to hide her dismay.

Alister gave her hand a last squeeze before he released it. 'The best surgeon for the tendon and ligament damage is on holiday. Hopefully, she'll put me back together again on her return. I hope then it will be only a few days before I get out of here.' He paused to tug at his bottom lip. 'I've been worrying about what happens then.'

'It's been on my mind, too.'

He passed a weary hand over his eyes. 'I expect I could get myself flown home but it would be unfair to leave you here with the kids.'

Leah almost fell off the big orange patient chair in shock. 'It's definitely not a good idea to leave me in France with the kids while you fly to England!'

'No, I understand.' Though his tone was soothing, Alister looked vaguely troubled by her vehemence. 'We'll aim to all go home together, but the fact is we have two vehicles and only one able-bodied driver.'

'I don't see what we can do but wait until Michele reappears. I know she won't like it but she'll have to drive The Pig home. I don't see another choice.'

'Not so much a choice as a last resort.' Then Alister had to swallow his alarm as the kids reappeared, pockets and mouths bulging with Milka chocolate. As if his emotional outburst had never happened, and being stuck in a foreign hospital was no more than a minor inconvenience, he joined in their chatter in his usual easy way. Leah admired anew his ability to de-escalate a situation and could imagine him sailing along school corridors refusing to be flapped by irate parents or over-excited children, as he solved problems with either hand.

She could relax and let Alister take on the role of chief adult while she went down to Outpatients to have her graze cleaned and redressed.

Most of the afternoon had gone when they met up with Ronan and Curtis at the main entrance, and Ronan tucked Leah's uninjured arm through his as they once again pulled up their hoods and prepared to jump the puddles all the way back to the tram stop. She wasn't sufficiently wounded to need anybody to lean on, not physically. But emotionally? She left her hand in the comforting crook of his arm.

Finally, when they'd made it back to Kirchhoffen, they congregated in the kitchen of the gîte. 'Bake off?' reminded Natasha, hopefully.

Leah sank into a chair, finding it hard to summon a smile. 'Let's gather back here in twenty minutes. I need coffee or something first.' Especially if the 'something' was wine.

She needed to wrangle her demons into submission. Alister had seriously considered leaving her in France with the children while he flew home! Just the thought was enough to make her want to run like a rabbit at a greyhound meeting.

As soon as the door shut behind the teenagers, Ronan slid his arms around her and pulled her against the solidity of his chest. 'You look freaked out.'

She closed her eyes and let herself be comforted by his

heartbeat. His strength and calmness made it easy to imagine being completely confident in climbing aboard any helicopter he piloted. 'I was hoping it didn't show. But since when was I considered fit to care for two unsettled teenagers in a foreign land?'

His voice rumbled in her ear. 'I can translate when you need it. The kids can hang out with Curtis whenever you want a break.'

'Thank you,' she whispered. 'I'm being pathetic. I need to just get on with it. Whether or not this is the life I want, it's the life I presently have.'

'You're being anything but pathetic.' He dropped a kiss on her hair. 'And I'm gloating fiendishly that fate has delivered you into my hands, encouraging you to not only spend time with me but –' he breathed in her ear '– be grateful for my help.'

Leah managed a weak giggle. 'Let's just begin with the spending time part.'

He loosened his arms, laughter lurking in his eyes. 'Shall I take Curtis off? I can claim to need a hand with something. In fact, I could take all three kids. You don't need to be bothering with all that baking malarkey.'

Cheered by the hug, she shook her head. 'No. Baking's good. Very calming.'

'All right, how about you and your crew bake dessert for tonight and I bring the main course? Then if you need any more hugs – or anything – I'll be here.' There was no laughter in his eyes, now. But there was something. Intent, glowing, interested and interesting.

Warmth filtered through her. 'It's a deal.'

Curtis made his tone casual, even bored, his gaze on the hooded figures in Jordan's Assassin's Creed Xbox game, a game kept hidden from Alister because it was an 18. 'So, are we supposed to be going down to the kitchen yet?' The suggested twenty minutes were definitely up but although he didn't want to look too eager to abandon the virtual street gangs in nineteenth-century London, Curtis's mind was elsewhere. He liked food tech at school and Leah seemed to have let him off the MILF remark so he'd really like to bake some cake. And, not long after, eat it.

Natasha glanced at her phone. 'Yes! Leah said twenty minutes and it's thirty.'

Curtis followed Natasha downstairs, chattering as usual. 'So, do you?' she demanded, as they reached the foot of the stairs.

Belatedly, Curtis realised he hadn't been listening. 'Do I what?'

'Do you think your dad's got a "thing" for Leah?'

Before Curtis could reply Jordan bounded down the stairs in three noisy jumps. 'Shut up, Gnasher. No one's listening.' He shoved open the door to the kitchen. 'Got the chocolate, Leah?'

In the kitchen, Leah was gazing at Curtis's dad across a corner of the table, eyes bright with laughter. Two empty coffee mugs rested close together. Curtis glanced at Natasha, rolling his eyes in an attempt to convey: *looks like Leah's got a 'thing' back*. Natasha giggled in reply.

Leah jumped up as if belatedly recalling their plans. 'Curtis, you'll need to tie up the long part of your hair. Hands washed, everyone, please. That's proper hand washing with real soap.'

Obligingly, Curtis gathered up his long front hair into a mini ponytail and hooked it behind his ear. Natasha giggled again and said, 'Cool.'

'Moron,' said Jordan, with grudging admiration.

Curtis's dad took one of those deep breaths that meant he was trying not to laugh. 'See you later.' He ducked out of the door.

Leah produced slabs of chocolate. 'Let's make lava cakes. We can incorporate a bit of food art to keep things interesting.' They went through the thing of unwrapping and studying the chocolate, snapping it and sniffing it before pronouncing it good enough to use in 'a product'. 'We should melt chocolate in a double boiler but I'm not sure about mixing you guys with boiling water so we'll do it in the microwave. Curtis, will you break the white chocolate into this bowl? Natasha, the dark chocolate into this one. And Jordan, maybe you could wash the strawberries? Dry them with clean kitchen roll but don't hull them till the last minute.'

'Awesome,' breathed Curtis, ripping into the big cream-coloured packet of the white chocolate, breaking off a square of chocolate and biting it in half.

'No, you don't.' Sternly, Leah twitched the rest of the block from his hands.

'Chocolate tasting!' he protested.

'Kitchen hygiene while we're baking. You should never put your fingers near your mouth, which means no eating. You need to wash your hands again.'

Curtis looked at the rest of the chocolate square in his hand, then flipped it into the air and caught it neatly in his mouth. 'My fingers didn't go near my mouth that time.'

It made Jordan and Natasha laugh but Leah sighed and pointed at the sink.

Curtis soon discovered that although the family referred to the session as a bake off they were all firmly on one team, calling 'What do you think, Chef?' to each other, and Leah strolling about with her hands behind her back to question their plans or offer advice.

The kitchen began to smell so good you could get a sugar rush just inhaling. Curtis mixed melted chocolate with butter, stirred in sugar, beat in eggs, sifted in flour and spilled so much down himself that Leah said, 'You ought to go in the oven with the cakes.' Natasha giggled furiously and Jordan made an obscene hand gesture in Curtis's direction when Leah wasn't looking, except she turned and saw him and went '*JOR-DAN MIL-TON*!' which made Jordan go red as fire. It was fun, everyone getting messy and teasing each other. Curtis supposed that this must be what it was like to be part of a family instead of one kid with various parents.

After Curtis had greased little dishes and coated the insides with sugar, Leah came over. 'Great. Divide the batter equally between five ramekin dishes. Lava cakes only take about fifteen minutes so we'll put them into the oven while we're eating our first course.'

'Am I staying for dinner? What are we having?'

'Your dad's in charge of the main course.' Leah turned to watch Jordan, who'd spooned melted chocolate into a piping bag and was drawing thick chocolate shapes on baking parchment.

Curtis snorted a laugh. 'Curry, spag bol or salad, then.'

'All sounds good.' Leah rounded on her niece. 'Natasha, if you eat one more strawberry I'm going to ban you from my kitchen. Eating is a separate activity to cooking. Wash your hands.'

Natasha, who'd been industriously dipping strawberries in melted white chocolate and then into edible glitter, stopped chewing and put on an innocent face.

Curtis found himself instructed to 'start the clean-down'. With a sigh, he began to gather up chocolate-coated bowls and batter-spattered utensils, taking surreptitious licks of the cake mixture when he thought Leah wasn't looking.

Then his pocket buzzed and he wiped his fingers on his shorts before fishing out his phone.

Mum: *Are you OK? What's the weather like? Are you doing anything fun? x*

'My mum,' he said.

Leah didn't look up from wiping down a counter in big brisk circles. 'Hope she's OK.'

'Yeah.' He tapped back:

Curtis: *Fine thx. Raining. Making chocolate cakes.*

Before he could even put his phone away, he received an answer:

Mum: *I suppose the house is a tip and you and your dad are camping out on the floor? Lol. x*

His mum and Darren's house was like something from one of those property shows on telly after a poncey designer had had his hands on it. That 'lol' didn't fool Curtis. Mum would think a few paint spots meant he was sleeping rough.

Curtis: *It's OK. Dad's put a new shower in and he's painting everywhere. We sleep in beds.*

Mum: *Glad to hear it.* ☺ *x*

Curtis shoved his phone away. Leah had begun the washing up so he helped Jordan transfer his sheet of chocolate shapes to the fridge while Natasha washed her hands free of glitter. When Curtis saw the shapes Jordan had made he snorted with laughter.

Jordan sent him a warning look.

Then they set the kitchen table with cutlery with coloured plastic handles and Leah showed them how to fold paper napkins into the shape of swans.

'Making paper swans is well easy,' Curtis marvelled, following her instructions closely and ending up with something that was recognisably a swan.

'Don't tell anyone. Let them think we're really clever.' Leah grouped the swans as if they were swimming down the centre of the table.

Jordan looked discontented. 'Forget paper swans. Where's dinner?'

On cue, Ronan called to be let in, his hands, when Curtis flung open the door, proving to be full of their two large stew pots, balanced one atop the other. 'Cool,' Curtis grinned.

'Actually, scalding hot.' His dad deposited the pots on the hob with a clang, dropping the towels he'd used as oven mitts.

'Mum texted.'

His dad's face did that funny flicker that tended to accompany conversations about Curtis's mum. But 'I hope all's well with her' is all he said.

'Yup, fine.' Curtis took a seat at the table. He hadn't asked her that specific question but she'd sounded fine. She'd lolled, after all.

The meal was leisurely. Leah relaxed and enjoyed the kids and their quirky worldview. After the main course, suspiciously giggly, they arranged glittery strawberries and Jordan's chocolate decorations on scoops of ice cream beside the lava cakes. Leah understood the red-faced mirth when she got a proper look at the shapes Jordan had created and realised they were unmistakeably phallic but decided that stern words would only give him the satisfaction of knowing he'd made an impact. Plus, Ronan's eyes were dancing and Leah didn't trust herself not to laugh.

'Delicious,' she pronounced, scraping the sides of her bowl a couple of minutes later. 'Curtis, your lava cakes were exactly right – firm on the outside but squishy in the middle. As you guys have worked so hard I'll do the final clean-down. You go and play pool or something.'

'Cool!' In three seconds the door to the hall was swinging and the kitchen was empty of teenagers.

Which left Leah alone with Ronan. Trying to pretend she hadn't planned it, she bundled up damp tea towels and put out clean ones. 'Teenagers are hard work. I love Jordan and Natasha but I've never had to spend so much time in their company. They talk all the time and fire questions, and you have to try not to swear and remember to be disapproving when they say or do something they shouldn't.'

Ronan glanced up from loading the dishwasher. 'Like making chocolate decorations in the shape of –'

'Exactly.' She felt a blush begin. 'Has Jordan been to Ann Summers for ideas?'

'Fifteen-year-old boys had ideas like that long before Ann Summers shops were around.'

Suddenly very conscious of the weight of his gaze, Leah paid assiduous attention to the hang of a clean tea towel. 'It's obvious that your wife's wondering about how Curtis is getting on over here. Nice for him that both his parents are obviously loving and concerned.' She turned around and found Ronan right there. A fizzing swept over her skin as if she'd lain down and rolled in Space Dust.

'Ex-wife,' he corrected softly but with emphasis. Backing Leah up against the kitchen table, he hooked his right arm around her waist and, with a quick heave, jumped her up onto the surface so that their eyes were level. 'It's over between Selina and me. Completely. OK?' His gaze moved between her eyes and her mouth.

'Right.' As he edged his body closer her dress hitched up by several inches. The denim of his jeans brushing the inside of her knees made it hard to think.

'You don't have to test me. We live separate lives.' Slowly, he brought his lips closer to hers. 'And now . . . I really don't want to talk or think about my very very *very* ex-wife.'

'Right,' Leah repeated.

'Because I want to kiss you.'

'Good.' As the heat of his mouth took hers, she closed her eyes and let herself feel the softness of his kiss, the sensual stroke of his tongue. There was no reason to fight the attraction she felt for Ronan. It would make this strange and uncomfortable holiday bearable. A French fling. A flingette.

Hooking him closer with her leg and hearing his breathing change she shut down to anything apart from his mouth on hers and his hands beginning a flesh-tingling slide up her body.

And the clatter of feet on the stairs.

Ronan sprang away and Leah leaped off the table, making sure her hem had fallen to its proper place, an instant before Curtis threw back the kitchen door.

'Natasha's crying lots,' he told Leah urgently. 'Jordan said would I get you cos he doesn't know what to do. She's really going at it.'

'I'll go up to her.' Natasha sprang to the forefront of Leah's mind, though her uneven breathing even before she ran up the stairs was a reminder of the snatched moment in the kitchen. That and the waves of heat still pulsing through her body.

She found Natasha draped across her bed, reams of damp toilet paper clutched in her fingers. Jordan crouched beside her patting her arm awkwardly. The look he threw Leah was defensive. 'I wasn't even horrible to her.'

'Good. Shall I have a chat with her?' Leah suggested softly.

With undisguised relief, Jordan gave his sister a last pat before slipping out through the bedroom door. Leah pulled the heaving little figure into her arms, smoothing her hair and kissing the top of her head. She didn't ask what the matter was. She just waited, ripping off fresh festoons of loo roll as each reached the limits of absorbency.

Finally, Natasha choked, 'I want my mum.'

Leah felt a peculiar sensation under her breastbone as if someone was very slowly pulling a thread that was attached deep inside her. 'I know. She'll be back. It's a difficult time for all of you.'

'I've texted her today and she hasn't answered.'

Leah fought to damp down a spark of sisterly rage. 'Maybe she's still having trouble with the signal. She said she was leaving her phone on all the time and that she was going to keep in contact with you.' It was actually what Leah had demanded. She wasn't quite so certain that Michele had agreed. 'Let's try and call her now.'

But the call went to voicemail once they'd heard the ring tone a few times, making Natasha sob anew. 'I'm so glad you're here, Leah.' Natasha held onto Leah tightly, smelling of chocolate and curry.

'So am I.' With a warm trickle of pleasure, Leah realised she meant it. There were few things sadder than an upset teenager and if her presence could make Natasha feel even a tiny bit better she was glad, even though her own heart was feeling oddly bruised.

As if it, too, wanted to offer comfort, Natasha's phone began to ring. She snatched it up. 'It's Mum!' she beamed wetly, fumbling in her haste to answer.

Almost weak with relief Leah withdrew to the doorway as Natasha exclaimed, 'Oh, you were in the bathroom?' and began to pour out the day's news, breathlessly mixing it up until it sounded as if they'd baked lava cake on a tram as it whizzed through the hospital. She even managed a few watery smiles. When Jordan crossed the landing with an expression of expectation Leah stepped out to meet him. 'Do you want a word with your mum?'

He gave a single nod. 'Might as well.' The eager light in his eyes belied his casual words.

Leah left him listening to Natasha's jumbled side of the conversation, putting in a comment here and there. Then she remembered Ronan and Curtis in the kitchen and, though feeling as if her emotions had had a quick whizz in a blender, jogged downstairs.

The room was empty. The stew pots had gone. On the table was a note written on the back of a shopping receipt. *Thanks for a great evening. Goodnight. R & C.*

There was little left to do but finish the last few chores, lock up, switch off the light and mooch back upstairs. She found Jordan's door shut. Natasha was already in bed, three-parts asleep but managing a sleepy smile. 'Mum's still icky but she's going to be OK,' she murmured before turning over and closing her eyes.

'That's fantastic.' Leah sought the sanctuary of her own room. She fished for her phone and rang Scott.

'About time,' he snorted mock-disagreeably, 'you've

hardly sent me any texts and you've been away a week. Is everything OK, you bloody annoying woman?'

'Don't give me a hard time.' But Leah smiled just to hear his funny, familiar, snarky voice. In the background she could hear a lot more voices and what sounded like a TV. 'Nothing's OK. The Milton Family Dramas just pile up.' She brought him up to date then, hearing a muffled roar go up in the background, demanded enviously, 'Are you at the Chequered Flag?' It was their favourite pub for a relaxed Saturday night watching Sky Sports and drinking with mates. A longing rolled over her to be there, sinking a couple of Budweisers and getting involved in pointless arguments that led to raucous laughter and more beers, close enough to home to walk back at the end of the evening.

'Yep.' Another roar. 'Watching a Superbikes race. Loads of dicing at the front. So you're still stuck out there?'

Easing the ponytail elastic from her hair, Leah lay back on her pillows. 'Stuck like superglue. And I don't know how we're going to get two vehicles back. I may have to drive The Pig home and fly back for the Porsche.'

Scott laughed incredulously. 'Don't leave the Porsche, Leah. Bring your favourite kid and make the other one stay behind.'

Although she knew he was joking, for a wild instant Leah imagined having to choose which child to leave alone in a foreign country, woebegone and desperate. She actually had to gulp back tears.

Scott's voice softened to a remorseful croon. 'Hey, hey, it was just a stupid joke. Don't get upset. You'll get everyone home somehow. There are trains, planes and coaches. The people are what count. Cars are just bits of tin.'

Leah was so astonished at hearing him term *cars* 'just bits of tin' that she even smiled despite her hot eyes. 'Wow. People more important than cars? That may take some getting used to.'

Though Scott laughed, he said, 'You know it well enough. That's why we all love you.'

Chapter Eight

As soon as she awoke on Saturday Leah rang Michele and listened to the far-off ringtone. She'd just resigned herself to the call going to voicemail when Michele answered.

'I'm glad you found time to speak to your kids last night.' Leah decided there was no point pulling punches. 'Natasha was getting upset.'

'I know. I'm sorry. I spent most of yesterday on the bathroom floor.' Michele sounded worryingly faint and wobbly. 'I can't keep anything down and I'm reaching the point of exhaustion. If I'm the same today, Bailey's going to find a doctor to give me medicine to stop the constant throwing up.'

Leah had rung with the intention of getting a firm answer as to when they might expect to see Michele back in Kirchhoffen and, meantime, discuss the fact that the last visit to the supermarket had mopped up most of the food kitty. Now concern for her sister overrode those things. 'You poor thing–'

Michele suddenly gasped. 'Oh . . . I've got to run!'

'I hope you soon feel bet—' The line was already dead.

Leah sighed as she shoved her phone in her pocket. The situation got worse all the time.

At Chez Shea, Ronan was spending his morning painting the walls of the third bedroom. The sunshine had returned to stream in as he painted the sloping patch above the window. That done, the upstairs would be finished and he could tackle the unappetising, time-consuming job of rubbing down the kitchen cabinets before applying fresh stain. Curtis hadn't put in an appearance and Ronan was allowing him to sleep in and indulge his wild teenage circadian rhythms.

Ronan pulled up the step in order to reach the upper edge of the wall and paused to release the stiffness in his left arm, rolling the shoulder, lifting and flexing the arm, stretching and flexing his fingers. The doctors had warned him about building his fitness sensibly and he'd cut down his usual running regime to jogging or walking while his collarbone healed.

Laborious labour. It was meant to free the mind to wander. Not that his mind needed any invitation; it'd been awake hours before it should have been, drawn like a magnet to the day the RPM needle on Buzzair Two had begun to flicker, leading him into going obsessively over whether he'd chosen the best of the farm fields spread below him for his forced landing, pulse accelerating at the memory of the dropping engine note and the warning flash of the *engine out* light, reliving the automatic movements of his hands and feet on the controls to take the aircraft into autorotation, the procedure every helicopter pilot practised until nursing a sick helicopter down could be done in their sleep. The ground had come closer at a rapid but controlled rate; he'd achieved exactly the right angle and speed of descent until he could execute a perfect flare and run-on landing.

Then had come the sickening instant when the aircraft dug in its toes and the world flipped, leaving Ronan hanging in his harness, his shoulder feeling as if it had burst into flames.

He recognised it was just bad luck that the crop had disguised the underlying bogginess of the spot he'd chosen. He knew he hadn't been incompetent. Stretching the glide in search of a more closely mown field hadn't been achievable. Yet first light slipping its shining fingers around the curtains had found him re-examining every detail of what had caused this frustrating break from flying and thanking his stars that at least his injury hadn't been career-ending.

He paused to drag the step along to the final couple of feet of wall. Irritated that he was mulling fruitlessly over the forced landing *again,* as he had last night and the one before, he directed his mind instead onto the subject of Curtis, wondering how the shyly smiling boy who, only a few years ago, had skipped hand-in-hand at Ronan's side had been replaced by a man-sized teen who dressed like a character from a graphic novel; as if he wanted everybody to look at him. Or nobody to see him. Particularly disenchanting was Curtis's occasional habit of treating Ronan as a joke. Ronan liked jokes, but didn't exactly see himself as one.

Ronan was pretty comfortable with his place in the world, his respected career, the responsibility he took for the life of every passenger who boarded an aircraft he flew. Yet he saw his greatest responsibility, his greatest achievement, the most important thing in his life, was Curtis. It hurt that Curtis was so obviously, even deliberately, growing away from him.

And then there was last night . . . Leah, the way her smile struck him in the pit of his stomach, how she'd felt in his arms: soft and curved in all the right places. He loaded his brush with cream emulsion and his mind flipped to Curtis's face when he'd almost caught them in a clinch.

Ronan had thought he'd unwrapped himself from around Leah quickly enough but now he wondered whether Curtis's eyes had narrowed suspiciously.

Tucking his left hand into his waistband to relieve his shoulder of its weight, Ronan used his right arm to sweep the paintbrush to and fro, to and fro, methodically covering the last segment of the wall before stepping down to check out his handiwork. Instead of seeing the bright new coat of emulsion, he remembered the edge to Curtis's voice on Thursday evening. *I've seen the way you look at her*.

In the three post-Selina years, Ronan's sex life had consisted of hook-ups with the kind of women who were happy for him to leave while the condom was still warm, a smile on his face and a head full of interesting memories. But none of the women concerned had been living in the house next door, as Leah was, so they hadn't appeared on his radar before. Maybe Curtis was alarmed at this first hint of Ronan as a man rather than just a dad? Ronan might one day want to introduce Curtis to a girlfriend but there was a difference between 'girlfriend' and 'holiday romance'.

He frowned over his thoughts as he cleared up his decorating paraphernalia and went downstairs.

It was a couple of hours later when Curtis finally made an appearance. By then Ronan was calculating the amount of work needed on the kitchen cabinets and mentally consigning it to the day's 'the doctor said not to push myself' category.

'What's up?' mumbled Curtis through the hair hanging over his face, swinging open the fridge and pulling out the milk.

Ronan passed him a glass in the hopes of encouraging him not to drink directly from the carton. 'Nothing much up with me. You?'

Shrugging, Curtis poured the milk. Despite the hot August morning he wore baggy black and white chequered trousers that tucked into boots laced up almost to his knees. Black braces dangled pointlessly from his waist and his black T-shirt depicted maggots wriggling through the eye sockets of a skull.

'Lunch?' Ronan took yesterday's baguette from the bread bin. He covered chunks of baguette with grated cheese and slices from a big red tomato, stuck them under the grill and helped himself to a bottle of Meteor beer.

Curtis poured a second glass of milk, plonked the carton next to the fridge – what good was next to? – and noisily dragged out a kitchen chair. 'What we doing today?'

Ronan was tempted to say, 'I've been up for hours and have finished emulsioning the third bedroom already,' but instead went with 'What do you want to do?'

Shrug. 'What are the others doing?' Curtis inclined his head in the general direction of the gîte next door to indicate the identity of 'the others', adding, helpfully, 'Cheese is burning.'

Locking expletives behind his teeth like a responsible parent, Ronan leaped for the grill pan. He'd only removed his attention for a split second and one hunk of bread had begun to catch. Having put that and another on his plate, he passed Curtis the more golden slices.

'Fanks.'

'Fink noffing of it.'

Curtis laughed as he chewed. 'Good banter, Dad.'

Feeling cheered by the applause, Ronan took the other chair and returned to the subject of the family next door. 'I saw them go out a while ago. Probably to visit Alister in the hospital.'

'Are we eating with them tonight?'

Ronan tried to get a handle on Curtis's feelings. 'Would you like to?'

Shrug.

Unhelpful.

When the toast was no more than a track of crumbs across the table Ronan tried again. 'Is anything bothering you, Curtis?'

Curtis looked mildly alarmed as he gulped down the last mouthfuls of milk. 'No.'

'Are we spending too much time with the family next door?'

Shrug. 'No. Jordan's cool. Natasha's OK. Leah makes good cake.' And, quite definitely, Curtis blushed.

Worry wormed into Ronan's stomach. Were Curtis's pink cheeks because he *had* caught sight of his dad and Leah glued together, last night? Or . . . surely not . . .? He took a fortifying draught of beer to help him tackle a horrifying thought. 'Do you . . . do you, you know, *like* Leah?' It made his stomach feel as if he'd just dropped into an air pocket to think that he and his newly-a-teenager son might have feelings for the same woman.

Yet, there had been that 'MILF' remark. Had Ronan been wrong to put that down to Curtis simply feeling, and expressing in basic terms, a thirteen-year-old's indiscriminate lust for any attractive female?

But Curtis was turning aghast eyes his way. 'What are you *on*?' he blurted. 'She's, like, *thirty* or something.'

'Thirty-five,' Ronan said, repeating what Michele had told him. 'Sorry.' He felt awkward. But also relieved. He tried a laugh. 'I didn't mean to embarrass you. It's just that when you first saw her you said she was hot–'

'I was winding you up!'

'And you were quiet last night–'

Curtis stumbled to his feet, clattered his glass and plate in the sink and strode through the door. 'I'm going on my laptop.'

Upstairs, Curtis threw himself on his unmade bed. It was proper gross when adults stuck their noses in. Curtis was *so* not going to share with his dad that he'd been quiet last night because of Natasha crying for her mum, her face all pink and blubbery. He hadn't wanted to leave without finding out if she was OK but his dad had said it was time to give the family their privacy.

To calm himself, he opened his laptop and went to one of his favourite sites, where the women wore sultry smiles and little else, immediately absorbed as he flicked from image to image. The sun moved round to look into his room and he had to get up and throw open the window.

Which was the moment his dad chose to knock and stroll in. 'Curtis–' His gaze landed directly on the machine temporarily abandoned in the middle of Curtis's bed.

'Dad,' Curtis breathed in horror. 'This sucks! What about my privacy?'

Ronan blinked. 'Oh . . . sorry. Um, that's a funny screen saver.'

Crimson, Curtis snatched up the laptop and slammed it shut on the image of a giggling woman with no top on. 'It's . . . it's an educational site.'

'Looks it,' said his dad, drily. 'We'll, um, talk later.'

Curtis cursed, every inch of his skin hot and sweaty as the door closed. Dads were so crap.

Then, to his horror, the door swung back open and his dad returned, pained apprehension warring with determination in his face. He untangled a segment of the bedclothes so he could sit on a corner of the bed. 'Actually, we need to talk about this now. I haven't quite got used to you not being a little boy and I didn't respect your privacy. I'm sorry, because I want you to be able to trust me – but I expect to be able to trust you, too. Curiosity about sex is normal but pornography sites are skewed and often exploitative, rather than being about what happens between a loving couple.'

The words turned to babble in Curtis's ears. His dad was giving him 'a talk'! He'd even paused to do that eyebrows-raised waiting-for-a-reply thing.

Burning with dismay, Curtis hurriedly shoved his laptop aside. 'I won't look any more.'

'That's great.' But, inexorably, his dad slid the laptop into his own hands and reopened it. He tapped away while Curtis waited anxiously. After several minutes his dad returned the machine along with a level look. 'I've made myself an admin and you a standard user and I downloaded software that allows me to block adult websites. This way, there can't be any accidents.'

Outrage bloomed hot in Curtis's chest. 'You've got to be kidding me! It's *my* laptop!'

'But my rules, mate. Porn sites are prone to computer viruses so making them inaccessible will protect your machine, too. Phone, now, please.'

Curtis slung his handset onto the quilt, glowering as his dad frowned over selecting and downloading a suitable app.

'There we go.' He handed back the phone, then came over totally dad-like and asked Curtis a list of cringe-making questions about whether he'd been frightened by anything he'd seen – yeah, *right* – or had anything he'd like to ask, now things were out in the open . . . so to speak.

'No!' Curtis kept his gaze fixed unhappily on his laptop, which somehow felt less precious, as if he'd been diminished in its eyes by having his status ignominiously reduced to *standard user*.

'Any time you want to talk . . .'

'Yeah, *yeah*.' Curtis knew his dad was providing him with time to bring forth any concerns but he refused to look up. The more silent he remained, the quicker his dad would go.

Finally, his dad said, 'OK, sorry to intrude,' which he *so* wasn't, and closed the door carefully behind him as he left.

'Bit late to think of privacy now, right?' Curtis hissed at the closed door.

Dropping into his bedroom chair, Ronan closed his eyes, a short-of-sleep headache developing to keep company the ever-present throbbing in his shoulder. Had that cheesy line about a screen saver really come out of his mouth? Had he said *any* of the right things to Curtis? Had Curtis noticed that Ronan's initial reaction had been to pretend it wasn't happening? Opening his eyes again he drew his own laptop from its place beside his bed and repeated the safeguarding just in case Curtis hit on the idea of utilising it instead to further his 'education'.

That accomplished, he went to a parents' site to check out the articles on what to do if you caught your kid viewing porn. It was reassuring to find that he'd ticked some boxes. Relieved that he may not have made a total botch of things, he turned to his email account.

To: Selina Worrall he tapped in, with the now familiar moment of noticing that she'd abandoned Shea and taken Darren's name, even though not actually married.

From: Ronan Shea
Subject: Keeping current
Hi Selina,
I'd appreciate a quick chat on Facetime or Skype when you have a moment. Would tomorrow evening work for you?
R

He tried to be conscientious about sharing anything that concerned Curtis in the hope that Selina would return the favour. Broadly speaking, this worked, except where Selina was pretty certain Ronan would disagree, such as facial piercings.

Clicking *send*, he moved on to check his inbox. A sender leaped out at him. Swiftly, he opened the email dated the previous day, 11th August.

To: Ronan Shea
From: Henry Brook [Buzz Sightseer]
Subject: Update request
Ronan,
I'm aware your next meeting with your orthopaedic surgeon isn't scheduled until September but if you'd update me on your state of health, it would help me gain a sense of progress being made (if any).
As I expected, the insurance company is asking a

lot of questions about your incident on 3 July now that the Air Accidents Investigation Branch's report's available.

You'll appreciate that there are financial ramifications from this unfortunate incident. These cannot be overlooked.

Henry

What the hell? Ronan stared at the email in shock. Buzz Sightseer might be Henry's business but Ronan had always been a huge part of it – though little trace of what he thought was his friendship with Henry filtered through this stilted, faintly admonishing communication. He'd given hundreds of unpaid hours supporting Henry through the start-up and establishing operational strategy. In exchange, Ronan had been given the title of chief pilot and directly employed, rather than working on a self-employed basis as did the other pilots.

Henry had all too obviously switched to 'let's do this by the book'. Grimly, Ronan hit *reply*.

From: Ronan Shea
To: Henry Brook [Buzz Sightseer]
Subject: Re: Update request

Henry,

Health situation is as we were told to expect – while healing, I'm performing physio as directed. You're correct re: my next scheduled meeting with the orthopaedic surgeon. As you're already aware, that's when I anticipate the surgeon OKing me to request my AME to pass me fit to fly.

Thank you for the information re: the insurance company. How would they process the claim without

asking questions? Isn't it the insurance company's function to mitigate the financial ramifications, via the claim?
Ronan

He scanned through the remainder of his inbox but Henry's email felt like a red flag. Something had changed . . . and not for the better. Henry had been quiet lately but that hadn't felt out of the ordinary. Ronan's absence from the hangar was bound to drop more work on Henry's shoulders and as they weren't currently living in the same town there would have been no point to *Fancy a drink after work?* calls.

So far as Ronan was concerned, his sick leave was merely an interruption to normal life.

Wasn't it? *Wasn't* it?

For the first time he felt uneasy that he'd chosen to spend his sick leave so out of touch with his job in aviation.

Chapter Nine

Next morning, Jordan loped into the kitchen, yanked open the fridge so that everything rattled, and pulled out two bottles of a peach fizzy drink the kids had fallen in love with. 'Curtis is coming round.' He added a handful of chocolate bars to his haul.

Gently, Leah relieved him of one bottle and all the chocolate bars. 'You've only just had breakfast.'

'But Curtis is coming.'

'I expect he's only just had breakfast, too.'

A rap at the kitchen door and Jordan abandoned the battle in favour of opening it.

Curtis shuffled in, wearing so much tin he looked as if he should be put out for recycling. 'Hey. Dad's here to talk to you.'

Leah turned, her arms still full of Mars Bars and fizzy drink. Ronan was standing just inside the door, all tanned skin and tight black T-shirt. He raised an eyebrow at the booty in her arms.

She rolled her eyes. 'Kids.'

'That's what they all say.' He stepped properly into the

room as Jordan and Curtis vanished upstairs. 'Do you have plans? The Sunday market in Muntsheim brings out Curtis's inner magpie. Fancy bringing Natasha and Jordan? Then, if you're planning to visit the hospital we can take the tram into Strasbourg and have lunch beforehand.' He took a quick peep out into the hall, eased the door quietly closed and lowered his mouth hotly to hers.

Unable to do much but let herself be kissed, her arms still being occupied with fizzy drink and chocolate, Leah had to grab a gap between kisses to make a breathless reply. 'That would be great. The kids are squabbly, probably because their mum's still away. At least with Alister they can see him and that he's brighter, shaved and in his own PJs.'

She rose up on tiptoes to nuzzle his jaw. 'Your phone number would be useful, by the way.' When the kids had vanished to their rooms last night Leah had gone to bed wishing she could call or text Ronan. She hadn't felt she could just rock up to his door. Curtis would be around and she was pretty sure she wasn't supposed to leave Natasha and Jordan alone late in the evening. She'd concluded, groaning, that she'd enjoyed more freedom when she'd been a teen herself: sneaking out had practically been her duty and, as the youngest, she hadn't been obliged to set a good example.

'Definitely.' Ronan wedged his foot against the kitchen door while he pulled her closer and kissed her harder and she let her head tilt slowly as his lips moved on along her jaw to the sensitive skin below her ear.

Footsteps began to thump on the stairs, voices raised in teenage-normal cacophony. Ronan, sighing, released the door and shifted himself around the other side of the kitchen table in three long strides. Leah got busy restoring the drink and chocolate to the fridge.

The door flew back on its hinges. 'Curtis says there's this market full of cool stuff. Can we go?' demanded Natasha.

Hot on her heels, Jordan looked equally eager. 'You can get big baked things called bretzels and eat them with cheese.'

'Sounds perfect.' Leah shut the fridge. 'But you can't possibly be hungry, Jordan. And you'd both better put your sunscreen on, it looks baking out there.' Then she winced. She sounded exactly like a mother.

The market was held at La Place de la Liberté in Muntsheim, transformed by stalls under green-striped awnings. A couple of snack vans lurked on the far side, as if hoping to escape the notice of the owners of Café des Trois Cigognes. Delicious-smelling bretzels were much in evidence, hanging up temptingly on the snack vans. Shoppers chattered as they pushed shopping trolleys past the fountains and around the stalls.

Leah took a cursory tour of the stalls to buy fruit to stow in a cool bag in the back of The Pig. Holiday money obviously burning holes in the pockets of Jordan and Natasha, she then bent what she hoped was a Deputy Parent-type respect-inspiring gaze on them. 'Find me when you've finished shopping. I'm going to sit out of the sun under a parasol at that café over there to see how many cups of espresso I can drink. Stay in the market square, OK?'

'Same for you, Curtis,' Ronan added.

'Yeah, yeah, yeah, totally.' Curtis moved off shoulder-to-shoulder with Jordan.

'Yeah, yeah,' Natasha supplemented happily, trotting after their departing backs.

At the café Leah and Ronan secured an outside table. Leah turned her face to the sun, taking the time to smell the flowers – literally, as there were frothy tubs of them all around the square – until a waiter arrived with a tray and the fragrance of strong coffee took over.

Ronan had fallen quiet, she realised, staring across the market as if not seeing it. Leah picked up her pretty pale blue cup. 'Something up?'

The smile he turned on her was rueful. 'Little bit. I'm worried for my career and Curtis is looking at porn.'

She felt her eyebrows fly up. 'Porn? Isn't he a bit young?'

Ronan heaved a sigh. 'If I were Curtis I'd say, "Duh!" and smack myself in the head. Of course he's too young in the sense that porn is bad for the developing mind and a poor view of the joys of sex but, self-evidently, not too young in terms of enjoying it. Or, it turns out, to sulk that I'm not giving him the privacy to enjoy it. He's currently punishing me with teenage insolence and eye-rolling.'

Leah felt her shoulders begin to bunch. Yet another potential challenge to add her guardianship list. 'Wow. Do you think that Jordan could be doing the same?'

'Who knows?' Ronan threw his arms wide in exasperation, then winced and rubbed his shoulder. 'There's software you can install to stop him viewing adult sites. I can show you. But why should it only be Jordan?'

She groaned, itching her elbow beneath its dressing where a scab was now forming. 'I suppose I think of Natasha still as a little girl but you're right. I'll have to install it on her phone, too. I'd better ask Alister's permission, though.' Leah sipped her coffee, which suddenly didn't seem quite so delicious, and fell to watching a young man who stood on a corner of the square making balloon animals, gathering a crowd of children who giggled as he held up a yellow-balloon rabbit. Leah felt a surge of panic at all the trouble teenagers could get into and yearned for Michele to stop throwing up so she could come and be responsible for her own kids.

Then the rest of Ronan's remark filtered back to her. 'Career worries? Are they more or less important than your Curtis worries?'

Ronan curled one eyebrow. 'Nothing's more important than Curtis, but the career worries are significant. My employer's attitude's bothering me.'

Leah tried to get a handle on what was carving the frown on Ronan's forehead. 'Over your accident?'

He took a deep breath before letting it out slowly. 'It wasn't an "accident". It was an incident, which I dealt with. When a helicopter's engine fails mid-flight you have to be proactive. You can't park in mid-air.'

Alarm jolted through Leah. 'Yikes. Is that the situation you had to deal with?'

Grimly, he nodded. 'One of our helicopters had been to the maintenance company for a hundred-hours check and my boss, Henry, asked me to fly it back to base, performing a test flight en-route. Eight minutes in, the RPM dropped and I got flashing lights and alarms – the whole emergency thing. To put it technically, the rotors weren't being driven at a level that would sustain normal flight.'

'So you *crashed*?'

He chuckled as if he found her dismay genuinely funny and proceeded to sketch her a technical explanation that she half understood. 'It sounds scary but any half-decent pilot will get down without undue damage to pilot or machine.' He used his hand to demonstrate the flight path. 'What I couldn't judge from the air was that the ground was sodden. The skids dug in and . . .' He flipped his hand.

Leah found herself clutching her heart. 'And you broke your collarbone?

'Yes, harness injury. Farm workers from the next field got the ambulance while I phoned base, then I went off to hospital and had a fixation device inserted, a bit like the operation Alister's waiting for but on a different body part. Getting an "unfit letter" from the AME – Aviation Medical Examiner – was a pretty sobering moment and until now, I've considered that my biggest issue.'

'It's not?' Leah reached for his hand. Remembering the kids she glanced in the direction of the bustling market and, by mutual consent, they shifted their clasped hands beneath the table.

'It's big enough.' He smiled bitterly. 'Right now it's Henry talking as if I have something to worry about. But my airmanship was good. It transpired that the cause of the RPM drop was that a nut had backed off, allowing an air pipe to slacken. It was disappointing work on the part of the mechanic who applied torque stripes as if everything had been tightened up and Henry ended up with a machine and a pilot out of action.' Finishing his coffee, he returned his cup to its saucer with undue force.

'I understood enough of that to know it's bad news,' she said, softly, reading in the lines of worry around his eyes how much of an anathema it was to have doubts hanging over him. 'I hope the insurance company can't find a way to blame you.'

'So far as I know, they're not even trying to! There's no suggestion of pilot error from the Air Accidents Investigation Branch and that's all that matters.' He laughed, mirthlessly. 'Hence the red flags at Henry's tone.'

Unthinkingly, Leah leaned forward ready to plant a consoling kiss on his cheek.

But, 'Look, Leah! I'm *la Gothique! Très* amazeballs, aren't I?' Natasha's voice burst over them, high and excited.

Executing a rapid change of direction and at the same time dropping Ronan's hand, Leah twitched around to view Natasha wearing black lipstick, incongruous with her dewy make-up-free skin and making her look rather as if she'd been sucking a faulty pen. Leah blinked, wondering what Alister and Michele would say. 'Mm, I suppose so.'

Jordan had his arms full of a virulent orange oversized ball in a net. 'I bought an exercise ball.'

'Right,' nodded Leah. 'I suppose you do exercise that doesn't involve screaming around a football pitch. I'm glad The Pig's parked here so you don't have to cart that great big thing about on the tram.'

Jordan nodded sagely, as if he'd thought the same. Leah would lay money that it hadn't even crossed his mind.

Curtis, bizarrely, had purchased a double row of reproduction medals and pinned them to his T-shirt.

Ronan looked pained. 'What do you have on your chest?'

'Nipples,' retorted Curtis unanswerably. 'Can we have bretzels now? They do them here as well as on the vans.'

Helping themselves to nearby empty chairs the children managed to cram around the table, debating how many bretzels would be enough and demanding cold drinks to refresh them after trailing around the market under a sky of unbroken blue.

'One bretzel each might be enough,' Ronan suggested. And, when Jordan began to protest, 'I thought you might like to be introduced to *Flammenküche* for lunch.'

Curtis closed his lips on his own protests and even forgot his sulk. '*Flammenküche*'s awesome. It's like the world's thinnest pizza. You'll love it, Jordan.'

Jordan looked tantalised but wasn't about to allow the

promise of an as yet unseen treat deter him from his immediate goal. 'But we still get bretzels first?'

'One each,' Leah said, firmly. Jordan was capable of stuffing his face until he literally couldn't hold what he'd eaten.

Ronan disappeared into the interior of the café to give their order and Jordan and Curtis began telling Leah of their adventures around the market.

'Where's the loo?' interrupted Natasha. A little of the black lipstick had worn off already.

Curtis pointed to the café door. 'Right through to the back.'

Natasha made a beeline for the facilities as Ronan and the waiter reappeared with drinks and a tray of bretzels. In the process of clearing the dirty mugs and distributing the food and drink, it took Leah several minutes to realise that Natasha hadn't reappeared.

Alarmed, she jumped up, leaving her fresh espresso untouched. 'I'll just check on Natasha.'

Never before having seen the inside of the café it took her a few moments to thread a path between tables and cake-filled glass cabinets to a tiny ladies' room, tucked away at the rear of the premises. 'Natasha?' she called.

'In here.' Natasha's voice came from behind the wooden door, high-pitched and tearful.

Leah felt a wriggle of alarm. 'Are you OK?' And then, when Natasha didn't answer, she knocked on the door. 'Natasha?' At the continued silence her heart began to pump. She rattled the handle. What if Natasha was ill? She began to conjure up visions of *les pompiers* being called to break down the door. '*Natasha!*'

'I don't know what to do,' Natasha wailed.

Relieved to know her niece was at least conscious, Leah sagged against the panelling. 'What's–?'

Just as Natasha opened the door.

Leah all but fell into the tiny room.

Natasha immediately slammed the door behind her and locked it again, her eyes big scared circles. 'I've . . . *started.*'

It took Leah a second to remove her attention from the oddness of being in a toilet cubicle with someone else and latch on to the significance of the words. 'What, your period? Have you got a pad or anything?'

Natasha's black-lipsticked lips trembled. 'I've never had one before. Mum gave me some pads to put in my drawer, ready, but they're at home in England.'

Heart melting at the anxiety all over Natasha's little face, Leah pulled her into her arms. 'Oh, sweetie, your first period? Don't worry. I'll go and get you a pad from my bag.'

Natasha sniffed dolefully, her face brick red. 'I need clean knickers.'

'OK, I'll run and find a shop. Why don't you come out and eat your bretzel while I do, then we'll get you sorted.'

'Really, Leah? *Really*?' With this savage teenage expression of scorn, Natasha unlocked the door, bundled an astonished Leah out of the room and flatly refused to do anything but remain locked in the only toilet, regardless of the potential discomfort of other café patrons, until Leah had procured the items necessary to 'sort her out'. With the command of 'And *don't let the boys know*!' ringing in her ears, Leah had to whizz back to the table, grab her bag, mutter about forgetting something, telegraph Ronan a 'Don't ask!' look and dash through the market to the pharmacy on the other side of the square, then hunt out a stall arrayed with underwear in pastel-coloured rainbows.

By the time she'd finally coaxed Natasha to rejoin the

party, Jordan was hinting about another bretzel and Leah's coffee was cold. 'Right, shall we get off to the tram stop?' she suggested, to give Jordan and Curtis something else to think about had they intended to demand what had taken so long. Natasha was silent as they made their way out of the square. Leah held her hand as she had when she was a little girl and made sure of seats together on the tram.

'I want to talk to Mum,' Natasha muttered in a wobbly voice as they whooshed smoothly away. 'I feel all weird.'

Leah whispered back, 'It might be better to wait till we get back tonight and you can have some privacy.'

'Can I go into the annexe, then, so Jordan won't hear?'

'Of course. But it's all perfectly natural and Jordan's old enough to know that it's something that happens to us girls.' She gave Natasha a reassuring squeeze.

Natasha's voice rose to an angry squeak. 'But he'll make fun! And he'll tell Curtis.'

As Leah could easily envisage both of these things she put up no further argument. 'OK, don't worry about that now. You can ask me anything you want to know, of course. But maybe,' she added, 'not when we're on a tram full of people with the boys wondering what we're whispering about.'

Natasha's mood flipped and she giggled, a little colour returning to her face. 'Let them wonder. It'll do them good to know that the world doesn't revolve around them.' With this wise pronouncement, which sounded exactly like one of Michele's sarky comments, she settled into pensive silence to gaze out of the windows as they continued their smooth journey into the ornate city of Strasbourg.

Focused on hospital visiting, previously they hadn't seen much of what Ronan termed 'the many pretty bits' of

Strasbourg. This time they alighted at La Place de l'Homme de Fer with its glass structure like a suspended stadium roof and where the armour-clad 'iron man' gazed out from a ledge above a pharmacy. Ronan led the way among tall picturesque buildings with steep roofs, past the painted carousel in Place Gutenberg, which earned more than one longing look from Natasha, until they reached the old half-timbered buildings of Rue Mercière, leading to the towering Gothic splendour of Cathédrale Notre Dame. Then it was hard to do anything but gaze up at the cathedral, carvings seeming to grace every inch of the centuries-old building.

It took only ten minutes of culture before Jordan switched his thoughts to more important matters, running an assessing eye over nearby pavement cafés. 'When's lunch?'

'Yeah, actually,' Curtis agreed. 'We need *Flammenküche*.'

Reluctantly, Leah turned away, as Ronan observed, drily, 'The inside of the cathedral's just as stunning, if you're ever here without starving teenagers.'

Heading for the river where petunias gave the bridges lace edges they found shade at a riverbank restaurant where tourist-packed barges glided past. Leah felt more relaxed than at any time during her stint as Deputy Mum. With Ronan to take on French language matters she even began to feel as if she were truly on holiday in France, his knee brushing hers beneath the table and the kids laughing and joking amiably and not winding each other up.

The *Flammenküche*, exactly like the world's thinnest pizza, as described by Curtis, was indeed awesome. Leah chose a topping of goats' cheese drizzled with honey and found it meltingly delicious.

Natasha, the impact of her rite-of-passage event apparently fading along with her black lipstick, embarked on her usual cascade of questions. 'Ronan, Curtis says you fly helicopters along the River Thames in London. That's the one on *EastEnders*, isn't it?'

'It is,' he agreed, gravely. 'Most of the area either side of the river is too densely populated for single-engined helicopters to be allowed to fly over, and following the river saves me getting lost.'

'Do you see the London Eye? I want to go on that.'

'The Eye, the Shard, the Gherkin, St Paul's, Tower Bridge, the boats on the water and the traffic crossing the bridges. It looks great, London laid out beneath you.'

Natasha beamed winningly at him. 'Can you take us on the helicopter, please?'

Ronan's dark eyes twinkled above the rim of his coffee cup. 'I'd love to. We just need to wait till I get back to work and we pay my boss a couple of hundred quid each.'

The winning smile vanished. 'How many hours is two hundred quid for?'

'Less than half.'

'Less than half an hour?' Natasha gave him an incredulous look. 'Call me when the price comes down.'

Ronan laughed, the breeze running its fingers through his hair. 'Helicopters are expensive things to buy and run.'

'And *especially* to crash,' interposed Curtis.

The smile slid from Ronan's face. He let his gaze rest on his son for several long moments. 'A forced landing is definitely costly in all kinds of ways, especially if the pilot gets hurt,' he agreed, softly.

Curtis flushed.

'Have you had a *crash*?' demanded Natasha, eyes alight with excitement, the tension between father and son – appropriately – whooshing over her head.

Ronan explained so briefly that it drew a verbal line beneath the subject.

But it was as if Curtis's remark, obviously intended to hurt, had changed the tenor of the afternoon. Leah tried to lighten the mood by promising that if they could find a shop selling balloons she'd show the kids how to make chocolate bowls later but Curtis withdrew morosely and Jordan and Natasha set their personal switches to 'bicker'.

Ronan, too, was quiet. Leah saw him rub his shoulder. 'I have paracetamol in my bag.'

'I can't be taking painkillers all the time.' He tagged on a smile, as if aware of sounding short.

Leah glanced at her watch. 'I ought to take the kids to see their father anyway, then you can get home and rest up.'

As they divided up the bill, the fun part of the day definitely over, Leah found her now familiar anxieties crowding back in about when Michele would return and what would happen at the end of Alister's stay in hospital.

She was shocked out of her thoughts by a sudden bellow from Jordan. 'Ow, *Natasha*! Cut it out!' Clamping his hand to his left eye, he glared at his sister with the other.

Natasha stared back with a horrified expression, then looked down at her hand as if astonished at it.

Aghast, Leah could draw only one conclusion. 'Natasha, did you just *hit* Jordan?'

A dark red tide swept up Natasha's face. 'No,' she denied, unconvincingly. 'I just, um, high-fived him . . . in the face.'

Curtis snorted a laugh. 'An eye-five? Mega excuse.'

Leah heard her voice crack out far too loudly. '*Nat-a-SHA!*'

Around them, people stopped and stared. Natasha burst into tears, tucking her hands into her armpits as if to make them safe. 'Jordan was picking on me and calling me Gnasher,' she wailed.

Though Ronan ushered Curtis ahead to give Leah space to deal with the situation it took the remainder of the trek to the tram for her to dry Natasha's tears and wheedle out of Jordan, in turns embarrassed and truculent, that he'd not only called Natasha 'Gnasher' but told her she was a stupid little turd with no brains.

Patting her red eyes with a tissue Natasha gulped, 'And that's why I hit him.'

Leah fixed her gaze on Jordan. 'Do I need to dig further back in the conversation to discover why you spoke to her like that?'

After a couple of moments to reflect, Jordan shook his head.

'Natasha?'

Natasha shook her head, too. Evidently, neither of them was convinced that their place in the squabble was on the moral high ground.

Leah, borrowing what had always seemed a really useful technique from Alister, said firmly, 'Right, let's have hush from you both for a few minutes,' and fell into silence herself, giving her charges not only time to wish their spat undone but to a) see that she wasn't going to pronounce lightly and b) wonder what came next. In fact, Leah was wondering the same.

Miserably out of her depth, she followed the bobbing shoulders of Ronan and Curtis ahead. This guardian thing really sucked when it didn't go well. It had been dropped on her with no training or handbook so how was she supposed to know how to handle its challenges? She thought longingly of the peace and quiet of a product development kitchen where there might be a raft of rules and protocols but also a pleasant temperature and she was left alone to make important decisions about whether a chocolate was more delicious when made with ground almonds or ground walnuts.

As that life currently seemed as distant as the moon she fell back on the bantering relationship she'd always enjoyed with her niece and nephew. 'Look, I know things are a bit crap but hurting each other's feelings just makes them crapper. So please stop, because you're making things crapper for me, too.' And, inspiration striking, 'I don't want to have to waste the time you'll have with your dad in asking him to speak to you both.' Masterstroke.

'Because that will crap things up for him too,' Natasha hiccupped, searching for a dry piece of her sorry-looking tissue.

'Totally.' Jordan hung his head.

'OK.' Leah gave each of them a hug. She suspected Alister would have ended the conversation with a frosty, 'Which one of you knows they should apologise first?' but that was probably advanced parenting. She was nowhere near that level.

When they reached the tram stop everyone queued quietly to get their tickets stamped by the little machine before hopping aboard the silver tram. Ronan and Curtis, heading straight home, remained in their seats when Leah took Jordan and Natasha off at Hautepierre to trek through miles of antiseptic-smelling corridors to Alister's bedside. There, they found a smiling woman in a navy suit already ensconced in the visitor's chair. Alister was propped up against his pillows, booted leg atop the covers.

'Ah, here's my family,' he said. 'Hello, Jordan, hello, Natasha! And this is my sister-in-law, Leah Beaumont.'

The smart lady rose to her feet and introduced herself as Myriam Lemaitre, who worked in hospital administration. While Alister chatted to the kids Myriam made explanations to a bemused Leah in English. 'M. Milton's insurance company desires me to complete a questionnaire so they can understand what is the best action to take upon his release from hospital.'

Leah felt a surge of relief at this first hint of progress. 'It'll be great if someone can clarify the situation.'

Alister sent the kids off to the cafeteria with enough euros to buy bottles of water and instructions to be back in half an hour when, he hoped, the paperwork would have been done. Leah was glad to note that she wasn't the only one who kept teenagers entertained by giving them something to drink or eat. As they left, she sent them both a stern look, which she hoped conveyed *Do this without arguing or fighting*.

Myriam Lemaitre opened the formalities by confirming Alister's personal details then got down to the nitty gritty. 'At your home in the UK, you live with others?'

'Not in the UK, not presently.' Alister, looking embarrassed, sketched in the brief facts of his recent separation.

She glanced at Leah. 'You do not live together?'

Leah wondered how much clearer Alister had needed to be about living alone. 'No, I'm his sister-in-law. We don't live together.'

Back to Alister. 'Before your accident, you had intended to stay in France for how long?' She noted his answer. 'In Kirchhoffen?' Another note. 'And, here in France, there are others in the household?'

Alister cleared his throat. 'My children and Leah.' Then,

after an assortment of emotions had flitted across his face, 'And my estranged wife, for some of the time, but she's away at the moment.'

Confusion creased Myriam's brow. 'Your wife?'

'Estranged.'

Myriam hesitated, glancing at Leah as if hoping for clarification.

'In the UK, they agreed on divorce,' Leah explained, uncomfortable on Alister's behalf at having to air the painful details. 'They both came on holiday so that they could each spend time with the children but Alister's wife, my sister, has gone travelling with a friend for a while. We're not sure when she'll be back.'

'Ah.' With an expressive shrug, Myriam wrote on her form for several moments. 'Your home in the UK, M. Milton, it is a house? Or an apartment?'

'First-floor apartment.'

'There is an elevator?'

Alister shook his head. His sad gaze flicked apologetically to Leah.

'In your holiday home, in Kirchhoffen, is there a place where you could sleep that is not upstairs?'

Leah sent him a rueful smile. 'Yes,' she answered for him. 'There's a salon with a sofabed on the ground floor.' The way forward became all too obvious if you just asked the right questions, she admitted to herself drearily. 'But you should be clear that we can't stay in Kirchhoffen indefinitely. The gîte is rented for the month of August. The children have to return to school and Alister to his job. I'm starting a new job, too. On Monday the 4th of September. In the UK,' she added, just to be crystal.

Nodding along, Myriam added to her copious notes. 'And you have a vehicle to drive home to England at the end of your stay in France? One in which M. Milton's leg can remain elevated?'

Leah nodded, though she added, honestly, 'But it would be much less tortuous for Alister to fly home.'

Gloomily, Alister shook his head again. 'I asked a doctor today and he said there's a significant risk of clots owing to the nature of my injury. I should go by vehicle.'

When Myriam had completed her questionnaire and promised to get it typed up and sent electronically to the insurance company she left, heels tip-tapping across the ward floor.

Alister broke the silence she left behind her. 'I'm rather afraid the insurance company will advise my staying in Kirchhoffen to recuperate for as long as possible before attempting the trip.'

Leah sighed again. 'And living alone right now wouldn't be the best thing. I'm not sure how we're going to get two vehicles home when the time comes, though.'

'Sorry, Leah.'

Alister looked so woebegone that Leah forced herself to smile. 'It's not your fault! We'll manage. Michele will just have to get over her fear of driving on the right.'

'Not with Jordan and Natasha on board,' he said, not joking about it this time.

'Right.' Leah frowned. 'I thought maybe Dad would fly over to drive The Pig back but he and Mum will still be with Mum's cousin in America.' Leah wished she could just ring their parents. It would be a huge relief to her to see her dad taking charge. He was a proper parent.

Alister nodded sadly. 'I thought so.'

'And you still can't see the surgeon till tomorrow?'

Alister looked still more morose as he shook his head. 'I'm even losing hope about tomorrow. A doctor's pointed out that August is a busy time on the French roads and there are always emergencies.' He stared unhappily at his elevated leg, which looked a bit bondage in its black boot and velcro straps.

Hiding her disappointment, as it seemed obvious that the faster Alister had his op, the faster he'd rejoin his family, Leah moved on to the next items on her agenda. 'Before the kids come back I have to ask you about a couple of things.'

At least Alister had been teaching too long to let anything concerning kids faze him and greeted her concerns over porn calmly. 'Controlling software installed on all family phones and computers. Don't worry.'

But he was unexpectedly emotional when Leah told him about Natasha starting her period. 'My little girl.' Misty-eyed, he shook his head. 'Bless. My little girl growing up.'

'I've promised she can talk to her mum tonight.' She was updating him on Michele's health as Jordan and Natasha bundled back into the room.

Rather than get upset about Michele this time, Alister gave Leah's arm a pat. 'You're a diamond, Leah. You've saved us all.' He sucked in a stabilising breath and turned to his children. 'So, tell me what kind of "water" you drank in the cafeteria.'

'Coke,' admitted Jordan, promptly.

'Pamplemousse,' declared Natasha with a giggle.

The three of them exchanged grins and Alister put his arms out for a hug, which Natasha snuggled into and Jordan looked embarrassed by, but accepted.

'I'll go down for a cup of coffee,' Leah excused herself. The kids and Alister would profit by family time – and she was sorely overdue a little Leah-time. *Sorely.*

Peace. Quiet. Headspace. Bliss . . .

But when she'd secured a fairly peaceful seat in a corner of the cafeteria where she could sip coffee and text Scott an update she was surprised that, rather than wallowing in the break, she felt odd on her own.

Chapter Ten

Once back at the gîte, the kids vanished straight upstairs. Leah had barely finished stowing the shopping when a man knocked at the back door.

'Ah, *bonjour madame*,' he began affably, waggling fulsome eyebrows and smiling.

'*Bonjour monsieur*,' Leah returned, cautiously, all too aware that the man, not unreasonably, would not expect the conversation to halt there.

'*M. Milton, s'il vous plaît? Ou Mme. Milton?*'

'*M. Milton est dans l'hôpital et Mme. Milton est dans Austria.*' Leah returned his smile, hoping it would make up for her shortcomings with the French language.

The smile vanished. The man's eyebrows knitted over his nose and he began barking questions. When she tried to tell him that she didn't understand and apologise for her bad command of his language, he barked the same questions but more loudly and slowly.

Patience thinning, Leah snapped, 'I thought it was only English people who did that. I won't miraculously understand your language just because you shout it.'

As the man began a further barrage, Ronan's top half appeared at the fence, frowning with concern. 'Are you OK, Leah? What in the hell is all this racket?' He said a few words to the man in French.

Jumping on this promise of effective communication, the man started again with many gesticulations and urgent movements of the caterpillar eyebrows.

Nodding along until the discourse wound down, Ronan turned to Leah. 'This world-class gobshite doesn't speak English but he's M. Simon and he and his wife own the gîte. He arranged with Alister that he'd keep the grass cut while your family was renting. As a matter of courtesy, the loudest man on earth here knocked on the door before he began, only to discover that his tenants have vanished and some crazy hot English woman is squatting in his property. He demands to know what your business here is and why he shouldn't have you turfed out in the street. Probably he's ready to call the *gendarmes* to arrest you for murdering Michele and Alister and burying them in his garden.'

Stifling the urge to giggle, Leah replied in the same mock-formal manner. 'Can you convey the disasters that have befallen us? Tell him that Alister and Michele will be back in a few days.'

His face cleared. 'Will they?'

She gave a short laugh. 'No, I doubt it, but it's probably best not to tell M. Simon. Get him to cut his bloody lawn if that's what he's here for and stop giving me a hard time.' She smiled sweetly at the gîte-owner, who began to look less annoyed.

It took Ronan a few moments to summon up sufficient French to convey all that needed to be conveyed. Then M. Simon clucked sympathetically, shook Leah's hand apologetically and dragged a big red petrol mower into view.

As M. Simon got busy, Ronan swung himself over the fence, keeping his weight on his right arm, bore Leah backwards into the kitchen and closed the door as the lawnmower yelled into action.

'Hello again,' Leah managed, suddenly breathless at finding herself at agreeably close quarters with Ronan's warm body. 'Don't you have to get back to Curtis?'

'My phone's in my pocket and he'll know I won't have gone too far. I'm grabbing five minutes alone with you.'

'Then let's hide out in the salon where we're less likely to be interrupted by marauding teens.' She led the way into the salon, shaded by the shrubbery outside at this time of day, cabinets of painted crockery standing like sentinels around the walls. 'It's a bit formal, which is why we stick to the kitchen and the games room, but I think when Alister's discharged from hospital he'll sleep in here on this sofabed.'

'Let's try it out for him.' Ronan's arm hooked around her waist and when she came down to earth she was sitting across his legs.

He kissed down from her temple, across her cheekbone, and Leah's head tipped back as he moved down to the sensitive skin of her throat. 'Should a man with an injured shoulder be hauling a woman onto his lap?'

'I used my other arm and kissing's a well-known healer.' His mouth moved on down to the first swell of her breast. 'The further south I get, the more effective it is.'

'Very believable.' She made a noise in the back of her throat when his lips tingled across the skin above the scoop neck of her camisole top. 'Natasha and Jordan are upstairs.'

He groaned, progress slowing. 'We're going to have to get rid of all these kids.'

With a sigh, Leah slid off his lap and onto the cushion beside him, the good feelings he'd begun to build in her fading away. 'I thought the whole thing about kids is that you're not allowed to do that. You're stuck with them until you have to pay a university to take them off your hands.'

He looked at her blankly, his hair ruffled above his eyes. 'It's not hard to get rid of teenagers. In fact, one of their missions in life is to gain liberty. You just set them clear boundaries.'

'Oh.' Leah felt idiotic. 'Of course. I've been so tense about taking responsibility for Jordan and Natasha that I've been thinking of them as if they were tiny. I'm so rubbish at this.'

He laughed, moved in on her throat again and licked hotly at the tiny hollow at its base. 'You do have to take account of the fact that they're not in their own country, but Kirchhoffen's a great village and very safe. There are all kinds of places for teenagers to get breathing space: the park, a stream they can fall into, and a few shops where they can blow their holiday money. Tomorrow we can get Curtis to show Jordan and Natasha around. And then –' he moved his face back up to hers '– maybe you and I can find a way to destress.'

Sinking against him, sliding her hand into the thickness of his hair, Leah had just begun to say, 'That sounds like something we could discuss,' when she heard footsteps on the stairs.

Heaving matching sighs, they disentangled. 'I'm going to end up doing myself damage,' Ronan grumbled, adjusting his board shorts.

The footsteps went into the kitchen. 'Leah?' bawled Natasha. 'Can I ring Mum from La Petite Annexe now?'

Leah groaned under her breath. 'I'd better go with her.'

'I'll leave.' Ronan kissed her again, not leaving.

'OK.' Leah kissed him back, then, trying not to mind that the burgeoning heat between them was being rudely interrupted yet again, raised her voice. 'On my way, Natasha.'

After wandering into the kitchen and saying a casual ''bye' to Ronan, Leah slipped her arm around her niece's narrow shoulders. 'We need to talk, by the way.' They stepped out into the late sunlight together, the scent of fresh-cut grass strong in the air. Leah smiled politely at M. Simon and he smiled and nodded, reining in his eager lawnmower at one edge of the grass to allow them to pass.

'Talk about Mum?' Natasha clung onto the arm Leah held around her as if to keep it in place.

'About you.' Leah unlocked La Petite Annexe, feeling a pang at the airless and unused stuffiness of the place. She pulled Natasha down onto the small sofa. This was the kind of woman-to-woman stuff where she felt on solid ground. 'You probably know that when you have your period, your hormones can be in a tizz.'

'Mm.' Natasha looked down at the floor, already blinking shamefacedly.

Leah tried to tread the line between being understanding and leaving no room for doubt. 'Well, I don't know what you've heard, but that doesn't mean having a period is an excuse to bitch-slap people who wind you up.'

'Yeah, no, but Jordan–'

In her pocket, Leah's phone vibrated but she ignored it to focus on Natasha. 'Including Jordan. I'll be letting him know he overstepped the mark today but I want to be able to ask Curtis to show you guys around the village tomorrow and enjoy a bit of your own space. I can't do that if I think you and Jordan are going to act like brats.'

'Lush! Do you think Curtis will?' Natasha cheered up so abruptly that Leah's conscience gave her a sharp kick for presenting as a treat something that she actually wanted for herself. She ought to check with Ronan or Alister whether parenting was really meant to include two-faced conniving.

'His dad seems to think he will.' To avoid looking at Natasha's guileless smile, she pulled out her phone to check out the text that had made her phone buzz a moment ago.

> ***Michele:*** *Had to see doctor again as throwing up so much. They moved me straight to hospital for a day or two for them to rehydrate me and give me anti-emetics to stop the hyperemesis. Really sorry. Waiting to see obstetrician now so I'll ring the kids when I've spoken to him but can you explain, first? Text me when you have. xx*

Leah's heart began a slow slither down to her boots. 'Fu— Oh, dear,' she murmured.

Natasha looked up with big eyes. 'What?

She gave Natasha's hand a compassionate squeeze. 'It's a message from your mum, sweetie. We can't ring her right now because she's still not well. She's got to have some treatment to try and stop her being sick.'

'In Austria?'

'That's right.' Leah assumed what she hoped was a reassuring smile. 'In hospital. I'm afraid they have to do this with pregnant ladies, sometimes. Being sick so much means they don't have enough body fluids. They'll give her some via a drip and give her some anti-sickness medicine, too, and she's going to ring you after she's seen the doctor again.'

Bottom lip beginning to quiver, Natasha's voice climbed. 'So Mum's in hospital *too*?'

'Just for a couple of days, till they get her sorted. We want her to be better as soon as possible, don't we?' Leah made to draw Natasha up into her comforting arms.

But Natasha shoved her away, face contorting into a rictus of grief as she burst into tears. 'I hate that baby! *I hate it!*' she bawled. 'I hate Mum!' Then, as Leah tried again to hug her, 'And I *hate you*!'

Then she proved that she hadn't been paying attention to the recent lecture because she eye-fived Leah in the face, too.

Chapter Eleven

In the morning, concealer and foundation took care of the bluish crescent beneath Leah's right eye but didn't help its tenderness, or her leaden feeling of despondency. It was the first time she could remember being on the receiving end of teenage contempt from either of the kids and it stung. Natasha's mood had been further blackened when Michele eventually rang last night, sounding weak and wobbly as she explained the obstetrician had ordered at least forty-eight hours under the eye of the medical world.

This Deputy Mum stuff was a world away from being Cool Auntie.

Cool Auntie got to take Natasha shopping for shoes or cheer Jordan on from the football pitch sidelines then fill the kids with cake and give them back to their parents. Cool Auntie didn't get smacked in the eye or feel sick every time she thought about how Jordan would react when he learned that Baby Three's dad was his beloved soccer coach. Cool Auntie didn't lie awake half the night feeling anxious that she was irreparably harming the kids with her bumbling Deputy Mumship. Cool Auntie was, however, glad Natasha's next period would be someone else's problem.

Even the prospect of *pain au chocolat* for breakfast wasn't enough to cheer Leah as she trailed down into the kitchen.

She was glad when her phone buzzed.

Scott: *What u up 2?*
Leah: *Feeling sorry for myself. Natasha and Jordan not dealing well with issues. Relying quite a bit on man next door, who has teen son and speaks French. Saviour!*

In seconds her phone rang and Scott began to demand details in his best put-on gossipy voice. 'Is he hot? While I'm driving to work for another week of crushing boredom are you enjoying a tumultuous holiday romance with the saviour next door? Tell all!'

Feeling better just for hearing Scott being an idiot, Leah laughed, though she felt an unexpected twinge of homesickness at the idea of him enlivening his morning journey by calling her on his in-car infotainment system while Bettsbrough, their hometown, bustled around him. Without her. 'Very hot . . . and there's not a thing to prevent the tumultuous holiday romance. Apart from awkward teenagers and a sister and a brother-in-law in hospitals in different countries.' She updated him on the latest dramas, loyally omitting the little matter of Natasha thumping her in the eye.

But Scott evidently felt he'd shown enough interest in Michele's family and interrupted, 'Are you picking up the "interested" vibe from the saviour?'

Memories of yesterday's snatched minutes in the salon

flashed through her mind. She fanned her face, hovering between being self-conscious and being smug. 'He's not exactly hiding it.'

'Ooh, get you.' Scott camped it up. 'You'll make me jealous.'

Pressing the button on the coffee machine to start it heating, she laughed. 'He's not your type. Not arty, bitchy or dodgy enough.' Although Leah only rarely met the men Scott hooked up with, he'd told her enough about them to know they weren't usually the dependable types. Oddly, although he was equal opportunities sexually, the women he saw were organised and sane. His declared preferences were men with a bit of risk, women with none.

'Judging your future by your past, dear, he'll be a deviant fibber, anyway.' Abruptly, he jettisoned his silly persona. 'Do you want me to fly over, if there's somewhere for me to sleep? I can help.' He made the offer in exactly the same casual way he might offer her a slice of his pizza.

Gratitude brought a lump to Leah's throat. 'That's really lovely of you, but don't spend your precious annual leave or your money helping clear up my family's mess. Just be ready for some marathon TV motor sport sessions when I get back in a couple of weeks.'

'Will do.' He had to raise his voice over the sound of a motorbike roaring past. She could envisage him stuck in nose-to-tail traffic in the one-way system en route to the admin job he didn't particularly like at the warehouse of a huge online retailer that nobody particularly liked either.

She had to swallow before she spoke again. 'You're a good buddy, Scott.'

The roar of the traffic continued. Without it, Leah might have thought Scott had moved into a signal-less area. 'You there?' she prompted, when his silence had stretched to several seconds.

'Sorry, yeah. Speaking as the goodest of good buddies, one who wants only good things for you . . . you're sure Hot Man Saviour is available?'

'His name's Ronan and yes, he's divorced.' She waited, pretty certain that she knew what was coming next.

More traffic. 'Really divorced? I don't have to remind you about Tommy?' Although there was a definite note of warning, Scott's voice also dripped with sympathy.

Leah reached down plates from the cupboard with the hand not holding the phone, prepared, as it was Scott, to indulge his protective streak. 'Ronan's really divorced and his ex-wife lives with her new boyfriend. He's a pilot.' She told him about Ronan's helicopter coming down.

'A supercool career and heroic tendencies! I'm well jel.' The teasing note was back in Scott's voice. 'There's nothing in the way of him being your next big mistake.'

Leah crowed a protest. 'You bitch, Scott Matthewson! He might not be a mistake.'

'Cling onto that thought and there's nothing to hold you back from a sizzling holiday romance, lucky girl.'

'Not a thing,' she agreed, brightening at the thought of the cunning plan Ronan had hatched to award the teens space and the adults privacy.

'OK, well, I'm at work now and it's one minute to nine, so byeeee!' And Scott was gone, back to his real life while Leah carried on like a square peg in a round hole. Making like a mum.

With a sigh, she stuck her head out into the hall. 'Jordan! Na-tash-a! Let's have breakfast!'

'Don't want none!' Natasha yelled back.

Leah debated whether to bother saying, 'Don't want

any,' as Alister or Michele would. Deciding that correcting grammar wasn't in her job description, she shouted back, 'No *pain au chocolat*?'

'No!'

'Cool. More for me.' Jordan clattered downstairs, almost spinning Leah like a turnstile in the doorway in his eagerness.

Natasha ran down behind him, hair half-brushed. 'I don't want Jordan to have mine.'

'Sit down and eat it then,' suggested Leah mildly. 'Jordan, there's plenty. You don't have to act as if you'll get no more food for a week.'

'Hot and melty.' Jordan crammed more than half of the pastry into his mouth in the first bite. 'Eat some, Gnasher. You're thin as a snake.'

'Bite me, fat boy.'

Leah was saved from having to intercede when Curtis and Ronan turned up to ask if Natasha and Jordan would like Curtis to show them around the village and maybe hang out at the park. Natasha threw down her pastry as if it was responsible for all the ills in her world. 'No, I wouldn't!'

'No?' Dumbfounded, Leah gazed at her niece's faceful of obstinate lines. She hadn't envisaged anything as fundamental as one of the kids refusing the treat. She was careful not to catch Ronan's eyes and make her dismay visible. 'Don't you want to hang out with the guys?'

Natasha pretended to stick her finger down her throat.

Irritation began to burn in Leah. 'Na*tasha*–!'

Jordan butted in cheerfully. 'That's a "no". Result! C'mon, Curtis. Let's go quick, before she changes her mind.' Ignoring Curtis's awkward mumbling about it being OK with him for Natasha to go with, Jordan raced upstairs for his euros in case they went near the shop, which Leah translated into 'The shop will be the first and most important port of call.'

When he skidded back into the kitchen Leah reminded him, 'Here by one, please, to allow time for lunch before hospital visiting. And, Jordan, you and I need a little word beforehand.' Belatedly she remembered her earlier intention to talk to him about his attitude to his sister and mentally smote her forehead. If that talk had taken place Natasha might not now be eschewing her brother's company so rudely. And inconveniently.

'Yep,' Jordan agreed cheerfully. The door banged behind the boys and their voices faded away.

Natasha treated the closed door to her most rancorous glare. Then, in slow motion, her face crumpled into a mask of woe and she began to heave with noisy, squeaky sobs. 'I just want to stay with you-hoo-hoo, Leah!'

Dragging up a chair, Leah pulled Natasha's head against her shoulder. 'You can stay with me. Of course you can. But there was no need to be like that with the boys. "No thanks" would've been fine.' Over Natasha's head, Leah met Ronan's gaze with helpless resignation. *Not going to happen.*

With a rueful smile, he mouthed, 'Later,' and let himself out quietly.

'I'm soh-soh-sorry I hi-hi-high-fived you in the face,' Natasha wailed. 'I lov-love you, Leah. Forevs!'

Eyes burning, Leah squeezed Natasha's slender frame. 'I love you forevs, too. Thank you for apologising, sweetie. I know it won't happen again.'

Natasha sniffed mightily. 'Is Mum going to be OK? We won't have to go home without her, will we?'

'She will get better and I doubt very much we'll have

to go home without either of your parents. I know it seems like a huge deal but this mega-sickness does happen. Do you know it happened before?'

Natasha lifted a blotchy face. 'No?'

Leah's hand began to circle comfortingly on Natasha's back. 'Well, here's the story: she threw up a lot, the doctors gave her medicine. She got better and had you, so she got something good out of it.'

Natasha gave a hiccup that might have been a laugh. 'But she wasn't split up from Dad.'

'That's true,' Leah admitted. She knew of no medicine to make Michele want Alister back.

Leaning her damp face against Leah's neck, Natasha sniffed. 'Can we ring her?'

'It's probably better if we text, isn't it? If she's in a ward with other people then her phone ringing would disturb people who are ill and need to sleep.'

Natasha ferreted in her pocket for her phone. 'I'll do it.'

Craning, Leah read the message as Natasha tapped it in.

> ***Natasha:*** *Are you OK mum are you still in hospital are you coming out soon are you coming back to us soon have you stopped honking xxx ☺ ☹ Best love and massive hugs forevs xxxxXXXXXXX*

She looked a bit happier when she'd fired her missive into cyberspace but still snuggled back into Leah's arms. 'I've got a bad belly, all heavy and achey.'

'Sounds like a normal period.'

'Every time?' Natasha sounded outraged. 'That sucks.'

'Truly does. Shall we watch a DVD?'

Natasha sat up and wiped her nose on her hand. 'Yay!

Pitch Perfect 2's upstairs in the games room but the boys don't want to watch it.'

'You should have told them it's full of hot girls.' Leah kissed the top of Natasha's head. 'We'll take crisps and lemonade but you go and blow your nose first because you're breathing like a dragon.'

With a watery giggle, Natasha headed up to the bathroom. Leah whipped out her phone and texted Michele.

> ***Leah:*** *When you can text, will you give me Bailey's number? I was so surprised last night I didn't ask for details like which hospital you're in. Would he keep me updated? Give my number to him. I hope you're soon feeling better. I saw the text Natasha just sent you – she's a bit emosh. xx*

Feeling better at attempting to put a contingency in place in case her sister's situation worsened, she was gathering up unhealthy snacks when Natasha returned. 'Mum hasn't answered.'

Leah glanced at her watch. 'Probably nap time. Can you carry the crisps?' They climbed up into the sunny room in the eaves, opening all the windows to blow out the stuffy air, then snuggled on the sofa to follow the fortunes of a girly singing group. The film didn't have enough cars in it for Leah, but it kept Natasha amused. It wasn't until they'd watched most of it that Leah's gaze fell on the DVD case and she realised she was letting a 13-year-old watch a 15-certificate film.

Just went to prove what a crap mum she would have made, she thought, sinking more comfortably into the squashy sofa. Deputy Mum was just about all she could handle. Her phone buzzed in another text.

Bailey: *Yo, this is Bailey. Michele forwarded ur text. Micheles still hurling but theyve put her on a drip to rehydrate her and give her stuff to help sickness. She feels slightly better. Shes in medical university of innsbruck.*

Checking that Natasha was still glued to the TV screen, Leah replied.

Leah: *Hi Bailey, this is Leah. Thanks so much. Michele goes in and out of contact so I'd appreciate any updates because we're all anxious, especially Natasha and Jordan. Thanks again.*

When the DVD was over, Leah went down to the kitchen. She was washing salad for lunch when Natasha bounced into the room with a beaming smile. 'Mum's text me! She says she's feeling slightly better and she'll ring again tonight. Can we visit her, like we visit Dad?'

Fighting the urge to groan out loud for not having anticipated this request Leah gave her niece a big hating-to-disappoint-you hug. 'That would be lovely but she's a long car journey away so we'll have to wait until she's well enough to come to us, won't we? Now, please can you text your brother and ask him to get his bum back here for lunch?' It wasn't one thirty yet but it would give Natasha something else to focus on. Deflecting teenagers from any given purpose was exhausting. Maybe it got easier with practice. Though what was she thinking? She didn't need practice! Soon she'd be Cool Auntie again and could happily leave parenting to others.

'But it's not fair not seeing Mum,' Natasha whined.

'Hey, I know what would be really helpful.' Leah beamed

encouragingly, though returning to Cool Auntie suddenly seemed a long way off. 'If you sorted out some bedding for your dad, because he's going to sleep in the salon. Would you do that?'

Natasha brightened. 'Yeah! Because he will come home soon, won't he? Then maybe Jordan won't be so sucky to me.'

When Jordan scuffed in at one forty, Leah was waiting for him with folded arms, having settled Natasha sorting through the enormous closet in her room, where the additional bedding was stored. 'I'm hoping you have an explanation for me.'

Jordan halted just inside the door. He had sugar at one corner of his mouth. His brow quirked upward. 'For what?'

'For the way you're treating your sister.'

A dark red tide inched up Jordan's neck.

'Because if you do have an explanation, I'm all ears. I'll be sympathetic to anything reasonably logical.'

Laughing uneasily, Jordan shuffled his feet. 'She's a douche.'

Leah didn't smile. She sat at the table and pulled out another chair, beckoning Jordan into it.

Reluctantly, he sat. She fixed him with a beady gaze. 'I expect you get sick of the "You're the eldest" stuff. I know your mum used to. But I obviously struck lucky because despite Nanna and Granddad constantly laying "You're the eldest" on her, my big sister was always on my side. I find that really admirable. And she earned my lifelong loyalty because of it.'

Jordan sat very still.

Leah hadn't finished. 'I'm floundering, here, to be honest. You know I'm not a parent. I don't know if you taking out your own anxieties on your little sister is acceptable, or understandable, or whether it will scar you for life if I tell you how disappointed I am that you're going out of your way to make things worse for her when she's upset already. But here's the thing. For now, *we're all each of us has got*. Remember what I said yesterday?'

'Don't make the crap crapper.' Jordan's face could get no redder.

She let herself smile. 'Our new family motto.' She patted her nephew's shoulder and then, because he was a kid, no matter how much he'd roll his eyes if she said so, she gave him a big hug. 'I think this is where your mum and dad would ask you whether you had any concerns to share. Do you?'

He heaved a great sigh. 'Yeah. Is it long till lunch?'

At Hautepierre, Alister greeted the news that Michele was in hospital with a shocked expression. 'Oh, dear. She's obviously quite ill.' Then he caught sight of Natasha's face. 'But the doctors know how to sort this out. They're very good at it.'

He raised crossed fingers. 'But at least I have better news from my side – it looks like surgery's tomorrow. Once I've got the pins in I just have to get over the op, show them I can get upstairs on crutches, then I'm outta here.'

Everyone began laughing and joking in relief until Jordan, reliably thinking of his tummy, asked to be allowed a drink and a raisin cake from the cafeteria and politely asked if Natasha would like to come, too.

Alister waited until they were out of earshot. 'What a bloody mess Michele's in,' he said, succinctly. 'What a horrible holiday for you.'

'Not as bad as yours,' she joked feebly.

Pain flashed across his face. 'It would have to go some

to be as bad as mine. And now I'm going to have to beg yet another favour. I've been trying to think of a way around it but I can't.'

He looked so miserable that Leah's heart, which had lightened considerably at Alister's op finally being scheduled, slithered back into her white flip-flops as she tried and failed to imagine the fresh responsibility looming. 'Just ask,' she managed, through stiff lips.

He flushed. 'Could you possibly do my washing? This is my last pair of clean pyjamas.'

Leah almost laughed in relief. 'That I can manage.'

Chapter Twelve

On Tuesday morning, Ronan checked his email, hoping for a reply from Selina, who was doing her usual fine job of winding him up, this time by ignoring all communications from him. Instead, he found another message from Henry.

To: Ronan Shea
From: Henry Brook [Buzz Sightseer]
Subject: Absence from the workplace

Thank you for updating me on your health situation and confirming your absence from your post is likely to be extensive.

I'm attaching an electronic copy of your salary slip. As a gesture of goodwill you were kept on full pay to 23rd July, which is the date you left the UK. NB No flying pay can be earned during an absence from work. You've been paid holiday pay for the weeks beginning 24th and 31st July as it has become clear that the two weeks of annual leave you had booked will fall during your extended absence from the workplace.

Your statutory sick pay began on 7th August.

Stunned, Ronan snapped, 'For fuck's sake!' After a glance across the landing to check Curtis's bedroom door was shut and he could consider his inadvertent F-bomb unheard, he switched his glare back to his laptop.

Rubbing his shoulder and wishing he could train himself not to sleep on it, he reread the message. *Statutory Sick Pay*? Since when? And he was pretty sure he couldn't be forced to take annual leave when sick – though that wasn't the biggest battle here. After opening the attachment and glancing at its unsatisfactory contents, Ronan began to type out his surprise and disappointment, and to counter that he proposed not only full pay but compensation in lieu of flight pay.

He paused. Charging into the situation furious and unprepared was as stupid as initiating a take off without having planned his flight. He opened a browser window to search for information, breathing deeply and giving himself the opportunity to calm down.

But by the time he'd finished reading the relevant government website he was, if anything, angrier. Henry was avoiding doing the right thing by hiding behind the letter of the law. He began to type again.

> *I don't have my contract to hand to check whether it contains reference to company sick pay or accident pay, so perhaps you could remind me?*

He was still combing the government website when Henry came back, quoting, with an air of finality, the relevant clause in Ronan's contract. What it boiled down to was that company sick pay and accident pay was paid at the company's discretion.

With the whiff of being crapped on strong in his nose, he typed a grim reply.

If being injured while in your service doesn't encourage you to exercise that discretion then I suppose I have no choice but to investigate other legal remedies open to me, such as making a claim for compensation.

Henry's response pinged back in under two minutes.

That's another matter for the insurance company. It's what employer's liability is for.

Ronan felt sick as he read and reread the terse message. Henry was looking for his most financially advantageous way to deal with the issue. Their friendship, the hours he'd put into supporting him when the business was new and Henry had needed an experienced shoulder to lean on, evidently counted for zip. Zilch. Zero.

He cast his thoughts back more than five years. He read contracts carefully but must have assumed that as he was at the core of Henry's start-up plan, Henry would exercise discretion in Ronan's favour. Because it was only fair.

Now he realised that fairness wasn't going to come into the transaction. He tried to give himself some small measure of satisfaction by meticulously listing 'pilot's personal effects' *to add to your insurance claim, Henry*. His headset alone would cost over a grand to replace.

As, this time, Henry returned no immediate reply, Ronan stoked his irritation by having another go at getting hold of Selina, trying Facetime on his phone and Skype and Facebook voice messaging on his laptop. Every single one of those channels proving unresponsive, he texted her:

Ronan: *Would appreciate that chat soon.*

Frustrated and unsettled, he performed his daily physio, working grimly through the heaviness and stiffness that came with challenging a post-operative area, and waited in vain for Selina to respond. Typical. She was always available when she wanted to put on him or change arrangements.

Circling his left arm slowly forward and back, he couldn't regret having made Curtis but it was hard to remember how it had felt to love Selina. The feelings seemed too far in the past to connect with.

When the fate of the marriage had been taken out of his hands and he'd supported Curtis over the worst of its end, Ronan had considered his life sorted, splitting the majority of his time between Curtis and the only career he'd ever wanted, content with whatever was left over for himself. Two sobering thoughts flashed into his mind: what would he be without the title of 'helicopter pilot'? And was Curtis the only living person he loved in a meaningful way?

Leah drifted into his mind.

She was there a lot these days, all golden brown hair and determined eyes. Through being married to Selina he'd learned to be wary of women who needed a lot of emotional support, so he was fascinated by Leah's contrasting ability to cope, whether with a roll of her pretty eyes or a rolling up of her sleeves.

Just for the intellectual exercise, because he and Leah were definitely in agreement that this thing they were trying to try out was just for the holidays, he found himself wondering how the title of 'boyfriend' would feel. To fall asleep with Leah snuggled up to him, wake up with her hair spread across the pillow next to his, have company at meals other than just when Curtis was around, uncover the mysteries of track days or watch a fiercely independent woman pushing on with her career.

In short, what his life would be like if the feelings he had for Leah weren't just for the holidays.

Curtis went in search of his dad and found him in his bedroom, stretching his arms about. 'OK for me to go round to Jordan's?' The atmosphere between them had thawed a bit but Curtis still wasn't totally over his dad taking control of his laptop.

Ronan paused. 'We could go and see.'

Curtis backed up. 'It's OK. You probably want to start work in the kitchen. I only want to see if Jordan wants to hang out down the park.' Really, he wanted to see if Natasha was over yesterday's weirdness. He'd been shocked at how hurt he'd felt when she'd pretended to gag at the idea of hanging out with him and Jordan. He knew the gesture had been aimed at Jordan but it had still caused a snag in Curtis's breathing, as if someone had poked him hard in the chest.

His dad proved difficult to sideline. 'I want few things less than to start work in the kitchen. It would be neighbourly to check whether Leah needs a hand with anything.' He kicked his way into deck shoes and picked up his wallet.

Curtis sighed. That was the dull thing about holidays. Grown-ups tended to be less preoccupied with their own crap than usual. 'I can ask for you.'

But his dad was already jogging downstairs and opening the front door. 'Has your mum texted you lately?'

Curtis sent him a sidelong look. 'Yep. This morning, like usual.'

'Right.' His dad frowned, but said no more as they

rounded the dividing fence that divided Chez Shea from the gîte.

They found Leah in the back garden of the gîte, hanging out washing and dancing to whatever sounds were coming through her earbuds. She shuffled a couple of steps to her right and bent to the laundry basket for the next item. Her gaze must have fallen on their shadows behind her because she spun around with a tiny yelp. Clutching at her heart, she dragged the earbuds from her ears, laughing. 'That was scary!'

Curtis didn't have a chance to open the conversation before his dad jumped in.

'Curtis wanted to see if Jordan's up for the park, so I thought I'd come and see if you need anything.'

'Only if you fancy joining me in doing the laundry,' she joked. 'Alister's having his operation today so we won't be visiting him.' She glanced at her watch. 'In fact, the op might have started.' Anxiety flitted across her face. Then she sent Curtis a smile. 'It would be great if you did get the kids out of the house for a couple of hours. They've never had a parent in hospital before, let alone have an operation. I think they feel a bit weird.'

'Right.' Curtis nodded, happy that she'd given him the perfect excuse to involve Natasha.

Clumping upstairs he found Jordan playing Assassin's Creed with ferocious concentration.

Five minutes passed as Jordan's thumbs worked on the controller and his on-screen persona leapt and kicked through gangs of rivals. Curtis had never really got on top of Assassin's Creed, what with Templars and Revolutionaries and everything. He got up and mooched over to the window that looked out over the garden. His dad was still standing watching Leah. He could tell they were talking by the way Leah kept looking around from her task. They laughed so loudly that Curtis could hear them through the glass.

He turned away. 'Want to hang in the village?'

Jordan's movements continued on the controller. 'When I've completed this. Better ask Gnasher, though. Leah gave me a hard time and I've got to be nicer,' he said, putting on a soppy voice.

'I don't mind Natasha coming.' Curtis wished Jordan *was* nicer to his sister. At his school there was a girl like Natasha who was obviously unhappy. For some reason, some kids thought that meant they ought to make her unhappier. Her brother stuck up for her and sometimes the kids who were mean to the girl found themselves with a fat lip. Curtis didn't have a brother or sister but, if he had, he'd have wanted the kind that stuck up for him rather than the kind who gave him added grief.

Jordan, eyes still glued to the TV screen, raised his voice to a bellow. 'NATASHA? WANT TO COME HANG IN THE VILLAGE WITH ME AND CURTIS?'

A door opened on the floor below. 'WHEN?'

As Jordan seemed to have reached a particularly gnarly point in the game Curtis went to the top of the stairs so he could see Natasha looking up at him from the floor below. 'When Jordan's completed this bit of Creed.'

'Right. Just a minute.' She flashed him her small uncertain smile and dived back into her room.

Then Jordan swore and tossed his controller on the sofa. 'OK,' he said, as if Curtis had been waiting for his permission before moving.

Natasha appeared as they reached her landing. Curtis jammed his hands in his pockets and gave her a smile. 'OK?' She was really pretty when she smiled back. Her hair was shiny and hung from a ponytail at one side of her head.

Despite his allegedly good intentions to be nicer to his sister, Jordan stipulated, 'You can come with us but don't yap on all day,' swinging around the banister and taking the steps down in twos.

'Give her a chance. She hasn't said a word yet.' Curtis began to take the steps in twos as well.

Jordan glanced back over his shoulder and frowned but he didn't challenge the comment and Curtis was glad he'd stuck up for Natasha, who was looking at him as if he was an Assassin who'd just slaughtered a Templar for her.

In the garden, Leah, put down her laundry long enough to hand Jordan twenty euros. 'Would you nip into the shop on your way home and bring back a lettuce and four of those big tomatoes, please? Then you can all have ice cream with the change. Be back by one thirty and we'll have lunch together, if Curtis and Ronan are free.'

'Cool.' Curtis nodded.

'That would be great, thank you,' agreed his dad.

As they turned into the lane, Natasha matched her steps to Curtis's. 'Our dad's having pins put in his ankle today.' Her eyes were big and apprehensive.

Curtis tried to cheer her up. 'Like a pin cushion?'

If she didn't quite laugh, at least some of the angst faded from her eyes and despite Jordan's earlier admonition, she began to chatter and ask questions as they meandered towards the village centre before turning left under the wooden arch to the park.

The park was a pretty cool place. It led on to the part of the woods with trails for runners and walkers. Curtis had grown up playing there, right from when he was young enough for his mum to take him, in the days before she'd gone off with Darren.

Today they elected to amuse themselves in the area designed for training circuits.

Curtis was pleased to do ten pull-ups without stopping but was chagrined to find that Jordan could do twenty.

'Do it at football training all the time,' Jordan panted as he jumped down, red in the face, rubbing his arms. 'Bailey, our coach, is the only one who can do more than me.'

Curtis felt better when Natasha could only do two pull-ups and thought ten was an amazing number.

When they'd exerted themselves enough, they lay in the sun, chewing blades of grass and squinting at the sun, Natasha sighing, 'I wonder if Dad's op's over yet,' at intervals.

Jordan didn't stand it for long. 'Can't you talk about anything else?'

'I wonder how Mum is?'

'Natasha! Don't give us all shit ache over Mum and Dad. Either shut up or *talk about something else*.'

Huffily, Natasha chose the 'talking about something else' option. 'I still think Curtis's dad's hot for Leah. He's always looking at her.'

Any good intentions towards his sister with which Jordan might have begun the day seemed to be eroding fast. 'Like you're hot for Curtis?'

'What?' Curtis levered himself up on his elbow to gape at Jordan.

At the same moment Natasha, face puce, yelped, '*What*?' in such overdone astonishment that Curtis realised, with a heady mix of shock, pleasure, apprehension and awkwardness, that it might be true. 'Shut *up*, Jordan, you douche!'

With a mortified glance at Curtis, Natasha leaped up and began to stalk away.

'You're just making it look true!' Jordan shouted after her. Then, 'Come back, moron, I was only teasing.' Natasha just picked up her pace. Jordan scowled. 'Shit. Little twat. She'll get me in trouble with Leah.'

Curtis sat up to stare at the older boy. 'What, just because you gave Natasha a hard time when Leah specifically told you not to? Really?'

Beginning to look sheepish, Jordan lifted his voice again. 'Come back, Natasha! I didn't mean anything.'

Without looking round, Natasha broke into a run, her long legs carrying her across the grass and into the shady tunnel of trees that formed the entrance to the wood. In seconds she was out of sight.

'Well done.' Curtis settled back down on his stomach, deciding that though his face was hot and his palms sweaty, pretending to be totally cool was the only bearable way out of this situation. 'You were well nicer. That "moron" was a masterstroke. Auntie Leah's going to be thrilled.'

For several silent minutes they waited for Natasha to re-emerge from the trees, Jordan snatching up bits of grass and throwing them down again, anger and unease warring on his face.

Finally, Curtis climbed to his feet and set off in Natasha's footsteps.

'She'll come back if you wait long enough,' Jordan snapped. 'She always does.'

Apart from flipping Jordan a farewell finger, Curtis ignored him. Partly he wanted to bring Jordan down a notch because he was always an arse to his sister; partly, he wanted to think about Natasha liking him. He hadn't been liked by a girl for ages. He'd liked Jen Lakey at school last year but she'd screamed with laughter when an old lady in McDonald's had asked him, 'Are you one of the fashionable children?' so she obviously didn't like him back.

Being liked by a girl made him feel as if his heart had been rolled in sherbet. Natasha was sweet and pretty. It didn't matter if she'd got to thirteen without knowing words like 'MILF'.

Once he'd reached the trees, he paused. It was pleasantly cool in their shade but he needed a few moments for his eyes to adjust. A lady strolled past with a little brown dog and said '*Bonjour*'. A man in a red T-shirt pounded down one track and up another. Curtis chose the centre track based on a feeling that a speeding Natasha would've simply taken the road ahead.

He was right. He hadn't been walking long when he heard a tell-tale sniff and the 'Uhhuh' sound of someone trying to stop crying. Catching a flash of pink through the trees, he made his footfall as quiet as he could and was able to get close to where Natasha hunched dolefully on a fallen tree trunk before she had the chance to spot him and run away again.

'Hey,' he said softly, folding up his long legs so he could sit beside her.

She dropped her face into her hands as if to shut him out.

'Jordan's a shit,' he added, conversationally.

Sniff, sniff. Uhhuh.

'Don't worry about him. I'm not.'

Cautiously, she opened the fingers over one eye. 'Where is he?'

Curtis shrugged, leaving time for Natasha to sniff back her last tears. A French lady with two little children stopped and, from her big mumsy backpack, gave Natasha a wet wipe to clean her face and a tissue to blow her nose. She seemed inclined to linger in her concern but Natasha smiled tremulously and said, '*Merci, merci beaucoup*,' and Curtis added, laboriously, '*Elle est blessée la tête, mais elle est bien, maintenant. Merci.*' The lady giggled, so Curtis guessed his French wasn't perfect, even apart from the fact that he'd lied about Natasha hurting her head because he didn't know how to translate 'Her brother's crappy to her'.

The lady's attention must have made Natasha conscious of her appearance, as, face attended to, she took her ponytail down and put it up again. She sent Curtis a bashful glance as if checking she looked OK. He smiled approvingly and her cheeks turned rosy.

'Want to see the stream?' Curtis got up and took a few steps toward a stile to a smaller, less used track, encouraging Natasha not to decide she ought to return to the park and make her peace with her brother. 'There are little paths where we can get right up to the back fence of the gîte, behind the annexe. We can go home that way.'

Sniff. Natasha wiped her cheeks one last time and, looking awed by this turn of events, slowly rose. Shyly, she smiled up at him.

At first they walked in silence, the sunshine blinking on and off through the trees. Curtis stamped down any encroaching nettles and told her about the summers he'd spent exploring the woods. His heart gave an extra beat at what came into his mind next, but he reminded himself that he already knew that Natasha *liked* him. So, cautiously, he took her hand. He felt his face go as red as fire, as red as Natasha's. But a smile blazed across her face and she didn't pull her hand away.

Curtis's phone bleeped a text alert. When he saw it was

from Jordan he switched his phone to 'do not disturb' and dropped it back into his pocket without replying.

A few more minutes and Natasha halted, cocking her head. 'Is that Jordan shouting?' The sound came from a long way behind them, carried on the breeze.

'I can't hear him. I might have gone deaf.' Curtis grinned, inviting her to conspire with him against Jordan. Natasha giggled and they wandered further along the narrow path where the trees were thick enough to make them feel as if they were in a green tunnel.

Curtis halted where the water ran alongside the path. They were still quite a way from the back fence of the gîte. 'Have you seen the big water rats that live here? They're called coypu.'

Natasha drew back. 'Rats? Bitey ones?'

Curtis kept hold of her hand. It was sweaty in his but if he let go he might not get up the courage to grab it again. 'Not like ordinary rats. They're cool because they used to be kept as pets and escaped into the wild. If we hang for a few minutes we might see one.' Sure enough, before too long a coypu obligingly shoved off from the opposite bank and paddled ponderously to a nearby clump of weed.

'Oh, *cutie*,' breathed Natasha, misgivings about rats forgotten at the sight of the thick brown fur and chubby body. 'He's like a little otter but with a string tail.'

They crouched down beside the stream, the leaves above allowing drops of sunlight to dance across the water. 'He doesn't usually like humans to know this but his name's Claude,' Curtis offered, solemnly.

'*Bonjour* Claude!' Natasha called, laughing. 'Oh, look, he's brought his babies!' Two smaller sleek brown backs glided in Claude's wake, just visible above the water.

'He's so busy being a new dad he hasn't told me their names yet. I think his wife's leaving everything to him.'

'Oh, one of those.' Natasha nodded wisely, then sighed. 'Let's hope that Claude has given his babies a Cool Auntie Leah. That helps.' Her smile flickered.

'*Une Tante Léonie, absolument*.' Curtis squeezed Natasha's hand and wished he could protect her from her parents splitting up, Jordan's mean moods and anything else that washed happiness from her face. It was a completely new feeling to him but he liked the tingly warmth of it.

He began to pull at the laces of his high-top Converses. 'C'mon. Let's get in. We can walk in the water and keep cool.'

Chapter Thirteen

When the teenagers had left and the last clothes were pegged to the line, Leah kicked off her sandals and flopped onto a lounger. 'How long do you think we have?'

Ronan lowered himself onto the edge of the same lounger, his hip against her thigh. 'They'll probably take all of the two hours but we can't rely on it. I'm thinking of tying bells round their necks.' He lifted up her arm to touch a kiss to her healing graze and fading kaleidoscope of bruises. His eyes smiled. 'You've no idea how much I've wanted time alone with you.'

She watched his lips move onto her fingertips, heartbeat beginning to hurry. 'I might have *some* idea.' Because she'd wanted the same.

He edged closer. 'And now that we have time alone – ouch!' He hurriedly switched his weight from his left arm to his right as his mouth moved in on hers.

Her skin tightened with the delicious onset of arousal and her arms, as if possessing wills of their own, slid up his lean body. Yet she couldn't keep all her mind on the job. So many bombshells had exploded recently and so often had she been required to put other's needs before her own. 'I'm fighting the urge to check my phone for texts that might herald the next disaster.'

Ronan glanced back over his shoulder. 'And there's always the spectre of the kids returning early.' He turned a speculative gaze on La Petite Annexe and then, with a slow smile, on her. His voice dropped. 'Will you invite me in?'

Whether he meant into the annexe or into her body, heat flared inside her. Her throat went dry. 'Consider yourself invited.'

With only one 'Ouch!' he got them both to their feet and in moments she was fumbling with the door handle. He placed his hand over hers and the door opened inwards. Once inside, Ronan bolted the door between them and the world with an air of finality.

'At long last,' Leah murmured, winding her arms around his neck and brushing his jaw with her lips, savouring the taste of him, taking the time to enjoy his heat without fear of interruption by inquisitive teenagers.

He groaned as he pressed against her. 'If this is leading where I'm desperately hoping it's leading I'm going to have to be creative with the shoulder. It doesn't do much weight-bearing.'

She smiled into his eyes. '"Creative" is appealing. Got any ideas?'

'A whole head full.' He nudged her in the direction of the sofa. 'They just involve sitting rather than lying.'

She laughed breathlessly as he pulled her down astride him. 'Go for it.'

He needed no second invitation. Hand and mouth working as a team he began flipping open the tiny buttons down the front of her top, pressing kisses on the skin he revealed at the base of her throat, the upper curves of her breasts, making her jump as he dipped his fingertips tantalisingly into the lace of her bra. 'You are so beautiful.'

Leah slid her hands beneath his T-shirt, earning a murmur of approval as her hand skimmed the contours made by the muscles either side of his spine, enjoying the feel of his warm skin. Her fingers halted as they encountered something thick and un-skinlike. 'What's this?'

He drew back sheepishly. 'Oh, yeah. Shoulder support. Helps with the aching.'

'May I see?'

'As you asked so nicely.' He arched away from the sofa to carefully pull his T-shirt over his head, Leah gently helping tease free the fabric that was warm from his body.

'Well, that's interesting,' she breathed when the shoulder support was revealed, neoprene and black, like one sleeve and a diagonal slice of a T-shirt. It was an unexpectedly good look, tight across his chest, accentuating his leanness. 'It's like the shoulder version of a pirate's eye patch. Are you in pain right now?'

His eyes half closed as she ran her hand over his shoulder, fingertips exploring where flesh met neoprene. 'All I feel is you.' Curling his body around hers he reached for her bra fastening, making her nipples gather in anticipation as he exposed her to the air and to his rapt gaze. Searing palms slowly traced the lines of her ribs before cupping her naked breasts. She couldn't breathe, couldn't think of anything but him and the building knowledge of what was about to happen.

His lips and tongue on her, his skin and hair beneath her hands, their breathing quickened as, careful of his shoulder, they managed to scramble somehow to their feet and slide free of the rest of their clothes. 'It's going to happen,' he breathed as if he couldn't quite believe it, caressing her behind and moulding himself to her, nibbling her jaw, brushing his teeth against the sensitive skin of her throat.

Tipping back her head to allow him greater access she slid her hands ooooh soooo sloooowly down his body, savouring his sinewy strength, until she could take in her hand his heavy, scalding hot flesh.

He groaned, rolling his hips against her hand.

'You have condoms, right?' Gripped in the shocking heat of arousal, she could scarcely form the words.

'Enough for that guy in Muntsheim to make balloon animals with.' He groaned again. 'I would really love to take things deliciously slow–'

'–but we don't know how long we've got,' she agreed.

He grabbed his shorts and dragged out a slim black pack from a zipped pocket. When he fumbled to open it Leah took over, excitement coursing through her, all responsibilities fading from her mind. For these stolen moments she and Ronan were safe, locked away, threatening nothing and no one, woman and man obeying the basic instinct to give and take pleasure.

His breathing almost stopped as she brushed his hands away and rolled the condom slowly into place. With a strangled sound he sank back down onto the sofa, pulling her down, turning slightly so that it was his right shoulder against the sofa back.

She paused, trying to keep her weight off him. 'Are you OK?'

He laughed, lifting incredulous eyes to her face.

'I mean your shoulder–'

'What shoulder?' He curled his hands around her hips and guided her down over him, murmuring his pleasure as their bodies joined. And began to move. Slowly. Then faster . . . More urgently. Finding their rhythm, fighting their breath, clinging, clinging, together, together, together.

Afterwards. They clung to each other, waiting for their hearts to stop hammering, glued skin-on-skin by a fine sheen of sweat. 'Wow, chemistry overload,' gasped Leah.

'Yeah. Combustible.' His voice was slow, satisfied, his eyes closed.

Conscious suddenly that she was draped all over him, she tried to shift her weight.

His arms tightened around her, keeping her exactly where she was.

'Doesn't your shoulder hurt?'

'Yeah.' His embrace grew tighter still as if, deep as he was inside her, it wasn't enough. 'But I'm still enjoying aftershocks.'

She laughed, making him groan again. 'Our time must be running out.'

Face pressed against her throat, he shook his head. 'Time halted for us. The universe is on "pause".'

'I wish.' She dropped a kiss on his hair. 'I may be only a deputy parent but I'm sure we're pushing our luck–'

'Leah!'

Her head snapped up. 'That's Jordan.'

'*Leah*? Where ARE YOU?' Urgency was unmistakeable in Jordan's voice.

Immediately, Ronan let his hands fall away, giving a stifled, 'Ouch,' as she scrambled clear of his lap.

'Sorry!' She snatched up some of her clothes fumbling to fasten her bra and the way-too-many buttons of her top.

Without even checking if Ronan was getting himself together, Leah shoved her knickers in her pocket and threaded her legs into her shorts as her phone began to ring. She managed to answer it as she wrenched at the door. 'Jordan, what? What's up? I'm in the annexe.'

In moments Jordan was hurtling down the garden, sweaty and red-faced, relief combining with anxiety in his voice. 'I couldn't find you!'

They met halfway up the lawn, both still clutching their phones. 'What's the matter?'

Jordan's chest heaved. He hesitated, apparently struck dumb now he'd located his quarry.

'*What*?' Leah had to look up to gaze into his face these days. 'Where are the others? Spit it out!'

He almost took her literally, spouting his words between gasps. 'Natasha went off into the woods in a strop, Curtis went after her, neither of them came back, they didn't answer when I went into the woods and shouted and they're not answering their phones, and they're not in the house.'

Although the day was warm, Leah suddenly shivered. 'How long ago did this happen? What woods?' Horrible possibilities began to flash through her mind's eye: everything from sinkholes to carnivorous trees to alien abductors.

A reassuring voice came from behind her. 'I expect he means the woods between here and the park. Curtis knows the area pretty well.' Ronan's clothes were miraculously back in place, his phone in his hand as he strode across the grass. 'Leah, you try phoning because they might not be answering Jordan if they've had a fall-out. I'll check my house in case they're there. If there's no joy I'll search the woods while you stay here in case they turn up.'

Steadying at his calm control, Leah headed for the gîte, trying Natasha's phone as she went. It didn't take long for her to locate it on charge and vibrating uselessly on

Natasha's bedroom floor. She ran back downstairs and met Ronan barging into the kitchen, phone clamped to his ear.

A rapid exchange of enquiring looks and shaken heads established that neither had a lead on the missing pair. 'Oh, hell,' Leah whispered, shaken right down to her core. A core that was still trembling in reaction to love-making that now seemed a stark contrast to the much less lovely emotions tumbling through her.

While Ronan quickly drove off, Leah paced up and down the garden, in and out of the kitchen, Jordan trailing, in turns sheepish and defiant as Leah fired questions at him. 'Why did Natasha go off in a strop? Why did Curtis go after her and not you?'

Jordan at first tried to scuff his feet and shrug but Leah persisted until eventually he admitted, 'I teased her a bit about liking Curtis. S'pose I should have been the one to go after her but I thought Curtis would bring her back.'

'You should definitely have been the one to go after her. Which one of you is her brother? Which one of you teased her?' Leah was too frightened to worry whether she was handling the situation as Jordan's parents would. She'd read the phrase 'sick with fear' but didn't think she'd actually experienced it until now. Her skin was clammy with it. Jordan made her a cup of coffee as a peace offering but she couldn't force even a mouthful down.

She knew Kirchhoffen was safe and that Curtis was familiar with the village, but still Ronan didn't ring and say, 'I've found them!' Still the teenaged pair didn't return.

As the minutes ticked past, Leah settled shakily at the kitchen table and covered her eyes. 'What the hell am I supposed to tell your dad when he comes round from his op? Or your mum when she rings tonight? "Oops. I've lost one"?'

'Dunno,' Jordan mumbled remorsefully. 'I'll go back and look–'

Leah removed her hands from her face to glare at him. 'You stay where I can see you. I'm not going to lose you, too.' Then her phone rang and she almost dropped it in her haste to answer. 'Ronan? Have you got them?'

He sounded baffled. 'No. Obviously you haven't?'

Her heart sank. 'Not a sign.'

'Shit,' he muttered. 'I've walked all round the park, including the main tracks in the woods. If they've strayed from the obvious areas it will be trickier to locate them. If ever I needed a helicopter!' He paused for several moments. 'I've driven all over the village I'm going to come back for now. I'll come out again if they haven't turned up in an hour.'

Leah's hand trembled as she put her phone down on the table. 'He can't find them. He's coming back.'

'Sorry,' Jordan offered hoarsely.

Seeing fear on his face, Leah took his hand remorsefully. 'And I'm sorry I snapped at you. I'm anxious.'

When Ronan returned he made more coffee and insisted Leah drink a little. He spoke reassuringly about how frequently kids did this, forgetting the time, wandering along in their own little bubble.

The next hour passed excruciatingly slowly. The youngsters were an hour and a half late when Ronan, grim-faced, picked up his car keys and opened the back door, turning back to say, 'I'll comb the off-track areas of the woods, this time,' when Leah's attention was caught by movement behind him, beside La Petite Annexe.

'There they are!' She felt as if a kangaroo had ricocheted off her chest, her relief was so great at seeing the tall figure of Curtis helping Natasha over the fence and starting up the lawn in step with the girl's much smaller frame. She flung open the kitchen door. 'Where have you *been*? Natasha, I've been worried sick. It's nearly three o'clock!'

'Is it?' Natasha gave a surprised little 'oof' as Leah dragged her into a hard hug. 'I left my phone on charge so I didn't know the time.'

Ronan was hugging Curtis, too. 'But you should have your phone, Curtis. I've been ringing and texting you.'

Curtis scuffed around in his pockets until he located his flat black handset. 'Oh, right. Mine's on "do not disturb".' He went red, glancing at Natasha.

'Sorry,' said Natasha, blushing just as hard. 'We just stopped to watch the coypu in the stream and didn't look at the time.'

Leah stepped back to look at her. 'How did you get so wet?'

Natasha's gaze slid away. 'We got in the water to paddle and I fell over so we sat on a fence in the sun while my shorts dried.'

'Or you got in a water fight,' snorted Jordan.

Natasha giggled and Curtis grinned at her. 'Little bit,' he admitted.

While this reassuringly normal interchange took place, Leah tried to get a grip on her emotions – joy, rage, fear, whatever bubbled to the surface first. But she watched Ronan give Curtis's shoulders another squeeze, look intently into his eyes and say, 'But you're OK?' and Curtis nod and shrug.

Ronan nodded back and that seemed to be it.

Deciding that Ronan was the one who had the parenting thing all figured out, so if he was over his anxiety she could give her adrenalin a chance to stop crashing round her system too, Leah groped for a mantle of calm as she squeezed Natasha's hand. 'Don't go out if your phone's not charged in future, right? I nearly freaked. What are coypu?'

'You know, like, otters? But they're rats.'

'Rats?'

'Cuddly rats. They have fat bodies and skinny tails.'

While Leah had been petrified, Natasha had been watching cute rats. She allowed her panic to drain away. Nothing awful had happened. The kids had had a spat and Natasha had gone off to sulk and got distracted by furry creatures. 'You'd better wash your hands and we'll have a late lunch.'

Jordan looked hunted. 'I forgot the lettuce and tomatoes.'

The least of her worries. 'Then we'll have egg on toast. You can help me scramble the eggs.'

'Can me and Curtis make more mug cakes?' Natasha clamoured. 'Have you rung the hospital yet?'

'Fine by me and no, I can't ring till after four. We'll have to be patient a little longer.'

'And calm down. We've had a lot of excitement,' Ronan added, catching Leah's eye.

'It's a wonder parents don't all need pacemakers,' she retorted. But she didn't need his barely perceptible wink to know the excitement he referred to wasn't entirely related to the adventures of Natasha and Curtis. She cast a glance at the annexe, remembering in a rush what had happened there, and turned back to find him smiling.

Ronan and Curtis taking little persuading to join the party, they prepared lunch together in the kitchen. Ronan sliced bread, Natasha and Curtis handled dessert, Jordan set the table and, mindful that poor Alister's sojourn beneath the scalpel should be drawing to a close, Leah kept a check on the time as she whipped up fluffy mounds of egg.

Finally, after consuming both eggs and mug cakes – Natasha's chosen variation had been chocolate laced with marshmallows and cornflakes – Leah made the call, Ronan taking over to get her through to the correct person.

Suddenly nervous for her brother-in-law, Leah found she had to swallow before asking for news. Blessedly, the ward nurse not only reported good news but did so in English. Leah was beaming when the call ended. 'Your dad's back on the ward, a bit tired but successfully pinned together. He'll ring later but just wants to rest now.'

'Yay!' crowed Natasha, eyes shining. 'That means he'll be back in a few days.' Despite her smile, she wiped the corners of her eyes.

'Thanks,' said Jordan economically, but his shoulders visibly unscrunched.

To add to the good news day, Jordan's phone rang while they were clearing up. 'It's Mum!' he said and, after listening for a minute, was able to broadcast better news from her, too. 'The anti-sick medicine's working and she hopes to be out of hospital tomorrow. She might soon be able to travel back in two or three stages.'

'Yay!' cried Natasha again.

The children abandoned the dirty dishes and moved in a body up the stairs, Jordan and Natasha passing the phone between them as they downloaded news of cake and coypu into their mother's ear – nothing about missing teenagers, Leah noted – and Curtis followed behind with the certainty kids seemed to have that they were never unwelcome.

Leah set about clearing the table, her heart lighter than it had been since Michele's abrupt departure. 'Light's beginning to glimmer at the end of the Jordan-and-Natasha tunnel. I don't think I can cope with too many more scares like today so thank goodness their parents might soon be available to take over their rightful roles so I can return to my own stress-free life.'

Ronan caught her up against him, his eyes dark. 'But I hope you're not in too much of a hurry?' His breath was soft against her hair. 'After today . . .'

She pressed against him, making him groan and tighten his arms. 'We have loads of time left. Two whole weeks.'

Chapter Fourteen

'How are things going with the hottie next door? Is he your type – a self-centred fibber?' Scott was again easing the boredom of battling the one-way traffic system by calling Leah with his usual brand of outrageous teasing.

Her headset allowing her to chat as she made up the bed for Alister in the salon, Leah laughed, shaking the duvet energetically, its pattern of large yellow daisies betraying it as Natasha's choice. 'I'm not a girl to kiss and tell but we did dip briefly under the teenage anti-adult-fun radar.'

'Seriously?'

Leah decided that for once she wasn't in the mood to have her leg pulled about her record with men and breezed on. 'I pick Alister up this afternoon. I've configured the seats in The Pig so he can prop his leg up. Apparently it feels as if it's going to explode, otherwise.'

After an instant's silence Scott accepted the change of subject. 'Messy. Have you worked out how to get back to the UK?'

'One problem at a time.' Leah reached for the sheet. It had ducks on.

Then, 'LEAH?' Natasha was evidently trying to locate Leah by the simple expedient of standing in the hallway and bellowing.

'Sounds like someone wants you.' Scott laughed.

'Leeeee-a-ah!' bawled Natasha.

'Welcome to my new world.' She lifted her voice. 'In the salon!'

Natasha appeared at the door. 'What are you doing? Who are you talking to? Scott? Oh, can I talk to him, pleeeease? I haven't seen him for ages!' Natasha spent the next five minutes laughing and chattering into Leah's headset, calling Scott 'Scottie Dog' and getting in the way while Leah finished the bed and heaved a small chest of drawers across from under the window to serve as a nightstand.

Finally, Natasha thrust the headset back. 'Scott wants to say bye. Are we having breakfast soon? What time are we fetching Dad? How far did you say Mum got last night? Is it OK if Curtis comes round?'

Laughing, Leah waved Natasha away. 'Yes; don't know; Zurich in Switzerland; and yes.'

'You sounded like a parent,' Scott accused, when she regained possession of her phone.

'Deputy parent only. When Alister reappears today normal service will resume.'

But when the afternoon arrived Leah began to suspect that normal service was still a way off. She successfully identified where to park to collect a discharged patient, but getting Alister into The Pig proved to be a mission. Leah and Jordan heaved, Alister hopped, and Natasha provided an anxious commentary about the new big black boot and were they being careful because of all the hardware in Alister's leg. Leah almost had sympathy with Jordan when he gritted, 'Shut up, Gnasher.'

By the time they'd got him home to the gîte, Alister was pale and terse and Leah had postponed her plans to move back into La Petite Annexe until the next day.

Flexing their muscles again, Leah and Jordan got poor Alister out of the vehicle and hauled an armchair and footstool from salon to kitchen for him, the occupational therapist now having instructed him to be out of bed during the day. For the rest of the holiday a nurse would visit daily to administer blood-thinning injections and a physiotherapist would call four times a week to torture Alister towards health. Just before heading homeward he'd return to Hautepierre for staple removal and for the boot to be replaced by a plaster.

It became plain to Leah that in all other respects she'd be first in line when it came to Alister's care until they were safely back in the UK. She closed her mind to what might happen to him back in Bettsbrough. She'd be back in her own home and deep into her new job.

Adjusting her thoughts to the present, she smiled reassuringly. 'I've made you a bed in the salon so you don't need to worry about the stairs.'

Alister, wincing, let himself down into the chair and lifted his leg onto the stool as if it were made of spun glass. 'Thanks.' He sighed as he let his head settle back. 'Actually . . . I didn't mention it at the hospital in case they refused to discharge me but –' he made a 'this is awkward' face '– there's no bathroom on the ground floor of the gîte.'

'Balls.' Leah was too appalled that she'd so overlooked the obvious to stifle the profanity, making Jordan laugh and Natasha reprove, 'Leeeeea-ah!' Leah even looked out into the hall as if hoping a magic bathroom portal might materialise. What she saw instead was the wooden staircase, no doubt looking like a polished Everest to someone on crutches.

Alister flushed uncomfortably. 'Don't worry! I'll just have to make it up to the first floor. That's why they'll only discharge you once they've seen you hop up and down a few steps.' But his gaze flicked towards the kitchen window and the garden.

Stifling the urge to rage 'Balls' a few more times, louder and more viciously, Leah sucked in a huge breath and dredged up a smile. 'There's La Petite Annexe but if you intend to base yourself here in the kitchen during the day you'll have to get yourself across the garden every time you want the loo–'

'Perfect.' Alister's face relaxed. 'I have to get up and potter around regularly, anyway. If you're sure?'

Leah felt her smile might crack. 'It's the only solution. Right, kids, let's get your dad's stuff moved.'

'Really?' Jordan groaned. But no amount of complaining altered the fact that they must transport Alister's things down the garden, the very same things they'd moved from top to ground floor that morning. As if to underline how much Leah's lovely private space was now neither hers nor private, Alister promptly shut himself into La Petite Annexe for a nap.

Leah was left to revise the afternoon's shopping plans. In her naïveté she'd thought it'd be possible to roar off to the supermarket in the Porsche once Alister was back at the gîte. Now she saw that there was no way she could consider Alister well enough to be in charge of the kids. She'd have to drive The Pig and take Jordan and Natasha. Her vision of being alone with her car trembled and vanished.

More importantly, as she shot a jaundiced look at the

closed door of La Petite Annexe, so did her vision of being alone with Ronan.

She felt conflicted about the remaining couple of weeks of the holiday. As time away from her real life they seemed too long. But as time left with Ronan? Her heart dropped.

Short. Very short.

That evening, Curtis was lying on his bed, alternately watching prank videos on his laptop and texting on his phone, when a tap sounded at his door. 'Yep?' he answered, enjoying the novelty of there being no just wandering in.

His dad's head appeared around the door. 'Heard from your mum?'

'Yep. She's been WhatsApping.' How many more times were they going to have this conversation?

Ronan's gaze fell to Curtis's phone. 'Is it her you're texting?'

'Nope.'

'OK.'

The head withdrew and the door shut. Curtis turned back to the conversation with Natasha.

> ***Curtis:*** *Dad just came in wanting to know if I heard from mum*
> ***Natasha:*** *My mums supposed to be coming back here I want to see her*
> ***Curtis:*** *Still miss her?*
> ***Natasha:*** *Yes being split up sucks do you miss your mum*

Curtis paused. His mum had texted or WhatsApped him most days. He was used to only having one parent at a time so if he ever missed the other one he'd stopped noticing.

Curtis: *I'll c her in sept. wuu2?*
Natasha: *Talking 2 u lol*

Curtis grinned and sent back a 'scratching head' emoticon and added X.

He felt his face flush hotly as he added the kiss and quickly pressed *send* before he could change his mind. Since he'd known that Natasha *liked* him and discovered he liked her, his mind had buzzed with how to progress. He hadn't kissed many girls. Two, in fact, and only one of those had been a successful proper kiss. The other had seen firmer contact with their noses than their lips.

Since the day he'd held Natasha's hand he'd felt wired all the time they were together. Jordan kept giving him looks because Curtis was spending so much time talking to Natasha. Next time they were alone, Curtis resolved, he'd kiss her. She was pretty and funny and the way she looked at him made him feel like a giant.

Downstairs, Ronan sprawled in the leather armchair that had once been his father's, drinking coffee and trying to ignore the bare floorboards that he hadn't stained and varnished yet because at every opportunity he was throwing off his work clothes and springing to Leah's side like the Roadrunner.

Now, using his left hand to rhythmically stretch the yellow elastic ribbon as per physio's instructions, he operated his phone with his right to check his email – nothing that required a reply and nothing from Selina: irritating, as Curtis seemed to be hearing from her regularly. Well, he couldn't do anything about that from France. He switched to texting Leah instead.

Ronan: *I didn't see enough of you today. x*
Leah: *Likewise. ☺ x*
Ronan: *The way things are going, I'm going to have to fly in and abduct you. x*
Leah: *Sounds great! But as you can't currently fly maybe we should focus on something more practical. Any ideas? x*
Ronan: *In the current situation, frustratingly few. Two intelligent single adults ought to be able to work out how to spend a couple of hours together without . . . distractions. x*
Leah: *By distractions you mean kids. How do parents get the privacy to have sex and create other kids??? ☺ x*
Ronan: *I think it's easier if the adults share a bed every night. x*
Ronan: *Just taking a moment to appreciate the idea of sharing a bed with you. x*
Leah: *Not a sofa? x*
Ronan: *Sofa, bed, up against the wall . . . x*

Her end of the conversation paused and Ronan got up for more coffee, pent-up energy to burn. Un-penting it with Leah didn't look likely to happen. It was ridiculous that they couldn't get together again. Apart from the annexe situation, he'd noticed that Jordan wasn't hanging out with Curtis and Natasha so much. Was it simply because his dad was home? Or had Ronan emerging from the annexe behind Leah that day telegraphed lascivious intent towards Jordan's aunt, making Jordan protective?

Leah's scheduled move back to her own space had been meant to herald more of the planet-tilting sex they'd shared in their all-too-brief bout of privacy. Under the guise of stepping up his fitness regime he'd planned to ask if Curtis could hang out with Jordan and Natasha under Alister's supervision some evenings while Ronan took a 'late night run' . . . that would lead discreetly to the annexe and Leah's bed.

Now that bed was Alister's–

His phone beeped a text alert.

> ***Leah:*** *Sorry. Had to stop WWIII between Natasha and Jordan. Kids! Argh! x*
> ***Ronan:*** *They get over it. Will I see you tomorrow? x*
> ***Leah:*** *Expect I'll be local. It would be odd to take the kids out and leave Alister now he's finally out of hospital. x*
> ***Leah:*** *Not being free to do as I want sucks, by the way. Totally sucks. Not what I signed up for. How do you cope with parenthood 24/7? I like to be the freest of free agents, the singlest of single women. x*

Ronan drained his coffee and reread this last exchange, cold dismay settling around his heart. Was Leah beginning to see the discrepancy in their situations as insurmountable?

Here in France, Ronan was effectively a single parent. Whatever strictures it placed on his liberty, he wouldn't dream of cutting a thirteen-year-old loose, other than a bit of freedom within the boundaries of the village.

'Single parent' was an oxymoron, because parents never had the luxury of being single. It sounded as if Leah might already be shying away from that.

Restlessly, he jumped up to prowl around the room.

Maybe it would be for the best. Hell, he'd already caught himself thinking about what it would be like if they were back in the UK. It would be wise, he admitted to himself as he dumped his empty cup in the sink and switched off the lights, to just smile whenever he remembered that hour in the annexe and accept that it was yet another one-time thing. Pushing for more was madness when Leah liked to fly free, and the only good thing he'd taken from his last relationship was a child who had first call on his time.

His resolve lasted for an hour. Until the next text message.

***Leah:** I like to sleep naked. x*

The reply flew from his fingers.

***Ronan:** I'd like to sleep naked with you. x*

Natasha burst into the kitchen the next morning when Leah was awarding herself a leisurely start to the morning after staying awake late to exchange increasingly heated texts with Ronan.

'Can we stay here today cos of not leaving Dad alone?'

Leah filled her mug with coal-black coffee from the filter jug then added enough milk so that she could drink the first cup straight down. 'Good plan. Almost the only place we've been lately is the hospital, anyway.'

Natasha assumed her wheedling voice. 'And can we invite Curtis for lunch? I'll make the meal if it's a lot of trouble for you.'

'OK,' said Leah, easily. 'You'd better include Curtis's dad. It would be rude to leave him home alone.' How easy it was to be co-operative when what was asked happened to be exactly what she wanted.

Natasha paused, giving her aunt a look that suggested she expected to have to be more persuasive than that. 'You could help me.'

'Maybe,' Leah teased as she prepared to carry her second coffee out into the garden and the inviting early sunshine.

'I'll text Curtis.' Natasha skipped from the room.

For once the morning idled by without a schedule. Temperatures soared towards the heatwave mark and Alister chose a shady garden lounger as his day bed, his leg cradled by fat pillows. Once an hour he rose gingerly, threaded his arms through his crutches and hopped around for five minutes before lowering himself, equally gingerly, back to the horizontal.

Natasha and Jordan, perhaps reassured by their dad's return, sprawled on the grass without arguing, making frequent forays into the kitchen for cold drinks and ice-lollies. Pretty soon Curtis ambled into the garden, hands tucked in the huge side pockets of voluminous black cargo shorts. He flopped down beside Natasha, mumbling in Leah's direction, 'Yes, please, for lunch, me and Dad, fanks.'

'OK.' With a feeling of wellbeing that had been noticeably absent so far this holiday, Leah prepared to laze in the sun and catch up with the Formula 1 news on her iPad, listening to the distinctive whine of an electric sander at work at Chez Shea. She pictured Ronan guiding the machine back and forth as its voice rose and fell. He was probably wearing the shoulder brace under his T-shirt. Or maybe he'd discarded the T-shirt altogether in the heat. The mental image made it hard to concentrate.

Just as she was considering making an excuse to go and see for herself, the sander fell silent. Glancing at her watch she realised it was nearly one. 'So what are we having for lunch, Natasha?'

Natasha looked around with an expression of alarm at being held to her earlier offer. 'What've we got?'

'Salad,' Jordan guessed resignedly.

'Chocolate cake, ice cream and crisps,' Curtis suggested hopefully.

'Anything that isn't hospital food,' Alister sighed longingly.

'I'll help. C'mon.' Leah pulled Natasha to her feet and encouraged her towards the kitchen.

Curtis followed them as if he'd been asked to. 'S'pose I have to wash my hands?'

'You're getting the idea.' Leah set eggs and pasta to boil then grated a block of Parmesan cheese while Curtis and Natasha dawdled over washing tiny tomatoes and rocket leaves, Curtis making bad jokes and Natasha giggling.

Eventually, impatient at their lack of progress, Leah biffed them out of the way with her hip. 'How about setting the table? I'll finish up in here and bring the food out.'

They gathered up plates, cutlery and cloth with no noticeable change of pace and vanished outside, still deep in their own conversation.

Shifting up easily to her usual kitchen speed Leah grilled goat's cheese on slices of bread and whizzed up walnut oil dressing with the stick blender. When the door reopened her attention was on tossing the pasta salad. 'Do we need something else?'

A hard arm snaked around her waist. 'There are so many things. They all involve privacy.'

Laughing, Leah turned around, capturing Ronan's just-showered smell in her lungs. 'Which seems unachievable.'

He held her close, their bodies nestling together as if remembering they knew each other. 'Nothing's unachievable if the incentive's great enough.'

They did, at least, manage a slow and tantalising kiss before Leah freed herself to swoop on the grill pan just as the cheese turned a beautiful bubbling gold.

Regardless of the frustrations of Leah and Ronan, lunch proved to be fun. Alister sat sideways at the table, his leg and its pillows on another chair, giving great *mmmms* of pleasure at every bite and not even minding that he couldn't risk being drunk in charge of a broken ankle by partaking of the red wine.

Leah, in no such danger, let the wine, warmed by the sun, trickle down her throat like nectar as she stretched out beneath the table to 'accidentally' brush up against Ronan. His bare leg replied by stroking slowly across hers, sending a tingling wave right through her.

'So what's for dessert?' demanded Jordan, smacking his lips as his last mouthful disappeared. 'I could make ice cream sundaes.'

'Yay!' Natasha cried.

Leah wrinkled her nose. 'Last time Jordan made sundaes it involved four types of ice cream, squirty cream, broken biscuits and chocolate sauce. Everyone felt sick.'

'Maybe you could make a nice fruit salad.' Ronan's leg came to rest against Leah's once more.

'Yuck,' said Jordan.

Alister laughed. 'I'm not sure "nice" is a word he'd use in connection with fruit salad–' But the rest of the sentence died in his throat. He stared in the direction of the house with such a flabbergasted expression that everyone twisted in their chairs to follow his sightline.

Natasha was the first to react, sending her chair and a glass of lemonade flying as she leaped up to race across the grass, arms outspread, shouting joyfully.

'MUM! You're back, you're back!'

Chapter Fifteen

It was a wan and gaunt Michele who opened her arms to receive her younger child. 'Darling! Sorry I didn't make it straight back. I came as soon as I could.'

Although she'd known that Michele was on her way, Leah felt somehow surprised to see her. Maybe some small mean part of her had suspected that all along Michele had been giggling in a big hotel bed with Bailey while she span outrageous lies designed to keep Leah deputising until it was time to go home. Or maybe it was just too much to grasp that suddenly here were *both* of Jordan's and Natasha's parents. Leah was free!

Leah felt like a spectator at a movie as Michele hugged and kissed her children, wiping the corners of her eyes and laughing, then hugging them all over again. For once, Natasha didn't seem to have a single question but just hung on her mum and looked tearfully ecstatic. Jordan wore a heavy scowl, which Leah recognised as teen-boy technique to force back any tears that might dare to leak out.

Finally, Michele's gaze fell on Alister and her smile faded.

'Poor you. Oh, Ally. Does it hurt a lot? I'm so sorry.' She stooped and dropped a soft kiss on his forehead. Alister looked stunned. Or haunted, or pained. Leah wasn't sure.

Finally, Michele reached Leah and fell to her knees to drag her into a fierce hug. 'Thank you! You are the best sister!'

It took several moments for Leah to return the embrace. It was too hot, too sweaty to be pleasant and the words that flew into her brain were better left unsaid. *That was a virtuoso performance. Have you been planning it all the way home?* Instead, she managed, 'How are you?'

For an answer Michele gave into her emotions, beginning on a wail then burping out big sobs that made Leah feel still more hot and damp as the tears soaked into her T-shirt. Over the top of her sister's head, Leah watched as the smiles of Natasha and Jordan faded uncertainly and Alister gazed pensively across the garden, chin on steepled fingers. Ronan sent Leah a sympathetic look, clapped Curtis on the shoulder and led him discreetly off in the direction of Chez Shea.

Finally, Michele unpeeled herself from Leah's shoulder and settled in the chair that Ronan had vacated, gathering up paper napkins for eye-wiping and nose-blowing purposes. Where her skin wasn't red from crying it was stark white.

She essayed a smile. 'Oh, dear. I'm sorry. Things got a bit much.' A tiny hiccup of a laugh. Spying the jug of water, she poured herself a glass and drank thirstily, then lifted her voice as if calling her class to order. 'Right. Well. I owe you all explanations.'

Jordan and Natasha returned to their seats.

Michele gazed at each person in turn. Only Alister refused eye contact. 'Right,' she repeated, 'you know I've been away to try and make decisions about the future, but my pregnancy sickness escalated into hyperemesis until I ended up in hospital.' A rueful smile. 'It wasn't how I expected to spend the time but you'll probably all be glad to know that it made it easy to see that things aren't going to work out with the baby's father.'

Jordan and Natasha exchanged uncertain glances, smiling then pulling their faces straight again as if smiling might be wrong.

Alister finally looked at Michele. 'Is the baby all right?'

She gave a tremulous smile. 'So far, so good.'

Alister nodded. Leah knew he was far too nice a man to wish harm on a baby but, even in profile, she could read pain through his veneer of courtesy. 'What did the doctors tell you? Do you have to keep seeing someone local?'

'I need to rest but I shouldn't need immediate medical care if I continue as I am, able to eat a little, rest a lot.'

'Have you notified your head teacher about the pregnancy?'

Michele shook her head. 'September's soon enough, so I can do it in person then. What about you? Have you told your head of governors about your injury? Are you going to be able to return to school in time for the new term?'

'No, it's a bit of a mess.' Alister shifted his leg as if even the act of discussing it made it hurt. 'I'm not allowed to return for health and safety reasons but we have an Ofsted due. My deputy head, poor Julia, will have to see it through. I can help with admin from home, of course.'

The stilted exchange made Leah's heart ache. They might have been teachers in the staff room making polite conversation. She supposed the screaming matches must have happened weeks ago, but watching the children watch their parents so politely not loving each other brought a huge lump to her throat.

Quietly, she stacked some dishes and headed for the kitchen. The family needed time alone. The kids would turn to their parents; Leah would return to being Cool Auntie Leah.

She was shocked at the heaviness inside her at the thought.

On the other hand . . . she paused to stare over the fence to the honey-coloured house next door.

Restless after the unexpectedly abrupt end to lunch, Ronan took to his sofa to check his email. Nothing from Selina and she still wasn't answering his phone calls. He even blocked his number so she wouldn't know who was calling, but she'd got wise to that one very early in their estrangement.

Henry had responded to Ronan's request that pilot's effects be added to the insurance claim: *Noted*.

'One word?' Ronan seethed. Snatching up his phone again, Ronan tried Henry's mobile. The call went to voicemail; irritating rather than surprising. He'd had the same result the last couple of times he'd tried.

Drumming his fingers, he brooded on the reasons that might be making Henry act like this. He should have no additional flying duties because of Ronan's absence – he was a pilot short but then he was an aircraft short, too. He debated calling the Buzz Sightseer landline but it made for too public an arena to air a private matter.

Kneading the tightness in his shoulder, he experienced a moment's intense nostalgia for the smell of Avtur in the hangar, the silver aircraft gleaming, the kick it gave him every time he met and briefed passengers who were revved up to be flying in a helicopter or in awe of even the simplest pre-flight check procedure. He missed the beat-beat-beat of the rotors, the incomparable sensation of a helicopter dropping its nose and lifting beneath him.

He wished he could shake the feeling that the future was like a slumbering dragon and it was only a matter of time before it woke up and he discovered he was on its menu.

He was jolted back to the present by a flash of gold-brown passing his window. With a lighter heart, he scrambled up to open the door, surprising Leah in the act of knocking. In an instant he'd grasped the hand she'd raised and dragged her through the door and into his arms.

She gave a muffled squeak. 'Pleased to see me?'

'Every inch. I thought you'd be deep in family stuff.' He kissed her soundly, kicked the door shut and led her back into the sitting room, where he dropped to the sofa and managed to land with Leah neatly tucked beneath his good arm. A stirring in his groin signalled his appreciation of her hip and thigh against his.

'I think the Milton family need to be alone. I started to do my kitchen-porter bit, then I suddenly thought –' she gave a shrug, her breasts rising and falling with the movement '– I'm liberated! It was a toss-up whether I came to see you or went out in the Porsche.'

'I won over your *Porsche*?'

She grinned. 'It doesn't kiss well.' She lifted her head, her hair sliding across the arm he'd curled around her. 'I was thinking –'

A door banged upstairs. Heavy footfalls thumped on the uncarpeted stairs.

With a neat sideways lunge along the cushions Leah left Ronan's arms and positioned herself decorously in the opposite corner of the sofa.

Curtis strode in, face alight. 'The others are coming.'

Sure enough, even as he spoke the tall figure of Jordan and slighter one of Natasha passed the window. In what seemed like a twinkling the room was full of teenagers.

'What about dessert, Leah?' Jordan folded down onto a black leather footstool, propping his elbows on his knees.

Natasha claimed the arm of the sofa and slid her arm chummily along Leah's shoulders. 'Are we going to make pudding? Or just have ice-cream? You didn't mean it about fruit salad, did you?'

Ronan felt a laugh climbing up into his throat at Leah's astounded expression. 'I thought you'd be with your mum and dad,' she managed.

'Mum's gone for a nap and Dad's on the phone to someone at school.' Natasha screwed her body around so she could gaze hopefully into Leah's face. 'What can we have? Can Curtis have some, too? And Ronan,' she added, perhaps realising it wasn't good etiquette to leave someone out of dessert plans when you'd wandered uninvited into their house and were doing your best to hijack his guest.

Ronan moved promptly to foil the hijacking. 'How about we stroll down to the *salon de thé*? I'll treat us all to cakes.'

A chorus of 'Cool!' attested to the popularity of the suggestion.

Having locked the door of Chez Shea, Ronan fell in step with Leah in the wake of the three teenagers as they led the way down the hill to Rue Paul Deschanel. 'It seems your niece and nephew don't see that your role as Deputy Mum has ended.'

Her eyes were hidden behind her sunglasses but her mouth curved into a smile. 'I can't have copied them in when I sent my letter of resignation.'

He laughed. 'I'm not complaining. It creates reasons for us to be together and I'd rather see more of you than less.' He let his arm brush hers and looked forward to an afternoon of what had become familiar: the company of this beautiful woman and three capricious teens.

When they returned in the late afternoon, the kids escaped into the gîte while Leah lingered with Ronan out of sight behind the shrubs in the front garden, a few minutes she would remember more for the heat of his mouth and the tingle of his fingertips trailing up her sun-warmed skin than for any words spoken.

When he'd reluctantly returned to Chez Shea to catch up on chores, Leah surveyed the detritus of lunch littering the garden table and wondered, despite the way she'd yearned for their return over the past nine days, how much she was actually going to enjoy having the kids' parents around if it meant two more people to look after, Alister being *hors de combat* and Michele having taken up extreme napping.

Unwashed plates and cutlery being an unhygienic affront to her soul, she cleaned down. And afterwards . . . well, that seemed the ideal moment to search out Michele.

Finding the door of her bedroom closed, she shoved it briskly open with the suspicion that Michele had reclaimed it as her own again.

Sure enough, Michele looked up from a prone position on the bed, magazine in hand. 'Hello, little sis.' She treated Leah to her widest smile. 'I was hoping you'd come up for a chat. I'll bet you're dying to know what happened.'

'If you want to tell me.' Leah began gathering up her things and stowing them in the bags she'd brought from the annexe. 'Looks like you've left me the choice of the salon's sofabed or Alister's old room in the eaves.'

Michele had the grace to look sheepish. 'Thank you for sleeping near the children and for holding the fort. You've been an utter star and I can never repay you.'

Leah just nodded.

'None of it was on purpose, Leah. I'm sorry you copped the fall-out.'

'But not so sorry that you'll move to another room?' Leah wound up the flex from her phone charger and tucked it in the pocket of a bag.

Politician-like, Michele blithely ignored the question. 'I knew I was doing the wrong thing almost as soon as I left. Bailey was so excited, as if he thought I was going away with him for good. He drove and drove, through France and into Switzerland, up into the mountains. I felt worse and worse, terrible for leaving Natasha and Jordan, sick from the travel and the pregnancy. I couldn't decide whether to tell Bailey to turn around or whether I had to stick it out and find a way through the horrible mess I'd made. In the end, all I could think about was getting Bailey to stop the car while I got out to heave.'

Drawn in despite herself, Leah abandoned her packing and perched on the corner of the bed to listen.

Michele's eye sockets looked sunken and shadowed. 'The sickness just went on and on, and Bailey was so useless. I had to tell him I needed a doctor, tell him to go down to reception and ask for help, tell him what to say on the phone. When I didn't get better he got petulant and impatient, like a kid.'

'He is a kid.'

Michele closed her eyes for several seconds. 'He's a man.'

'Only in age. Emotionally he's a few years behind.'

Michele opened her eyes again with a sad little laugh. 'I'll give you that one. I'd never realised he was so disorganised. He began to run out of money and his credit card was maxed. His boss rang him because he'd only booked a few days off and just hadn't gone back to work. He sulked and wanted me to make him feel better whereas I wanted to talk about the baby, about Natasha and Jordan, about what being a father means. He seemed surprised that Jordan and Natasha were even a consideration. Out of that conversation I suddenly realised we had no future. I don't know who was more stunned – him or me.'

Leah's stomach dropped as if she'd just stepped unexpectedly down a hole. 'So you don't love him after all? That's it? After everything you've put us all through, it was just–'

Michele slapped her hands over her eyes. 'If you say infatuation, I'll scream! I do love him, but not enough to give up Natasha and Jordan, and he loves me, but not everything I am already. He's unreliable, but I love him, he's a weak reed, but I love him, he's immature, but I love him! I just can't have him because having him would be wrong for my children. All three of them.' She sagged back on her pillows, tears trickling from the corners of her eyes.

Seeing that Michele had realised what the right thing was at last, however close she'd come to doing the opposite, Leah stretched out on the bed and opened her arms. 'Oh, Shell,' she murmured as her sister's face crumpled. 'I'm so sorry.' However much of a mess she'd made, however she'd followed her heart rather than her head, Michele was paying a high price for committing the age-old crime of falling in love with the wrong person.

It took a while for the storm to blow itself out but, at last, Michele lay quietly in Leah's arms. 'He's on his way back to England. He says he'll never get over me. I know I'll never get over him.'

'You won't be able to make a clean break because of Baby Three, I suppose.'

'Of course not. He'll want to see his child.' Michele wiped her eyes.

Leah sighed for her poor troubled sister and looked for a more cheering direction for Michele's thoughts. 'Your kids have been fantastic, by the way, considering everything they've had to cope with.' Disregarding every cross word, mutinous moment, terrifying absence and high-five in the face she related the heart-warming episodes, the funny moments, how grown-up the children had been when Alister broke his leg and Natasha had her nasty experience in the lake. It felt almost like updating a colleague whose work she'd covered while they'd been on holiday, handing over the responsibility. And, in this case, putting down the guilt.

But Michele remained resolutely uncheered. 'Do you think they'll forgive me for going?'

'You might have to work on regaining their trust. Show you're prioritising them.' Leah tried to be honest but diplomatic.

'Of course I am!'

Leah smothered the '*Seriously*?' that jumped to her lips along with a pithy observation that Michele taking herself off for a nap almost immediately she returned and leaving the children to search out Leah to fulfil their dessert needs didn't really come under the heading of 'prioritising'. Michele had to work these things out for herself.

Michele sat up. 'Where are they now?'

'Up in the games room with Curtis, I think. Do you want to come clean about Bailey? I'll fetch them down if you do.'

'Not yet,' Michele groaned, clenching her eyes tight shut. 'One agony at a time, Leah. Jordan looks up to him. He's not going to take it well.'

Understatement. 'But if Bailey's to be involved in the life of Baby Three . . .'

Michele heaved a huge sigh. 'I can't deal with it yet.' She peeped at Leah under her lashes. 'I don't suppose you could tell them?'

This time, Leah didn't bother to bite her tongue. '*Seriously*? You actually think that would be OK?'

'I guess not. I have to face them myself. I've just got to screw my courage up first.' Michele fished in her pocket and came up with Leah's phone. 'Anyway, you left this on the table. Scott rang so I answered.' She gave a watery smile. 'He wanted to know if you were off having sex with the hot man next door. Were you? Are you and Ronan embroiled in a holiday romance?'

Leah snatched her phone back. 'He has Curtis and I've had Jordan and Natasha. Teenagers are worse than chastity belts.'

'Sorry.' Michele gave Leah's hand a squeeze. 'But are you?'

'Yes,' Leah admitted crossly.

'Then tomorrow I'll invite Curtis here for the evening. I'll barbecue and do a quiz, with prizes, and you can slip next door and, um, spend a little time with Ronan.'

Irritation fading, Leah's frown flipped rapidly into a smile. 'That sounds too good to be true. You'd really do it?'

'Unless you think Ronan's unwilling?'

Leah felt herself blushing. 'Doubt it.'

'That's a plan, then.' Michele sounded almost eager. 'I owe you a thousand favours. I'll go upstairs now and invite

Curtis. Then we ought to change the bedclothes on this bed.'

'*We*?' But Leah was smiling as she jogged downstairs to dump her stuff in the salon and text Ronan with the good news.

Chapter Sixteen

'So, all proper happy now your mum's back?' Curtis tried not to pant and groan as he heaved himself up on the pull-up bars in the park.

'S'pose.' Jordan fought to raise himself too, waggling his legs as if he could gain a foothold in the air.

Natasha watched, sitting cross-legged and reminding Curtis of a dainty elf amongst the dandelions and daisies. She wrinkled her nose. 'She's all clingy, though. You know, this morning? She was like, "What do you want to hang around a park for?" Leah just let us come if we wanted.'

Jordan dropped to the grass.

Curtis ground out one more chin-up, then did the same, rubbing the sting from his hands. 'Do you think she'll stop us hanging out?' He dropped down beside Natasha.

Natasha looked horrified. 'Why? Has she said that to you, Jordan?'

Jordan shrugged, moodily. 'No. Shut up.'

'Why don't you?' demanded Curtis, too outraged at the hurt in Natasha's eyes to consider whether it was wise to antagonise the older boy. 'Earth to Jordan, some big brothers are nice to their sisters.'

Jordan flushed and turned to Natasha with an elaborate show of patience, as if it was Curtis disrupting a perfectly good conversation. 'Mum's invited Curtis round for this crappy quiz thing tonight, hasn't she?'

Deciding not to push his luck with further hostility Curtis wrinkled his brow. 'Yeah. What's with that? Does she do this stuff because she's a teacher?'

'Not usually.' Jordan snorted. 'But nothing's usual any more.'

Curtis checked out Natasha's expression. Jordan's words had brought new uncertainty to her face. Trusting his movements were hidden in the longish grass, he put a comforting hand close to hers. 'But she's not going to get together with the boyfriend, so that's good, right? You don't have to worry about living with him.'

'There's still the baby though.' Natasha shifted so that her delicate pinky finger rested against Curtis's much bigger hand.

'The shit ache baby,' Jordan agreed. He levered himself forward on his elbows to peer around Curtis. Curtis quickly shifted his hand. Jordan snorted again. 'I have noticed you two, you know! You don't have to freaking pretend. You're both twats. You deserve each other.' But he was grinning now, without the horrible hard look he got when he was giving out shit ache.

Curtis let his fingers overlap Natasha's again. 'Twat yourself.' It wasn't the world's greatest comeback but he felt as if he and Natasha had passed some kind of coolness threshold at which Jordan was the gatekeeper.

Jordan went on to prove he hadn't had a personality transplant, though. 'You look well odd together. Hannah Montana meets Nightwish.'

Curtis felt incredibly flattered at being likened to one of his favourite Goth bands and though Natasha instantly objected, 'Hannah Montana's way more blonde than me,' she looked pleased, too. Then she looked thoughtful. 'Mum won't let me get piercings or Goth gear but I could wear the black lipstick again.'

'You don't have to.' Curtis wasn't sure what impact black lipstick might have on his kissing plans.

A smile stole across her face. 'I've just thought of something better.'

Leah waited until she was alone with Alister in the kitchen before asking him how he was. He looked up from his now familiar post in the armchair with his foot up and his laptop humming. 'Do you mean "How's your leg feeling?" Or "How are you coping with realising that your wife ripped the family apart for an affair that's dead already?"'

'All of the above,' she admitted truthfully, heart going out to him at his grim stoicism in the face of pain of all kinds.

'My leg feels as if an elephant jumped on it. As for the other . . .' He sighed. 'I think the elephant gave me a glancing blow to the nuts. But no amount of feeling sorry for myself will change history so I'm consoling myself with the joys of pre-term admin.'

Alister turned back to his screen with an air of the conversation being over so Leah decided it was kindest to leave him alone. To make the most of not being adult-in-charge at the gîte she took the Porsche out, satisfying her need for speed. The hedges and wildflowers flew past and she wallowed in the hop-skip-jump feeling of knowing she had a great evening ahead. With Ronan. It actually felt like being on holiday.

As a bonus, on her return she discovered that Michele had prepared lunch for all the family, even Alister, and all Leah had to do was eat. Alister didn't make a single snarky comment and it was all quite civilised.

Afterwards, Leah got a bucket and a cloth and was enjoying sluicing the dust from the Porsche and leathering the glowing scarlet paintwork squeaky clean when Ronan's low voice came from behind her. 'Beautiful.'

Leah swung around to find him at the fence, T-shirt and hair dusty. She gave the scarlet paintwork a proud rub. 'She is, isn't she?'

He grinned. 'The car, too.' He brought his hands from behind his back, exhibiting a bottle of Fischer beer in each. 'I'm sick of sanding cabinet doors. Have you worked hard enough to earn a break?'

'Definitely.' Leah abandoned her wash-leather in her rinsing water.

He waited while she ran around the fence then led the way to two mismatched garden chairs in his back garden. 'The kids are all up in Curtis's room.'

Leah took a long gulp of the cold, light beer that cut beautifully through the dust in her throat. 'So we need to behave in case we're observed.'

'I'm getting way too much practice at behaving.' He lifted the hem of his T-shirt to wipe sweat from his forehead, giving her a glimpse of the flesh above the waistband of his jeans.

Leah didn't pretend she wasn't looking. 'But later–'

His smile was slow. '"Later" is very much on my mind.' Then his attention shifted and both voice and gaze turned abruptly to ice. '*What on earth?*'

Puzzled, Leah swung around to see Curtis and Natasha standing beside Ronan's back door.

With matching dyed-black hair.

'Oh, shit,' she gasped. The grins on the faces beneath the stark blackness wavered.

'Quite.' Ronan rose and stalked over to his son. 'I hope you're going to tell me that colour's not permanent.'

Curtis's cheeks bloomed angrily. 'It's dye, isn't it?'

Natasha edged closer to Curtis. 'We like it.' Uncertainty made her sound even younger than her years.

Leah gazed in distaste at Natasha's usually shining mane, dull and lifeless in the grip of nasty cheap dye. 'Did it say permanent on the box?'

'Don't know.' Natasha sniffed. 'We got it from the village shop and the instructions were in French.'

A clatter heralded Alister hopping up to the fence on his crutches, obviously having overheard. 'Na-*tash-a*!' He sounded no happier than Ronan. 'This is completely unacceptable behaviour.'

From another direction, Michele marched up to join the scene, halting sharply. 'Natasha! What on earth were you thinking?'

Michele, Alister and Ronan began simultaneously to point out the hard truths about school and dyed hair. Alister so far forgot himself as to stigmatise Curtis's Goth look as a bad influence on Natasha then apologised stiffly to Ronan for the implied criticism of his parenting. Ronan bit out, 'I understand' in a voice that suggested he didn't.

Leah regarded the two teens at the centre of the storm as they listened, miserably in Natasha's case and defiantly in Curtis's. Thoughtfully, she tilted her head. 'I suppose if we shaved their heads they'd both have an eighth of an inch of naturally coloured hair by the time they went back to school.'

Everybody stopped arguing in favour of looking appalled. Natasha, whose locks hung down to the small of her back, burst into noisy tears.

Leah was unmoved. 'No? Then how about we waste no more time quarrelling and get you to a salon to see if the colour can be stripped out?'

Curtis put up a half-hearted argument for keeping the dye job at least until it was time to return to school but Ronan snapped 'Not an option.'

Against a background of Michele making unhelpful comments about colour stripping turning hair green it was decided Ronan and Leah should take the errant pair into Muntsheim, Ronan because he spoke French and Leah because she couldn't bear to let Natasha go without the support of a family member, Michele having declared that the chemical smell would make her sick.

'Withdrawal of privilege, Natasha,' Alister broke in to say. 'I'm not sure about this quiz night–'

'But that won't be fair on Jordan,' put in Leah, seeing her lovely evening with Ronan going up in a puff of hair dye. 'Come on, let's get going.'

Soon they were embroiled in the tedious process of locating a salon in Muntsheim and negotiating with staff that had to hide smiles as they consulted the appointment book in order to accommodate emergency colour removal. The colourist explained to Ronan that she had a new product that was efficient . . . but expensive, and would take the rest of the day. Ronan's expression progressed from grim to grimmer.

After a couple of hours of mixing gloop in bowls and working it onto hair, a long job in Natasha's case, and covering heads with plastic shower caps, the hair turned shocking orange. Natasha began to cry again, which brought the colourist and a shampoo boy fluttering around her with tissues and a glass of iced tea.

Turning as always to food to improve the situation Leah went out to fetch pastries. Her return route through the plate glass door brought her up behind Curtis and Natasha. With a jolt, she realised that their fingers were linked and Natasha was sending Curtis a watery smile full of trust and adoration.

Returning to her place beside Ronan in the waiting area, Leah whispered an explanation of what she'd just seen under cover of passing him *pain au chocolat*. 'Are they having a thing?'

'Oh, save us,' Ronan groaned wearily. 'He's definitely at the age to discover girls but I really don't think he should dye them to match his clothes.'

Leah had to turn her snort of laughter into a cough when two pairs of teenaged eyes swivelled to regard her through the mirror.

Much washing, protecting and drying later, teen hair had turned pale amber.

'Cool.' Curtis regarded his reflection with satisfaction.

But Natasha looked aghast. 'I look like an orangutan!'

The colourist returned with a request, routed through Ronan. He turned to Curtis and Natasha. 'Please find recent photos of yourselves on your phones so this lady can assess your natural look. Then she'll match the colour as closely as she can.'

Natasha looked visibly relieved but Curtis hadn't finished being awkward. 'I'll keep this, thanks.'

'Curtis.' Ronan employed his low scary voice and Curtis, snorting like a bull about to lose its rag, snatched his phone out of one of his many pockets.

Soon the colourist began again with fresh gloop. The shampoo boy brought Leah and Ronan coffee.

Ronan checked his watch. 'We'll be lucky to be out of here before midnight.'

Trying to get him to lighten up, Leah whispered, 'Shame. I was looking forward to finding out if you'd use that impressive growl this evening.'

'If you like it, you can be damned sure I'll use it,' he murmured. 'That's if we're ever alone long enough in the eleven days we have left together.'

Leah spluttered with laughter but she didn't know whether to be more startled that the days left in France were disappearing so quickly or that Ronan had counted them. She looked at the salon clock. It was already nearly four. Another day was passing fast.

It was nearer six when they were finally ready to leave, Curtis and Natasha sporting approximations of their natural hair colours, though their tresses were decidedly lacklustre and stiff despite copious conditioning treatments. Ronan and Leah trailed in their wake, stunned at the mammoth damage done to their credit cards.

'Michele and Alistair can reimburse me for that little lot,' she muttered to Ronan. 'Above and beyond the role of Deputy Parent.'

Getting ready that evening, Leah found she was nervous. She smoothed down her dress with slightly damp palms. She'd chosen a simple summer dress – her vampy dresses and killer heels were all in the UK anyway – but put on her make-up because there was 'simple' and then there was 'not trying'. Her hair lay in a newly washed, shining river down her back.

A perfunctory knock on the salon door and Natasha burst in and threw herself on the bed. 'Can we be girls against boys in this quiz?' She'd brushed her hair back into a tight bun, probably operating an 'out of sight, out of mind' policy until her parents calmed down a bit over Dyegate.

Leah gave her a hug. 'I'm not involved, sweetie. This is something your mum wants to do for you kids.'

'Aw! She won't mind if you come!'

Leah managed not to sigh. Having a teenager monitoring you was inhibiting. 'I'm good, thanks.'

'Are you going to hang with Dad? Or go for a drive?'

In the face of Natasha's searchlight gaze Leah gave up trying to keep her plans on the down-low. 'I said I'd eat with Ronan.' She tried to make it sound as if *of course* she'd be in on quiz night if it weren't for Ronan being desperate for a dining companion.

Natasha obviously wasn't fooled. Her eyes danced. 'He *likes* you, doesn't he? Do you like him? Is it going to be a candlelight dinner? Soppy music and champagne?'

Laughing, Leah hushed her. 'More like salad with a couple of glasses of plonk and whatever he has on his iPod. He's invited me over because the rest of you have your own plans.'

'I know, right, but he hasn't invited Dad.'

Leah improvised quickly. 'Your dad's busy with school admin on his laptop.'

Natasha laid her head on Leah's shoulder and sighed. 'Do Ronan and Curtis live very far away from us in England?'

Perceiving a change of mood, Leah stroked Natasha's poor tortured hair, stiff and coarse instead of soft and silky. 'They live east of London so it's a couple of hours by car to Bettsbrough.'

'Your car's very fast so it's probably less. We could all keep seeing each other.'

Although Leah had allowed herself the occasional stray thought along those lines, she began, 'I don't know, sweetie–'

Then a voice sounded in the kitchen and Natasha whisked free, face suddenly glowing. 'Here's Curtis.'

In ten minutes Michele had herded the kids off up to the games room, taking much of the contents of the fridge with them, judging by her dry commentary. A fizzing combination of indulgence, liberation and anticipation building, Leah gave them a few minutes to settle and then slipped out of the gîte and through the dewy evening fragrances of grass and roses to Chez Shea.

The front door stood ajar. Knocking, she stepped tentatively in. 'Ronan?'

'What took you so long?' Ronan strode into the hallway and swept her up on her tiptoes against the wall, body warm and hard, lips soft but purposeful as he swung the door shut behind her. Letting her bag drop to the floor she wound her arms around his neck and kissed him back, the heat of him settling low in her belly.

'Mm,' she managed, after several blissfully uninterrupted minutes of kissing, their stroking hands roving as if to commit each other to memory, 'smells to me like something's burning.'

'Crap!' One last hard kiss and he bolted for the kitchen, leaving her to get herself together and follow, butterfly-fluttery, sloughing off the memory of all Scott's teasing remarks that this would inevitably go wrong. It felt so right.

In the kitchen, Ronan ruefully regarded a grill pan of blackened lumps. 'You didn't want garlic bread, did you?'

'Never touch it,' she declared, untruthfully.

'I should have done salad.' He thrust the smoking pan

outside on the paving and closed the back door on the remains. 'I was trying to resist feeling intimidated by feeding a chef. Sit down and pour the wine and I'll check whether the pasta's edible.'

The pasta proved to be entirely edible, a safe but competent carbonara that went down as easily as the contents of a bottle of crémant. By the end of the meal their legs were entwined beneath the table and Leah was feeling as if her skin hosted microscopic fireworks that went off even at Ronan's most casual touch.

'I'm kind of waiting for an interruption,' Ronan admitted, glancing up the hallway, 'for your phone to go off with your next family emergency or for three teenagers to show up with their hair dyed green.'

Leaning in to leave kisses at each corner of his mouth, enjoying his freshly shaved skin against her lips, Leah grinned. 'My phone's on silent and Michele promised to provide such good prizes that the kids will be glued to the quiz until at least ten.'

'There are no such prizes.'

'There are. They're called euros.'

His eyes crinkled. 'Then maybe I have faith in her plan.' He lifted her hand and kissed her fingers, the warmth of his mouth putting a spike in her pulse rate, checked his watch and gathered up their glasses. 'I don't do my best seduction in a kitchen.'

'It's definitely your best seduction I'm looking for.' Leah laughed huskily, floating on a cushion of happy anticipation as they made their way up the hall.

His room was at the top of the stairs, its windows open to let the sultry evening breeze filter over his elderly wooden furniture. Curious to see his personal space Leah looked around at the laptop and pot of pens that suggested the dressing table doubled as a desk, the mirrors on the old-fashioned armoire cloudy with age and the king-sized bed that dominated the space.

Although the window looked out only onto the twilight shadows of the garden and woods beyond, Ronan closed the shutters and lit a lamp before he turned to her. The lamplight sharpened his features with shadows. 'Let's take this slowly.'

Her senses absurdly heightened, she felt as if his body heat touched hers before his skin actually made contact.

He touched her gently, tracing her cheekbones, the sides of her neck, the dips above her collarbones. His gaze roved from her face to her body, watching as his hands slid down over skin, over fabric, to her breasts.

Her breath fluttering, she lifted her arms to pull him closer, needing to feel his body against hers. 'I wasn't born to be patient.' His laugh was low as she pressed against his arousal, bunching up the fabric of his shirt, glad that even if France had brought her a lot of hassle and scary moments it had brought her this man to remind her that there was more to life than cars and chocolate. The fire burning in her was better than cars *or* chocolate, in fact. This man was on the same page as her mentally, physically and emotionally. Like her, he didn't expect 'forever' but intended to savour every moment of 'now'.

He didn't try to take over as she began to unbutton his shirt, only removing his hands from her body long enough to help her slide the fabric down his arms. He wasn't wearing his shoulder brace and the fresh pink scar of his recent operation interrupted the smooth line of his collar-bone. Leah pressed her softest kiss on the puckered flesh before skimming her hands over the tight planes of his chest, savouring the texture of his skin, her fingertips finding and following the trail of hair down towards the waistband of his jeans.

'You're getting behind here.' Gently, he turned her to face the mirrors, his front against her back, his erection pushing against the curve of her behind through his jeans. 'Look how beautiful you are.'

Then he watched his reflection undress her.

Leah almost stopped breathing at the intensity in his expression. The slow unzipping of her dress was like liquid excitement down her back. His fingers brushed the sensitive skin he'd exposed, touching, stroking, and following the contours of her spine to caress the tingling nape of her neck then back down between her shoulder blades.

Leah's heart skipped a beat as, with the smallest of movements, he flipped the catch on her bra.

Gently he gathered both bra and dress together and nudged them off her shoulders. Down her arms. In the mirror his eyes looked nearly black, fixed on the slow falling forward of the summer-blue lace of her bra, the slither of the dress over the curves of her belly and hips. Then, the fabric pooled at her feet, she was naked but for a skimpy thong, her skin tingling in the air.

'Jeez, you're something.' He smiled at her in the mirror as he caressed her, fingertips trailing up to her breasts and setting her on fire.

Leah, feeling as if she were bursting out of her skin at the feel of his hot mouth on the back of her neck, was mesmerised by the sight of his tanned hands on her white body. Hands that cupped and stroked then travelled down over her stomach to hook into the tiny scrap of lace that was all that was left to cover her.

When she was naked, she turned in his arms and began again on him, unbuttoning, unzipping, easing him out.

Catching random glimpses of their reflection as skin moved over skin, heartbeats quickening, Ronan touching her almost everywhere and kissing her everywhere else, twining his hands in her hair, groaning as he explored her until she could hardly think, could only react to his hands and mouth.

'I know we've got to work around your shoulder but I'm not sure my legs will hold me upright much longer,' she gasped, riding a wave of pleasure against his hand.

'We've already trialled a good alternative,' he murmured. Drawing her with him he seated himself on the edge of the bed and grabbed a condom from the bedside.

Slowly she sank down on him, gasping at the wave of sensation, trying to watch the desire and excitement in his face but seduced into closing her eyes to concentrate on his movements beneath her, inside her, against her, on and on. And on. Tipping her head back, she let the bliss swamp her, gasping, 'Oops, sorry!' when she realised from his strangled gasp that she was clinging onto his damaged shoulder.

He gasped a laugh. 'Worth it. Leah you are – this is –'

'So *gooooood*,' she finished for him.

'Amazing. Fantastic–' Then he stepped up a gear and it all became about urgency, about deeper, harder, faster, until the joy took them completely over the edge.

It took a while for Leah to come down to earth, breathing like a train and hooked over Ronan, boneless.

'Sorry, but shoulder,' he groaned, and they somehow managed to ease down onto the bed so that Ronan could lie on his right side. He held her close, hands cupped comfortably around her behind. 'That,' he murmured, kissing her temple, 'was off the scale. And your sister did her stuff. We didn't have a single interruption.'

Leah had just begun to say, 'Don't jinx us!' when the

sound of the front door opening and closing floated clearly up the stairs. But the voice that floated up after it didn't belong to Curtis, Jordan or Natasha.

'Hello-oh, Curtis? Ronan?' It was unmistakeably a woman's voice.

Ronan froze.

'Who is it?' Spell well and truly broken, Leah eased away, a chill on her skin that wasn't wholly accounted for by the open windows.

'It can't be.' Ronan sounded stunned.

'Are you here, guys?' the voice called louder.

Leah rolled free and scrambled up to stare down into his stupefied face. 'Who *is it*?'

His eyes were glazed with astonishment. 'Selina!'

'Your *wife*?'

'*Ex*-wife.' He reached, fumbling, for his jeans and shirt. It was the only time Leah had seen him looking seriously rattled.

Chapter Seventeen

Ronan stormed to the head of the stairs as if in a bad dream. 'Selina? What are you doing here?' It wasn't a warm welcome but when you'd been divorced for three years you didn't expect your ex-wife to march into your holiday home unannounced. It was particularly unsettling when you were making love to another woman, one you'd pretty much been exploding with desire for.

Selina appeared at the foot of the stairs. Her face was pale and exhausted but there was relief there, too. 'I was beginning to think there was no one here. Where's Curtis?'

'Hanging out with the kids next door.' Ronan jumped down the stairs two at a time. He stopped short as his bare feet hit the tiles of the hallway and he spied two big bags at Selina's feet. 'What's going on?'

'I'm sorry.' Selina's eyes filled with the easy tears he remembered too well.

Then the front door flew open behind her and Curtis barrelled in. 'I've just had a text from Mum to say she's in a taxi – oh, you're here! Hey, Mum.'

Selina threw her arms around him, having to stand on

tiptoe to place a smacking kiss on his cheek. 'Hello, sweetie! Mwah! Bet you didn't expect to see me.' She pulled back to regard him quizzically. 'What's happened to your hair?'

'Never mind that now,' Ronan snapped. Then, mindful of Leah stranded upstairs, changed tack. 'I'll make coffee.'

'But his hair looks funny.' Selina smoothed down her own salon-blonde tresses as she let herself be ushered into the kitchen.

Ronan grabbed the kettle and turned on the tap as if wringing something's neck. His heart was a trip hammer as he tried to absorb the abrupt change from having a soft, vibrant, naked Leah in his arms to having his ex-wife pop up in Chez Shea like a pantomime demon. 'What on earth are you doing in Kirchhoffen?'

Selina pulled out a chair and dropped into it, her eyes huge and tragic. 'Me and Darren have lost our house.'

Ronan set the kettle down with suddenly numb fingers. The dismay that slithered coldly through him made him entirely omit to comfort or commiserate. 'The house you put your share of *our* house into?'

Miserably, Selina nodded.

Curtis, who obviously wasn't getting the import of his mother's words, glanced up and grinned in the direction of the hallway. 'Hey, Leah!'

Ronan heard a swallowed cluck of exasperation. Then Leah's voice, tight with strain. 'Hey, Curtis.' Her desire to get away almost vibrated to Ronan through the air.

Curtis, oblivious to such nuances, swung the door further open invitingly. 'My mum's here, look.'

Reluctance in every line, Leah stepped into the room, clutching the bag that Ronan vaguely remembered her dropping to the floor at the beginning of the evening when the perfect hours had stretched out before them like a dream come true. 'Hello.' Her smile looked about as natural as Curtis's hair.

'Gosh, hello.' Selina glanced at Ronan. 'I didn't mean to–'

'You didn't. I'll leave you guys in peace.' With another plastic smile and not even looking at Ronan, Leah turned and hurried out. Ronan listened helplessly to the sound of the front door swiftly opening and firmly closing. Considering his audience, he couldn't think of a single thing to say to stop her. But he knew with an almost suffocating dose of reality that leaving was the last thing he wanted her to do. It felt as if they'd been lovers for months; tonight they'd simply known each other – and, watching her leave, he realised that the electric connection wasn't something he'd want to end on the last day of August.

Selina looked apologetic. 'I really didn't mean to . . .'

'Of course not.' Anger fading to hollow disappointment Ronan made the coffee mechanically. The urgency had gone out of demanding answers from Selina. The shutters over Leah's gaze had told him what damage had been done.

He listened as Selina and Curtis did their catching up: the holiday, Curtis's hair, the weather. Curtis gave a jumble of information about the family next door: parents, kids, aunts, accidents and break-ups. 'Can I go back for a bit? I've won twenty-three euros. Michele says we're finishing at ten.'

'Fine,' Ronan said, before Selina could block it.

Curtis leaped up, then halted, his gaze falling on his mother. 'But are you staying? Or . . . ?' He looked uncertainly between his parents, probably beginning to grasp the out-of-the-blue and unprecedented character of his mother's visit.

Ronan forced a reassuring smile. 'I doubt your mum's going anywhere tonight.'

'Cool beans.' Curtis beamed and loped from the house in Leah's tracks.

In the silence he left behind, Ronan studied the woman he used to call his wife. It was odd to see her dressed down in jeans and flat shoes. Her usual look was more about heels and bling. 'Tell me what's going on.'

Ready tears began to ooze from her eyes. 'I'm sorry. I didn't know where else to go. You know how ill Dad is since his stroke; it's not fair to put on Mum when she has him to care for. I had a bit of cash so I took the Eurostar to Paris then the train to Strasbourg, the tram, then a taxi from Muntsheim.'

Mentally, Ronan translated. *There's nowhere else I wanted to go. At my parents' I'd be expected to help with Dad's care. I've stayed out of contact so you couldn't stop me coming; likewise the taxi instead of phoning for a lift.*

'What happened with your house?'

She gulped back more tears. 'Darren's business got in trouble and his loan was secured on it.'

Ronan's heart felt like a rock. Nothing would be served by reminding her that what she'd lost was the lion's share of the house he'd once called his. When you married someone, you shared your worldly goods. When you divorced, the law didn't allow you to take those worldly goods back. He forced himself to focus on the present situation. 'Where is Darren?'

She blew her nose. 'He did a moonlight and left me to sort it all out. I tried to tell the building society that it was all Darren's mess but they didn't care. They were all "penalty payments" and "arrears charges" and "the mortgage payments are still your responsibility". So I handed the keys back.'

He rubbed his shoulder, which was pounding now. If

he'd still been upstairs with Leah he wouldn't have felt it half so much. 'You must have co-signed the second mortgage on the house.' He had a lot more questions as to whether voluntary repossession had been the best option and whether there'd be anything left for Selina after the house sale but it would be cruel to fire them at her now. She needed time to regroup and, perfectly obviously, he couldn't turn her away. There was nowhere for her to go.

At least she seemed sincere when she burst out, 'Ronan, I'm sorry! You must hate me for landing myself on you and interrupting . . . whatever I interrupted. But I'm desperate.'

'I understand.' No doubt he'd have to add helping Selina sort out her mess to his other worries. 'Take your stuff up to the spare room. Get some rest. We'll talk tomorrow.'

'That's fantastic of you! But where are you going?' She looked alarmed as he started towards the door.

'To talk to Leah.'

Ignoring her expression of surprise tinged with resentment, Ronan was soon clambering over the fence, ignoring fresh protest from his shoulder at the way he was treating it this evening. Eschewing good manners, he let himself in through the gîte's kitchen door. Knocking or telephoning first seemed to be asking to be politely barred.

He half-expected to find Leah in the kitchen, baking something comforting. But there was only Alister, tapping at a laptop, pausing, his fingers in the air above his keyboard, as Ronan strolled through with an unceremonious 'Evening'.

Ronan halted only when he reached the door to the salon, which he knew to be Leah's present abode. He knocked. 'It's me.'

Silence.

After a moment he turned the handle, intending to discover whether she was refusing to answer or there was no one in the room.

Leah lay on her bed, phone to ear, hair fanned across her pillow.

She glared balefully at him. 'Looks like I'll have to ring you back,' she said to whoever was on the other end of the call. 'Yes, he is. Yes, I'm sure. And I don't need you being smug about having called it right, OK?'

He watched her press the red *end call* button. 'I've come to explain.'

'You don't need to.' She didn't bother to sit up, just lay as if exhausted by events.

'We *are* divorced.'

'I know.'

'I had no idea that she was about to turn up but it seems she has nowhere else to go.'

'I heard.'

'I can't throw her out.' He was conscious of repeating the same point in different words but Leah was so oddly unemotional that he wasn't sure she was getting it. He wanted to join her on the bed and cradle her against him but hesitated at the remoteness of her thousand-yard stare.

'She's Curtis's mother,' she finished for him. Slowly, she rolled to her feet, but it seemed as if that was only so that she could keep the bed between them.

He tried a different tack. 'She'll leave again.' He hoped, when he'd worked out the best way to effect that.

'Where will she go?' Her golden eyes were sombre. 'I heard her say she's lost her house. If she's come all the way to Alsace, after you've been divorced for so long, she's in trouble.' She edged back another step. 'Your wife might be ever so ex, but she's Curtis's mum and in your house. That's not a situation I'm remotely interested in messing with.'

'But–' Ronan scoured his mind for some persuasive argument, something that would counter her implacable, unanswerable logic.

She waited.

Then, very softly, she said, 'I think you need to go home, Ronan.'

After he'd gone, Leah fell back on her bed and screwed her eyes shut against visions of Selina's unhappiness; Curtis's beaming pleasure at being able to introduce his mum; Ronan's astonished hurt as, after holding Leah's gaze for what had felt like a year, he'd turned and silently left her room.

In her hand, her phone began to ring. 'Sorry,' she said, putting it to her ear. She knew it would be Scott, too impatient to wait until she re-established the conversation.

'What the hell did he want?' he demanded, wrathfully.

'Came to apologise.' She shut her eyes. 'But it's all moot. I don't want to be involved.'

'Right.' Scott hesitated. 'Are you OK?'

'Yeah.' Drearily.

'No, you're not. How fucking craptastic. Had you actually *just*–?'

Fresh misery welled at the all too vivid memory of her clothes sliding off her body and Ronan sliding into it.

'Yeah.' She tried to wish they hadn't. But failed.

Sprawled on the games-room sofa, Natasha frowned. 'Your mum's here? Why?'

Curtis thought she looked cute when she was confused. 'She says she's lost her house.'

'*Lost her house?*' Michele looked so astonished that white showed all the way around her brown eyes.

Natasha's eyes did the exact same thing. 'Like, she can't find her way home?'

Curtis paused, suddenly uncertain. Till now, he'd processed events of the evening sketchily. 1) Mum texted to say she was in Kirchhoffen; 2) she was!; 3) he was surprised, but glad; 4) his dad got that waiting air of wanting to speak to his mum without Curtis listening; so 5) he'd returned to the gîte.

Michele explained in his stead, voice hushed and sympathetic. 'It usually means the person can't afford to keep the house.'

'Oh,' Curtis, Natasha and Jordan said together.

Curtis grappled with the concept. 'So what happens to it?'

'The bank or building society sells the house to pay back any money owing on the mortgage.'

He grappled harder. 'So, like, my mum's *homeless*?'

Natasha's eyes grew rounder than ever. 'Doesn't that mean you are too?'

'Of course not.' But shock rippled through him. 'I live part of the time with my dad, anyway . . .' It literally hadn't occurred to him that his mother losing her house meant *she didn't have a home any more*. And her home was his main home. The reality washed through him. Dimly, he recognised the feeling as that of being scared.

Jordan chimed in. Even he was wearing an odd expression, as if comprehending things that Curtis wasn't. 'Will your mum live with your dad? Where's her boyfriend? At your dad's house, too?'

'Don't be stupid.' Because surely someone would have mentioned if Darren was moving into Chez Shea, too? And surely it would be totally weird? Curtis gave up trying to compute complicated thoughts about husbands, wives and boyfriends and snatched up the euros he'd won. 'Thanks for having me round,' he mumbled.

Michele gave a bright smile. 'Try not to worry.'

There was nothing like adults telling you not to worry to make your stomach gurgle. Curtis hurried out into the garden, clambered over the fence and burst through his back door. He found his mum making a sandwich in the kitchen, jumping guiltily as he burst in. 'Are you homeless?' he demanded.

'Oh, darling, don't worry about that.' Carefully, his mum cut her sandwich into four triangles. She lowered her voice. 'Dad's in his room. He hasn't asked if I want anything and I'm starving, so I've helped myself. Do you think he'll mind?'

'But are you?'

His mum sank slowly into a chair, her eyes shining as if she was about to cry. 'I suppose I am.' She began to explain something boring about Darren's business.

'But where's my stuff? Our stuff?' he interrupted.

'In storage. One of Darren's mates came with a van and took our personal things to his lockup. I got a house-clearance firm to come and give me a price for the furniture, so I'd have some cash.'

'What about Darren?'

She shook her head and dragged out a bit of tissue to blow her nose.

Curtis sat down right in front of her so she couldn't not look at him. 'So you've come to live back with Dad?'

His mum pulled the sandwich towards her again and toyed with it. 'We'll have to see. I mean, yes, for now. But Dad . . .' She gave a tremulous smile. 'Presumably that was his girlfriend who was here? Leah?'

'Oh, she's just staying next door on holiday.' Curtis

found himself dismissing any link between his dad and Leah, no matter how much he, Natasha and Jordan had agreed they liked one another. After all, he'd never so much as seen them kiss or hold hands. 'What about me?' He tried to laugh. 'Am I half-homeless?'

She stroked his hair out of his eyes – which really got on his nerves, actually, as he grew it that way on purpose. 'Your dad wouldn't let that happen!'

'He wouldn't let anything happen to you, either.' As he said it, Curtis realised it was true. The only time his dad had failed him was in unaccountably letting his mum get together with Darren.

But now she was back Curtis realised how much he wanted her to stay back. He even put his arms around her, and repeated, 'He wouldn't let anything happen to you, either.' It gave him a feeling of solidity and warmth, of fear receding from his world.

Chapter Eighteen

Leah woke feeling as if a lump of lead had formed in her tummy, reminding her that something bad had happened.

It took only a second for yesterday's debacle to come crashing back. Ronan had turned from hot heaven to hard heartache. Selina was here: pretty, blonde, in trouble, and Curtis's mum.

On a masochistic impulse she checked her phone. *3 messages.*

> ***Scott:*** *Chin up. You'll be home before you know it. x*

She replied:

> ***Leah:*** *I know. Sorry for the long whiney conversation last night! And thanks for not saying I told you so. Even if you did tell me so. x*

The second message was more surprising:

__Bailey:__ Is Michele OK? Shes not answering texts. Shes not being sick again is she?

She left that unanswered until she could talk to Michele, and turned to the message she'd deliberately left till last:

__Ronan:__ Now the dust has settled on the bombsite that yesterday evening became, can we talk? xx

She stared at his words. She showered and dried her hair and read the text again before she allowed herself to reply.

__Leah:__ I'm sure we'll bump into each other before I leave but I don't think there's any point in more.

Then she went in search of Michele, locating her sipping fizzy water and nibbling dry crackers in the kitchen. Leah showed her Bailey's text. Michele sighed, propping her pale cheek sadly on her fist. 'I told him I didn't want to get involved in long heartbroken messages. It only prolongs the agony.' Her voice was thready with tears.

Out of the blue, Leah found herself experiencing empathy with Bailey's sore heart. 'But shouldn't one of us text him to say you're OK?'

'I will.' Michele gulped. Then she turned a sympathetic eye on Leah. 'But what about you? Last night . . . well, Curtis said his mother arrived. That was a shock, I take it?'

'Yup.' Leah swallowed a lump in her throat. 'I don't know the full story because I didn't hang around. I want to steer clear of Ronan today but I don't know how best to do it. If I take the kids out it will leave you with Alister; if I take you and the kids it will leave Alister on his own. I suppose we could all go out together if you can put up with each other but Alister has to wait in for the nurse to arrive and give him his injection.'

Michele pulled Leah into a tight, squeezy, sisterly hug, the kind that made you hug back really hard. 'Or you could take yourself off for the day and leave us all to fend for ourselves. You've certainly earned it.'

With a gush of relief Leah realised that to be alone, to brood miserably and come to terms with the hollow horribleness of what had happened was exactly what she wanted. To get completely and utterly away from other people and the responsibilities, undercurrents, hopes and disappointments that had invaded her life this summer. 'Wouldn't you mind? I love you sometimes, Shell.'

Laughing ruefully, Michele gave her a final squeeze. 'You love me all the time, which is why I was able to put on you so disgracefully. Go on, jump in your pose-mobile and clear off.'

Leah was already reaching for her bag.

In other circumstances, she would have adored her day, beginning with a long drive through villages dotted along country lanes like beads on a necklace, stopping to breakfast on two croissants and two cups of espresso at a pretty pavement café with green wooden tables and an extravagant number of flower tubs.

Breakfast over, she drove on, following the Porsche's long nose through towns, villages and countryside, crossing the Canal de la Bruche via a stone bridge. But for once the throaty hum of the engine and the power beneath her right foot failed to soothe her so she circled back to Muntsheim with the intention of catching a sleek silver tram into Strasbourg in time for lunch. She'd do something touristy like walk by the river or take a boat ride to gaze at the picturesque buildings decked with window boxes bubbling with blooms. She could even go up inside the cathedral.

Shying away from the memory of that being Ronan's suggestion she found herself parking the car and, changing her mind about Strasbourg, mooching through La Place de la Liberté, thinking vaguely that she'd never had the leisure to properly explore the town centre. She strolled past the fountains towards a row of arches with shops beneath. There, tucked away in a corner, she discovered an English-language bookshop café, Le Café Littéraire Anglais, its window display bright with guidebooks and holiday reading. Assailed by sudden homesickness, she pushed the door and went in. A very British snack menu was chalked on a board with ploughman's lunch as the day's special. 'Pork pie,' she breathed, suddenly longing for something so totally and unmistakeably British.

A cheerful girl with 'Kat' embroidered on her black apron paused in delivering two fat white teapots to a crowded corner table to nudge out a chair invitingly. 'Pork pie, Branston pickle and extra mature cheddar with Jacob's cream crackers, if you want.'

'Sold.' Leah's spirits lifted a few degrees as she dropped down at a table, its placemats depicting English countryside scenes of hay carts and shire horses.

Kat returned. Her dark curls, caught up by a black bandana, trembled like springs atop her head.

Leah didn't have to browse the menu. 'Ploughman's and a big pot of builders' tea, please.'

The meal was bliss. The cheddar cheese nestled against fat shiny pickled onions as well as the promised Branston and the precisely perfect amount of jelly joined the meat to the pastry in the pork pie. She was wiping up the last crumbs from the Jacob's cream crackers when Kat brought her a fresh pot of tea. 'You're a new face. Are you an expat? Or just visiting?'

Leah responded easily to the open, friendly smile. 'I've been holidaying with my sister's family in Kirchhoffen but we leave on the twenty-ninth.'

Kat's face fell. 'Shame. It would be nice to know someone my own age here. I love it,' she added, hastily, 'and Graeme and Katherine, the owners, have a lovely lot of friends. Just . . .' With a sly look at the occupants of the corner table she mimed bending over a walking stick and clutching her back.

A howl of outrage went up from the group. 'We are not old! We're like the cheese – mature!'

'Or crumbly,' Kat teased them.

Though Leah joined in the laughter, English voices exchanging English banter only intensified her feeling of homesickness.

She lazed away the afternoon wandering around what Muntsheim had to offer – churches, a park hosting an open-air concert, half-timbered buildings and a food market.

Leah was soaking up the sun over coffee at another pavement café, reading a paperback purchased from Le Café Littéraire Anglais, when the real world intruded in the shape of a text.

Michele: *Do you know when you'll be back? There's a big surprise waiting for you.*

***Leah:** Nice surprise or horrible?*
***Michele:** Nice!!! Come back, I'll make crepes for dinner.*

Although she suspected that Michele's real motive was to get Leah to make the crepes, she was intrigued enough to drink up her coffee and close her book. Less than an hour later she drove up the hill to the gîte and hopped out of her car, aiming to hurry safely indoors without looking over to Chez Shea.

Before she'd taken more than a few strides, her 'surprise' came lounging around the corner of the gîte. It had spiky mouse-brown hair and a wide grin.

She halted in her tracks. '*Scott!*'

Laughing, he threw his arms wide and in a second Leah had dived into them, fighting an absurd urge to cry at the sight of his dear, comforting, lop-sided smile. 'It's great to see you! But what are you doing here? When did you arrive?'

He hugged her nearly breathless. 'This afternoon. I've come to hang out for a few days then share the driving home.'

'Oh, Scott! Seriously? You're such a million-watt star. And I'm just so glad you're here.' To her horror, she found her throat closing, the disappointment of the previous evening surging up in a hot well of tears.

'Hey,' he chided gently, stroking her back. 'You didn't think I'd let you leave the Porsche here and make a double trip, did you? No, I'm going to make you drive The Pig while I drive your Porsche.'

Leah swallowed her tears and laughed ruefully. 'You are one of the few people I'd make that deal with.'

Then the door of Chez Shea thumped open and Ronan shot out.

He stopped short when he saw Leah in Scott's arms.

'Oh. I was going to . . .' For several heart-thuds his eyes clashed with Leah's.

Swiftly Scott set Leah free and approached the fence, offering his hand. 'Scott Matthewson.'

'Ronan Shea.'

Though he shook Scott's hand, Ronan looked stiff and pained, making Leah wonder if his shoulder was hurting. Shocked that she'd begun to observe him so minutely she watched the two men sizing each other up, conscious of having feelings for them both.

But such different feelings.

She swallowed any unsteadiness in her voice. 'Right. Well. Apparently Michele's cooking so–'

Ronan returned his dark gaze to her. 'Do you have a minute first? Please.'

'You heard what she said, man.' Scott hooked his thumbs in his pockets. 'It's dinnertime. Maybe your other half's cooked for you?'

'I don't have an "other half". Just an ex-wife. Not that it's any of your business.' Ronan's voice was low and inflexible, the way he spoke to Curtis when he didn't expect to be messed with.

Leah hesitated, wanting to keep a safe distance but no less drawn to Ronan than she'd ever been. Maybe, in order to be able to keep that distance, she had to give in one more time to her compulsion. She looked into Scott's dear, pugnacious face. 'Do you mind giving us a little space?'

Scott looked as if he did mind but he shrugged and vanished back around the house.

Ronan waited until he was out of earshot. 'Take a walk with me?'

'I suppose so.' Silently, sadness skulking between them like a third person, they walked without talking up the lane and away from the village, birdsong from the hedges adding an incongruously cheery note, until they reached a stile leading onto a footpath.

Leah propped herself against the wooden rail and Ronan positioned himself squarely in front of her, gaze level, stance open as if trying to reassure her that he had nothing to hide. 'I had no idea that Selina was on her way. It was as much a shock to me–'

'I know.' She smiled to take the sting out of cutting him off, attempting to project a calm it was hard to feel. 'I don't suspect you of lying or cheating. I'm just not going to get involved in your family.' She injected into her voice all the finality she could muster.

'But nothing's really changed.'

'Your wife's in your house.'

For an instant his lips tightened but he corrected her with calm deliberation. '*Ex*-wife.'

Leah closed her eyes, reading the hurt in his. Hating it. Wanting him. 'But she's here and it's made everything way too heavy for something that was only ever just for the holidays.'

Then his body heat was touching hers and she popped open her eyes to find him right in close. 'But the thought of calling it quits is chewing me up.' His breath brushed her cheek like a caress. 'We live only a couple of hours apart. That barely counts as a long-distance relationship. It's half an hour in a helicopter!'

Mute with shock, Leah stared at him, at his rueful expression. 'Are you completely going back on everything we've talked about? You don't do long-term relationships.'

'I haven't for a while,' he acknowledged. 'And the reason for that is currently an uninvited guest at Chez Shea. Your friend Scott just called Selina my "other half" but she was never the other half of me. We shared a home and we share a child but it went no deeper. Make me understand why you won't give me time to deal with Selina's situation and give us a chance.'

Closing her mind to the exhilarating vision of him whizzing through the skies to be with her, to the temptation of giving herself a chance to see whether he was going to prove the exception to her rule, Leah knew exactly how to make him understand. It meant trusting him with her secret but maybe he deserved that. 'It's because of what happened with Tommy,' she blurted, before she could change her mind.

'Tommy lied about being divorced. I didn't.'

'I know. But I didn't tell you the whole Tommy story. It's . . . unsavoury.'

Surprise flashed in his eyes.

She took a long breath. 'When Tommy's wife turned up . . . well, I might not have known about her but she knew *all* about me.' Leah paused, seeing in her mind's eye the woman whose name she'd never known, salon-blonde, gym-toned, sly triumph all over her perfectly made-up face. 'She thought it was funny that I hadn't caught on. That she had to explain that they were one of those couples who get their jollies by going off on sexual adventures and then sharing the juicy details with each other. Tommy even had a blog called "The Sexpeditions of a Salesman" and everything we'd done was recorded there, in lurid detail. The only saving grace was that he'd referred to me as Lily instead of Leah.'

Silently, Ronan took her hand.

She laughed without humour. 'She described me as a naïve little mouse being played with by two sophisticated, libido-driven, manipulative cats. That she, the strong queen cat, was the one who decided when they were going to move on to fresh prey and Tommy would now simply look around for something else to stalk. The name Tommy was a joking reference to being a tomcat and I hadn't been given his real name.'

Ronan had become totally, unnervingly, still.

She swallowed, miserably. 'I went round in a daze for weeks. Then I realised I might be pregnant. Maybe I panicked or perhaps I was immature enough to use the possible pregnancy as an excuse to try and contact Tommy. After all, *he* hadn't told me we were over. The woman had. What if it was all lies, what if she wasn't even his wife . . .? I might have paid for pigs to take flying lessons if it would've provided an explanation other than Tommy being a lying, cheating creep. So I emailed to tell him that there was a chance he was to be a father.' Her stomach twisted at the memory of the old humiliation. 'When the email bounced, I texted, and left voicemail on his phone. Nothing. Then my period arrived so I stopped clinging to pathetic hope and faced the fact that not only was I dumped but he'd changed his contact details so I couldn't talk to him. I suppose he and his wife were experienced at having their perverted fun then cutting themselves free of possible repercussions.'

Ronan's hands were tight on hers now, fury darkening his face. 'The cruel bastards. I can see why you're so wary! But that was Tommy, Leah. Not me. It's not how life normally is.'

'Yeah. I realise.' Rather than face the sympathy in his eyes she gazed over his shoulder to the long grass and wild flowers, to the hills turning to shadows in the early evening. 'I grew up a lot after the Tommy episode. And thinking, even for a couple of days, that I was pregnant, taught me something: I like being childfree. I like being unmarried.'

He dropped her hands to slide his arms around her. 'Nobody says you have to be anything else but–'

Hands against his chest she fended him off, scared to feel him against her in case she couldn't let him go. '*But*, though a baby wasn't what I wanted, I would have taken on the role of single mum. I would have done what was best for the baby because it would have deserved it. Like I did my best for Natasha and Jordan these last few weeks. Like you're going to do what's best for Curtis.' A picture of Curtis swirled in her mind's eye, man-sized but very much a boy. 'And now you and Selina are sharing a home again, with the son who belongs to both of you, you'll have to go through the Selina leaving thing all over again.'

Ronan hunched his shoulders. 'Bullshit. She's only in my house out of desperation. When she's straightened herself out, we'll return to our separate lives.'

Leah managed the tiniest of smiles. 'Get back to me if that happens but I've got to be honest . . . Selina turning up has reminded me why a man with a kid isn't my Plan A.'

He recoiled as if she'd slapped him. 'Nobody gets their Plan A! Most of us are approaching Plan Z! We've had relationships that failed; we've compromised on our careers, where we live, who we love. Look at Michele. I'll bet she was supportive about Tommy, wasn't she? She knows life never goes to plan.'

Leah flushed. 'Scott's the only one who knew the whole story. He let me weep and wail all over him.'

He was silent for several seconds. When he spoke again his voice was low and tight. 'You know he's in love with you, right?'

'What?' She stared into Ronan's face, reading anger and

frustration there. *In love?* Scott? Scott, who'd alternately listened, counselled and teased until she'd finally been able to learn from the Tommy episode and move on? Scott, who'd never told a soul but just spent the next decade being her friend, funny and outrageous? Scott, who shared almost all her interests? A wave of resentment broke over her, making her shove blindly at Ronan's chest as she scrambled to get out from between him and the stile. 'Scott may be the only successful long-term relationship I've had with a man, but don't try and make it something it's not! We're friends, that's all.'

Ronan let himself be thrust rudely aside and jammed his hands into his pockets as if to ensure he didn't yank her back. 'I don't think I'm trying to make it something it's not – I recognised the way he looked at you in a second. And he was like an alpha male chimp, all bigged up and trying to stare me down.'

'*It's not like that with Scott*!' she hissed in frustration. 'You're just like all the others – can't bear me to have a male best friend.'

He snorted. 'I could bear it with perfect equanimity if I thought that's all he was. But he's in love with you and you're using him as an excuse for past relationship failure. And as a barrier.'

Leah backed away, heart thundering in ears that could scarcely credit what they were hearing. If she'd had to guess, she would've expected Ronan to take her standpoint about Selina quietly, though perhaps not hiding his disappointment. She hadn't expected angry statements that would cut her to the bone. Or for his flash of temper to ignite hers. 'A barrier against what, precisely?'

'A barrier against anyone who might make you put

Tommy down to experience and give a proper grown-up relationship a try.' His usual expression of calm control had been wiped away by contempt. 'It's a bit fucked up, to be honest.'

Chapter Nineteen

His last, unwise words ringing in his ears, Ronan watched as Leah stormed back down the lane, ponytail swiping the air behind her as if prepared to strike at him if he followed too closely.

He gave her a five-minute head start while his blood pressure dropped to its normal level. Then he trailed in her wake, dragging his black mood behind him in the dust and cursing his big stupid mouth.

When he finally arrived back at Chez Shea he discovered Selina had been busy. Table and chairs, scrubbed after languishing neglected in the shed, were set out on the lawn. Risotto bubbled fragrantly on the hob.

In his current frame of mind it was hard to assume the polite veneer he usually maintained with his ex, let alone share a cosy meal with her.

He was angry and shocked at himself for the hard words he'd just spat at Leah. Where had they come from? Was this churning sensation jealousy? If so, he didn't think he could have suffered from it before. He cringed to remember that his rage had actually escalated at Leah's grief that her precious relationship with Scott was being questioned.

Now he was expected to watch Selina playing at homemaker. 'You shouldn't have gone to any trouble.'

Uncertainty stole across her face. She looked more like herself today in a dress and make up, her feet arched prettily into wedge-soled sandals. 'I thought as you hadn't begun dinner I could do something useful.'

He checked his watch – it was past seven. He hadn't begun dinner because he'd been too intent on pitching his case to Leah to think about it. He managed to mutter, 'Thanks,' because his black mood wasn't with Selina, even though, he reflected bitterly, she was the catalyst for this entire shit storm. As usual.

Selina was all about bad decisions. Abandoning university without completing her degree. Having a child with Ronan to pressure him into marriage. Dumping Ronan for the high life with Darren that had collapsed like a house of cards and brought her running scared on the edge of debt-driven desperation.

Each and every one of those choices had turned Ronan's life upside down, and either she wasn't aware of it or didn't see it as important.

As she bustled around the kitchen as if she still had a right to, he leaned against the counter. 'We need to talk.' He'd tried to initiate the conversation a couple of times already but she'd skittered away from his overtures and he'd reasoned it was kinder to give her a day to calm down after what were undoubtedly traumatic events. 'OK?' he pressed, when she didn't answer.

She nodded jerkily, avoiding his gaze. 'Dinner's ready. Would you call Curtis, please?'

Though she was as capable as he was of shouting

'Curtis!' in the general direction of Curtis's bedroom, Ronan did as requested. Shit storms were not calmed by throwing in unnecessary shit.

Twilight loomed as they gathered at the table and the scent of lavender filled the air. Ronan's frustrations had shrunk his stomach. Selina, too, pushed her food around half-heartedly. Curtis was the only one who wolfed his food as he chatted happily about the game he'd been playing online with a schoolmate.

Interrupting him, Selina dropped her fork with a clatter. 'Ronan, I know me turning up must have been a shock and I'm really grateful that you didn't chuck me out on my ear. You deserve total honesty in return.'

Prickling with alarm at the light in his ex-wife's eyes, Ronan frowned. 'But maybe–' He looked pointedly at their son in the age-old parental communication: *don't forget who's listening*.

Curtis had paused mid-chew, expression enquiring.

Selina's face set in the all too familiar lines that told Ronan she wasn't about to be hinted off-course. 'I wasn't honest in the past, not even with myself.' She paused to gulp her wine. 'I shouldn't have left you. I shouldn't have begun anything with Darren.'

'Selina–!' Ronan started again, full of misgivings at what was about to come out of her mouth.

But Selina talked over him, rushing her words out onto the air. 'I was an immature idiot. I couldn't be satisfied with the things you'd provided, including security, because I wanted every day to be a passionate love affair. I was too much of a princess to understand that even a good marriage isn't like that. That you showed your love for me and Curtis by working hard and looking after us.' Though Curtis's sandy eyebrows had flipped up to meet his hair, she seemed oblivious of there being things he didn't need to hear.

Ronan was all too aware, though. 'Selina, this isn't the appropriate time!'

'The truth is,' she ploughed on, 'I still love you. Maybe I went off with Darren to make you jealous, to make you fight for me. But it backfired, didn't it? Because you kept your dignity, hid your hurt and gave me a divorce because that's what you thought I wanted. You're the father of my son, the most decent man on earth, yet I went off the rails because Darren seemed exciting. But he was also scarily unreliable.' Tears streamed down her cheeks, dragging at the corners of her mouth.

Ronan made his voice as firm as a man could while teetering at the edge of the trap he'd just seen yawning at his feet. 'We shouldn't be having this conversation in front of Curtis.'

'I'm sorry!' Selina wailed, 'I can't do anything right. But I'm not sorry I told you. I didn't ever stop loving you!' She stumbled to her feet, shedding a sandal, knocking over her chair as she ran for the house, her sobs floating behind her.

Not for the first time, Ronan was left to face Curtis, quashing the fury that bubbled inside him like black bile while he tried to explain the inexplicable, defend the indefensible, absorb the bitter realisation that she'd chosen her moment precisely *because* Curtis was listening. Words, once heard, couldn't be unheard. And now thirteen-year-old eyes were looking to him for illumination, for the protection and stability that Ronan had always provided. He groped for an explanation that wouldn't let Curtis see that the mother he loved had just put on a masterclass in manipulation, that her tears were those of a crocodile and her instincts those of a leech.

But a beaming smile slowly broke across Curtis's face. 'Does that mean you're back together?'

In his room, Ronan paced morosely, mind spinning. This crap situation was all about womanly principles. For Leah too many and Selina too few.

His roaring need to make things crystal-clear to Selina couldn't be satisfied with Curtis in earshot and, unfortunately, he was past the age of having an early enough bedtime to allow his parents a low-volume, high-voltage row.

Selina hadn't reappeared since her dramatic exit from the table an hour ago and the need to beard the ex-wife in her den burned through him. He took out his phone and, gambling heavily on Leah coming through for him now and asking questions later, began to text.

> ***Ronan:*** *I'll explain as soon as I can but please is there any way you could get Curtis invited to your place for a couple of hours? I apologise in advance but I think you'll understand when you know my reasons.*

And then, because he was nothing if not optimistic, he added three kisses. And then two more.

He opened his bedroom door and pretended to check email while he waited. In two minutes Curtis bounded onto the landing. 'Going next door, right?'

'Oh, I don't know . . .' floated out uncertainly from behind Selina's door.

Ruthlessly, Ronan talked over her. 'Yes, great. Be back by ten.'

Curtis began to clomp down the stairs in great strides. 'Laters!'

Before the echo of the front door had died away, Ronan was rapping grimly at the spare room. 'Talk time, Selina.'

Her response took so long that Ronan had raised his fist to bang harder when she opened the door. She'd re-applied her make-up so all signs of her earlier tears, real or crocodile, had already vanished. Her mouth was set mulishly. 'I can't do this now.'

He smiled in false geniality. 'I have to insist.'

Clouds gathered on her face. 'You can't.'

'Let's not get into what I can and can't do. Let's go downstairs and talk things through like two civilised people.' He stood back and gestured her politely ahead of him.

'Don't try to browbeat me!'

This time, he didn't waste a smile. 'If I were trying to browbeat you I'd be in there packing your bags and tossing them down the stairs.'

Selina gave him a look that should have flayed his skin. Then she thrust her nose in the air and stalked past.

Ronan waited until she'd seated herself at the kitchen table before taking the chair opposite. '"Disappointed" that you chose to enact your drama in front of Curtis doesn't even begin describe how I'm feeling. We both know you don't love me and that you left because you were happier with Darren. I wasn't hurt, because I don't love you either.' He paused to let that sink in before going on more gently. 'I understand you're justifiably frightened of the situation Darren's put you in and I'm willing to let you stay until we go back to the UK. I might be able to help you sort yourself out. But don't try and manipulate me via Curtis, because he's our child, not a weapon or a tool.'

Gaze sharpening, Selina responded to only one aspect

of Ronan's speech. 'Help me? What, financially?' She glanced around the kitchen as if assessing the worth of its contents.

Fighting for calm, Ronan shook his head. 'There isn't a tap on the settlement that you can turn on again now you've thrown away your portion of what were our joint assets. I'm simply offering to help you discover your rights and what people do in your situation.'

'Rights? Oh, thanks.' It wasn't quite a sneer but she could almost have been thanking him for putting a turd in her shoe.

But he could see the fear in her eyes. Selina was used to nice things. She'd been the only child of doting parents. As an adult, first Ronan had provided for her, then Darren. How must it feel to suddenly find herself with only her wits to live on? 'You might be entitled to support from the state. Or maybe you could get a job now Curtis is old enough.'

'What kind of job?'

'Anything you want.'

'I left university to have Curtis. I don't have qualifications.'

'You did enough of your degree to get your HNC and you have your GCSEs and A Levels.' *If you don't like that, you shouldn't have made your unilateral decision that we were making a baby.*

The washing up was still in the sink, smelling faintly of risotto. In the silence, a fly buzzed in through an open window and settled happily on the debris. Selina gave a great sigh. 'Perhaps I ought to go and live with Mum and Dad.'

Her parents lived in Lancashire but Ronan wasn't too alarmed by the thinly veiled threat. The last he'd heard, his ex-father-in-law, Perry, needed help with everything from eating a biscuit to visiting the toilet. Hardcore nursing wouldn't appeal to Selina. Still, Ronan saw no harm in dismissing the idea from the outset. 'Aside from the terms of the shared custody stipulating that you'd need my consent to take Curtis away, I know you're much too good a mum to uproot him from everybody and change his school. Unless you mean to leave him with me?'

'In your dreams!' But then Selina dropped her head in her hands. 'Sorry. I didn't mean to snap. But I have literally nowhere to go. I don't have a roof to put over my son's head or food to put on his plate. You're wrong that I'm frightened.'

Her voice wavered and broke. 'I'm terrified.'

Chapter Twenty

'You'd better not let your parents hear you say it, that's all!' Leah's voice shook with the effort not to giggle but it was hard when the teenagers were crying with laughter. When Curtis knocked and walked in, Natasha and Jordan just laughed harder.

Gazing at them as they wiped tears from reddened cheeks and Scott grinned from his perch on the corner of the kitchen table, Curtis scratched his chin. 'What's up?'

Jordan waved a packet he was holding. 'Look! "Shit ache mushrooms"!'

'They're not shit ache mushrooms!' Leah protested.

'Let's see.' Curtis snatched the packet to read it then threw back his head with a huge guffaw. 'It *does* say "shit ache mushrooms". Have you been eating them, Jordan? You always give me shit ache.'

'Shush!' Leah tried to reprove. 'It's *shiitake*.' She emphasised the pronunciation. 'Shee-tarky!'

'No,' said Curtis, solemnly. 'He definitely gives me shit ache.'

Natasha collapsed in fresh giggles, Jordan pretended to

punch Curtis in the face and Scott's grin grew ever broader at Leah's failed attempts to restore order.

She fell back on chocolate. 'As we're all going out tomorrow, shall we make brownies for a picnic? Would you like to join us, Curtis? Oh, but . . .' A lurch of misery reminded her that things were no longer that simple. 'Your parents will have their own plans, of course,' she backtracked feebly.

'Isn't it weird?' Natasha smiled up at Curtis. 'Our parents are split up but living together – and now yours are! Ours aren't arguing any more, though. Are yours?'

Curtis took the seat beside hers with a flick of his waist chains to avoid sitting on them. 'Yeah, *but* . . .' He paused dramatically. 'Mine are talking about getting back together.'

Leah, who had her head in a cupboard searching out ingredients for the brownies, almost dropped the flour. A thin, high-pitched whine began in her ears.

'Seriously?' Jordan and Natasha chorused.

The bag of flour was a cold weight in Leah's hand as she turned in slow motion and caught Scott looking at her with overflowing sympathy.

Curtis's smile blazed. 'Mum said she still loved Dad and wished she'd never got involved with Darren. Dad was hovering when I came out, watching the door to her room. I think he was waiting to go to her.'

The high-pitched whine became an angry buzz and Leah had to grope for the counter top to steady herself. She hadn't in her wildest dreams foreseen reconciliation as the reason Ronan had asked her to get his son invited over.

From a distance, she heard Scott suggest that the kids hang out upstairs. She didn't bother reminding them about baking brownies, just carried on clutching the flour as if it were a life jacket and she was in deep water while the kids clattered around grabbing drinks and making last jokes about shit ache mushrooms.

Eventually, their footsteps faded up the staircase. Leah felt Scott's arm slide around her shoulders. His voice was soft. 'Bit of a bolt from the blue?'

She turned blindly to burrow her face against his T-shirt, the blood still pounding in her ears. 'Bit.'

Scott hugged her close. 'Good job it happened before you got in too deep.'

'Good job,' she agreed, bleakly.

Upstairs, Jordan and Natasha were besieging Curtis with questions. 'So, seriously, you think your parents might get together again?' demanded Jordan. 'But haven't they been split up for years?'

Curtis took glasses from the cupboard but Jordan was obviously waiting for a reply before he was ready to share the two-litre bottle of fizzy grapefruit juice he'd grabbed from the fridge. 'Doubt Mum would've told Dad she loved him if she didn't. And he's been seriously weird since she turned up. He–' He glanced round apologetically, knowing he was about to say something uncomfortable about their cool auntie. 'He went off with Leah this afternoon and I watched them come back separately. She looked mega pissed-off; he looked grim. I think he might have, you know. Told her. About still having feelings for Mum.'

'Crap.' Jordan slammed the bottle down on the counter so hard that bubbles frothed to the top.

'Poor Leah,' mourned Natasha. 'I think she really liked him.'

'I thought he liked her, too,' Jordan maintained. 'You agreed, Curtis.'

Curtis shrugged. The idea of his parents being together was taking proper shape in his mind and his heart was hopping at the idea of being a family again. 'I must've got it wrong. It's going to be amazing. No more trying to remember which house I'm supposed to be going to after school, no more wanting stuff that's at Dad's house when I'm at Mum's or at Mum's house when I'm at Dad's. No more stepdad and stepfamily. No more . . .' He struggled for words that would adequately express his joy. 'No more shit ache!'

'Well jel,' said Natasha, in a tiny voice. And burst into tears.

'Curtis, you arse.' Jordan put his arm around his sister.

Astonished, Curtis looked from the heaving shoulders of one to the grim scowl of the other. 'What? Why are you crying, Natasha?' He knew Jordan was Natasha's brother but if anybody in the room should be hugging her, shouldn't it be Curtis? He even took a step towards her, preparing to sidle in and take over.

Jordan's scowl turned to a snarl. 'Just piss off and play happy families. You don't have to ram it down our throats. I thought you were meant to be "with" Natasha? Why'd you upset her?'

A nasty little pin of remorse began to threaten Curtis's bubble. 'I wasn't! I was just saying.'

Natasha began to wail. 'But you've been spouting off about parents splitting up being OK when you got use-used to it! Double Christmas and two holi-holidays!'

'Oh.' Curtis saw suddenly that boasting about his parents getting back together might not be fun for others who weren't so fortunate. 'It sort of is OK . . . and I am going to miss double Christmas . . . though not having three parents to buy for rather than two,' he added, honestly.

Natasha cried harder than ever and Jordan wrapped his other arm around her. 'Just get lost, Mr Shit Ache. Go check your mum hasn't run off with a new man.'

'At least I know who my mum ran off with!' Ashamed, angry, mortified, Curtis turned and stormed from the room.

Natasha and Jordan really knew how to spoil a good mood.

Leah had settled down for a couple of consoling glasses of wine with Scott when a red-faced Curtis burst into the kitchen, stalked through the back door and slammed out of the gîte.

'It's all going on in your family,' Scott observed, drily.

Leah sighed. 'I suppose I ought to go up and see what's happened.'

'Shouldn't Michele?'

'You'd think so.' Leah cocked an ear in the hope of catching the sound of Michele emerging from her room. Instead, she heard a sniffling snuffling approach down the stairs. Then Natasha crept in, woebegone and pink-eyed.

Leah opened her arms and Natasha flew to her, straddled her lap as if she were still small and buried her face wetly in Leah's neck. Leah hugged her close. 'Had a row with Curtis?'

'No.' Sniff. 'Jordan did.'

'What happened?' Leah's hand made comforting circles on Natasha's thin back.

Sniff. 'Jordan told Curtis to pee off. And Curtis did.'

Lifted out of her own misery, Leah tried to fill in the blanks. 'You're upset because they rowed?'

Natasha shook her head. 'No. Because Curtis's mum and dad are back together.'

'Right.' Leah rested her cheek on Natasha's hair. She couldn't tell Natasha not to cry over that. She might do it herself.

Chapter Twenty-one

Tuesday morning saw Ronan staring at his laptop screen, reading about homes being repossessed. He was desperately seeking some hint that Selina hadn't done exactly the wrong thing by handing over her house to her lender without seeking advice or applying for help as homeless – although he wasn't sure he could live with thinking of her living in a hostel, and he would gnaw his own head off before seeing Curtis in a place like that.

But that hadn't happened, had it? Because Selina had handled the situation in typical fashion: run to someone else and expect help.

As he read, a conversation he'd had with Selina last night swam through his head. 'But they're selling the house,' she'd argued with Ronan. 'I couldn't sell it myself because it would have meant waiting for Darren to surface.'

He'd tried not to frighten her too much. 'But can they sell it without Darren?'

She'd looked uncertain. 'They said something about court.'

'What happens if they sell for less than you owe?'

Her hands had tightened to fists. 'That would be morally wrong.' It had been distressingly plain how little idea she had about responsibility for residual debt.

'But what if they do?'

Selina had burst into tears and run up to her room. No, *not* her room, he'd told himself as he prepared to follow and encourage her to return to the conversation. It was the *spare* room. Selina had no room in this house. He'd tried to quiet the voice of his conscience that whispered . . . *or any house.*

Then Curtis had made that difficult by skulking in, frowning ferociously and uttering only grunts and monosyllables before banging the door to his room.

Ronan had resorted to putting on his running shoes and getting the hell out into the velvet evening just turning dark, but all jogging around the village had achieved was to send him to bed tired but unable to sleep for the pounding of his shoulder even though he'd popped pain pills. And now, this morning, he was too tired to think his way out of this nightmare.

He crossed the landing to Curtis's bedroom door and knocked, looking contemplatively at the spare room from which Selina had not emerged this morning.

'What's up?' shouted Curtis, from within.

'You OK?' Ronan poked his head into Curtis's room. The curtains were still shut, the room dim and musty.

Curtis lay in bed, laptop propped on his knees, a games controller in his hands. 'Yep.' He didn't look up.

'Breakfast?'

'Not yet, fanks.'

'You didn't stay out long last night.'

Curtis shook his head, thumbs busy on the controller, eyes still fixed to the laptop screen.

'Can you pause that a minute, please?'

With a barely concealed sigh, Curtis did so. 'What?'

'I got the feeling you were upset.'

A shrug.

'Were you?'

He shrugged again. Then, 'I sort of upset Natasha and Jordan had a go at me.'

'Ah, right.' Ronan moved properly into the room. 'Want to talk about it?'

'Nope. I text Natasha this morning and said sorry.'

'Right,' Ronan repeated. Curtis didn't tell him Natasha's reaction and Ronan instinctively shied from asking. Curtis was growing up, forming some kind of relationship with a girl. Ronan loved Curtis no less than when he'd been a helpless baby but Curtis was making it obvious that things were different now. He wasn't helpless and he was entitled to some control over his own life. 'You know where I am if you want me,' Ronan said, eventually.

'Yeah, yeah, yeah, fanks.' Curtis turned back to his laptop with obvious relief.

Back in his bedroom, Ronan glanced restlessly out of the window. And paused. Leah was in the garden of the gîte, hanging out washing. In fifteen seconds, Ronan was letting himself out of his back door.

'Morning,' he said, from his own side of the fence.

Leah turned briefly with a cool greeting then returned to her task. She was wearing shorts with a fringed hem, the silky strands shifting to give tantalising hints of her skin beneath.

Ronan refused to let himself be dismissed. He vaulted the fence and closed the distance between them. 'I owe you an apology.'

She didn't pause, just took a damp garment from the

basket, shook it, pegged it to the line. 'Don't bother.' Garment, shake, peg.

'I want to explain–'

'I don't want to hear it.' Garment, shake, peg.

He thought he could detect tears in her eyes but it was hard to be sure when she was so studiously refusing to look at him. Nonplussed, he tried to find another route around the barriers she'd thrown up. 'Curtis seems to think he's upset Natasha.'

Leah grabbed a blue shirt and stepped along to an unused stretch of washing line. 'I suggest you share any concerns you might have with Natasha's parents.' Then she left the rest of the washing lying in the basket and whisked away indoors, snapping the door shut behind her.

Ronan was still staring blankly at it when he caught a movement from the corner of his eye. Scott was unfolding himself from a lounger and heading straight in Ronan's direction.

'Oh, great, did you get all that?' Ronan asked, tiredly.

Scott sauntered closer, hands in pockets. 'Haven't you done enough, sending your son round last night to break the news that you're back with your wife? Till then, I think Leah may have had the impression that you cared for her.'

Dismay struck coldly into Ronan's gut. He cursed himself for not foreseeing that Curtis would seize only on Selina's manipulative words and lose no time in making it seem real by talking about it. 'I didn't sent him round with that message because I'm *not* back with my ex-wife.'

'Yeah. That's what they all say.'

Anger bloomed in Ronan's chest and he switched his attention from the closed door to Scott's cold gaze. '*I am not married.* That's the big difference between me and Leah's old boyfriend. Tommy.'

'Difference between crooks and thieves from where I'm standing.'

Ronan's breath hissed between his teeth. 'Why don't you butt out?'

Scott edged right into his space. 'Because I want what's best for Leah and you're not it.'

Ronan struck blindly back. 'Neither are you. She only thinks of you as a friend.'

Scott's expression didn't alter. 'Best thing for her. Anything more would hardly be fair.' He hesitated, hunching his shoulders. 'Leah's probably already mentioned that I'm bisexual. Some of us find it hard to be faithful to one gender when we're attracted to both. You can read all about it on the Internet.'

Ronan paused, feeling a reluctant respect for honesty from someone with so much sadness in his eyes. 'If you mean you're prepared to do what's best for Leah even at your own expense and I should do the same–' Then he forgot Scott as the door reopened.

Paralysed, he watched Leah approach, her hair blowing, her face composed. She held his gaze until she halted in front of him.

He tried to jump in. 'I only asked you to invite Curtis here so I could have a row with Selina–'

She held up both hands. 'It's rude of me not to listen but you need to face facts. Whatever *you* think the situation is between you and Selina, Curtis thinks you're likely to get back together. She's living in your house and Curtis is thrilled. That's a mess I don't want to step in. Let's part on good terms.' Then she tiptoed up and kissed him impersonally on the cheek and turned and vanished back indoors without a backward glance.

Ronan stood frozen to the spot for several seconds as

grief and outrage warred in him with the echo of what he'd just said to Scott . . . *to do what's best for Leah, even at your own expense* . . . Finally, he met Scott's contemplative gaze. 'Look after her for me,' he mumbled, his heart the only part of him that wasn't numb.

'I always look after her – but not for you. Bye, fly boy.'

Leah stood back from the kitchen window so that Ronan wouldn't see her watching him. The slump of his shoulders as he slowly turned and moved out of sight made her let go of a breath she hadn't realised she was holding.

From the armchair Alister sighed. 'I feel I ought to congratulate you on doing the right thing but you don't look as if you enjoyed it.'

'Not much.' She glanced around at the rest of her audience, all frozen in place like one of those games where a whistle blows and the action halts. Michele and both kids were gazing at her with expressions that dragged at her heart. 'Well,' she said brightly, because if she acknowledged the compassion in their hearts she'd burst into tears. 'I'll finish hanging out the washing and drag Scott from his sun bed, then we can get off to the water park.'

'Will that be OK?' Natasha looked at Leah as if worried her aunt might disintegrate if called upon to whizz down a slide.

'You bet! The grown-ups can sit in the shade while we have fun.' Leah paused, her hand on the door handle. 'I don't think we can invite Curtis, though. With your dad's leg up on a seat, we won't have room.'

Natasha studied her fingernails. 'That's OK.'

The planned brownie baking had never come to fruition but the kids made do with bretzels from the water park snack bar while Alister and Michele, who'd found a way of co-existing lately without exchanging barbed comments, claimed an umbrella and loungers in red and yellow.

Jordan and Natasha bore Leah and Scott off to whoosh down the corkscrew maze of turquoise waterslides with screams of joy. Though they all laughed, though the sun beat down to offset the exhilarating rushes through chilly water, Leah was aware of both Jordan and Natasha being quieter than usual, glancing over at their parents on the loungers as if checking they were still there. Michele read, her magazine resting on the growing mound of her tummy. Alister worked on his laptop, probably on one of his interminable spreadsheets, exchanging the occasional word with Michele and even making her smile.

'I'm exhausted,' Natasha said, suddenly. 'I'm going to lie on a lounger.'

Jordan fell into step beside her and they edged between sunbathers around the frothing splash-down pool until they reached the patch the Miltons had made their own.

Leah felt the water drying on her skin as she watched them grab their towels and pour drinks, the last vestiges of family unity clinging to their actions. 'I think we're surplus to requirements.'

'Yeah.' Scott fished in the waist of his swimming trunks and pulled out a twenty-euro note. 'It's a bit soggy but I'm sure they'll take it at the bar.'

While Scott bought the drinks, Leah secured a couple of tall stools at a counter facing the pool, propped her chin on her hand and watched Michele towelling Natasha's hair and Jordan craning to see something on his dad's laptop screen.

'Bloody shame about your sister's crowd.' Scott plonked a bottle of Fischer in front of Leah and hitched his backside onto his stool. 'Do you think there's any chance of them getting back together? They just look like any other nice family enjoying their holiday.'

Leah sighed. 'Maybe if Michele wasn't having a baby by another man. I just don't think Alister . . . could.'

'Yeah. Hard to take on someone else's kid.' Swigging from his beer and smacking his lips, Scott nudged her. 'You doing OK?'

She nodded and took a swallow of beer. 'Just unsettled. I've had an email from Chocs-a-million's HR department setting up my orientation, my first-day meetings with my boss and my team, asking my size for chef whites and arranging for my electronic pass to get around the facility. I'm ready for this so-called holiday to be over.' And to be where she couldn't fall over Ronan at any moment; see his smile, hear his voice. Lock gazes with him.

Loyally, Scott responded only to what she said out loud. 'Get you and your posh new job. Bet you can't wait?'

Leah felt a fresh twist of homesickness. 'Really excited.' She could hear a distinct lack of excitement in her voice. 'Only a few more days before we begin the long trek home. Can't wait to see everyone down the Chequered Flag.' She took several long pulls of her beer.

Scott squeezed her hand gently. 'You'll feel better at home, Leah.'

Leah nodded, blinking furiously, thanking her lucky stars for a friend who always had her best interests at heart, and always understood how she was feeling. 'It's the first F1 race after the summer break this weekend. We can get it on pay TV on my computer.'

'I always like the second half of the season when the championship begins to hot up.' And they fell to talking about who was likely to drive for McLaren next season and whether Williams could qualify a car on pole position this year.

It was a couple of hours before they rejoined the others. Alister, although he'd been seated with his leg up all afternoon, was becoming pale and cranky and was desperate to go to bed for an hour with his favourite painkillers and a book.

'I'll bring The Pig up to the entrance.' Leah threw her dress on over her costume.

So Scott and Jordan helped Alister into the rear-most seats with his leg propped up in the middle row for the drive back to Kirchhoffen. A full load of passengers did nothing to enhance The Pig's performance. 'It'd go better if we cut holes in the floor and ran, like the Flintstones,' Scott scoffed, to wind Michele up.

'But we wouldn't get seven people in yours and Leah's pose-mobiles, would we?' retorted Michele as they drew up in the drive.

Scott wasn't going to stand for slurs on his current 'pose-mobile', a lime-green Focus, and they bickered amiably as the car began to empty. Scott and Jordan helped Alister, and Michele put out a hand to catch the door as it tried to blow shut on his injured leg.

It was almost – but not quite – as if things were going to be OK, Leah thought, as Alister smiled and thanked Michele for her help.

And that was when a shadow detached itself from the shrubs at the front of the house and took on man form.

Michele gave a little 'Oh!' of surprise.

Leah halted in horror.

But it was Jordan who gave voice to the collective astonishment. 'Bailey? What are you doing here?'

Chapter Twenty-two

Leah looked on with a sickening feeling of inevitability. No bright smile and plan to make cake would distract the kids from the horror show she could see was about to unfold.

Natasha and Jordan looked bewildered; Michele frozen; Alister as if his worst fears were about to be realised.

'Why?' breathed Michele, at last. Leah knew what her sister was asking. Not why had Bailey turned up when Michele had ended things, but why had he barged into the spotlight when her children and her ex-husband were in the audience?

Bailey's pleading eyes were fixed on her. 'I turned back. You didn't answer my texts. I didn't know if you were OK. If the baby's OK.'

Michele's hand dropped to her stomach as Jordan, almost in slow motion, turned on her with an incredulous stare.

Natasha, slower at joining the dots, frowned. 'Jordan, what's your footie coach doing here?'

Still in slow motion, Michele opened her arms, as if to

draw the kids into a safe harbour. Or to plead for forgiveness. 'Bailey's the baby's dad,' she whispered. 'I'm sorry I haven't told you yet. I wanted to, but–' She swallowed. 'I didn't know how.'

Jordan jerked back as if she'd raked him with her nails. 'You have to be kidding! *Bailey?*' He turned to his father. 'Did you know?'

Alister leaned against the side of the car looking grey and defeated. 'I suspected, but I'd hoped to be wrong.'

Jordan turned to Bailey with a snarl. 'You dick.'

Bailey looked hurt. 'Jordan, man. Me and your mum couldn't help it. We love each other.'

'Bullshit.' Jordan turned on his mother with such an expression of loathing that she flinched. 'You . . . *cougar.*' Shoving past Scott he stumbled blindly down the side of the house. Natasha, freckles standing out like paint on her poor white little face, scampered in his wake. Settling his crutches, Alister started slowly and painfully after them.

Leah, deciding that she was *de trop* in a conversation that was obviously overdue between Bailey and Michele, ran to catch up as Alister steered the kids towards the annexe. Once inside, she swiftly pulled up two chairs for a pallid Alister to heave himself and his leg into.

Brushing away angry tears, Jordan propped his back against the wall. 'Did you know, Leah?'

Alister's and Natasha's heads snapped her way.

Leah's stomach disappeared down a lift shaft. She straightened up to face a row of accusing eyes. 'I found out the day before Michele went off,' she admitted. She paused to lick her lips, feeling suddenly the worst kind of worm. 'I honestly didn't feel it was my secret to tell and she said she'd explain everything when she came back.'

'But she didn't,' Natasha whispered. 'You still didn't tell us.'

Miserably, Leah shook her head. 'No, I asked her again to do it but . . .' She'd been too taken up with slithering out from her Deputy Mum role and into bed with Ronan to persist.

Jordan slid down the wall and covered his eyes. Natasha stared at Leah, looking as stricken as if her aunt had punched her in the face.

Alister gazed blankly at the floor. 'You were in a difficult situation and we shouldn't blame you for your loyalty to your sister. It's the foundation of everything you've done for us this summer.' When he did look at Leah, his eyes were blank with pain. 'But perhaps now you could leave me alone with my children?'

Leah made it up the garden on legs that felt made of wool. Scott waited near the door, for once unsmiling.

'Shit hit the fan,' he observed economically, following her into the deserted kitchen.

Leah tried to agree but, instead, began to cry. 'The kids are gutted because I knew and didn't tell them.'

He slid his arms around her. 'You were between the proverbial rock and hard place. They'll see that in a while.'

Feeling her phone vibrate in her pocket, Leah dragged it out to read its text message with a sudden hope that one of the occupants of the annexe was reaching out to forgive her. But instead:

Ronan: *I still want to talk. Please?*

'Oh, no,' she hiccupped, showing Scott the message. 'Like I'm going to have Curtis on my conscience, too. Today's a shining example of why I'm neither married nor a mother.'

'Just delete it.' Scott snatched the phone and did exactly that. 'Make him gone.'

If it wasn't for the human need for food and drink, Leah reflected, there was no telling how long the family might have remained in fragments. As it was, all she had to do was remain in the kitchen and, over the hours, everybody came to her.

First, Michele, eyes red and swollen, uttering a tragic 'My children hate me,' and flinging herself into Leah's arms. 'Should I go to them?'

Automatically, Leah held her tight. 'They don't hate you. But they feel betrayed and I think you need to wait till they're ready to talk.'

Judging by Michele's renewed sobbing, she didn't find that advice particularly comforting, but Leah, exhausted by her own sorrow, had limited capacity to be Michele's emotional trampoline. She doled out what sisterly comfort she found herself capable of, sat Michele at the table with a cup of camomile tea, then continued her task of transferring food from the fridge to a huge saucepan. Her eyes burned as she wiped the shiitake mushrooms. The hysterical laughter they'd caused seemed part of a different world. 'You've been a while. Where's Bailey?'

'I had to convince him to go.' Michele blew her nose. 'It really is over.'

Twenty minutes later, as if smelling the red wine sauce spiked with rosemary, Alister and the children edged in through the door.

Michele leaped up, hands clutched together so hard the knuckles whitened. 'I'm so sorry! There just seemed no good time to tell you. I was scared. But letting you find out the way you did made everything ten times worse.'

Leah put down the knife and the tomato she'd been about to slice. 'Maybe you guys ought to be on your own.'

'No.' Alister made his crutch-hop way to the table. 'You're part of this. We need to do some air-clearing.' He dropped down into the chair furthest from Michele.

The children stationed themselves in the chairs either side of him. 'We're sorry we were angry at you, Leah,' offered Natasha. 'You've been fantastic all holiday.'

Jordan nodded. 'Yeah. We get you were stuck in the middle.'

'Thank you,' Leah whispered, no more than marginally comforted. The words were delivered as if rehearsed and almost without expression.

'So.' Alister winced as he settled his leg, not meeting Michele's eyes. 'We need to talk about next steps.'

Leah didn't hesitate. 'Let's go home.'

Light crept into Michele's expression. 'Yes, let's.'

Jordan and Natasha nodded.

'I was thinking longer term than that but I have to confess that it sounds a wonderful idea.' Alister rubbed his hand over his eyes. 'Hopefully I can manage the stairs at my flat. I'm getting stronger every day and maybe I can get by if I order ready meals from Tesco.'

'I'll stay with you to help,' Jordan offered. His eyes slid to Leah. 'If Scott's driving your car home, can I go with him?'

'But you will come home when Dad's better, Jordan?' Michele's face was furrowed with grief.

Jordan just shrugged without looking at her.

'What about you?' Alister took his daughter's hand.

Natasha shrugged, face woebegone. 'You've only got one spare room. I suppose I'll be OK with Mum.'

Alister nodded understandingly. 'I'll be buying somewhere bigger when Mum and me get the finances straight.'

While Michele sat, dumb with misery, watching her children turning her a cold shoulder, Alister took refuge in business-like efficiency. 'That's agreed, then. If we pack this evening we can get off early tomorrow. I'll change the ferry bookings online. I can telephone my nurse from the car in the morning to explain that I'm going home and email M. Simon to say we're vacating early. We can fuel the cars in Muntsheim en route to joining the Autoroute de l'Est and, traffic allowing, have a late lunch on the ferry. If the drivers aren't too tired to go on we'll be in Bettsbrough tomorrow evening.' He smiled at the children. 'Do you want to go next door and say bye to Curtis?'

Jordan and Natasha exchanged glances. Natasha shrugged. 'We'll text him when we're home.'

Alister turned an enquiring gaze on Leah.

Silently, she shook her head. She wouldn't be going next door to say her farewells, either.

'Then,' he said, 'there doesn't seem to be much keeping us here.'

Chapter Twenty-three

Although he'd checked his phone every few minutes since sending last night's text, Ronan jumped when his phone rang at 9 a.m.

It wasn't Leah. Damn.

But it was a call he had to take. 'Henry! Mr Elusive.'

Henry was all business. 'Sorry not to get back to you. It's not an easy time for me.'

'Nor me, owing to my injury and the consequent lack of company sick pay,' Ronan replied grimly, equally direct.

'OK, well, the good news is that you're entitled to claim expenses, losses and compensation for pain and suffering. Your losses can include both basic and flight pay.'

Ronan felt a stirring of optimism. 'That's great!'

'No skin off my nose. The insurance company pays under the employer's liability,' returned Henry, bluntly. 'The rest is bad news. I'm afraid you've written Buzzair Two off.'

The optimism, appropriately, took a nosedive. 'I did the best that could be done with a sick engine.'

Henry snorted. 'Reducing my fleet from four to three,

involving me in untold work and stress – and all the time my supposed chief pilot is sunning himself abroad.'

Between his eyes, Ronan could feel rage fermenting. He quashed it ruthlessly. Letting rip would only cloud his thinking.

'It's a nightmare,' Henry went on. 'The broker has taken weeks and now the insurance company's seeking to subrogate the claim via the maintenance company. The maintenance company is *not* happy. I have a deductible of 2.5% on the hull insurance, and what about betterment charges? My premiums are set to rocket–'

'That's all bullshit.' Ronan spoke quietly but it did halt Henry's tirade. 'Claims *will* take a long time if you use cheap companies. If the aircraft's written off there can *be* no betterment charges. The maintenance company *is* at fault *and* you can reclaim your deductible from them. Your premiums cannot be affected.'

He listened for several seconds to Henry breathing, a feeling growing that there was more wrong with this conversation than he'd yet grasped.

Abruptly, Henry changed tack. 'Look, Ronan, you've been a good employee till now, so I'm going to give you the opportunity to resign. Then, when you find another job, I'll be able to provide a reference. Wouldn't that be best for us all?'

Ronan's rage erupted. 'No, it fucking wouldn't! Why should I resign, as if my airmanship was at fault? And what's going to happen if I don't?'

Another silence. Then, 'I think you'll find resignation's the best course.' Henry ended the call.

Gripping the now silent phone as if he'd like to grind it to dust, Ronan stared out of the window, noting low altitude cumulonimbus cloud and thinking, absently, that it wouldn't be the best day to fly a helicopter. The ranking of the formation suggested a cold front or a squall. Maybe lightning.

When would he be up among the clouds again? He was beginning to feel a vast emptiness where his career used to be.

Still staring out of the window, he discarded his phone and began his physio, arms above his head, to the side, up his back. The flexion behind his back was still the weakest function. As he worked on it he realised that he was no longer studying the clouds. Maybe lightning had already struck him because he was watching the garden next door in the hope of catching a glimpse of Leah, the woman who'd turned the walls around his heart to dust. But no washing danced on the line, no lounger supported her curvy figure.

He checked his phone again. No reply to his text.

From behind him came Curtis's voice. 'I'm hungry.'

'We'll get breakfast.' Turning away from his sad and fruitless vigil, he managed a smile for his son.

Down in the kitchen Ronan cast a jaundiced eye over the cabinet doors that still needed refinishing. He'd have plenty of time for them if Leah kept up her policy of non-communication. 'What date do you need to be back at school?'

Curtis, who'd taken the juice carton from the fridge and was drinking directly from it, managed a shrug.

'Fifth of September.' Selina was hovering in the doorway, as if unsure of her welcome.

Ronan felt a sudden twinge of conscience. She was no longer his wife and he hadn't invited her to land herself on him but it was wrong to make her feel so unwelcome that she didn't want to venture into the room. He took down a mug and plate for her. 'Coffee? Toast? Cereal?'

'Fry up?' suggested Curtis hopefully.

'OK, we'll call it brunch.' He began collecting eggs and sausages from the fridge.

Selina opened the bread bin. 'I'll make toast.'

It was weird for Ronan to find himself sharing a kitchen with Selina again, reaching for the cutlery drawer together – 'Sorry, you first' – or turning to warm the plates and finding her already doing it.

At the end of the meal, Curtis laid down his cutlery and burped. 'I might go round and see if Natasha and Jordan want to hang.'

'Not literally, I hope.' Ronan decided not to suggest that Curtis might like to help load the dishwasher first. Curtis 'hanging' with Natasha might somehow prise open the door to Ronan making contact with Leah.

Selina sipped her coffee. 'The people from the gîte? They left early this morning.'

'Oh. Must've gone out for the day.' Curtis looked disappointed, took out his phone and glanced at it as if hoping to see a message. Ronan had to restrain himself from doing the same.

But Selina was shaking her head. 'I think they've gone home. They woke me up, clattering around, and I watched them loading cases and everything into the cars. Then they went.'

Curtis gazed open-mouthed at his mother. Ronan, afraid that the same almost comical expression of consternation was mirrored on his own face, clapped a hand to his son's shoulder. 'You could text Natasha and find out.'

Ungraciously, Curtis shrugged him off. 'I know, right.'

Upstairs, Curtis fell onto his bed. His mum must be talking crap. She must be. He checked his WhatsApp and Snap

Chat in case he'd missed anything, then, thumbs flashing over his phone screen, texted Natasha.

Curtis: *Where u at?*

He checked to see if Natasha or Jordan were playing online. Nothing. He took out his laptop and messed around with Moviemaker, because he was supposed to have begun a project before he joined Year 9 IT.

An hour crawled by while he waited for a reply, importing video clips from his phone of Natasha making faces and Jordan pigging an ice cream. He reversed the second segment so Jordan seemed to spit the ice cream back into the cone, which was gross but proper funny.

He frowned at his phone. Remembering the Find Friends app, he opened it and typed in *N-a-t*. A flicker, then a map jumped onto the screen, an orange icon flashing. He frowned harder.

Curtis clomped downstairs and homed in on his dad working in the kitchen. 'Look.' He thrust out the phone.

His dad glanced up from the cabinet door he had laid out on newspaper on the floor. 'Map of France.'

'See the orange head? That's where Natasha's phone's at.'

His dad began to turn his sandpaper to a fresh spot. 'Oh?' Then he dropped the sanding block. 'Natasha's in *Calais?*'

Curtis searched for *J-o-r*. He tilted the phone to show his dad. 'And so's Jordan.'

'Shit.' His dad must have been annoyed because he almost never swore in Curtis's hearing.

'Mum was right. They're on their way home. Do you know where they live?'

'In Cambridgeshire. It's a couple of hours from Orpington, by road.'

Curtis felt lead settle in his belly. They'd probably never see one another again.

His dad sighed, then, grabbing a can of Coke and a bottle of beer from the fridge, beckoned Curtis out in the garden. It was beginning to spit with rain but they sat down at the table as if it was a sunny day.

Curtis yanked his ring pull and sucked the froth from the top of the can.

His dad smiled but it didn't make him look happy. 'Henry called, acting oddly, trying to make me responsible for something that I'm not. I think we ought to go back to England so I can sort it out. How would you feel about that?'

'Would we all go? All three of us?'

His dad didn't quite answer the question. 'It's a tricky situation because Mum hasn't got a house right now. I've been trying to help her sort out her rights and that will be easier to do in England, too.'

Curtis wanted harder facts than that. 'If we go back to England, where's Mum going to live? And what about me?'

His dad gave a reassuring smile. 'You'll live with me full time, at least until Mum gets sorted.'

Curtis waited. Finally, his dad said something that was more what Curtis wanted to hear. 'Don't worry, I won't toss your mum out on the street.'

'Cool. I don't mind if we go home.' Curtis found himself beaming. Wow. They really were all living together again.

His dad looked serious. He spoke very slowly, as if picking his words. 'Curtis, this is difficult but it would be wrong to let you think that me and Mum are getting back together.'

‘Oh.’ The wave of happiness subsided a bit. ‘So you don’t love her back, then?’

‘I’m sure we’ll always have affection for each other but when she said she loved me she was emotional, frightened at what had happened with her house.’ His dad’s voice became gentler with every bit of bad news he gave out. ‘Even if she lives at my house for a bit, we’ll have separate bedrooms.’

‘I get it.’ Curtis still smiled on the inside. His parents *were* going to live together. With him. He didn’t care about them sharing a bedroom. Gross or what?

After Curtis had gone indoors, Ronan sat on in the garden as the wind patted at the trees with giant invisible paws and the sky turned as dark as his mood.

He took stock. His career had gone from being on hold to being in trouble. He’d just agreed to his ex-wife living with him. By her presence – and by Darren’s absence – Selina was a siren trying to lure Ronan back onto the rocks of a relationship he’d been glad to see the end of but Curtis so obviously wanted back.

Ronan felt like a bastard.

His feelings were all for another woman, a woman who’d distanced herself by hundreds of miles physically and much more than that emotionally. Leah’s smile, her walk, her sunny personality, had all vanished back to the life she’d put on hold for the holidays. A life that didn’t include Ronan Shea.

Chapter Twenty-four

England in October

Leah had been back in the UK for nearly six weeks and had already spent a month in her new job. The leaves on the trees outside the window of her new product development kitchen had turned golden and were drifting down to eddy across the staff car park in the autumn breeze.

At her bench she perched on a tall stool, setting up a trials table from a Chocs-a-million template on her computer. Commensurate with her status, she wore chef whites and a bandana along with her hairnet. Through the glass she could see technicians in the lab coats, caps and protective glasses that she, 'the creative', was excused.

Her workspace boasted both gas and induction hobs let into the stainless-steel work surfaces, three fan ovens, two microwaves and two fridges.

She was working on a new range, boxed chocolates to be branded 'Chocs-a-million Airs'. The accent on lightness, the range would be aimed at those tempted by a hint that this luxury chocolate product would be healthier or less fattening than others. Biscuit bases baked in Oven A, ready to be topped with puffs of lemon meringue and swirled with the all-important chocolate tomorrow for a product trial.

Her working day would be over when the timer light went out and Leah's attention was already straying to the evening ahead: Natasha had texted to invite herself for supper and Scott had done the same.

She tabbed along to *Name of trial* and typed in *Chocs-a-million Airs – Lemon Meringue* – then paused, trying to think airy. *Nibble? Light?* Both done to death. She made it *Lemon Meringue Fresh*. Marketing would probably change it anyway. That seemed to be their job. Her job, her shiny new job was proving to be quite different to her old position in a small chocolatier. At Chocs-a-million she was finding herself just one cog in a big machine; a vital cog, as she'd been assured when headhunted, but still only able to move when the other cogs moved.

Before, she'd been less constrained and the workplace had had a warmer, inclusive feel. As if they were all one big family.

A vision swam into her mind of 'family' – the gîte kitchen in Kirchhoffen: Natasha trying out mug cake recipes, Curtis licking the bowl, Ronan trying not to laugh at Jordan's phallic chocolate decorations.

Her Chocs-a-million co-workers were friendly, too, she reminded herself, and the salary was great. Revelling in moving to the next level professionally, and loving her high-spec product development kitchen, she found it rewarding to be involved in not just new product concepts but entire ranges.

It wasn't the fault of Chocs-a-million that she wasn't feeling settled; the memories of the holiday were fading more slowly than her suntan and the joy she'd expected at returning to her own living space was slow to make its presence felt.

Maybe it was because Natasha had sent her an iMovie slideshow of the holiday and Leah couldn't stop looking through it at Ronan's dark eyes smiling at the camera. Maybe it was because Leah still nursed anxieties about Michele's family and was so preoccupied with each of them trying to find their way through the maze of after-break-up reality that she sometimes didn't sleep well.

Michele, worryingly, had had plenty of reasons to rue wobbling off the straight and narrow. She'd returned to school to a couple of uncomfortable interviews with her head teacher about her far from ideal circumstances. Many of her students knew Bailey from his coaching at the community centre so salacious gossip was a concern, and the chair of governors, though she kept assuring Michele that she wished her well with her pregnancy, was anxious that her conduct was going to reflect badly on the school. Fuelling these concerns, in the aftermath of rejection Bailey had begun, in Michele's words, 'acting like a kid', vocal about his impending fatherhood but quieter on the subject of financial responsibility.

Jordan and Natasha were slow to forgive their mum for breaking up the family and exposing them to the wagging tongues, and showed few signs of preparing to welcome their sibling.

Jordan still lived with his dad in silent rejection of his mum's situation though Alister, in a normal plaster now, was hopping gamely around, still on sick pay until he was off his crutches in a few weeks.

Natasha had remained with Michele so far, but Leah had become accustomed to her frequent *Can I come round yours?* texts. Full of compassion because Natasha hadn't asked to be caught up in her parents' problems, Leah answered *No prob!* whenever possible. Michele was accepting of this facet of the adjustment period. If not entirely happy at home at least Natasha was safe with Leah, for which benefit Leah was prepared to compromise her customary degree of solitude – especially with Scott hovering to support her through any lingering regrets about Ronan. Scott was a good friend.

Being brutally confronted with Baby Three's young father seemed to have flicked a switch in Alister. When Leah had gently asked if there might ever be a prospect of reconciliation he'd actually raised his voice to her. '*Michele's having her toyboy's child!*' Whether it was resignation, humiliation or a loss of respect for Michele, he now appeared content to spend his sick leave chafing to return to school and instigating divorce proceedings.

The timer flashed and Leah slipped her hands into silicone gloves to slide out the oven trays in a hot sugar-smelling cloud. The tiny biscuit bases slipped easily onto a cooling rack: round, square, diamond, oval and rectangle, some plain, others cocoa. She'd already experimented with the topping so tomorrow she'd whip up a fresh batch of meringue and coat with a range of Chocs-a-million chocolate, label each batch and enter the details in the trial table ready for the initial product evaluation meeting where the chocolates would be nibbled, sniffed, rolled about between fingers, photographed, scrutinised and discussed before detailed evaluation forms were completed. No doubt someone would point out that she hadn't trialled a triangle.

Ingredients would be scrutinised, too – cost, availability and sourcing, and the ever-present consideration of nut allergy.

A lab assistant would collate everyone's feedback for

discussion. Leah would study it, tweak the recipe, include a triangle, and the cycle would begin again, moving on presently to the sensory evaluation suite, where tasters in cubicles would provide more focused feedback.

Having shoved the day's trays and utensils into the dishwasher she closed her kitchen and zipped along a glass corridor to the female changing area, waving her pass at the appropriate aperture to open the door.

So it wasn't her new role, she told herself, changing into street clothes and dumping her whites in a laundry hopper. It wasn't her home life. Her car was running well and she had a weekend watching touring cars with Scott to look forward to.

She just felt . . . She paused to check her phone.

She just felt pissed off because once she'd recovered from her long drive from Kirchhoffen, unable to stop thinking about him, she'd texted Ronan to apologise for leaving without saying goodbye.

Sucking in her cheeks and scratching her head over the correct blend of friendliness and disarming sincerity, she'd said she regretted things hadn't worked out and appreciated Selina had put him in an untenable position. It had been an olive branch, an acknowledgement that Leah might have been inflexible-verging-on-unreasonable.

And Ronan had replied . . .

. . . with silence.

A month of silence. She slapped her locker door shut.

The evenings were getting cooler and she put the Porsche's heater on as she drove home from the industrial park on the edge of Peterborough.

A week ago Leah had given Natasha a key to her house, uneasy at finding her niece waiting like a delivery on the step outside, so today Natasha was already indoors, TV blaring, a glass of orange juice making rings on the table. 'Hey,' called Natasha, curled in a corner of the cream leather sofa, long legs encased in thick black tights, having established her coolness by being sent home from school on the first day for bare legs.

'OK?' Leah paused to drop a kiss on her niece's hair, which was only now beginning to regain a natural gloss. 'Scott's coming, so I'll get the chicken and pasta on.' She pulled off her jacket and made for the kitchen.

'Random.' Natasha's gaze didn't move from her phone screen.

Leah decided not to argue that Scott scrounging a meal wasn't random, it was commonplace. Her mind was more on starting up the coffee maker and preparing chicken thighs to be sandwiched between the plates of the contact grill.

Doorbell. Knock-tat-tat. Scott's usual signature tune.

Natasha yelled. 'I'll go!' Leah added a drop of olive oil to the water for the pasta and listened in to the usual banter that followed the sound of the opened door. 'What you want, Scottie dog?'

'Good company. Have to wait till the child goes home.' The door closing, Scott's voice approaching.

'Company was good till you showed up.'

Then a dog-like snarl and a squeal of laughter.

Scott appeared in the kitchen, grin at the ready. He brought with him a smell of outdoors and a bottle of gin. They'd lately discovered the charms of gin produced by a small local distillery. A brief hug, then he raided the fridge for Fevertree tonic and the freezer for the ice cubes Leah froze around slices of lime. 'Coffee? Fantastic. I'll set the table. Work's been shit. Here.' He passed her a gin with not much tonic, topped up her coffee, then returned to the sitting room. 'What're we watching, Natasha? *The Thundermans*? Cool.' A grunt of satisfaction as he fell into the reclining chair he considered his own.

Leah took out fresh pasta. 'What was that about setting the table?'

A sigh. Then, murmured, 'You do it, Nat, eh?'

'How much?'

'Two quid.'

'Pay up first.' A pause, then the chink of change followed by the clinking and clunking of cutlery being grabbed from the drawer and clashed onto the small glass table by the windows.

Chopping sage and coriander, Leah wondered idly whether she should object to Scott bribing Natasha. She settled on the positive: at least Natasha was learning the value of money by working for it.

Once the meal was ready, Scott, revived, refreshed the gins and even poured Natasha fresh juice without trying to get his two quid back in exchange.

Scott and Leah shared news about their workdays. Natasha, having established Leah hadn't brought sample Lemon Meringue Fresh chocolates home, changed the subject. 'You didn't ask what was random.'

Leah tasted the sauce. Just the right balance of mushroom, cream and mustard. She liked the hint of tarragon, too. 'What was random?'

'Curtis text to ask whether we're speaking.'

Leah's heart bumped so hard that it shook her voice. 'And are you?'

Natasha went pink and busied herself with picking out the crispiest chicken. 'He was a bit sucky when his mum turned up but I've text back.'

Though the reminder of Selina in Curtis's and Ronan's

lives shivered through her, Leah managed, 'Good. How's Curtis doing?' *Get him to ask his dad why he hasn't answered my message.*

'Got in trouble at school for his piercings and had to take them out. Says it hurts every time he puts them back.'

'His mum and dad still back together?' Scott interjected, chasing peas and pasta through his sauce.

'Curtis says it's cool to be living like a family again, so think so.' Natasha looked at Leah under her lashes. 'How far did you say it is from Bettsbrough to where they live?'

Leah took a hefty swig of the gin and tonic, averting her gaze from Scott's so he couldn't read fresh misery in her eyes. 'Couple of hours.'

'Oh,' Natasha sighed. 'With Mum being pregnant and Dad being broken, they won't take me.' She tried her aunt with a winning smile.

Leah's breath fluttered as she let herself toy with the idea that if she offered to take Natasha to see Curtis she, Leah, would have a reason to see Ronan. 'Maybe you could Facetime him?' With a pang, she watched Natasha's face fall.

Ronan's first action after being declared fit to return to work by his orthopaedic surgeon was to ring his Aviation Medical Examiner with the good news.

'Glad to hear,' the doctor responded breezily. 'Feeling generally fit?'

'Never better,' Ronan fibbed, deciding that feeling jumpy could be forgiven when your ex-wife came to stay and your boss turned inexplicably hostile. Add to that a frustrating end to a nearly love affair with a woman who seemed to have gripped him equally by the heart and the –

The AME interrupted his thoughts. 'Grand. Email me

the surgeon's report. If it's satisfactory I'll send you your "fit letter" on the basis of information received and you can notify your employer.'

'Can't wait to.' He'd do it immediately. In person.

It felt odd to drive to the airport after a three-month absence. The familiar buildings and hangars housing flying schools and London shuttles glinted in the autumn sunshine; London landmarks rose up in the mid-distance. Aircraft, private and business, fixed-wing and rotary, lined up on aprons outside hangars like some fantastic toy collection.

Ronan didn't park outside Buzz Sightseer. Instead, he chose to stroll the last hundred yards and enter the hangar via the personnel door. Two of the aircraft, company call signs Buzzair One and Buzzair Three, stood in the hangar in gleaming livery of silver with green and purple flashes. Presumably Buzzair Four was out. Buzzair Two would be in the hands of the insurance company.

He paused to breathe in the Avtur and the peaceful atmosphere of the hangar. Liam, the ground engineer, had his wheeled tool chest alongside Buzzair Three. The client lounge at the side of the hangar was unoccupied but Ronan glimpsed people moving beyond the next window: Cindy's fair head, a rotund body that would belong to Janine. Then a lean male frame that passed purposefully by the window, heading out of the office.

Moving swiftly, crossing his fingers that Liam wouldn't see him and give him away by calling out, Ronan crossed the concrete and reached the offices at exactly the moment the door opened.

'Whoa!' Henry skittered back a step.

Ronan assumed a genial expression. 'Hi, honey, I'm home. Surgeon says I'm fit to return to work. AME's sending me my "fit letter".'

'I'm on my way to a meeting–'

'Great.' Ronan stood back to let Henry pass. 'I'll just talk to Cindy about my return to work on Monday and get Janine to arrange my base and align check.'

'Hang on.' Henry looked taken aback. His chest, under the Buzz Sightseer logo on his neat black sweater, rose and fell.

Ronan lifted a brow. 'Shouldn't you be getting to your meeting?'

Henry narrowed his eyes. 'We'd better sort this out.'

Ronan followed him across the tiny foyer but paused at the door to the main area. 'Cindy and Janine! How's life treating you?'

'Ronan!' they called, sounding surprised but pleased to see him.

Waiting with exaggerated patience for Ronan to follow him through the door to his private office, Henry made a performance of tidying paperwork and minimising windows on his computer.

Ronan waited calmly. At least outwardly.

Henry finally shuffled aside enough paper to make room for his elbows on his desk. 'I have to admit I was expecting you to have resigned by now, after our telephone conversation.'

'But all you did was talk bullshit, Henry. You're going to have to do better than that.' Ronan watched his boss carefully and, to his satisfaction, a couple of beads of sweat popped on Henry's brow. Ronan kept his voice even but firm despite the anger spiralling inside him. 'Don't insult my intelligence. Tell me what's going on.'

A clock on the wall ticked.

Henry looked down and fidgeted with his computer mouse.

Ronan watched him.

Henry sighed. 'OK. Here are the hard facts. I no longer have enough business for four aircraft. If I run three, I can use the insurance money from Buzzair Two to pay off one of my loans, reducing my outgoings and my exposure.'

Ronan processed the information. 'Fair enough. What I'm still missing is why it's me you want to see gone. I'm the only pilot that's directly employed. The rest you call on according to bookings and pilot hour limits.'

Henry rolled the mouse in precise little circles. Finally, he sighed and caved in. 'You're also the most expensive, with the national insurance contributions, pension and everything.'

A chill crept over Ronan. 'So you thought you'd try and "encourage" me to resign so you can get away without paying redundancy money? After all my support, Henry?'

Henry fidgeted and sighed some more. Then he switched on a pleased expression, as if in the grip of a wonderful idea. 'How about you go self-employed? Then I can use you, especially in summer, when we take on additional VIP travel to Ascot, the British Grand Prix and Cowes week.'

Ronan had to fight not to bang his fist on the table. 'A zero-hours contract is no good to me.'

'It's all I'm in a position to offer.' Henry cheeks were mottled red now.

Ronan watched him dispassionately. 'As you've relied on me for many a business decision I'll do you a favour and point out that you're trying to contravene employment law. *Law.* I'll get ACAS and the legal people at the British Airline Pilots' Association on the case.'

For the first time since entering the office Henry met

Ronan's gaze squarely. 'Then I have to tell you that I don't have money for a court case. I'm not being greedy or mean. I *don't have the money.* If you pursue this you'll close us down.' Desperation crept into his voice. 'You know a competitor set up in spring. If I can shed all the expenses and obligations of an employee it will help.'

'So you'd shaft the guy who helped you build up this company?'

Henry literally wrung his hands. 'I've gone about this the wrong way and I apologise. I've been clinging on by my finger ends and I thought I saw a lifeline so I had to follow the old saying about there being no place in business for friendship. But do you actually want to put me out of business?'

His words rang in the following silence. Ronan's mind churned. Although Henry had acted like a weasel he was probably speaking the truth now his optimistic little scheme had been uncovered. It had often taken Ronan's cool head to manage cash flow so he wasn't sure why he was so shocked to hear that Buzz Sightseer was flying close to the wind. It was a bitter pill that the unconventional solution Henry had seized upon involved hanging Ronan out to dry, but that didn't mean he'd willingly be the one to put Buzz Sightseer under, throwing Cindy, Janine and Liam out of jobs and losing other pilots significant flying hours.

One way or another, Ronan was going to be looking for a new employer before too long.

He shook his head in disgust. 'I can't resign or people will assume my forced landing was pilot error. You're going to have to find the money to make me redundant. But first, *on my existing contract,* you're going to put me through my base and align check so that I'm current when I apply for other jobs.'

Henry looked first relieved, then dismayed. 'I'm not sure where the money would come from.'

'The insurance payout? I don't care, so long as you do it.' Wearily, Ronan clambered to his feet.

Henry held out his hand. 'I owe you, Ronan.'

Ronan looked at the hand without taking it. 'I predict you'll be in some other shitty situation within three months of my leaving. But then you won't have me to pass you the paper.'

The hangar air seemed less clean as he walked back through it. Liam looked up and started forward but Ronan just raised a hand in greeting and strode on. Time enough to be pally when he came back to work. Right now, he had to get away from the place before he lost his customary calm and broke something. Possibly Henry's nose.

Fury was still tingling beneath his skin when he pulled into his drive. Windows stood ajar upstairs to give Curtis's music full access to the air. His neck bunched, not because his teenager was behaving like a teenager but because he knew that indoors he'd encounter the same situation as he had every day since returning from France.

Selina: alternately moping about the crap life had handed her and being evasive about her next step.

Curtis and Selina: blithely acting as if the elephant of divorce was not in the room. Selina had even offered to move into Ronan's bed, 'if it would make a difference'.

'A *difference*?' He'd gazed at her in fascinated horror. 'Like it would un-divorce us? Or somehow rationalise your presence here? No! Just sort yourself out.' S*ort yourself out* was a vague phrase he used to encompass whatever it would take to get Selina out of his house in such a way that Curtis was both happy and living in the area.

He slammed his car door and let himself into the house to find Selina reading a magazine in the sitting room.

'How did you get on today?' He threw his jacket over one chair and dropped himself into the other.

Selina looked vague. 'Get on?'

'In trying to sort yourself out.' That ambiguous phrase again.

She sighed. 'Darren hasn't surfaced.' Her eyes strayed back towards the glossy pages in her lap.

Ronan stretched out and gently removed the magazine to help her focus. 'You were seeing the lawyer today, the one the Citizen's Advice people lined up. Didn't he or she have any helpful information?'

'Not really.'

Ronan didn't bother to suppress his sigh. 'If you can't get a job you must go to the DSS and find out what benefits you're entitled to. Including housing benefit.'

His heart sank as he watched her eyes fill with practised tears. 'You'd see your son existing on benefits in some horrible last-ditch accommodation?'

'Stop wheeling Curtis out like a weapon. There are perfectly nice rental properties available, through the council, housing associations and private landlords – I showed you the page on the Citizen's Advice website about that. And you know I always pay my way with Curtis. When you're not living in my damned house,' he added. 'Have you applied for any jobs?'

As the piteous tears hadn't worked, she set her mouth in an obstinate line. 'I'm not qualified–'

'Not true and, anyway, you left me and we divorced. You must see it's not on to expect me to support you because your new life hasn't worked out. It was unpleasant, what happened, but I've given you weeks to get over the shock and it's time you took back responsibility.'

'Curtis likes us being together.'

'*We're not together.*' He had to fight not to bellow the words. 'You're a guest in my house on a strictly temporary basis. *Temporary*,' he emphasised, sweeping up his jacket as he headed for the door.

But her next words halted him. 'The lawyer did have one very interesting thing to offer. If you want me out and I don't want to go, you may need to evict me. And you can't do that until twenty-eight days after you give me formal notice to leave.'

Stunned, Ronan turned slowly. 'What?'

'Actually, two things,' she amended, picking up her magazine. 'She was interested that you're not currently paying child maintenance.'

'But I've taken sole responsibility for supporting Curtis!' he protested in outrage. 'You're not paying for his food, clothes, shelter, heat or anything else. It's common sense that I don't pay you to maintain him when I'm the one doing it.'

She shrugged, licking one finger and turning a page. 'You didn't clear it with the Child Support Agency, did you?' She paused, looking struck. '*Three* things – I can go back to court to ask for child support to be reassessed, owing to my changed circumstances.'

Slowly, Ronan came back and sat back down. For the second time in one day someone was trying to shit on him, undeterred by the fact that he'd always played fair and had done not one thing to deserve being shat upon.

Well, here was where it stopped. 'Unfortunate for you that I'm being made redundant, then, eh?'

The magazine slid off Selina's lap as her head jerked up. 'You can't be.'

'Of course I can. Henry's reducing his fleet. I'm the casualty.'

'But what will you do?' Selina demanded, looking genuinely dismayed.

'Look for another job because I've been on statutory sick pay for weeks so the piggy bank is almost empty. I'm going to struggle to make the mortgage and the household bills. There's a rocky ride ahead.'

As he strode from the room, Ronan at least had the satisfaction of seeing the smile wiped from his ex-wife's face. He recognised that she was manipulative rather than malicious but she sometimes took thoughtlessness and self-interest to dizzy heights.

He halted abruptly as he came face to face with Curtis in the hall. Damn. He'd have preferred Curtis not to overhear the confrontation. He stretched his mouth into what he hoped was a reassuring smile. 'Looks like I'll be moving on, job-wise.'

Curtis nodded. He was wearing his most recent fashion statement, a long black coat with military-looking brass buttons. He pushed his hands into its pockets, looking younger without the facial piercings the school had, as predicted, banned.

Ronan went on, 'You don't need to worry but we'll have to be realistic about money until I see what my next step is. Good job we've had our holiday! But try not to break anything expensive for a while, OK?' His conscience twanging at having made things sound slightly worse than they were for Selina's benefit, he gave Curtis a big man-hug. Curtis actually responded for several seconds before letting go.

Filled with warmth, Ronan enjoyed the hug while it lasted, then went to grab his laptop because although he had financial reserves – he'd had no conscience at lying to Selina about that – they wouldn't last for ever. He'd need to put out feelers for another job.

Chapter Twenty-five

Climbing back into the cockpit on Monday morning was like coming home.

Ronan's hands took charge of the collective and cyclic levers, his feet settled on the rudder pedals, the array of instruments read as clearly to him as a child's book as he performed his checks and set the rotors spinning, the noise climbing until the only way it was possible to speak to the examiner beside him was via headsets. In minutes the fabulous machine put its nose down and surged into the air and he regained the thrill of which he'd never tired, one that, in some dark moments over the past couple of months, he'd thought he might have lost. They swooped up above the buildings and bridges, pedestrians and cars, and Ronan was totally at one with his machine.

Heaven.

Once back on the ground the examiner duly ticked the boxes on behalf of the Civil Aviation Authority and stamped and signed the precious piece of paper that was Ronan's licence. *Yesssss!* His rating as a commercial helicopter pilot was current once more.

Back to earth in more ways than one, and having read a lot of advice to employees since Henry became no kind of a friend, Ronan went into the hangar and rapped on Henry's office door. Once admitted, he formally requested an early meeting and equally formally expressed his willingness to be made redundant. 'If we call this meeting the consultation, you can serve me with notice of redundancy.'

'I'm aware of the procedure,' Henry responded, testily, from behind the barricade of his desk.

Still, to ensure no later misremembering of events Ronan went out into the outer office and emailed Henry a summary of the meeting, copying Janine in.

In response – or perhaps retaliation – Janine, looking acutely uncomfortable and clearly acting on Henry's instructions, printed out a formal notice of redundancy to tell Ronan to expect the bare legal redundancy payment equal to about a month's basic salary, no allowance for flight pay, and one month's notice to begin with immediate effect.

'Not a lot for all the effort I've put in,' Ronan remarked, coldly.

'Your first passenger air tour's scheduled for this afternoon,' responded Henry, with equal chilliness. 'And in accordance with company policy following return to work after a significant absence I'll be along as observer.'

As far as Ronan was aware no such company policy had existed till today and it was no doubt designed to piss him off.

It worked.

As Henry not only sat in the back of the helicopter for the flight but hovered at Ronan's shoulder during the pre-flight checks, Ronan went home fuming. There he found Selina in a matching bad mood.

'Any news?' she demanded, as he walked in the door.

He flung his jacket over the banisters. 'About?'

'Redundancy.'

'I got notice today. Finish in a month.'

Selina folded her arms. 'Do you get a payout?'

Ronan paused to marvel, not just that it obviously didn't occur to Selina to show any sympathy or concern, but that he'd once been in love with this ungracious freeloader. 'Not your concern.' He brushed past her into the kitchen.

She followed. 'But what's going to happen to us?'

Turning swiftly, Ronan shut the kitchen door so that Curtis wouldn't hear. 'There's no "us",' he snapped. 'What's going to happen to *me* is that I'm going to search hard for another job to pay my mortgage and support my son. How about you do something along the same lines?'

Eyes flashing, Selina threw the door open. 'Stop harping on!'

Ronan again shoved the door shut. He needed to take a couple of deep breaths before he could control the volume of his voice. 'We're angry with each other but, please, can we try not to let Curtis hear it? It's not his problem. It's ours. Till your recent issues we managed to put him first, to share his care, to each create a home for him. I would very much like to return to that arrangement.'

'Well, we don't always get what we want, do we?' Selina stared at his hand on the door until he moved it.

Ronan watched her flounce out. He was troubled by the deterioration in relations and knew his flash of temper had accelerated it. Sinking down at the kitchen table he gave his heartbeat a chance to return to normal, rubbing his hand wearily over his face.

The scene hadn't all been Selina's fault. He'd mismanaged the conversation by being confrontational because although he'd put a front on for Henry's benefit, his heart was heavy at losing his job. He could comfort himself that if Henry hadn't found a way to see off the competition then Buzz Sightseer would have been heading for oblivion anyway, but the fact remained that until the day he and Buzzair Two had somersaulted in a field, he'd loved his job and Henry had been his friend.

Funny how life treated you. It let you care deeply about something – job, friend, woman – and then took it all away.

Curtis wandered towards home, his backpack dangling from his shoulder, his phone in his hand.

> ***Curtis:*** *Getting out of Saturday footie club early*
> ***Natasha*****:** *Wuu2*
> ***Curtis:*** *Forgot to take piercings out this morning and they won't let me play case I get hurt*
> ***Natasha:*** *Couldnt u just take them out*
> ***Curtis:*** *I only just put them in yesterday after school so I dint want take them out again*
> ***Natasha:*** *Lol will u get dropped from team*
> ***Curtis:*** *Not just for missing one week. Wuu2?*
> ***Natasha:*** *Going to leahs soon*
> ***Curtis:*** *Not home with ur mum?*
> ***Natasha:*** *Not til later leah says shes brought new choc from work for me to try its lemon merang*
> ***Curtis:*** *Kool beans*
> ***Natasha:*** ☺ *laters*

Curtis put his phone away, wishing he could just walk into Leah's kitchen as he had in France. It was awesome that he and Natasha were talking again. He was spending half his time thinking of things to say to her and the other half checking his phone to see if she'd answered.

His steps slowed as he neared his dad's house and he thought of the raised voices he'd heard last night.

Now his mum was grumbling that she'd no idea what would happen because Ronan had lost his job. Neither had Curtis but he hated it when his mum moaned about his dad because his dad never dissed her. And his mum had made it sound as if his dad had done something wrong but redundancy wasn't the same as getting sacked, was it? His dad was stressed enough.

Quietly, Curtis let himself into the house. The TV was on in the sitting room but he could hear his mum on the phone. She didn't break off, so he guessed she hadn't heard him. Good. He crept along the hall towards the stairs, heading for his laptop.

Then he halted as he heard his mum's next words. 'Darren, before I commit I need to know where we're going. What would we live on?'

Curtis held his breath, edging towards the crack in the door until he could see her, feet planted, hand on hip, frowning as she listened to what was being said on the other end of the phone.

'But at least I have a room and board here,' she broke in. 'Where would I live with you?' Then she laughed as if she wasn't finding things funny. 'Yeah, you make fun of him, but *he* never left me to pack up everything I owned and drop the keys to my home at the bank.'

Finally, her voice softened. 'I love you, too. But I'm not sure. You let me down so I had to go crawling off to my ex. And what about Curtis? I'm not going anywhere without him. Are you sure things will work out?'

I'm not going anywhere without him? Where was she

thinking they might go? Curtis's heart began to beat so hard that he had to strain to listen over it.

'I suppose it'll be worth it in the end,' his mum went on, 'if you're certain it's a way of leaving the financial mess behind. But you're talking about a whole new place . . . Of course it's you I want to be with. I said I love you, didn't I? But I'm not going to say yes till I've talked to Curtis. *Nothing* happens till I've talked to Curtis.'

Curtis's heart plummeted. *A whole new place . . .*? He didn't want to live in a new place. He liked Orpington, where his friends were, his school, his footie team.

In a dizzying rite-of-passage moment he understood that his parents were not back together – and would never be. It felt a bit like when one of his mates gave him a nipple tweak, but deeper, right inside his heart. He blinked back tears. He'd been a stupid kid, shutting his eyes to the fact that his parents had stopped loving each other a long time ago.

And now, apparently, his mum was considering going to a new place and taking him with her. But he couldn't leave his dad! For a month he'd suffered a crappy hollow feeling over missing Natasha, and missing a parent would be much worse. His knees went funny and he realised he was frightened.

Breath sticking in his throat, Curtis crept towards the stairs while his mum carried on making plans with Darren. In his room, he was surprised to see that his hands were shaking as he opened his laptop. Getting a grip on himself he began tapping. After a while he had to tiptoe to his mum's room and find her handbag, keeping an ear on the reassuring rise and fall of her voice that confirmed she was still on the phone.

Back at his laptop, he input the card numbers. It was

wrong borrowing his mum's card but it was wronger to take him away from his dad.

He gathered up his cash from his pockets and his tin in the wardrobe. £10.32. Enough for lunch. He tipped his footie gear out of his backpack and stuffed in two T-shirts, underwear, a pair of jeans, his laptop, his phone charger and his ear buds.

Any slight anxiety about making it out of the house undiscovered was allayed by his mum running upstairs and into the bathroom, handily enough. Once he heard the hiss of the shower, Curtis dragged on a hoodie and made for the stairs, snuck out of the door and marched along the car-lined streets. He'd never done anything like this and he didn't like the knots of apprehension in his stomach. But he also felt a defiant sense of liberty.

For once he wasn't going to wimp around waiting for his parents to make decisions that affected him but were made without him. This time he'd act. Let them react for once!

Chapter Twenty-six

Leah was spending Saturday with Scott and Natasha, both of whom seemed to half-live at her house at the moment. Sprawled in a chair, Scott had the Odeon's programming for that evening open on his phone and Natasha, perching on his chair arm, was putting together her most persuasive arguments to be included in the arrangements, preferably after a visit to Pizza Hut.

'But if we take you, we have to see some PG nonsense,' Scott teased.

'It could be 12 or 12A, too.' Natasha treated him to her most winsome smile.

'And we have to pay for you.'

'I might be able to get some money from my dad. Or I'll wash Leah's car and then she can pay for me.'

Leah lounged crosswise on the other armchair. 'My car's clean. Wash Scott's. It looks as if he rolled it in a field.'

Solemnly, Scott shook his head. 'She's not tall enough to reach the roof.'

'I am!' Natasha shot to her feet and extended an arm over an imaginary Ford Focus.

'That's not right to the middle.'

'It *is*–'

The doorbell bing-bonged and Leah tutted at this disturbance to her lazy Saturday afternoon. 'Get that, Natasha, and we'll discuss you coming to the cinema.'

'Awesome!' Natasha darted into the hall.

'She's coming to the cinema,' Leah told Scott, giving him a shove with her toe. 'It's you who's in doubt.'

'Awwwww pleeeeease.' Scott made his biggest eyes and saddest face. 'I'll waaaash your caaaar.'

From the hall, they heard Natasha's excited treble. 'AweSOME! What're you doing here?'

Leah raised her eyebrows. 'Who's awesome enough to be told they're aweSOME?'

'Justin Bieber? Hannah Montana?'

Natasha burst back into the room, eyes sparkling. 'Look!'

A tall sandy-haired figure sidled into view.

Leah sat bolt upright, feeling as if the floor had shifted beneath her chair. '*Curtis*? How did you get here?'

Curtis let his hair swing forward. The sides of his head were freshly shaved. 'Train.'

Leah licked suddenly dry lips. 'Who's with you?'

He shook his head.

Natasha rounded on him, ponytail flying, voice shrill with excitement. 'You came on your own?'

He nodded.

Leah swung her feet to the floor, her 'trouble' antennae vibrating frantically. 'Sit down,' she invited. 'Natasha, how about you get drinks?'

Natasha danced off to the kitchen as Curtis lowered himself to the sofa, gaze darting around the room as if loath to encounter anybody else's.

Leah made her voice friendly but firm. 'It's fab to see

you but what's going on? Do your parents know where you are?'

'I wanted to see Natasha. It's not that far.' He glanced over his shoulder at the door. Leah's stomach lurched on an uneasy suspicion that he might be contemplating vanishing back through it.

Natasha, bless her ingenuous little socks, had simply accepted his presence as an unexpected treat. Leah would pretend to do the same.

She turned to Scott, who was regarding Curtis warily. 'Maybe Curtis would like to come to the Odeon with us. Why don't you show him what's on?'

'Right.' Scott's smile was stiff but he tilted his screen so that Curtis could study it.

Leah slipped out through the hall and into the front garden. She fumbled with her phone. This time she'd ring. A phone call might be less easy to ignore than a text. She tapped Ronan's name in her list of contacts and held the handset to her ear.

But all she heard was a beep. She checked the screen. *Number unobtainable*. What? Impatiently, she opened an internet browser window and looked up the phone number for Buzz Sightseer. That, at least, rang. A man answered.

'Is Ronan Shea there, please?' Leah was dismayed to hear how breathless she sounded.

'He's busy.'

'I'm Leah Beaumont, we met in France–'

The man sounded irritated. 'Tell him to keep his holiday romance out of the workplace.'

'It's not–' The dialling tone.

'Moron,' she snarled at the phone.

Behind her, the door opened and closed. She turned to

find Scott, hands deep in his pockets. 'Ringing Curtis's mum?'

'His dad. I don't have his mum's details. But I'm getting number unobtainable.' She tried Ronan's number again, exhibiting the screen message to Scott. 'Could he have blocked me?'

Scott shrugged. 'Get the mum's number from Curtis.'

'But I don't want him to know what I'm doing until I've talked to one of his parents. You don't think he's here with permission, do you? And what if he goes off again? Worse, what if Natasha goes with him? The hair dyeing showed that she's capable of doing stuff just to please him and she's as unsettled at home as he is.' She tried Ronan again. *Number unobtainable.*

'Let me try.'

'What good will that do?'

But Scott took the phone, tapped a few times, and handed it back. The screen message had altered to *Calling Ronan.*

Slowly, Leah positioned the phone. 'How did you do that?'

Scott shrugged.

In her ear, Ronan sounded surprised but warily pleased. 'Leah?'

She snapped her attention to the situation she needed to focus on. 'Curtis has just shown up at my house.'

A moment's silence, then rank disbelief. 'In *Cambridgeshire*?'

'I guessed you wouldn't know.'

Ronan growled, 'Too bloody right I don't. Can you put him on?'

She hesitated. 'He doesn't know I'm calling. I'm worried he's a flight risk, and there's even a remote chance Natasha might go with him because things are still troubled for her family-wise. Can you or Selina come?' Her heart sank an inch at her acknowledgement that Ronan and Selina would forever be coupled up by sharing Curtis.

'Can you keep him there?'

'If I can keep Natasha here I probably stand a good chance. They lit up like Christmas trees when they saw each other. I'll get them making something chocolatey.'

'Fantastic.' Relief rang in his voice. 'What's your address . . .? OK, got it. And . . . Leah? Thank you. I want–' He paused, then said hoarsely, 'Just thank you.'

The call over, Leah turned her gaze on Scott. 'So what was the issue with my phone?'

Scott shrugged and scuffed a foot.

Heart sinking, Leah recognised the signs of Scott closing up. 'OK. I need to stabilise the Curtis situation before anything else. But after that we *definitely* need to talk.' She hurried back into the house, following the sound of Natasha's high-pitched giggles to the kitchen, making sure she entered as casually as if they were back in the gîte. 'Want to make chocolate baskets? It's more fiddly than making chocolate bowls but you get to pop balloons.'

Curtis grinned down at Natasha. 'Cool.'

Her face shone as she beamed up at him. 'Amazeballs.'

Automatically, Leah moved to the sink to wash her hands. 'I think I've got plain, milk and white chocolate so we can really be artistic. We can add food colouring to the white chocolate, too.'

Natasha gave a series of bunny hops to join her at the sink. 'Rainbow chocolate! What shall we put in the baskets?'

'Ice cream?' Leah suggested. 'Or we could make mini muffins while the baskets set in the fridge.'

'Muffins!' Curtis tied up the front of his hair without a single glance at the door and Leah felt her anxiety cool a few degrees.

As she was supervising the blowing up of the balloons and the breaking up of chocolate, Leah realised that Scott hadn't followed her back into the house. She checked through the window . . . but he wasn't standing on the drive where she'd left him.

His car had gone. Her heart performed a slow, unhappy flip-flop.

'What colours have you got?' demanded Natasha.

'Several, I think. Open that cupboard and you'll see them.' Leah turned away from the window. Her conversation with Scott would have to wait.

But it would take place. Because something wasn't making sense in the largest possible way, sending butterflies swooping unpleasantly in her stomach.

But focus, focus. There was a more urgent situation to be dealt with. Chocolate duly melted and the white batch laced with red and blue food colouring, Leah left the teens happily drizzling it criss-cross over the bulbous end of the balloons to form spiky chocolate baskets while she phoned Michele to rapidly update her on the situation. 'So I need to keep Natasha here to keep Curtis here. Is that all right?'

Long years as a teacher of adolescents had made Michele reassuringly pragmatic. 'Of course it's all right. What a monkey Curtis has been! His poor parents must be frantic. Are both Ronan and Selina coming?'

Leah kept her voice light. 'We'll see who turns up.'

Call ended, she stared at her phone contemplatively. Then, as a test, she pulled up Ronan from her contacts and sent a text.

***Leah:** Just confirming address: 28 Grace Road, Bettsbrough, Cambs.*

She only had to wait a minute before her phone beeped.

***Ronan:** Got it, thx.*

Test conclusive.

Ronan phoned Selina from the apron outside the hangar. A small white private jet taxied past him towards the runway while he waited for her to answer.

She sounded impatient. 'What?'

He replied equally tersely. 'I've had a call from Leah to say Curtis has turned up at her house. He got to Cambridgeshire by train.'

Several seconds of silence. Then, 'What?' in a quite different tone, the mixture of astonishment, dismay and fear that parents reserve for the exploits of their children.

'Where did you think he was?'

'Footie practice. Although he is a bit late back. I was about to text him.' Then Selina seemed to collect her wits. 'Is he all right? How did he get the money for the train?'

'Don't know about the money but he's OK. Presumably he was feeling lovesick and knew we wouldn't let him go to see Natasha, so used footie practice as a smokescreen. Hopefully Leah can keep him with her till I get there.'

'Pick me up. I'll come with you.'

Ronan was in no mood for Selina to order him around. 'It doesn't need both of us. What if I have to put up in a hotel? I haven't got the money to splash about renting two rooms.'

Impatience returned. 'We've shared before!'

'We're not going to share now.' He took a breath. 'I understand why you want to come but we know he's safe and in good hands. I'll keep in touch with you.'

'And you want another crack at Leah,' she snapped.

Mentally, he counted to ten. 'I would value the opportunity to try and put things right between us, yes. Having my ex-wife in tow really won't help and I think I deserve your co-operation. I've been pretty good to you, considering that you owe me a lot, including the roof over your head.'

'Are you suggesting that if I don't co-operate you'll hoof me out?'

'No. I'm suggesting that you might wish to repay my kindness with a little of your own.' *And if I don't pick you up there isn't a whole hell of a lot you can do about it.*

She blew out a ragged sigh. 'All right,' she agreed, grudgingly. 'Ring me –'

'– the second there's something to tell. Yes.'

Tucking his phone away, Ronan ran into the hangar and stormed into Henry's office without knocking. 'I need to charter a helicopter – at cost would be nice.'

From behind his desk, Henry lifted a supercilious eyebrow. 'Why the hell should I charter you a helicopter at cost? You're down on the rota to take the three thirty. If you don't, it'll mean an official warning.'

'Curtis has taken himself off to Cambridgeshire alone by train. He's turned up at a friend's house and I want to get to him before he gets the wind up and vanishes.'

'Oh. Crap.' Henry sat back. He even looked vaguely sympathetic when he added, 'Bloody kids!'

Sensing capitulation, Ronan played his trump card. 'I'll

resign with immediate effect if that'll swing it. But I must get to Curtis.'

Henry gave a wintry smile. 'Even I'm not that much of a shit. Take Buzzair Three. I'll call someone in to cover the three thirty.'

Relief sent adrenalin surging through Ronan's veins. Tossing back, 'I might not get back today,' he strode out to tell Liam that Buzzair Three was going to need fuel to an airfield near Peterborough. He grabbed the keys to the cabin and his emergency travel kit from his locker, then on the chart identified an airfield about twelve miles south-east of Bettsbrough. After planning his route he rang Leah back.

She answered guardedly. 'Hey. I'm busy making chocolate baskets right now,' which let him know Curtis was still there and obviously within earshot.

Deep relief swirled through him. 'Is there anyone to pick me up from Conington Airport? The flight should take me thirty to thirty-five minutes and the aircraft's almost ready to go.'

'Let me see what I can arrange and I'll text you,' she answered.

'Fantastic.' For an instant he let pleasure wash over him at the knowledge he'd soon see Leah again. Then Liam came to give him the thumbs-up and Ronan headed out to the apron and the silvery bulk of Buzzair Three to stow his kit and embark on his pre-flight checks, not allowing his emotions to compromise thoroughness and method. Satisfied, he climbed into the left-hand seat and worked through his instrument checks before switching on, feeling the familiar shudder as the rotors began to revolve. He slipped on his headset. 'London City, this is Buzzair Three preparing for take-off, heading north over the London stub.'

London City came straight back and in less than a minute Ronan was performing a visual check that he was clear to bring the helicopter into hover. Henry, Liam, Cindy and Janine had come to stand at the mouth of the hangar. Henry even raised a hand in farewell, as if their friendship wasn't entirely dead.

For the next half hour Ronan lost himself in the familiar tasks of flying: calling Stapleford Airfield, then Stansted, as he passed through their zones, then London Information for the simple last leg of the journey. It was a nice easy approach to the local airfield and he requested permission to land and leave the aircraft, possibly overnight. He was soon in the helicopter parking area, putting the engine through its two-minute cool down.

He hardly noticed the silence as he stowed his headset and retrieved his bag. As he stepped down and secured the aircraft he spotted the unmistakeable pink bulk of The Pig near the airfield admin buildings and a figure waving. He never thought he'd be so glad to see Michele.

'This is exciting! I feel as if I'm in a James Bond movie,' she called, as he jogged up. Wasting no time, she climbed up into the driver's seat, her top stretched over her now visibly pregnant belly.

He hopped into the passenger side. 'Thanks.' He got his breath as she drove up to the barrier and off the airfield. 'How long will it take us?'

'About twenty minutes. So, apart from your son running away, how's everything with you?'

He blew out his cheeks. 'Oh. You know.'

She laughed softly. 'Leah's been miserable, too.'

He was so cheered by her response that he didn't mind her spending the rest of the journey sighing over the fact that Jordan was still living with his dad. Ronan had to text Selina and tell her he'd landed, anyway, and Henry to confirm where he'd left Buzzair Three.

The chocolate baskets were setting in Leah's fridge and Curtis and Natasha were watching *The Hunger Games* on Leah's laptop in her little conservatory off the sitting room when a woman's voice coo-eed, 'Helloo-oo,' from the front door.

Curtis squeezed Natasha's hand. 'That your mum?'

Natasha stuck out her bottom lip. 'I hope she hasn't come to take me home. If she has, I'll ask her to let you come, too.'

'Right,' he said, hollowly. Somehow, he doubted that Michele would accept him as unquestioningly as Leah had. Leah was cool. Michele was a teacher. Now the satisfaction of making his destination and the excitement of being with Natasha again were fading, he'd already begun wondering what came next.

He wasn't left wondering for long. A familiar voice said, 'Hello, Curtis.' And it certainly wasn't Natasha's mum.

'Hey, Ronan!' Natasha twisted around to beam at him, not seeming to realise that Ronan might not be very pleased over Curtis's surprise visit.

''Lo,' Curtis added, cautiously.

His dad came in and sank down in a cane chair, fixing Curtis with an uncomfortable stare. 'I'm glad to see you safe. We need to talk.'

Curtis felt his face heat up. 'OK.' His dad never got shouty or sweary like some dads did, but the inflexibility of his voice told Curtis to expect a bumpy ride over the next few minutes.

Leah spoke quietly from the doorway. 'Natasha, can you help me clear the kitchen, please?'

'S'pose.' Natasha sighed and paused the film with exaggerated patience. The sliding glass door between conservatory and lounge closed behind her, leaving Curtis alone with his dad.

His dad didn't smile. 'When Leah rang me to say where you were I nearly had a heart attack. What made you come without asking anyone?'

Curtis fiddled with one of the studs on his trousers. They were cool trousers, bought from Camden Market. 'Wanted to see Natasha. Didn't think you or mum would let me.'

'It would be irresponsible of either of us to let a thirteen-year-old travel up here alone without any arrangements in place for when he arrived. Anything could have happened.'

'I knew where Natasha was from the Find Friends app and nothing did happen. And I'm nearly fourteen.'

'True. But I wouldn't let a fourteen-year-old boy travel up here alone, either, so the point is moot.'

Curtis couldn't remember much about moot points, though he knew they'd done them in English last year, so stuck to the part of the argument he understood. 'But nothing *happened*. I looked up the trains, I bought the ticket and I got here. Orpington to Victoria, tube to Liverpool Street, train to Bettsbrough.' He didn't mention the knots in his stomach from fear and the moments that he'd at least half-wished that he'd stayed home and simply told his dad what he'd overheard his mum saying, and wait for the adults to sort it out. 'So, maybe you ought to, like, trust me.'

His dad raised an eyebrow a couple of millimetres. 'How did you pay for the ticket?'

Curtis let his gaze drop. 'Mum's credit card.' He brought out his nearly empty wallet and handed it over. 'I only kept it because I needed it to pick up the ticket from the machine.'

His dad's voice was like silk. 'Using someone else's credit card without their consent is deception, a criminal offence. And you want us to trust you? But we can circle back to that. You got here, you found Natasha at Leah's – thank goodness – and you made yourself an uninvited guest. What did you expect to happen next?'

Curtis shrugged. He hated it when adults asked unanswerable questions then waited with exaggerated patience for the answer.

'Where would you stay tonight?'

Well . . . here?

'What would you do for food?'

Leah always had loads of food.

'When did you expect to come home? Have you bought a return ticket?'

Unexpectedly, Curtis felt his eyes begin to burn. 'No. Where's home, anyway? Have I got one?' His nose burned, too, and he had to give a giant sniff.

His dad frowned. 'Of course you have a home! With me.' Then his voice gentled. 'Is there more to this than taking off to see your girlfriend? Are you in trouble? Has something worried you? You can tell me. Whatever it is, I'll help you sort it out.'

'Yeah, yeah, yeah,' Curtis said dolefully.

'I will, you know. There's nobody more important to me than you. You'll have a home with me as long as you want it.'

The love and concern in his dad's voice turned the key on everything Curtis had been keeping tightly shut away. When he opened his mouth, what came out was suspiciously like a sob. 'Mum's planning to take me somewhere.

I heard her on the phone to Darren. She said she was leaving as soon as she'd talked to me about it.' Another treacherous sob escaped between his words. 'I thought if she couldn't talk to me, she couldn't go. I thought she didn't care what I wanted. I thought I might never see you again.'

Then somehow his dad was kneeling beside him and pulling him against the comfort of his chest, growling, 'I will never let that happen.'

Curtis realised to his horror that he was proper crying, and every sob was so loud he was sure Natasha would hear.

But he couldn't stop.

His dad just hugged him harder. 'There's got to be some explanation for what you overheard. Mum's never purposely let you down.'

'But I heard her.'

'OK. When you're ready, we'll put my phone on speakerphone and talk to her together.'

Curtis nodded and blew his nose on tissues from a box under Leah's table but the tears took a while to stop.

Finally, he got over himself, feeling sort of cleaned out but headachey. His dad rang his mum and put the phone on the table between them. Haltingly, encouraged by his dad, Curtis explained how he'd overheard her plans. He had to blow his nose again and take a gulp from his glass of Coke.

His mum's squawk of dismay sounded tinny over speakerphone. 'I didn't say I was going off somewhere and taking you with me!'

'You said you were going to a whole new place!'

She had to pause and blow her nose herself, which made Curtis feel a bit guilty. 'Darren does want me to live with him again but what we were talking about was us declaring bankruptcy.'

'Is that when you lose all your money, like in Monopoly?'

'Kind of. But there's more to it. It's a financial state – Darren's been talking to the Insolvency Service about it. You acknowledge that you can't pay your debts and it means you can't have certain things like a normal bank account or a mortgage. It's good from the point of view of letting you leave your debts behind but it's bad because of all the financial restrictions it brings with it. So that's what I meant when I said it would take us to a "whole new place". A new way of living.'

'Oh.' Curtis tried to digest the information. 'I was scared you were going to take me away with Darren and I wouldn't see Dad any more.'

'Oh, Curtis!' gasped his mum, tearfully. 'It was your dad and me who split up. Neither of us has ever tried to stop the other seeing you. I might have made a lot of mistakes but I chose you a good dad.'

It was his dad who had to blow his nose this time.

When the phone call was over, Curtis wiped his face for the last time and drained his drink. 'Sorry,' he offered.

His dad smiled the first proper smile since he'd arrived. 'Promise me you won't do anything like this again. You can't run away from problems and put yourself in danger.'

'I wanted to see Natasha, too, though. She didn't speak to me for weeks then when she did I just wanted to be with her.'

'I know. Heartache sucks, eh?'

Curtis felt suddenly old. Or, at least, a bit more grown up. 'Is that how you've been feeling about Leah?'

His dad looked rueful. Then he looked as if he was fighting with himself. Finally he admitted, in that growl that he used when he really meant something, 'Yes.'

'Because Mum spoiled it when she turned up in France?'

His dad shrugged but his eyes looked as if he'd like to say 'Yes' to that, too.

Curtis felt that rocky feeling inside that came with awkwardness between his parents. 'Mum was desperate.'

His dad nodded. 'I know. And whatever has gone on between Mum and me, I won't let her sleep in doorways. We'll work something out.'

Curtis got another glimpse of how it was to be a grown-up, to realise someone was protecting you by saying what you wanted to hear. And to suddenly see things from that person's point of view. He sighed. 'But that's not fair. She's got Darren, so you should be able to have a girlfriend, and Leah only went funny when Mum turned up to live with us.'

Chapter Twenty-seven

It was past seven when Ronan ushered Curtis into the kitchen where Leah was wiping surfaces, Natasha drifting about vaguely as if she were helping, and Michele drinking coffee at the table. Ronan looked tired but managed a smile that felt as if it were just for Leah.

Natasha swung round when she saw Ronan. 'You're not going to take Curtis away, are you?'

'Not till tomorrow.' Ronan smiled. 'How about I take you guys up for a flight experience before we head back?'

'Did you fly here?' Curtis demanded, having apparently given no thought to his dad's method of arrival till now. 'Cool beans!'

'Amazeballs!' breathed Natasha, eyes alight. 'We can, can't we, Mum? Can Dad come?'

Voices rose in a babble as everyone tried to establish how many the aircraft seated – six and the pilot – and whether a pregnant woman and a man with his lower leg in plaster would make good passengers.

Leah listened quietly as Ronan joked about getting Alister in the helicopter by shoving him in bum first, one thought having absorbed her while the father-son talk took place in her conservatory. *Ronan had arrived without Selina.*

And she'd have to be blind not to see the hunger in his eyes whenever he looked her way. In fact, she shied away from meeting his gaze in case he could read hers just as easily, the jumble of thoughts and emotions that she hadn't yet acknowledged the full meaning of, even to herself.

Taking refuge in what she did know about, Leah began supper.

'Is Curtis invited? And Ronan?' demanded Natasha.

'Of course.' Leah clattered busily with a heavy based pan.

'To stay over?' Natasha pressed hopefully, ignoring reprovingly raised eyebrows from her mother.

'They can have the spare room if they want to.' Leah reached down her chopping board.

'That would be incredibly helpful, if it doesn't put you out.' Ronan didn't bother hiding his relief.

'Awesome.' Curtis grinned.

'Can I stay, too?' added Natasha. 'I could sleep on your sofa.'

Feeling somehow that there might be safety in numbers, Leah agreed. 'If your mum says it's OK and you sleep on the chairbed in my room.'

Michele glanced thoughtfully from Leah to Ronan. 'It's OK, if she's not in your way. But I've got a mountain of marking so I'll go now and see you tomorrow.'

'Great,' returned Natasha, unflatteringly, as Michele made for the door. '*Hunger Games*.' And the kids disappeared back into the conservatory, shutting the adults out with the sliding door.

The kitchen was suddenly ultra-quiet. The safety-in-numbers strategy hadn't quite come off, Leah thought, as she foraged in the fridge for red and yellow peppers, courgette, onion, carrot, mushrooms and a lime.

Ronan came up beside her. 'Let me help.'

His voice, so close to her ear, scrambled a squadron of butterflies. She decanted into the sink the veg and a handful of coriander from her pots on the windowsill. 'Thanks. These need washing.' Breezing around as if in a working kitchen, she collected her eight-inch knife, olive oil, soy sauce, chilli oil and a pack of fresh noodles. When he brought over the washed veg she put a light under the pan and added a splash of olive oil.

After topping and tailing the onion she slit the jacket and shucked it off, halved the acid flesh, arranged the two parts flat side down and ch-ch-ch-chopped them in a couple of seconds. Then she threw the coriander on top, cross-chopped the two finely, tossed the mixture into the hot oil, shook and tossed it again, then began on the carrot and peppers.

Ronan watched as Leah reduced the vegetables to a shredded rainbow across her chopping board. 'I don't know whether to be impressed or scared.'

As he seemed at ease in the moment, not referring to what had gone between them in the past or might in the future, Leah relaxed enough to grin as she used the flat of her knife to scrape the veg into the pan. 'Could you put plates in to warm, set the table and get us drinks? You've got about four minutes before you need to wrench the kids away from the DVD.' She tossed the noodles and added soy sauce and chilli oil, halved the lime and squeezed the juice into the mixture.

Five minutes later they were seated at the table, forking up sizzling stir-fry and chatting to Natasha and Curtis.

Leah's heart felt peculiar and bouncy. It made her leap up as soon as the stir-fry had vanished. 'Chocolate baskets! We didn't get around to making muffins so let's go with fresh fruit and chocolate sauce.'

The next hour passed in a happy clamour as Leah demonstrated how to artistically arrange strawberries and grapes they had washed and halved, before she whipped up chocolate sauce on the hob. Then Curtis and Natasha took phone videos and before-and-after photos as Leah swooshed on the hot sauce and the baskets began to melt. Then every scrap was eaten, even the fruit, since it was satisfactorily coated in chocolate.

The clearing up was accomplished with lots of slacking, giggling and getting in each other's way. Ronan tried to send the kids off to finish watching *Hunger Games* but they were too hyped to settle and brimmed with noisy jokes and laughter. With mixed feelings about having almost no time alone with Ronan, Leah embarked on meeting everyone's needs in the way of bedclothes and towels and, finally, what seemed like hours later, the teens yawned enough to be despatched to their respective beds.

Finding herself in a queue for her own bathroom, Leah slipped back downstairs to brew a nice solitary cup of fresh mint tea in the hope it would help her sleep, even with Ronan in the next room.

She was just deciding that now was the ideal time to text Scott, having waited in vain for him to contact her with an explanation that would stop her feeling hollow and dismal whenever she thought about him, when Ronan padded into the kitchen and shut the door.

He was still wearing a white shirt with epaulettes and black trousers but his feet were bare. With no regard for whether she wanted him in her personal space, he moved straight into it and took her hands. 'I'm so grateful that Natasha was at your house and for the app that brought Curtis to her. Thank you for being someone he saw as a safe harbour and giving him a place to be until I got here. For giving us somewhere to stay. And just for being you.' He lowered his head and brushed a kiss against her mouth, moving closer until their bodies fit together as if they'd never been apart. 'You smell of chocolate,' he murmured. 'The rich, dark, slightly bitter kind.'

Leah's stomach flipped like a pancake and she melted against him as he made the kiss deeper, stroking her tongue with his, cradling her as if she were precious. Growing hard against her and making the sort of approving noise that wasn't a word but said a lot.

By the time the kiss ended he was breathing hard. 'And thanks for not asking me to apologise for that.' He backed away. Slowly.

Leah, watching him turn and head back upstairs, wasn't sure she could speak anyway.

Leah woke on Sunday morning to the sound of a man's voice. Natasha was an unmoving bump under her covers so Leah crept to the top of the stairs to listen. Ronan was standing in her hall, sounding assured and professional, arranging for fuel and notifying someone of his intention to take a family up on a flight experience.

As he ended the call, Leah bolted for her bedroom to dress. When she made it downstairs it was to find coffee brewing and Ronan flipping through an *Autosport* magazine that Scott had left a couple of days ago.

Ronan, though his expression said he had other things on his mind, was back to treating her with restrained courtesy. 'As we're not all going to fit into your Porsche, do you think Michele would drive us to the airfield in The Pig?'

Leah nodded. 'But I think her mob could do with a little time together so I'll take you in the Porsche.' She made the necessary calls to Alister and Michele then made pancakes to eat with fruit for breakfast, because she hadn't expected all these houseguests and really didn't have much else.

During the drive to the airfield, Ronan chatted about his return to work and how his boss had been prepared to let Ronan take a fall to help him out of a financial cesspit. 'To be fair, he came good in letting me bring Buzzair Three to find Curtis, but it still stings.'

'What a shit.' Leah glanced away from the road. 'Aren't you furious?'

He shrugged. 'I was. Now I'm just sad our friendship meant so little to him.'

Friendship. It made Leah think of Scott, who still hadn't contacted her, even though she'd left messages. She parked at the airfield and when The Pig lumbered up to disgorge its passengers the mood was all excitement over the impending flight as everyone oohed and ahhed over the gleaming silver helicopter, watching Ronan perform mysterious checks that on occasion seemed as basic as giving bits of the aircraft a shake.

'Right, come on,' Ronan called, when he was satisfied, and they scurried to join him, except Alister, who hopped, having stowed his crutches in The Pig. Ronan gave a briefing about what to expect, then got Alister in first. He continued to allocate seats and harness people into them until only Leah remained. He closed and fastened the back doors, then opened the front and showed her where to put her foot and hand to swing up into the co-pilot's seat, a stick between her knees and her feet cradled by rudder pedals. He fastened her harness, managing to barely touch her, and then set everyone up with a headset.

As he took his own seat, Leah suddenly found her heart pounding. It wasn't from fear of flying – or crashing. It was from the sinking realisation that she and Ronan had talked about nothing important and after this flight was over she would be left on the ground, waving goodbye as he whirred off into the sky to fly Curtis back to their real life in Orpington.

Ronan swung up into his seat and performed an audio check, voices loud in Leah's ears as everyone acknowledged into their microphones. He explained some of the dials on his instrument panel, Jordan asked where the parachutes were, Natasha giggled a lot. Then everybody went quiet as the power came in and the rotors whup-whup-whupped above them, first slowly, then escalating into a blur as Ronan talked officialese to the tower.

Afterwards, Leah had trouble recalling the take-off. She remembered the helicopter dropping its nose as if for a last look at the ground and the slow sweep to skim above the ground away from other parked helicopters. Then suddenly she was high above the world, the kids all talking at once over the headsets.

Ronan's reassuring voice broke into the babble. 'So we're up at about fifteen hundred feet. Is everybody OK? If I was doing my own job, this is where I'd start pointing out London landmarks. But as this is your home turf, maybe you can do the honours. We're approaching Bettsbrough now.'

It didn't seem possible that they'd covered in three minutes in a helicopter what took twenty minutes in a car. It was amazing, Leah thought, as Natasha and Jordan competed to identify churches and supermarkets. The aircraft bobbed and banked like a giant bee and Leah watched the scenery scrolling beneath them.

Ronan's voice intruded on her thoughts. 'The others can't hear us.'

She removed her gaze from between her feet where she'd been watching toy cars threading along a toy road. 'Why's that?'

His smile was boyish. 'I've turned off their audio. I have some stuff to tell you. I'm trying to make it hard for you not to listen.'

'Oh!' she squeaked, warmth spreading inside her. Risking a glance around she saw the others all gazing raptly about them.

Ronan's eyes roved constantly between the space around the helicopter, the ground, his instrument panel. And her. 'Selina came back with us to England. We've all been living in my house.'

'Oh.' Leah's stomach dipped as if the helicopter had hit an air pocket.

'But in separate bedrooms, *obviously*, and straight back into the old routine of getting on each other's nerves and trying not to let Curtis know. It's taken a while for Curtis to come to terms with the fact that we're not "together" but now he definitely has. He knows his mum's talking to Darren about moving back in with him. Unfortunately, that's the conversation that set him off on this adventure, thinking Selina had a plan to remove him from Orpington . . . See anything you recognise? Am I covering the right neighbourhood?'

Leah looked down again at the world in miniature, so intent on his relationship update that she'd almost forgotten they were up in the air. 'Where the little lake is, that's a park quite near Michele's house. And over there's Tesco's and the retail area.'

'Good.' The engine note changed and their progress slowed. 'It was a shock when Selina turned up in France. It was a shock when you shut me out. But it was seriously bloody painful when you left without saying goodbye and then ignored me when I tried to call or text.'

Guilt rose in Leah. 'I shouldn't have left like that. But I texted you to explain! Why didn't you answer?'

He frowned across at her. 'You didn't text me. Not even once.'

'I did but then something screwy happened–'

Michele's hand came through from the back, tapping on Ronan's seat. Michele pointed to her headset, mouthing, 'Can't hear you!'

'Sorry,' Ronan mouthed back. Then, to Leah, 'Do you think you could ask your annoying sister to invite Curtis to her place for a few hours?'

Heart skipping, Leah nodded, and Ronan did something at his instrument panel and said, 'Is that better, Michele?'

'Yes, that's it,' she agreed over the headset. 'We haven't been able to hear you for ages.'

He smiled. 'That's OK. I haven't been saying anything you needed to hear.'

Chapter Twenty-eight

When Michele was approached to entertain Curtis for a few hours she blew out her cheeks. 'I don't have much in for lunch.' Then she glanced at Ronan's expression and rushed to add, 'But supermarkets are open on Sundays and I owe my sister a favour. Or twenty.'

Leah hugged her. 'You could invite Alister and Jordan. Build a few bridges.'

Michele wrinkled her nose. But she did take everyone away in The Pig, leaving Leah to drive Ronan home.

He didn't broach whatever was on his mind until they were inside her house. Then Leah found herself led firmly to her own sofa and fixed with Ronan's darkly direct gaze. 'If I'd received your text, I'd have answered. I've nearly worn the screen out looking for your messages. I never received a thing.'

'Something happened.' Leah had to swallow before she could explain how she'd received 'number unobtainable'. Until suddenly she hadn't. 'It took Scott seconds to put me back in contact with you.'

Ronan's gaze narrowed. He stared at her for several seconds before he asked, 'By magic?'

Dolefully, she shrugged. Then, more honestly, 'No, he knew what he was doing. I suppose it's possible I'd inadvertently put a block on you and he just took it off but . . .' She had to blink heat from her eyes when she thought of any other explanation.

His grunt was scornful. But then he looked into her face and drew her closer, holding her, making his body a safe place for her to rest. 'When a friend lets you down it removes a layer of skin,' he observed, softly. 'Did you ask Scott for an explanation?'

She let her cheek lie against his warmth as she thought about confronting what she absolutely didn't want to believe. 'I didn't get a chance – he left without telling me. He's not answering at the moment.'

'Let's stop talking about other people.' He scooped Leah up against him and kissed her.

'Your shoulder –' she protested.

'– is fine, now. Mainly. Shall we talk about how we're going to make things work?'

Leah's breathing rate doubled. 'Things?'

Shifting her around so that he could look into her face, he tangled his fingers her hair, teasing the strands apart, letting his hand brush her neck, her shoulder, her breast, his expression serious. 'I think it's more than chemistry overload between us, Leah. Borrowing a helicopter was a one-off but we're just a couple of hours apart by road. I want us to be together. So if that's not going to happen –' he ran gentle fingertips along her jaw '– it's because of you.'

Her eyes closed as tiny explosions of desire followed in the wake of his touch. 'Because I'm no good at relationships.'

His hand fell away. 'That is a huge heap of stinking horseshit.'

Leah's eyes flew open again. 'It is not!' she retorted indignantly. 'How the hell do you think I've got to thirty-five so incredibly single?'

'So you're an independent woman! You haven't met the right man before. And Scott–!' He glowered down at her.

'It's easy to blame Scott.'

'Yes, it is, if he's been messing with your phone. You should just be the woman you want to be. It's your choice.' Then he actually moved himself along the sofa, away from her.

'But I *am* the woman I want to be. Single. Child-free. Always the bridesmaid and never the bride. Totally independent. By *choice*.' Hadn't he been paying attention?

His eyes were bleak. 'You're so caught up in declaring your independence that you're actually not making choices at all. Maybe you should think less about what you think you should do and more about what you want to do. You're just living up to an image of yourself you created years ago.'

'I am not!'

'Of course you are. So blindly sticking by Plan A that you won't acknowledge that Plan B can be about development, not selling out. Aren't you strong enough to realise that people change? Grow? If you don't want to be a wife, fine! You also have the options of lover, girlfriend or partner.'

'Maybe I'm too selfish,' she tried, weakly, unable to cope with the ground shifting so abruptly beneath her. 'Too self-orientated.'

'Yeah, right,' he scoffed, scrubbing a hand across his face. 'Why do Natasha and Jordan adore you? Look at everything you did for your sister's family this summer. Look at the way you pulled out the stops to keep Curtis safe. So far as he's concerned you'd be a fantastic "my dad's girlfriend". In fact, I'm offering you that very position. We do have chemistry overload – I'm surprised my mirror didn't melt the last time we got together.' His gaze softened. 'But it's more than chemistry. I love you. You're the one, Leah.' He shifted closer but only to drop a kiss on her hair. 'You need to think hard about everything we've just talked about. I'll get a taxi to Michele's and pick Curtis up, then go on to the airfield.' He climbed to his feet.

'Already?' Leah scrambled up, giddy at his change of mood.

'Things to do. I need to get Buzzair Three back, let my lad clear the air with my ex-wife and help her get the hell out of my house.'

'I'll drive you.'

'No. Let's make this quick and clean.' He turned and dragged her into a big hard hug that felt as if it might be goodbye. His voice was muffled against her hair. 'If it turns out that all we had was just for the holidays, I'll never regret it. But I'll always be angry and disappointed because it could be so much more. If you'd choose it.'

'I can't–'

'Sweetheart, it's not *can't*, it's *won't*. If you don't recognise the difference then nobody can explain it to you – you've got to work it out.'

He kissed her gently, slowly, and strode out of the house.

Chapter Twenty-nine

For the past two weeks Leah had had just about all the personal space she could wish for.

Scott had been completely silent. Leah hadn't even known he was capable of it. None of their friends had seen him down at The Chequered Flag. Her messages had gone unanswered, including a sarcastic:

> *Leah: I'm not getting messages from you. Wonder if someone's been messing with my phone?*

In addition, Natasha's visits had tailed off because Michele had agreed that she'd drive Natasha down to Orpington soon, which had sufficiently improved mother-daughter relations for Natasha to have less need for a bolthole.

Single, child-free woman gets her life back. Yay. Leah could eat what and when she wanted, go where she wanted and watch motorsport in total silence.

When the freedom had nearly driven her demented, and even Saturday qualifying for one of the last F1 races of the season had failed to hold her attention, she texted Ronan.

Leah: *I understand Natasha wants to meet up with Curtis again. I might offer to bring her in a couple of weeks to save Michele the stress. x*
Ronan: *Fraud. You're making excuses to do things you want to do instead of choosing them honestly. x*
Leah: *I'm helping my sister!*
Ronan: *Bullshit. You're trying to avoid admitting anything I said is true, that it's down to you to make a choice. I'm onto you. x*
Ronan: *PS But I still love you, if that helps the making of the choice. xxxxx*
Ronan: *PPS And I'm prepared to keep telling you I love you, even though I can't help but notice you haven't said it back. xxxxx*
Ronan: *PPPS NB Falling for someone against your will is hard to come to terms with. But it's allowed. xxxxx*

Another week passed, then it was Ronan's turn to text first.

Ronan: *Have you seen Scott? x*
Leah: No. *x*
Ronan: *Maybe you're not the only one to avoid facing difficult situations. x*
Leah: *I am not!*
Ronan: *I don't agree. xx*

Unsettled and grumpy, Leah tramped to Michele's house, kicking through fallen leaves with her hands shoved in her pockets and her heart in her comfortable AirWair boots.

She knocked and let herself into the kitchen, shouting hello. Jordan ambled in. 'Hey, Leah, brought any chocolate?'

'No, sorry.' Leah gave him a hug instead.

'Disappointing. Mum's in the sitting room.' Jordan pulled on a jacket, swung through the back door and was gone.

Glad that Jordan was at least visiting his mum, Leah wandered into the room at the front of the house and found Michele at the computer, arms folded on her baby bump as if it grew there as a convenient ledge to lean on. She glanced up. 'How are you with spreadsheets?'

'Crap.' Leah dropped into an armchair.

'I hate them.' Michele pecked at the keyboard then paused to peer dubiously at the screen.

'Jordan was here?'

A smile overcame Michele's spreadsheet frowns. 'We're getting on better.'

'I'm glad.' Leah watched as her sister began to peck the keyboard again. After a minute she observed, 'Lots of changes for you, this year.'

Michele blew out her cheeks. 'You're not kidding.'

Leah tried to sound casual. 'Do you regret any of your choices?'

Swivelling her chair, Michele patted her tummy. 'Baby Three's more of an accident than a choice and much more good than bad. But I know some of my choices were rash and, unfortunately, other people have paid a price. Now I'm making sure that my decisions are more considered and I'm going forward with what I believe is called a "reimagined family" with a mixture of hope and regret.'

Leah mulled that over. 'What's your biggest regret? Upsetting the children? Losing Bailey?'

Grief fluttered briefly across Michele's face. 'It's that I can't see a way to have them all. Are you pondering the meaning of life?' She turned back to her screen.

Leah heaved a sigh. 'The meaning of my life, perhaps.'

'Ah. I thought that might happen. Have you heard much from Ronan?'

'Little bit.'

'Is it enough?'

Leah climbed heavily to her feet. 'That's a big question. I'll leave you to your spreadsheet.'

But Michele rose too and hugged Leah awkwardly around the big firm tummy that would one day emerge to be called something other than Baby Three. Another child for Michele to love. And Leah to love, too. 'Because we've started talking about you instead of me? Leah, if you've still got choices it's a blessing. Having no choices left? That's when you know you're in trouble. Even some of the choices you think you have turn out to have a sell-by date.'

'We're not talking about a cake!'

'Cake or man . . . they don't stay on the shelf forever. If you don't grab them, someone else might.'

Leah removed her head from her own cloud of worries for a moment. 'Are you trying to "grab" one?'

Michele gave a half-laugh. 'Bailey will get over what's happened and look elsewhere. Alister's "seeing a lot of" a woman he met in the fracture clinic, did he tell you? I've only one choice I can live with at the moment – to be a single mum to my three children.'

Leah stepped blindly back into Michele's hug, lost for words to encompass the enormity of how her sister must feel but admiring her for putting her kids first, born and unborn. The irritation she so often felt with Michele popped like a bubble as the arms she'd known all her life held her tight.

'So make your choices while you can,' Michele whispered, before she stood back to let Leah leave.

Stepping out of Michele's house, Leah fastened her coat against the gusts, turning over in her mind all that Michele had told her, not knowing whether to be glad or sorry that Alister was dating again. He was a good man and deserved some happiness but it snuffed out any spark of hope that he and Michele might one day get back together despite Baby Three.

Bailey seemed as if he might be a greater source of grief, always in contact with Michele as the dad of Baby Three but moving on to new loves, maybe getting married. Bettsbrough was a small town with only a couple of senior schools. If Bailey had more children they could one day be in Michele's class!

She trudged aimlessly around the streets, burrowing into her coat against the early November chill, unable to think of any way to help Michele's situation.

Her mind slid inexorably back to her own.

What she wanted. What she didn't want. What she could have. What she couldn't have. What she'd give up if she had to. And what she never could.

She halted to gaze at the streets she'd known all her life. Safe. Familiar. 'This is a moment of truth,' she told the trees that lined the pavements, while they tossed their heads as if forced against their will to listen. 'Was it just for the holidays?'

It was another half-hour's trudging before Leah arrived outside the red-brick block where Scott had his apartment.

She buzzed the intercom and he answered, almost to her surprise. But there was no camera facility to his entry system and she supposed he wouldn't have been expecting her.

'Ready to talk?'

A long hesitation, then the intercom buzzed and the heavy front door clicked undone.

He met her at the door to his flat wearing an expression that was a mixture of uncertainty and bravado. 'Long time no see.'

'Whose fault's that?' She followed him into the apartment that was almost as familiar as her own house, the untidy sitting room and his 'man chair' with the TV remote on one arm and a mug of coffee on the other.

'Been busy,' he offered unconvincingly.

Leah didn't sit down. Her stomach was jumping as it did when waiting for bad news. 'I need you to explain why I couldn't get in touch with Ronan on my phone when I left France. Then you did something to my phone and suddenly I could.'

He gave a big, put-on shrug and a wide wobbly smile. 'Technology, eh?'

'Technology is operated by humans.'

Five seconds passed. Ten. Then Scott deflated before Leah's eyes, sinking into his chair, every line of his face drooping with misery. 'I know your pass code so I changed Ronan's phone number and email addy in your contacts. I blocked him from ringing you, too.' His throat worked as he swallowed.

Shock shimmered through her, even though she'd known it must be something like this. It was hard to absorb the words falling reluctantly from Scott's mouth. 'Why?'

'I thought it was best for you to make a clean break. I

didn't want him to be able to cause you more grief. I'm sorry, Leah.' He wiped an eye. 'Don't hate me. I just wanted you not to be hurt any more.'

She took in a steadying breath, feeling sick that Scott, supposedly her best friend, could do something like this. 'If you hadn't happened to be here when Curtis showed up I wouldn't have known how to get Ronan and something bad could have happened. But, that aside, don't you know *anything* about me? You cannot run my life! Ever. *Ever.* EVER. Friends don't make each other's decisions. How *dare* you try and manipulate me and pretend it's for my sake?'

A long aching silence drew out. Leah's mind ran up the paths of logic his confession opened up. She could hardly bring herself to ask the next question because the answer might hurt too much. 'Did you do that with Tommy, too?'

'The trick's to transpose just a couple of characters, so it's not obvious,' Scott prevaricated.

She swallowed. 'Is that a yes?'

He surged to his feet, red-faced. 'Tommy was an arse! I wanted to stop him being so sleazy with you. When you thought you might be pregnant –' he paused to blow his nose '– I was waiting for my opportunity to change it back, but then you weren't, so . . .'

Leah sweated through a fresh wave of nausea. 'So you felt justified in deciding that I shouldn't contact Tommy again? Or Ronan? In making my decisions? Meddling? Interfering? *Controlling*?'

Scott flinched. 'I was protecting you,' he whispered, miserably.

'Bollocks,' she spat. '*I* make my choices, Scott!'

Another tiny tear escaped from Scott's eye. 'I'm sorry.' Then, when Leah made no reply, 'Where's your pilot now?'

'Back where he belongs,' she admitted.

Like magic, Scott's face cleared. 'Good! Oh, hell, but honestly, Leah, he's a *father*, for fuck's sake. A proper dependable adult with ties and responsibilities he'd want you to share. If you hooked up with him you'd be like a *mum*. He'd want you to go on family picnics instead of track days and he probably doesn't understand Formula 1.' He laughed. 'You can't half pick 'em, girl! But that's you, isn't it, always with the chemical reaction instead of common sense . . . hey, where are you going?' The relief that had burst over his face morphed into dismay as Leah began to back towards the door.

Tears burned in her eyes but she managed a wobbly smile. 'Wherever I choose.' She threw up a hand to ward Scott off as he made an impetuous move towards her. 'Building in failure to my relationships has become second nature to you. You've just shown me how unhealthy our friendship was and how negatively you've been influencing me. Because, actually, I can "pick 'em". Or one at least.'

'But Leah–!' Scott pleaded, scurrying behind her as she flung open his front door, his skin pink and sweaty and terror in his eyes. 'I have feelings for you,' he almost wailed. 'Proper feelings, all right? And before you tell me it won't work, I know! I know I'm wrong for you because of my orientation. That's why I've done what I've done.'

Leah's heart didn't melt for him but she felt a new sadness as she realised his confession, his last roll of the dice, the confession he'd probably had to rip out from his deepest hidden places, didn't actually change anything. 'I'm sorry, Scottie. You're right that it won't work but it's nothing to do with your orientation. Loads of bisexual people are happily monogamous. If you know you couldn't be faithful to me then there's something else getting in the way. And–'

She took a deep breath. 'I only ever loved you as a friend. No amount of trickery or manipulation will give me feelings for you that I don't have. I'm sorry.'

Chapter Thirty

Ronan answered the door in his Buzz Sightseer uniform after an air tour along the Thames in the late autumn sun. When he saw who was standing on his doorstep his heart gave a giant leap but his body stayed absolutely still.

Her golden-brown hair writhed in the wind as her eyes travelled over his pressed black trousers and the crisp white shirt. 'You scrub up well but I kind of miss the shoulder brace.'

'If you've got a thing about uniforms the bad news is I'll be made redundant on Friday.' He stepped back to allow her in.

Though her eyes widened sympathetically Leah stayed where she was. 'You didn't tell me.'

'I'd told you enough to be going on with.' He edged a bit further back.

She still didn't move. 'Selina . . .?'

'Has moved into a rental.'

Leah nodded slowly. The gold lights in her eyes glittered in the sun. 'Will Curtis be living with her?'

Apprehension gnawed at Ronan's belly. Was this the

deal-breaker? The final hurdle he was about to fall at? 'Just as before. He'll live here sometimes, there sometimes.'

Leah nodded again. Then, to his relief, she stepped through the door. 'Sounds good.'

He led the way to the sitting room and waited while she shucked off her coat and sat down. If he spoke first he might spout about how much he'd missed her and how many times he'd nearly phoned or jumped into the car. Or even chartered a helicopter.

He focused on her hands, laced in her lap. No long, painted nails, like Selina's. He supposed they didn't really go with working with food.

'How's your new job?' he asked.

'A definite step up from the old one. More responsibility and creativity. More money. The facilities are amazing.'

'Oh,' he replied, hollowly. 'That's fantastic. Congratulations.'

'Thank you. I hope you find another job you like soon.'

'I've got my feelers out already.'

The polite little conversation ground to a halt.

In the silence, Leah's hands clenched and unclenched. 'On the way here I composed a whole speech but now I've seen you, I can't remember it.'

He watched her, the jumble of emotions flitting across her face as if she were surprised to find herself here, even maybe a little aggrieved. But there was something else in her eyes when she looked at him, something like happiness. It made him smile to imagine her tussling with herself. 'I probably know it. Would I sulk when you go on track days? No, I wouldn't. Do I realise the only way to watch Formula 1 is in silence? Yes, I do.'

Her smile flickered. 'Glad we've got the basics down.'

'And I'll understand if you've forgiven Scott whatever chicanery he's been up to. He's your friend.'

Sadness stole into her eyes. 'Was. Turns out he's been euthanising my relationships. It's not that I'm no good at them, it's that he's brilliant at making me believe I'm not. If teasing and manipulation didn't do the trick he transposed a few characters in the appropriate contacts listing, to make sure.'

His heart twisted and he felt no satisfaction in murmuring, 'I thought it must be something like that.'

'Effectively, he's been making choices for me. Turns out, that's what's made me angriest with him.' Tentatively, she edged closer.

Pulse stepping up its rhythm at the prospect of their bodies making contact, he lifted his arm so that she could slide up against him. He chose his words carefully, as if she were a wild animal, ready to vanish in a flash if he put a foot wrong. 'You know how I feel about you making your own choices.'

She raised her eyes to his, golden and honest. 'Do I still have the choice you offered me, for us not to be just for the holidays?'

Mouth suddenly dry, he nodded.

Her solemn gaze didn't waver. 'Then that's what I choose.'

His heart began thundering so hard he could hardly hear his own voice. 'But you know I'm tied to this area for Curtis's sake for some years to come?'

'That's a hard one,' she acknowledged, sighing. 'My family, my job, they're important. Just not as important as you! Whether we decide on a long-distance relationship or whether I relocate down here sooner or later, however much time we spend together and apart, you're the one.'

It was everything he'd yearned to hear yet he seemed

totally unable to stop giving her excuses to backtrack. 'It's massive for you. You'd be the one doing all the giving up.'

The smile returned. 'Is there something wrong with your hearing? I want my job, my family, my home and my liberty but I want you more. I'm choosing you *over being single*! Everything else will fall into place somehow. There are other jobs and my family will be at the other end of a car journey. You'll owe me, obviously,' she added teasingly. 'Be amazing in bed. That kind of thing.'

He felt a huge smile taking charge of his face. 'I'll pay that price.' His hands, as if exercising muscle memory, slid down to curve around her bottom and pull her against him as he took her mouth, soft and wanting under his.

With a moan of welcome she wrapped herself around him, making it natural for his hands to reverse their direction and find their way inside her top, impatient for the heat of her skin.

Then a bang at the front door heralded a clamour of adolescent boys' voices in the hall.

'Hell's bells,' Ronan hissed.

Leah began to giggle, yanking her top to its proper position as she jumped away to create a decorous distance between them.

'Dad?' shouted Curtis's voice. 'Can Jack and Noodle sleep over? Their mums say it's all right.' His head appeared around the sitting room door. 'Hey! Leah!' He glanced rapidly around the room. 'Natasha here?'

Leah jumped up to give him a hug. 'Great to see you, Curtis. I've missed you! Sorry I haven't brought Natasha this time. I'll bring her soon.'

His face fell. 'OK. We'll go and play on the Xbox then, right?' A clattering on the stairs suggested his friends were already blazing the trail to the holy Xbox grail.

'Right,' Ronan agreed easily, marvelling that his still crazy heartbeat wasn't making his voice shake.

But Curtis ventured further into the room. 'Or how about a bake off, Leah? Jack and Noodle totally like food tech. We could show them mug cakes.'

Leah's eyes were dancing. 'Do you think you have the ingredients here?'

Curtis pulled a dubious face. 'Probably not. We need chocolate with high cocoa solids and good quality cocoa powder, right? Have we got any self-raising flour, Dad?'

Ronan pulled out his wallet and extracted a twenty. 'Not a speck. Why don't you, Jack and Noodle go to the supermarket for what you need?'

'Cool beans.' Curtis grinned as he finally exited through the door.

Ronan slid back up the sofa and dipped his head to touch Leah's earlobe with his tongue. 'Despite the teenage invasion I'm still a good choice.' He didn't know if he was reassuring her or himself.

But Curtis returned. 'Leah, what's good chocolate and cocoa powder here in England?'

'Green & Black's? Or Lindt.' Leah's voice sounded strained, as if she were bursting to laugh from within the cage of Ronan's arms.

'OK.' Once more Curtis made as if to leave. But then didn't. His gaze travelled over them, Ronan frozen half-curled around Leah. 'So are you, like, Dad's girlfriend, now, Leah?'

Ronan held his breath.

'Just discussing it,' she said tentatively. 'How would you feel?'

'Cool.' Curtis sounded surprised that anyone would think anything else. And finally he quit the room, hollering for Jack and Noodle 'because Leah's going to help us make totally amazing chocolate mug cakes and we need to buy stuff. What? Oh, she's Dad's girlfriend.'

'Hear that?' Ronan whispered, tracing her breast through her clothes, feeling her nipple tighten beneath his fingertip. 'We've been approved.'

Another clatter on the stairs. 'Laters!' Curtis shouted.

Ronan had barely dragged Leah into a proper deep kiss when his phone rang. Swearing, he saw *Curtis* on the screen. 'Yes?' he answered tersely, resisting the urge to snap, 'What now?'

'Can I get marshmallows?'

'Yes.'

Leah was giggling again as he ended the call. He looked down at her ruefully, this beautiful woman in his arms. 'I am a good choice. I am.'

She dropped her hand casually in his lap. 'You are. And everything you bring along.'

'I want to remind you how good,' he breathed, absolutely not wanting her to move her hand away but knowing the realities of the situation. 'But I know Curtis's long legs will eat up the distance he has to cover too quickly to allow me to make love to you now the way I want to make love to you.'

'Later,' she agreed, the golden glints in her eyes bright in the late autumn sunlight streaming in through the window as she gazed into his eyes. 'I'll still choose you.'

When the lads returned with bulging supermarket bags Leah had little choice but to pretend she wasn't aching for Ronan to make good on his promises and instead quickly find her way around his kitchen. It was very functional – a microwave, an oven, an easy-to-clean induction hob, a huge fridge-freezer and a basic collection of utensils.

‘So, what do we do first, Curtis?’ she tested him.

‘Wash our hands,’ Curtis sighed. ‘And, Noodle, you’ll have to tie your hair back. Jack’s is OK ’cos it’s short like a bog brush.’

Jack grinned, as if being a bog brush was a compliment, while Noodle, who rocked a short-on-the-left-long-on-the-right style, said, ‘Right,’ agreeably and secured his hair with a twist-tie from the kitchen drawer.

It was surreal to lead them through the same kind of ‘bake off’ she had so often with Jordan and Natasha, addressing each of them as ‘chef’ and allocating hands-on roles while her heart boinged about her chest every time she caught the heat in Ronan’s eyes.

Ronan had elected himself cameraman and filmed with his phone, interjecting the occasional, ‘So, Chef, what are we doing here?’

When he turned the camera on Leah she laughed and blew him a kiss, filled with a sense of rightness. Of belonging.

‘So, you’ll bring Natasha soon then, right?’ Curtis brushed aside their flirting as he sieved flour so enthusiastically that his black combats turned grey.

‘Soon,’ Leah promised.

Curtis looked contented as he reached for the cocoa powder. ‘You staying over tonight?’

Leah glanced at Ronan in alarm, hoping he could magically signal the right reply. But Ronan was looking no surer of the situation than she was, one eyebrow quirked, phone forgotten in his hand. Obviously this was another learning curve she had to hit without training, regardless of Noodle and Jack forming an interested audience. She peeped into Curtis’s face, heart fluttering. ‘How would you feel about it?’

He shrugged. 'Will you make breakfast tomorrow?'

And suddenly she knew that it was going to be all right. When you came right down to it, you could manage any situation via food. 'Eggs and bacon.'

'Awesome!'

Behind Curtis's back, Ronan, smile blazing, mouthed, 'Love you.'

Without even having to think about it, she mouthed, 'Love you back.'

'Yuck, not in the kitchen!' Curtis grumbled.

Leah laughed. And then the first mug was ready for the microwave and she had to concentrate on the important stuff. Chocolate cake.

The Lengths a Novelist Will Go To …

When I posted on Facebook that I was beyond excited because a pilot was going to take me up in a helicopter and pretend to crash it, I received around 70 comments.

The majority of them said, '*You're mad*!'

But they were all wrong. I was *thrilled*.

As you already know, my hero Ronan Shea in *Just for the Summer* is a helicopter pilot recovering from a shoulder injury after a forced landing. During my research, I was lucky enough to be introduced to Martin Lovell who owns a helicopter maintenance company, SkyTech Helicopters, and is also the company's test pilot.

If the engine begins to fail in a single-engine helicopter the pilot has to take prompt action because he can't park in mid-air. When Martin offered to take me up and demonstrate how the pilot retains full control via the art of 'autorotation', bringing the aircraft down at such an angle that the air passing over the rotor keeps it going, I could not believe my luck. I *love* helicopters and had always wanted to be flown in one. That my first flight was a pretend crash deterred me not one whit.

I arrived at the airfield on a beautiful day. We walked through the hangar to the black Hughes 500 helicopter in need of a test flight. Martin performed the pre-flight checks and suddenly the door was opened and I was invited inside . . .

Martin strapped me into my seat and gave me a set of headphones before beginning a running commentary on the instrumentation and which switches he was flicking and why. The engine started and the *whump whump whump* as the rotor began to turn became faster and faster until the blades were a blur above us. A little hover, then we were turning, tip-toeing across the grass to the runway.

I don't fully remember the take off. We just whooshed along and up and somehow we were above a village, above a reservoir, above the fields. The Hughes has great visibility, including what's passing below your feet. Apart from this all-round vision and the fact that we were whizzing along at altitude, the cockpit felt a bit like a car – comfortable leather seats, a heater and a sat nav – but with a lot more banking and swooping.

Once up at 2000 feet Martin told me he would begin the autorotation. He wouldn't actually switch off the engine (prudent of him), but would proceed as if he had. The RPM died, there was a fast initial drop then we swooped down on a diagonal flight path towards the ground.

It came up to meet us VERY quickly!

At the point where coming down to earth with a bump seemed almost inevitable, Martin 'flared' the aircraft and halted the momentum as surely as if he'd been able to apply brakes. In a real autorotation, he would then have performed a run-on landing and the helicopter should have sat down nicely on its skids (unless, as in Ronan's case, a hidden land hazard was there to trip the helicopter up).

'All right?' Martin asked.

I gibbered something like, 'Yes! That was fantastic! Amazing! Wow! That was fantastic-amazing-wow. That was *really* fantastic-amazing-wow.'

He turned us around again. 'Now we'll do it a bit more realistically, as if the engine's cut without warning and the pilot has to act fast. That was just a gentle mock-up.'

Up we went again. And wheeeeeee! We swooped down to Earth a lot more rapidly this time. Someone in the cockpit went 'WHOOOOOOOOHOOOOOOOOOOOOOOOOOO!', and I don't think it was Martin.

He pulled up at about ten feet and recreated the run-on landing this time. His accuracy was amazing because when we turned and flew back I could see the parallel lines where the skids had parted the longish grass but not touched hard ground.

Pretending to crash in a helicopter was truly awesome. I was exhilarated but never scared. I felt totally secure in the skill of the pilot.

I assumed that we'd pootle back to the hangar but instead we circled up again and flew on (ground speed about 100 knots, so not so much of a pootle), over the town where I went to senior school and over a supermarket my mum had texted me from an hour before, picking out churches and a golf course, ticking off the villages as we flew over them to the town where I now live. We circled over my house and then headed back to base.

I think it took about three minutes to get back to the airfield, a trip that had taken me twenty by car. We flew low-level along the runway so I could get an idea of what speed really feels like in a helicopter (rushy), then came back around and landed tidily outside the hangar.

Everything went quiet . . . apart from my heart, which was still whirring at full knots.

Pretend-crashing in a helicopter? Awesome.